UNSEEN PREDATOR

Laura left her chair and crossed the study. She stepped out into the hallway and tried the light switch. The domed fixtures that hung along the ceiling of the corridor remained dark. Apparently, the entire house was devoid of electricity.

A moment later she had descended the back staircase to the kitchen. A sudden burst of cold air told her that something was amiss. She found the back door standing halfway open. The wood around the deadbolt was splintered. Frightened, Laura grabbed a chair from the breakfast nook and wedged the edge of its back under the knob of the back door, securing it. Then she entered the utility room to the left of the kitchen. Again she found her suspicions justified. When she checked the fuse box, she found that most of the fuses had been taken. As if that was not enough, the carton of spare fuses that Rick had set on top of the water heater for just such an emergency was also missing.

Laura suddenly wondered if the intruder who had forced his way inside and deprived the house of its electricity was still around.

Cautiously she left the utility room and crossed the kitchen to the phone that hung next to the pantry door. Quickly she lifted the receiver and punched the preset button that would instantly dial 911. She was no longer hesitant about calling the local police; the broken lock and the stolen fuses were reason enough to alert the sheriff's department.

Yet no matter how many times she tried, she couldn't get a dial tone.

The phone was completely dead.

HAUTALA'S HORROR–HOLD ON TO YOUR HEAD!

MOONDEATH (1844-4, $3.95/$4.95)
Cooper Falls is a small, quiet New Hampshire town, the kind you'd miss if you blinked an eye. But when darkness falls and the full moon rises, an uneasy feeling filters through the air; an unnerving foreboding that causes the skin to prickle and the body to tense.

NIGHT STONE (3030-4, $4.50/$5.50)
Their new house was a place of darkness and shadows, but with her secret doll, Beth was no longer afraid. For as she stared into the eyes of the wooden doll, she heard it call to her and felt the force of its evil power. And she knew it would tell her what she had to do.

MOON WALKER (2598-X, $4.50/$5.50)
No one in Dyer, Maine ever questioned the strange disappearances that plagued their town. And they never discussed the eerie figures seen harvesting the potato fields by day . . . the slow, lumbering hulks with expressionless features and a blood-chilling deadness behind their eyes.

LITTLE BROTHERS (2276-X, $3.95/$4.95)
It has been five years since Kip saw his mother horribly murdered by a blur of "little brown things." But the "little brothers" are about to emerge once again from their underground lair. Only this time there will be no escape for the young boy who witnessed their last feast!

Available wherever paperbacks are sold, or order direct from the Publisher. Send cover price plus 50¢ per copy for mailing and handling to Zebra Books, Dept. 4368, 475 Park Avenue South, New York, N.Y. 10016. Residents of New York and Tennessee must include sales tax. DO NOT SEND CASH. For a free Zebra/Pinnacle catalog please write to the above address.

RONALD KELLY

THE POSSESSION

ZEBRA BOOKS
KENSINGTON PUBLISHING CORP.

To my aunt, Dorothy Williams;
a true belle of the South.
Thanks for being there
when I needed you the most.

ZEBRA BOOKS are published by

Kensington Publishing Corp.
475 Park Avenue South
New York, NY 10016

First Printing: November, 1993

Printed in the United States of America

Prologue

The cold bleakness of winter had a firm and icy grasp on Tennessee that December morning of 1864.

Pockets of old snow lingered in the shadows of gently rolling hills and backwood hollows, as did the occasional body of a dead horse or an unfortunate soldier who had been overlooked rather than buried with those who had fallen alongside him. Rich bottomland and pasture that had once boasted a variety of crops and herds of beef cattle now lay barren. Fine whiskers of frost coated the brown grass, and underneath that silvery blanket, the ground was frozen solid, nearly as unyielding as stone. Everywhere upon that rural countryside the earth was scored by the telltale wounds of battle. The hard mud held a multitude of scars and indentations, the footprints of thousands of marching soldiers and the deep ruts left behind by supply wagons and cannon alike.

Colonel Braxton Heller sat on his coal-black roan atop a wooded ridge, engulfed by the harsh weather and the even harsher surroundings of the violated region. He pulled the folds of his greatcoat closer around him and attempted to ignore the winter's bite, instead focusing all his attention on the devastation that sprawled across the valley below. The man could scarcely believe that this was, indeed, his beloved Magnolia. The plantation no longer resembled the idyllic memories he had taken with him when he endorsed the secession of Tennessee from the Union nearly four years ago and, trading in the fine duds of a planter for the gray uniform of the Confederacy, joined his brethren in the War Between the States.

Magnolia had once been paradise on earth: lush and green, and plentiful with cotton and tobacco, fruit orchards, and the leather-leaved trees that provided its name. But now it was utterly desolate, a lifeless landscape of raw earth and jagged stumps. Even the main house, standing two and a half stories tall and constructed of whitewashed brick and chiseled limestone, no longer resembled the proud structure he had once known. Most of the roofing had been burned away, and the once immaculate walls and columns were now scorched and stained with black soot. Braxton felt a painful hitch in his chest at the sight of his boyhood home. It looked like the bones of some exotic animal that had been cruelly slaughtered and then set afire.

The colonel found that he could remain on the ridge no longer. He spurred the flanks of his mount, urging the horse down the embankment toward the valley. As he rode, Braxton recalled the letter he had received several weeks earlier from a neighboring planter named John Herbert Ashworth. Ashworth had told him of General Hood's attempt to wrestle Nashville away from the Union and General Thomas's strategy to prevent the Confederates' march to the state capital, a strategy that had turned Braxton's own township of Franklin into a bloody battleground. He had also informed him that the Heller plantation had been forcefully taken by a Yankee colonel named Bates. Magnolia had been turned into one of several command posts for the duration of the battle, then was looted and set on fire after the skirmish had ended.

The last paragraph of Ashworth's letter had been the catalyst that caused Braxton to ask for an emergency furlough from Lee's army and travel home by horseback. It had read, "*When I thought it safe enough to venture out, I rode to Magnolia and found the place in blackened ruins. I searched the entire property, but could find no sign of Miss Jessica there. The few slaves that remained on the premises could tell me little about her whereabouts or what had become of her.*"

For the past fourteen days, Braxton Heller had made his

way cautiously through the battle-torrid states of Virginia, Kentucky, and Tennessee, the maddening mystery of his beloved Jessica's fate foremost in his mind. He had ridden through snowstorms and forded icy rivers to reach the valley three miles south of Franklin, and the strain of the traveling had taken its toll on him. As he reached the dirt road that led to the Heller plantation, Braxton was gripped by a fit of coughing that nearly rocked him from his saddle. The wet rattle of consumption sounded deep down in his lungs and an ache like a cannonball pressing against his chest threatened to double him over. *Press on, damn it!* he cursed inwardly, forcing himself to sit tall. *Press on, if only for Jessica's sake!*

Braxton slowed the roan to a trot and moved down the center drive of hard-packed earth. Once the lane had been lined on either side by dense groves of tall magnolias, but both the severity of winter and the destructive flames of Yankee torches had utterly destroyed them. Now there were only dozens of blackened trunks bearing but a scattering of ashen limbs and burnt leaves. The acrid stench of smoke still tinged the air, even though it had been nearly a month since the attack on Magnolia, according to Ashworth's account.

"The godless heathen!" declared Braxton in anguish. He reined his horse onward to the plantation house.

The structure looked no better up close than it had from a distance. The central walls and high Roman columns were intact, but the stone and mortar were dyed a dusty black. Slowly Braxton swung down from the roan and tied it to an iron hitching post. The horse snorted nervously, the strong scent of ashes causing its nostrils to flare in protest.

Braxton unfastened the flap of his side holster and withdrew a Colt Navy .36 that he had taken from the body of a Union cavalryman at Antietam. He thumbed back the hammer, then ascended the cluttered steps of the main entrance.

The double doors of heavy oak were splintered and hung loosely on their iron hinges. He stepped inside and saw that the house had been virtually gutted. All that was left of the regal architecture and furnishings of the dwelling were charred timbers and heaps of gray ash. He stared overhead, toward the upper story, and saw the pale light of early morning filtering down through the naked rafters of the pitched roof.

A fear like none he had ever experienced, even in battle, suddenly welled up within him. "Jessica!" he shouted. His customarily robust baritone no longer came as easily as it once had. It now seemed weak and past defeat, heavy and thick with the phlegmy congestion that occupied his lungs.

Like a lunatic, Braxton Heller stumbled through the dark belly of the mansion, calling for his absent wife and angrily swinging his pistol at anything that obstructed his progress. Timbers that had once stood sturdy and strong now crumbled and flaked apart. Several times, fragments of the floor above rained down, missing the Confederate officer by mere inches.

He reached the parlor where his beloved Jessica had spent many an afternoon, drinking spiced tea and reading her books. It no longer resembled the elegant chamber of crushed velvet and imported French wallpaper. Now it was only a smoky black hole choked by darkness. The smothering pall of stirred ashes sent Braxton into a renewed fit of hacking. He leaned over, hands on knees, attempting to force the thick liquid from his lungs, but without success. As he stared down at the debris of the floor with tearful eyes, he spotted something lying half-buried in the ashes.

Braxton reached down and picked up the object. It was a silk fan that he had bought for Jessica during a purchasing trip to Memphis. The gay colors of the Oriental fan had been turned black by flame, and even as he held the treasure, it withered away and dissolved, claimed by a cold draft that swept through the shattered windows. The wind moaned mournfully, matching the same pitiful tone that issued from Braxton's throat.

Abruptly, he heard a rustling behind him. Light footsteps on cinders. "Jessica?" he whispered hopefully, and turned.

He was disappointed to find not his beloved wife, but a mangy skeleton of a dog picking through the ruins of the house. Enraged, Braxton lifted his revolver and fired. His aim was faulty, though, and the bullet only kicked up ashes a foot or so from the dog. With a yelp, the frightened animal turned tail and ran. Braxton set out in pursuit, screaming hoarsely and snapping off shot after shot at the half-starved mutt.

A moment later, Braxton was back outside and chasing the dog through the flower garden, toward the stock barn and the outbuildings beyond. Even after the dog had eluded him, the man continued to fire his revolver, allowing the hammer to impotently strike the spent caps of the chambers. Braxton was stumbling past the barn when he heard a low groan echo from the vicinity of the slave quarters. He returned his gun to its holster and drew his cavalry sabre from its scabbard. Sword in hand, Braxton made his way through the gathering of single-room cabins until he located the source of the noise.

"Who's there?" he demanded, standing outside the partially closed door of a shanty. "Tell me, or as God is my witness, I shall run you through with my blade!"

"It only be me, Massa Heller," answered a feeble voice that was familiar to the colonel. "Jist ol' Sassy, an' no one else."

Braxton opened the door of the cabin and stepped inside. The room was dimly lit by a coal oil lamp which was nearly down to its last drop of fuel. He walked over to the old Negro woman and stared down at her. Sassy had been the Hellers' resident cook for the past forty years and had been a fixture of the household a decade or so before Braxton had even been born. She had once been a large, sturdy woman, but now she looked ancient and shriveled, scarcely anything but flesh and bones. Her tar-black face was coated with the sweat of fever, and her eyes were dull and yellow.

The young colonel returned the sabre to his belt and knelt beside the corn-husk bed upon which the old woman lay. "What ails you, Sassy?" he asked.

Sassy shuddered, her breathing labored. "Mah leg, Massa. Dem no-account Yankees, dey done maimed me. Took a sword an' hacked mah leg clean in half."

Braxton moved his hand to the cloth poultice plastered across her left thigh. He grimaced at both the sight and the odor of the wound. Sassy's leg had been cleaved in two by a cavalry sabre just below the knee. The horrid injury had been cauterized in an attempt at preventing infection, but despite the treatment, gangrene had set in. Greenish-yellow pus seeped from cracks in the charcoaled flesh, and the thigh was swollen to three times its normal size. Braxton studied it for only a moment before covering it once again.

"What happened here, Sassy?" he asked her. "Where are the other slaves?"

"Dey done up an' gone, Massa," she told him. "Reckon'd it were too risky for 'um ta stay 'round hereabouts. Jist upped and left ol' Sassy ta die, but I ain't done so yet. Reckon I's jist too dadblamed ornery ta give up da ghost."

"And Miss Jessica?" asked Braxton reluctantly. "What became of her?"

" 'Twas them thieving bluebellies, Massa Heller," she moaned. "Dey came in da dead o'night, dey did, an' took da place o'er. Big ol' mean Yankee named Bates, he cast me and da others outta da house. I tried to fight 'um, I shorely did, but Bates took his blade ta mah leg an' crippled me. Mah boy, Samuel, he carried me here ta this shack, then went back to save Miss Jessica. She was still in da house with dat devil an' his men."

Braxton knew who she was talking about. Samuel had been one of the Hellers' most loyal and trustworthy fieldhands, a strapping, blue-gum buck heavy with muscle and well over six and a half feet tall. "What happened then?" he urged. "After Samuel returned to the house?"

"Can't say dat I rightly know," she told him truthfully. "I's heard da most godawful screaming I ever did hear in all mah born days. Sounded like po' Miss Jessica running from da house, screaming to da high heavens and dat bastid Bates laughing like Ol' Scratch him ownself. Through da doorway yonder I saw Samuel pull dat big ol' ax from da choppin' stump an' run to da house. After dat, I can only guess at what happened. I heard Samuel yell out, angry-like, and dat Yankee's laughter, it stopped cold. Then I heard dem soldiers yelling out ta 'git da nigger.' Dat's when I passed out from da pain o' dis here sword wound. I reckon I never will know what dem bluebellies done to mah po' Samuel."

"But what became of Jessica?" he asked once again.

Panic shown in the woman's feverish eyes. "Dey went an' kilt her, Massa. Dey kilt her an' buried her somewhere hereabouts."

Dread nestled in the center of Braxton's chest, cold and heavy, like a well stone. "But *where,* Sassy? Where did the sons of bitches bury the body of my beloved?"

"Lawd, Massa Heller, I don't know," she said. Grievous tears bloomed in her jaundiced eyes and rolled down her dark cheeks. "Could be pert near anywhere, I suppose. I's in too much o' a hurting ta leave da here bed, an' none o' da other niggers would go near 'nough ta dis house ta see. All I know is dat dem Yankees buried her and set da whole blamed place afire. Burnt down da house an' ever one o' dem beautiful 'nolia trees. Den dey rode away."

Braxton questioned Sassy for a few minutes more but found that further interrogation was pointless. She was out of her head and near death. He was about to cover the frail woman with a woolen blanket when her claw of a hand dug into his arm. "Ain't no use in tryin' ta comfort me, Massa. Naw, I's done past comfortin'. Yo' can't do nary a thang for ol' Sassy but put 'er out'n 'er misery."

The man was appalled by her request. "I can't bring myself to do that, Sassy. I simply can't."

Sassy's eyes pleaded with him. "Shore yo' can, Massa Heller. Yo' an' yo' pappy was always real kind an' thoughtful to all'un us niggers. Please, jist do dis one thang fo' me? Send ol' Sassy down dat golden path ta glory. You'd do as much fo' dat fine black hoss 'o yers, now, wouldn't ya?"

"Yes," agreed Braxton sullenly. He drew his empty pistol from its holster, then took a hand-rolled cartridge from his belt. Braxton tore the paper open with his teeth and loaded a single chamber of the .36 with powder, ball, and firing cap. He lowered the blued octagon barrel toward her temple, then paused. "Close your eyes," he told her, his voice hardly more than a whisper.

The Negro woman smiled softly and did as he asked. "Remember, Massa, ol' Sassy, she's always loved ya, e'r since you's jist a little tadpole."

Although he would have never returned such a sentiment toward a slave before the war, Braxton saw no reason to deny her it now. "I love you, too, Sassy," he said. Then he cocked the hammer and fired.

Braxton extinguished the lamp and left the drafty shack. He breathed in deeply, but despite the bracing winter air, could not drive the pervading stench of gunsmoke and death from his nostrils. He recalled Sassy's words, knowing well the dying have no cause for lies. He cast his eyes around the vast acreage of Magnolia, half of it blackened by flames, the other trampled and trodded by men, horses, and wagons. Somewhere out there, Braxton knew that his beloved Jessica was buried beneath the frozen ground. The very thought maddened him, for he had no earthly idea where to look first. There was no need to search for a grave; most of the plantation looked like a raw mound of recently turned earth.

He knew, however, that he must not let such a barrier prevent him from finding her. Suddenly, all that consumed him was the need to gaze upon Jessica's face once again, whether it be livid with life or pallid with death. He wanted to hold her in his arms again and run his hands through the coppery spill of her auburn hair, even if those simple acts brought him nothing more than fistfuls of cold earth and decay.

Braxton Heller walked to a narrow shed next to the stock barn and opened it. Much of its contents had been looted by the Union brigade, but he did find a rusty shovel and a broken pickax in the far corner. He took the tools and walked a few yards toward the mansion. The possibilities were enough to boggle the mind, but he was determined not to let that sway him from his self-appointed task.

He picked a spot, then forcefully brought the pickax down against the cold ground. The point scarcely bit into the icy surface, but that failed to deter Braxton. Frantically, he struck again and again until, slowly, the earth finally began to yield.

The third day after Braxton Heller had returned to Magnolia, John Herbert Ashworth decided to ride to the neighboring plantation and check on the young man.

The elderly planter had refrained from visiting Braxton, simply out of respect for the grieving. In his heart, Ashworth knew that Jessica Heller was dead; that those marauding Yankees had murdered her, after performing only God knew what other atrocities. For the past two nights, Ashworth had watched from the windows of his home and spied the distant light of a lantern moving hither and yonder across the length and breadth of the Heller plantation.

Ashworth had no idea what the man was doing out there, and at first figured that it was really none of his business. But on the third day, after a night of bitter cold and steady snowfall, he figured that it was his Christian duty to ride his dappled gray to Magnolia and see if the young colonel was well.

Upon arriving at the plantation, Ashworth knew that Braxton Heller was not in a stable frame of mind. When he rode through the encompassing grove of torched magnolias, he found a dozen or so holes chiseled into the winter earth. It looked as if a battalion of grave-diggers had invaded the property and performed the haphazard excavation. But secretly, John Herbert Ashworth knew that one man and one alone had been responsible for those holes. At first, the old man could hardly fathom an obsession of such magnitude. However, after a moment's consideration, he began to understand how the death of a loved one could drive someone to such an extreme. Had not he himself experienced a similar fit of madness when he and his wife had discovered their only son, Alexander, mortally wounded only a stone's throw from the Ashworth homestead? He had endured watching their courageous Alex die in their parlor a mere day after the Battle of Franklin had ended. Had not insanity touched

Ashworth's own mind that moment when his son had coughed violently and breathed his very last?

Ashworth's mare skirted the profusion of open pits, carrying its rider to the fire-ravaged mansion. The elderly man climbed from the saddle and, taking a twelve-gauge muzzleloader with him, carefully mounted the icy steps of the Heller house.

It did not take long to locate the one he was searching for. An explosion of feeble coughing drew Ashworth's attention and he picked his way through the blackened debris to the rear parlor. He found young Braxton lying on a scorched sofa, deathly pale and burning with fever. The sweat of his sickness had frozen in the low temperature, and his raven black hair and moustache were matted with ice. Ashworth laid his scattergun aside and removed his coat. He draped the garment over Braxton's shivering form, although it was clear to see that such an action was fruitless now. Braxton coughed violently again. Ashworth could hear a wet rattling in the young man's lungs and knew that he was in the final, suffocating throes of pneumonia.

Ashworth knelt next to the divan and took Braxton's bloody, dirt-caked hand. Weakly it grasped the old man's fingers. Braxton's eyelids opened, the slate-gray eyes of his heritage staring at Ashworth until recognition registered there. "Thank you, Mister Ashworth," he rasped hoarsely. "Thank you for waking me." He attempted to sit up as if intending to rise from his makeshift deathbed.

It took little effort on Ashworth's part to restrain the ailing man. "Lie still," the old man told him. "You've done enough work for twenty men in the past couple of days. Now it is time for you to rest. You deserve that much."

"But I am *not* deserving!" protested Braxton Heller. "I've failed miserably . . . failed to locate the remains of my lovely Jessica. I must rise and continue the search. I simply must!"

"No, son," said Ashworth firmly. He pressed Braxton back onto the burnt cushions of the sofa and held him there. "To search for her in such a way is pure insanity. Rest, and soon you will be with her again. Believe me, the Lord Almighty will see to that."

"Of course," muttered Braxton. "You are right. I will meet her again . . . on the far side of that heavenly realm."

Ashworth could sense that the time of Heller's passing was near. "Surrender, young Braxton," he urged softly. "Surrender and claim your reward."

Then, abruptly, Braxton's glassy eyes brightened with a clarity that Ashworth could only describe as celestial. For a brief moment, the colonel's face was full of rapture, as if he were staring at the supreme wonder of Paradise. Then that expression of boundless joy faded, turning instead into horror. "Oh, dear God in heaven . . . *no!*"

"What is it?" Ashworth asked. "What is wrong?"

"She is not there!" cried the young man. *"My beloved Jessica . . . she is lost!"*

John Herbert Ashworth never knew precisely what sort of vision Braxton Heller had been subjected to during his final moment of dying, for an instant later he was gone. A long, shuddering gasp escaped his blue lips and he settled slowly back to the blackened cushions of the velvet divan. Shaken, Ashworth stared at Braxton's expression of torment. It held none of the peace that had possessed his own son's features during the time of his passing. Braxton's face was forever frozen into a rictus of anguish and mortification. Somewhere beyond the realm of the living, the young colonel had glimpsed something that had horrified him to the very depths of his immortal soul.

The elderly man sighed and stood. At the foot of the sofa he spotted the shovel and pickax that had been Braxton Heller's only companions for the past two days. He picked them up, knowing that one final act of compassion was required of him before he returned home. With some effort, he slung Braxton's body over his shoulder and made his way carefully through the blackened ruins of that once proud and regal mansion.

As John Herbert Ashworth stepped out into the gently drifting snowfall and headed toward the fenced plot of the

Heller family cemetery, a cold wind swept through the shattered windows of the dwelling he had just left. The breeze moaned around the charred timbers and scorched columns, seeming almost to separate, to multiply and intensify.

A chill ran through the old man, for that simple intermingling of winter gale and hollow desolation conjured an extremely discomforting illusion—the illusion of several voices in union, each one equally tormented, but somehow different; ghostly voices that either cried longingly for one another or clashed bitterly, as if screaming out for some heinous sin to be set right.

PART ONE

BURNT MAGNOLIA

Chapter One

Laura Locke had feared Magnolia before she'd desired it.

She had been a child then, perhaps ten, maybe even twelve years of age. Like the other children who lived on the rural farms south of Franklin, Laura had seen the old Heller mansion for exactly what it appeared to be: a desolate and forgotten dwelling that stood forlornly amid a dense grove of wild magnolia trees. Surely to such youthful eyes it appeared to be the perfect example of the classic haunted house. The plantation known as Magnolia had lost the magic of its history. It lacked the regal beauty of its mysterious past, yet was abundant with dark shadows, cobwebs, and the foreboding atmosphere of a place that life and laughter had not occupied for nearly a century and a half.

When Laura looked at the place that Magnolia now was, she could not believe that she could ever have regarded it as being ugly or evil, although she'd certainly held such an opinion at one time. Of course, Laura had been a totally different person then: a skinny, freckle-faced girl with honey blond hair tied into pigtails, and dressed in threadbare secondhand clothing that always seemed to be a size or two too small for her lanky frame. She had been considered to be from the wrong side of the tracks back then, one of a dozen children in her school born of poor, tobacco-farming families who lived outside the circle of Franklin's immediate community. True, Laura had been special even then—a young girl brimming with imagination and academic potential—but that had been overshadowed by her classmates' cruel catcalls of "barefoot hick" and "white trash." Her gawky looks, the slang of her speech, her social awkwardness . . . all had been sore spots at that tender age, causing her to withdraw from the popular crowd and spend her time with those who, like herself, had been chastised and ridiculed simply because they had not been raised in precisely the same way as the children in town.

Laura remembered the Halloween night when she and Bobby Perkins and the Shaffer twins had, upon a mutual dare, gathered the nerve to approach the Heller house after dark. After an evening of trick-or-treating, they had crossed the two-lane blacktop of Highway 31 and approached the dense undergrowth of the magnolia grove and the sturdy but skeletal structure of the plantation house that stood beyond. The four children had still been dressed in their homemade costumes—Laura recalled that she had been a scarecrow that year—and two had sported flashlights that they had secretly taken from the glove compartments of their fathers' pickup trucks.

The thicket that surrounded them had seemed ominously dark and claustrophobic outside the scope of those battery-powered lights. Everywhere they turned, another shadow reared before them, potentially threatening and perhaps even supernatural in nature. The old tales of Civil War ghosts that their grandparents had told them preyed on their young imaginations, turning leafless mulberry bushes into skeletal specters and swathes of moonlit honeysuckle into shrouded maidens; long dead Confederate colonels and Southern belles who had been tragically separated, yet continued to search for one another, their love for each other crossing even those boundaries that death had erected between them.

Laura remembered reaching the two-and-a-half-story house with its empty windows and towering columns of stone, all four overgrown with vine, yet still stained a dull grayish-black from the fire that had engulfed the building in that bitter November of 1864. She recalled how she and her friends had stood on the verge of entering the shadowy doorway, only to be driven—half-screaming and half-laughing—toward home by the hooting of a white-faced owl and the distant howling of a bluetick hound on the trail of a coon a good mile or so away. The sounds had certainly been recognizable, but at that moment, they had not held such innocent resonance. No, in their frightened minds, Laura and her pals had given the noises much more sinister origins. Instead, they had heard the moaning of the dead resurrected and the ghoulish wails of souls in eternal torment. So complete was their terror that Bobby had nearly twisted his ankle sprinting over the uneven ground of the magnolia grove and the Shaffer twins—who had portrayed the Siamese twins Chang and Eng, that All Hallows' Eve—had ripped their shared costume completely in half in their haste to escape the horrors of the Heller house.

But those unexpected sounds had not been the only frightening occurrence, at least, not in Laura's case. Laura had seen—or *thought* she had seen—something strange as she glanced back at the ruins of the old mansion. Laura was certain that she had seen a woman standing on the second-floor balcony. A balcony whose floorboards had burned away long ago.

She had glimpsed the woman for only an instant, but the image had been forever seared into Laura's mind by a mixture of fear and fascination. The lady was dressed in a silken nightgown of delicate pink. The sheer garment appeared to be torn and soiled. The woman herself was quite lovely. She was young, perhaps in her early twenties, and was slim and petite in build. Her skin was unblemished and as pale as alabaster, its light pallor heightened further by the dark copper of her auburn hair, which spilled luxuriantly across her bare shoulders and down upon her small breasts.

The expression that gripped the woman's face was one of severe pain and distress. At the sight of that disturbing expression Laura felt utter loss. The woman's eyes, full of panic and despair, stared across the dark expanse of Magnolia as if desperately searching for something . . . or someone . . .

Laura had turned back toward the magnolia grove and

called out to her friends, but they'd refused to listen, continuing their mad dash through the thicket toward the safety of the highway. When Laura turned around again, the apparition was gone. No woman clutched frantically at the ornate banister like a drowning sailor grasping the rail of a sinking ship. There was no one up there . . . nothing but motionless shadows and the strands of creeping ivy that grew rampant along the weathered columns and the sagging framework of the balcony.

When Laura finally reached the main road and joined her friends, who giggled as they attempted to catch their breath, she almost told them about what she had seen. Almost. Before she could, she thought better of it. They would have laughed at her if she'd told them of the ghostly woman on the balcony and undoubtedly razzed her mercilessly for days afterward. Laura decided to keep the strange sighting her own personal secret.

As she lay in her bed later that night, she thought of the woman again, of her disheveled appearance and tormented demeanor, and wondered if perhaps she'd been the ghost of Jessica Heller, the Southern belle who the old folktales said had been brutally murdered one snowy November night and thoughtlessly buried somewhere on the grounds of the plantation. Despite her initial fright, Laura thought of the wandering spirit and found her plight to be appealingly romantic, even if tragically so.

Laura had visited the Heller house many times after that night, unaccompanied by her childish friends and always in the light of day. She no longer feared the place. Instead, it was a site of interest and exploration. As she crossed from adolescence into young adulthood, Laura began to become increasingly taken with that distant era of love and hatred known as the War Between the States. She frequented the town library and read everything she could find on the subject, hoping to discover something concerning Magnolia and its former inhabitants. Laura uncovered little about Jessica Heller or her chivalrous husband, Braxton, but the books she read on the Civil War did stimulate her imagination. She began to dream up her own scenarios of tragic love in the face of bitter conflict, and eventually committed them to paper. By the time she had graduated high school and won a scholarship to the University of Tennessee, Laura knew that she wanted to be a writer.

Like most who pursue that often maddening and unrewarding profession, Laura Locke spent many fruitless years behind the typewriter, refining her talent and perfecting her literary style, learning her trade through hard work and constant rejection. During her junior year in college, she submitted her first novel—a historical romance—to a New York literary agency, hoping for the best. Success did not come instantly. It took nearly three years of sending the manuscript from one publishing house to another, but finally the word came, congratulating her on the acceptance of *Embittered Passion* by a major paperback firm. The advance she netted for the novel was a modest one, but to Laura it seemed like a small fortune. All the years of heartache and patience had paid off. Soon she joined the ranks of published authors.

Laura spent the next four years working as a feature editor at a Knoxville newspaper and writing romance novels in her spare time. It was after the publication of her fifth book, *Fallen Desire,* in hardcover, that she decided to devote all her time to her writing career. She found herself enjoying a degree of critical praise and financial success that was bewildering, yet more then welcome. Soon *Fallen Desire* had reached the seventh spot on the New York Times bestseller list and she was sent on a thirty-city tour, signing copies of her books at shopping mall bookstores. She attended writers' workshops and literary conventions whenever she found the time, and it was at one such Southern conference that she met her future husband.

As she had confined her social contacts mainly to the genre in which she had specialized, Laura had previously not known Rick Gardner from the Man in the Moon. She was soon enlightened as to his reputation and availability by a friend and fellow writer of gothic romance, Peg Winters. Rick was a popular artist in both paperback and hardback circles, specializing mainly in the fantasy, science-fiction, and horror genres. After a ten-year career that had included stints as a draftsman and comic book artist, Rick had done wraparound covers and inside illustrations for editions by some of the leading authors of science-fiction and horror.

Upon first meeting him, Laura had not been all that impressed. Rick was a shy, introverted person who was modest about his accomplishments and painfully embarrassed when praise was directed his way. However, after a single meal and a leisurely conversation, Laura and Rick connected. A whirlwind romance followed, and three months later, the two were married. Laura decided to keep her maiden name to avoid confusion in her writing career, and Rick had been considerate and understanding enough to respect that simple request.

During the next five years, their careers reached new heights of success, providing them with creative freedom and financial security. Rick's art grew more popular as he slowly moved into the mainstream, while Laura continued to turn out lusty novels of historical romance and gradually made her way toward the top of the bestseller list.

And during it all, a dream that Laura had possessed since she was twelve finally approached a chance of becoming a reality. As her fame increased and her bank account grew more healthy, she saw that her secret desire since adolescence and the catalyst that had forged her into a popular author was, indeed, attainable.

Magnolia.

Laura had always dreamed of owning the five-hundred-acre plantation and its weathered shell of a house. Following her bizarre encounter on Halloween night, Laura had spent countless hours imagining how she would re-create the mansion; how she would restore the sturdy floors, walls, and ceilings of the ancient structure and return it to the regal palace it had been during those years before North and South had battled each other for all the right and wrong reasons. She used to imagine the remodeling down to the very last detail; the color and texture of the wallpaper and draperies, as well as the quality and styling of the furnishings. Back then it had been only the fancy of a poor country girl whose sole claim to fortune lay within her vivid imagination. But now the fortune was well within her grasp and ready to be put to good use.

The process of acquiring Magnolia had not been nearly so difficult as she had first suspected. Braxton and Jessica had been the last surviving members of the Heller family, so the federal government had claimed the property during that vengeful process known as Reconstruction. The land had lain in disuse for decades before a farmer named Matthews had purchased most of the plantation's acreage to raise tobacco and corn around the turn of the century. Matthews had lost the property to the Williamson County Trust and Loan during the Great Depression. For the next sixty years, Magnolia was in the possession of that financial institution. Gradually, eighty percent of the acreage was divided and sold to local landowners. Due to its high price tag, all that remained on the market were twenty-five acres and the dilapidated plantation house that was located in their midst.

After consulting with her attorney, who assured her that the lien-holder was ready to sell and that she could acquire the place for half the asking price, Laura went to Rick and discussed the possibility of purchasing Magnolia and moving to her hometown of Franklin. Her husband was aware of her desire for the property and its antebellum mansion, and was all for turning her dream into a reality. Besides, it really made no difference where they lived. The flexibility of their careers gave them the option of setting up shop wherever they wished. So, with that typical good-natured grin of his, Rick gave Laura his blessing on the project, and together, they set to the task of making Magnolia their permanent home.

A year had passed since the deal had been made and the deed was signed over to Laura Locke. In the next few months, the overgrown acreage and the neglected house that stood on it were the subject of an amazing transformation. The plantation grounds had been cleared considerably. The burnt stumps that had been left behind by the destructive Union troops a hundred and thirty years before were pried from the earth and disposed of. The fruit orchard and the encompassing grove of tall magnolias were once again restored to the stately manner they had once possessed. The rutted dirt road that connected the plantation to the state highway was paved and branched into a circular drive in front of the main house. The walkways of the rear garden were recobbled with new brick and the ground tilled. The freshly turned earth of the flowerbeds awaited Laura's green thumb when spring rolled around. It now lay beneath colorful blankets of autumn leaves, shed by the maples and poplars that flourished on the property, as well as the huge and ancient oak that grew in the very center of the garden.

The house itself had undergone a wondrous revitalization. A crew of master carpenters, plumbers, and electricians had worked eight solid months to restore the Heller house to its former beauty, as well as provide it with a functional comfort that could never have been dreamt of during the 1850s and '60s. Of course, some of the house's former luxuries were sacrificed in favor of practicality. The money that could have been spent on expensive marble floors and delicately carved woodwork was put to better use. Copper pipes, state-of-the-art insulation, and central heat and air conditioning were installed. However, those modern additions were not conspicuous enough to overshadow the authenticity and charm of the antebellum decor.

It had taken much planning and many man-hours to transform a scrubby and useless piece of real estate into a showplace that was destined to grace the pages of *Better Homes & Gardens* and *Southern Living*. It had also taken a lot of effort on the part of Laura Locke, but she had performed the task and performed it more than admirably, with the same labor of love and imagination that she breathed into each and every one of her novels.

Chapter Two

When the Mayflower movers had carried the last of the furniture and labeled boxes through the front doorway of the big house, the driver, a husky fellow named Andy Jones, held out the service invoice for Laura to sign. "Right there on the bottom line, Ms. Locke."

Laura accepted the clipboard and pen from the man and signed her name. "I really appreciate the way you and your men handled our move from Knoxville," she told him sincerely. "This is Rick's and my first full-scale move, and we'd both heard horror stories about getting things lost and damaged."

"I've heard those kind of stories, too," said Andy. He carefully tore off a carbon copy from beneath the original and handed it to her. "But I've been in this business for nearly twenty-five years now, and take it from me, they're pretty much the exception to the rule." The middle-aged man smiled at her. "Besides, I told these guys a couple days ago that they'd be standing in the unemployment line if they got butter-fingered around your stuff, Ms. Locke. Can't have a famous writer like you PO'd at us. It wouldn't be good for business."

Laura was a little surprised. "But I didn't think anyone—"

"Oh, we know who you are, Ms. Locke. My superior recognized your name right off." Andy returned the pen to the pocket of his gray shirt and reddened slightly in embarrassment. "Uh, now that our business is all squared away, I was wondering if maybe you could do me a favor?"

Laura recognized that flustered look. She had grown accustomed to it over the years. "You want me to sign something for you, right?"

"Just a few books for my wife," said Andy. "You don't have to if you don't want to, but I'll likely end up sleeping on the couch tonight if I don't come home with at least a couple of them autographed."

Laura laughed warmly. "I'll be happy to, Andy."

After she had personally signed half a dozen books for Andy's wife, Laura watched as the driver and his three helpers climbed into the roomy cab of the big semi. "Are you sure you guys can't stick around for some coffee?" she asked. "Rick's plugging in the coffeemaker right now."

"No thanks, Ms. Locke," replied Andy. He peered through the windshield at the fading light of the autumn sunset. "We've got a long drive back to Knoxville, so I reckon we'd better be going. I wish you much happiness in your new home." He cranked the bright yellow diesel into life. "Oh, thanks again for signing those books for me."

"It was my pleasure," Laura assured him. "And please, give my best to your wife."

Andy waved, then shifted the truck into gear. He made a slow, graceful turn around the circular driveway, then headed through the long shadows of the magnolia grove toward Highway 31 and the interstate beyond.

Laura turned and regarded the towering front of the old plantation house. It looked much different than it had that Halloween night so many years ago. The brick walls had been repainted an immaculate white, the trim of the eaves and overhangs had been restored with new wood, and the great limestone columns had been completely reconditioned, the sooty stain of that long-ago fire having been meticulously scrubbed away by sandblasting. Tall, multipaned windows had been securely set in sills that had gaped empty for decades and twin doors of polished oak with shiny brass knockers were installed in the broad front doorframe. Ornate banisters and a new floor replaced the rotted boards of the second-story balcony that had overlooked the plantation grounds during the years before civil war had thrown the state of Tennessee into the heat of conflict.

She crossed the downstairs porch with its old-fashioned cane-backed rocking chairs and entered the open doorway. The shadows of evening gathered like a dark congregation in the large entrance hall. Laura reached over and snapped on the wall switch. A huge chandelier of cut crystal blazed brightly overhead, driving all gloom from the chamber. Laura had been hesitant about hanging the fixture there at first, wondering if it might seem a little too extravagant, even in such an antebellum setting. But after several months of searching for just the right touch, Laura found that a house like hers demanded such an extreme form of lighting. It complimented the molded floral pattern of the plaster ceiling, the walls of eggshell white, and the staircase that swept in a graceful half-loop from the ground floor to the story above.

Laura shut the double doors behind her, then turned back to the main foyer. She closed her eyes and breathed deeply. The odor of fresh paint and new wood was thick, almost cloying, but she savored it all the same. Laura had never lived in a house she could truly call her own. The drafty farmhouse where she had grown up had been passed down by generations of Lockes, and even when she had attended college and worked for the newspaper in Knoxville, she had always rented places where faceless others had dwelled before her. Even the house that she and Rick had leased in Knoxville had been a rental property for nearly ten years before they'd moved in.

But those times were past. Magnolia and its mansion was theirs now, hers and Rick's, and it always would be. Before undertaking the lengthy process of turning Magnolia into a livable domicile, Laura had made up her mind that she would spend the rest of her life within the shelter of the house she now stood in. Her children would, she hoped, be conceived and raised there, and after they had grown and pursued lives of their own, she and Rick would grow old there together, holding hands and rocking contentedly in the chairs out front.

Smiling at the idyllic thought, Laura crossed the foyer to the doorway that led into the kitchen. As she entered the long room with its oakwood cabinets, butcher-block counters, and authentic stone hearth, she detected the strong odor of coffee. Laura expected to find Rick standing amid cardboard boxes of kitchen appliances and utensils, waiting for the Mr. Coffee to finish brewing its pot. Instead, she found that Rick had already performed the task and left the kitchen. The coffeemaker's glass pot was nowhere to be seen, and neither was her husband.

Playfully, she checked the walk-in pantry, thinking that he might be hiding there. But it was unoccupied. "Rick?" she called out. "Rick, where are you?"

"I'm upstairs." His voice echoed faintly from the narrow staircase that connected the kitchen to the upper floor. "Come on up and join me."

Laura climbed the steps. She soon stood in the upstairs hallway. The long corridor with its tastefully papered walls and varnished hardwood floor stretched the entire length of the second floor, giving access to the house's eight bedrooms, four facing the front of the house and four facing the rear.

"Where?" Laura called out again. The aroma of coffee grew stronger the further she walked down the hall.

"The master bedroom, of course," teased Rick. "I'm sure not sitting in the toilet with a steaming pot of Folger's."

Laura stopped halfway down the hall and entered the master bedroom. Her cherrywood bedroom suite—highboy, dresser, nightstands, and the unassembled pieces of her canopy bed—stood around the large room, waiting to be put in their proper places. She also noticed that one object was not where the movers had left it. The box springs leaned against a far wall, but its king-sized mattress was gone.

A gentle but cool autumn breeze ruffled her blond hair and she turned toward the twin French doors that led onto the front balcony. Both doors were open and beyond the doorway was the mattress . . . with Rick lying comfortably on top of it.

Sitting next to him was the pot of coffee and two mugs he had liberated from a cardboard box downstairs. Laura eyed the empty space on the mattress's left side and assumed that the spot had been reserved for her.

"So, that's where my coffee went to," said Laura with a smile. She stood in the doorway for a moment and stared down at her husband. Rick was a handsome man, but not strikingly so. He was of medium height and carried a slight paunch that was characteristic of a thirty-five-year-old male who spent more time sitting at his art table than working out in the gym. He had the pale complexion of someone who spent more time indoors than out. His coal-black hair was shaggy in the back, but thinning in the front, and his clean-shaven face was a little soft around the jawline. His eyes were blue, but of a peculiar washed-out shade that seemed always to give him an expression of bland disinterest. True, he did not possess the bronzed physique and sharply chiseled features of the shirtless heroes who graced the covers of Laura's books, but then, such killer good looks were much more common in fiction than in real life.

"You didn't mind if I changed into something more comfortable, did you?" Rick asked with a wink.

Laura studied his choice of apparel. Rick wore faded jeans, scuffed Reeboks, and that ugly flannel shirt that he always worked in, the one with about ten years' worth of accumulated acrylic and oil paint on it. "Ooooh, baby," she whispered in a husky voice as she sank down on the mattress next to him. "You know how hot and horny that shirt makes me."

Rick detected a hint of sarcasm in her voice, and frowning, glanced down at the front of his shirt. "What's the matter with it?" he asked, taking a sip from his coffee mug.

"Nothing, except that it's older than dirt and has more shades of paint on it than Sherwin-Williams carries in its entire inventory. When are you going to throw it away and buy yourself a new one?"

Rick looked shocked. "Get rid of my lucky shirt? Never! I was still a starving artist when I started wearing this, and look where I am now. Believe me, some day the Smithsonian will be begging for this humble Kmart special with a career's worth of history on it."

"Dream on, sweetheart," said Laura. Laughing, she leaned over and kissed him, then poured herself a fresh cup from the coffeepot. "They'll want that eyesore about as much as they'll want my writing outfit."

"You mean that old pink sweatsuit with the peeling decal of Scarlett O'Hara and Rhett Butler on the front?"

"The one and only," she said. "Speaking of which, I think I'll slip into it and make myself comfortable, too." Laura glanced back through the doorway at the stack of clothing boxes that stood in the center of the bedroom floor. "That is, if I can ever find it."

Before she could get up, Rick reached out and lazily took her hand. "Forget that blasted sweatsuit. What I had in mind was that slinky negligee of yours. You know, the silky peach one with all the revealing lace down the front."

Laura giggled and sat back down on the mattress. "I wouldn't have thought you'd be in such an amorous mood tonight. We did get up at four o'clock this morning to finish packing before the movers arrived."

Rick shrugged. "Why do you think I brewed this pot of coffee?" With a sly grin he reached out and ran a hand along the curve of her thigh. "Besides, isn't it a longstanding tradition for a couple to make love the first night in their new house?"

"It seems like I've heard something like that before," said Laura. A sudden breeze snaked through the openings of the balcony railing, causing her to shiver. "But don't you think we ought to do it right and have our fun *inside?* It *is* sort of nippy out here this evening, wouldn't you say?"

Rick smiled and shook his head. "And you're the one who's always getting on *my* case for being a party-pooper. Anyway, I thought this would appeal to your romantic side. Don't you think the couple who lived here before the Civil War did the wild thing out here on the balcony at least once, during some torrid night of unbridled passion?"

Laura thought of the people Rick referred to. Lying there

with the darkness of night fast approaching and the massive pillars of the limestone columns standing around them, Laura used her imagination. Yes, she could almost picture Jessica and Braxton Heller making love where they now lay. Although she had no idea how either one looked, she could easily conjure up their images in her mind, softly beautiful and ruggedly handsome, entwined nakedly, moving rhythmically, flesh against flesh. In the darkness of some distant Southern night they might very well have abandoned the prim and proper restrictions of a bygone age and coupled passionately, the scent of magnolia blossoms serving as a heady aphrodisiac, spurring them toward the heights of ecstasy.

"Uh-oh. Do I sense those creative wheels turning in that pretty head of yours?" asked Rick. He recognized the dreamy look that appeared in Laura's eyes when she sat at her word processor, working on a particularly naughty sex scene.

Laura leaned over and tenderly gave him a kiss. "Does that answer your question?"

"I guess so," said Rick. He stifled a yawn and took another sip of black coffee as he watched her stand up and start toward the bedroom.

"You're not going to fall asleep on me, are you?" she asked. "We have had a long day, you know."

"Don't worry," Rick assured her. "I'll be here when you get back."

Laura left the balcony and entered the master bedroom. She read the scribbled writing on each clothing box until she found one labeled "lingerie." She opened the carton and rummaged through the dozen or so nightgowns until she found the one she was looking for. She went into the adjoining bathroom and turned on the light. It was fairly modest compared to the extravagance of the rest of the house. No marble Jacuzzi or European bidet; just his-and-hers vanities, a combination bathtub and shower, and a commode.

She undressed, folding her dingy clothes and laying them on the counter next to the sink, along with her bra and panties. She stood there for a long moment, appraising herself in the full-length mirror affixed to the door of the bathroom closet.

Laura was thirty-two, but fortunately most people, friends and fans alike, mistook her for someone several years younger. Her face was clear and devoid of lines, her shoulder-length hair was a warm hue of honey blond, and her eyes were deep azure blue in color. Unlike most women her age, Laura was satisfied with her body, as far as both weight and shape were concerned. She was a devout believer in proper diet and exercise, and worked out diligently four days a week. She was lean and firm from head to toe. Her figure showed none of the sagging around the breasts and butt that prematurely afflicted a lot of women over thirty.

Laura slipped on the flimsy peach negligee and mussed up her hair a little, producing that wild look that turned Rick on. She spotted her makeup caboodle where she had placed it on the vanity earlier that afternoon. Laura searched through the jumble of lipsticks, liners, and eyeshadow cards until she found a small bottle of her favorite perfume. She sprayed on just enough in just the right places to tease her husband, hoping that it would have the intended effect on him.

To tell the truth, Laura had been a little surprised by Rick's sudden flare of desire that night. During the past year or so, something had changed between the two. There certainly was no loss of love between them; they were as committed to each other now as they had been the day of their wedding. But sexually speaking, their attention toward each other had waned considerably. During the first few years of their marriage, Laura and Rick had made love almost every night, like clockwork. But lately, the time and inclination for intimacy had decreased. Laura tried to remember exactly when they had last made love and decided that it had been the middle of the previous week. And even then, there had been little foreplay. The entire act had lasted no more than fifteen minutes, and afterward, Laura had returned from the bathroom to find Rick sound asleep.

Laura attributed most of it to the increasing volume of their professional commitments, and the stress and intense focusing that their individual careers sometimes required. But on second thought, Laura could not help but wonder if something else was to blame—namely, their desire to have children and their frustrating inability to produce any. They had been trying for three years now, but to no avail. Maybe it was the numerous visits to fertility doctors, as well as the confusing confliction of diagnosis and advice they had received, that had taken the edge off their love life. Laura recalled the months of desperation that had followed those visits, the constant monitoring of her ovulation cycles and the almost clinical way they had been forced to regard the act of making love. Perhaps it was the constant pressure of having to perform on command that had dampened Rick's desire for sexual contact. Or maybe it was the fear of failing again that had cut their passionate rendezvous down to once a week, or even less often.

"Well, let's hope that the spark isn't gone entirely," she told herself.

Laura walked back into the bedroom and turned off the lights. Then, in the soft glow of the twilight's half moon, Laura made her way to the open French doors, moving as provocatively as she could.

But when she reached the balcony, she found that her sultry performance had been in vain. Rick was stretched out, flat on his back, his eyes closed and his mouth wide open.

"I should have known," she said aloud. A mixture of disappointment and annoyance drove away her mounting arousal as she sat down on the mattress next to him. Rick answered with a long, deep snore that sounded like a rusty chainsaw.

Her irritation lasted for only a brief moment. Then she eased the coffee mug out of his hand, set it aside with the steaming pot, and smiled wearily at the expression of exhausted peace on his face. "So much for tradition," she said softly, then kissed him on the forehead.

She rose, and with some effort, dragged the king-sized mattress—snoozing husband and all—through the French doors and into the bedroom. But before joining him, Laura returned to the balcony. She crossed the landing to the banister and stared out into the deepening nightfall.

A stiff breeze, somewhat cooler than before, swept through the magnolia grove, ruffling the thick, brown-edged leaves and whistling sharply around the vast limestone columns and the upper eaves of the plantation house. Goosebumps prickled her bare arms and cleavage, reminding her that October was already under way and that winter would soon be upon them. She stared down at the circular drive and cobbled walkways that extended around either side of the mansion and into the flower garden out back. They intended to install floodlights around the plantation house, for both atmosphere and security, but had not gotten around to it yet. That night only patches of moonlight illuminated the grounds below.

Laura closed her eyes and breathed deeply, drinking in the crisp country air. The excitement and anxiety of that day's sojourn finally left her body, and in its place settled a gentle peace. She truly felt as if she was home now. After years of renting apartments and other people's houses, Laura finally knew how it felt to stand in the shelter of a structure that she could honestly call her own.

She left the chilly night air, and returning to the bedroom, closed the French doors behind her. She looked down at her sleeping husband and suddenly felt a tremendous weariness overcome her. She had hoped that maybe they could have done some unpacking that night, perhaps set up the furnishings of the bedroom if nothing else, but she no longer felt the need to exert herself anymore that day. All she felt like doing now was curling up next to Rick and getting a good night's sleep.

Again she searched the cardboard cartons. This time, she found the one that held bed linens and blankets. She dug through the contents until she found an old patchwork quilt that her Grandmother Locke had sewn for her nearly twenty years ago. She took a moment to pry Rick's grungy sneakers off his feet; then, lying down next to him, she draped the heavy cover over both of them. An instant later, she was as sound asleep as her exhausted husband.

Chapter Three

On October 26th, Tyler Lusk received a phone call that he had been waiting three years for.

The young black man was working in the office of the Detroit bowling alley he managed, when the phone rang. He laid down the paperwork he was filling out and picked up the receiver. "Westside Lanes. May I help you?"

"Tyler, this is Professor Hughs," came a deep voice full of rumbling bass.

The monotony of that morning's work faded at the sound of the authoritative voice. "Yes, sir? How are you doing today?"

"Fine," replied George Hughs. The professor of ethnic history and the head of the University of Michigan's black genealogy department was usually as somber and humorless as a judge, but there was a definite hint of excitement in his voice that morning. "I have some good news for you, Tyler."

Suddenly Tyler Lusk could say nothing. A lump as large as a baseball lodged in this throat as the purpose of Hughs's unexpected call became clear to him.

"We found it," said the professor. "We finally found it!"

After a couple of attempts, Tyler gradually found his voice. "Are you sure?" he asked, although he knew very well that Hughs would not have called him if he had not been absolutely certain.

"I have the proof right here on my desk. If you want to

stop by and take a look at it, I'll be in my office until three o'clock this afternoon."

The university in Ann Arbor was about twenty-five miles west of Detroit. Tyler checked his watch. "I can be there by twelve-thirty."

"Excellent," said Professor Hughs. "We can have lunch together. I'll order a couple of sandwiches from the cafeteria. I recall that you're partial to ham-and-swiss subs."

"Right on the mark, as usual," said Tyler. "I'll see you in a while. And thanks for calling, Professor."

"It was my pleasure," said Hughs. Tyler could detect a tone of great satisfaction in the rumbling voice.

Tyler hung up and sat behind his cluttered desk for a moment, shaking his head incredulously. "Well, I'll be damned," he said softly.

He left his office and walked to the front counter. His best clerk, Hazel Schwartz, was handing a pair of size-eight shoes to a bowler who had just come in. He surveyed the alley's twenty-four lanes and saw that only a third of them were in use. Luckily for him, it was a slow day.

When the woman had assigned the bowler his lane, Tyler caught her attention. "I'm going to take a long lunch today, Hazel," he told her. "I should be back around two o'clock."

The dark-haired woman with the horn-rimmed glasses looked surprised. "Now I've seen everything!" she said. "Mr. Workaholic taking some time off. That's about as rare as a solar eclipse. What's up . . . or is that private business?"

Tyler shrugged. "Not really. You remember I told you that I've been trying to trace my family's roots? Well, I just got a call from a professor at the university, and he has some information for me. I thought I'd take a drive out there and see what he uncovered."

"So that's why you're in such a hurry?' Hazel asked jokingly. "Just because you want to find out which julep-swigging plantation owner enslaved your great-great-grandpa back during the Dark Ages?"

Tyler laughed. "I wouldn't expect you to understand, Hazel. You know exactly where your heritage lies. But my knowledge has always been severely limited. Hell, if I hadn't found those old letters in my grandmother's attic, I wouldn't have gotten this far in tracing my genealogy."

"Yeah, I know what you're saying," said Hazel with a smile. "I hope that professor found what you've been looking for. Let me know how it turned out when you get back, okay?"

"You've got it," said Tyler. He went back to his office, reached through the door for his jacket, then headed for his Camaro in the parking lot outside.

As Tyler buckled up and hit the road for the drive to Ann Arbor, he thought of how he had come to the decision to search out his family history in the first place. He'd been a senior at the University of Michigan three years ago. He was there on a basketball scholarship, but a knee injury in his second season had dashed all hopes of a career in professional sports. Fortunately, he was as promising in the classroom as he'd been on the basketball court. He majored in business, while dabbling in the subject of black history in his spare time.

It was the interest in history that had first prompted Tyler's desire to uncover the mystery of his own heritage. When he was a child, Tyler recalled his Grandmother Lusk telling him stories about the slave days, passed down to her from her own mother. The stories had never held very much detail as to names or locations, and Tyler had been much too young then to really care. Then, after his grandmother's death during his third year of college, he and his mother had been going through some junk in the attic of her house, when he'd come upon some old letters from a Great-Aunt Josephine. The letters were nearly illiterate, the handwriting crude and childlike, but Tyler had eventually deciphered them.

From what he'd gathered, Josephine and her mother, Allie, had fled north during the final year of the Civil War. Two other names were mentioned—those of Sassy and Samuel—and Tyler figured out that they referred to his great-great-grandmother and his great-great-uncle, who had been husband to Allie and father to Josephine. Other than those few gems of information, no other clues to the mystery were revealed in the letters. Tyler did not even know what part of the South his people had originated from, the information was that vague and unrevealing.

Then, during his last year at the university, Tyler had met the college's celebrated professor of black history, George Hughs. The man had taken an instant liking to the young student, seeing him as someone who truly appreciated his black heritage and desperately wanted to know the whole story concerning his ancestry. In his free time, Professor Hughs headed a nationwide genealogy network aimed at putting black students in touch with their roots. Through the magic of computer processing, Hughs had links to a number of other universities, as well as hundreds of black historians, librarians, and writers. During the past fifteen years, Hughs and his staff had revealed the hidden histories of over two thousand black families.

At the beginning of his senior year, Tyler had submitted what little information he had to Hughs, figuring that the history professor would have an answer for him within a day or two. Instead, the search had taken three long years. The names of Sassy and Samuel, as well as those of Allie and Josephine, had been cross-indexed with the multitude of files in the genealogical network, but nothing concrete had ever surfaced. That was, not until that morning.

Tyler hit the freeway and poured on the speed, anxious to get to the university as soon as possible. He could hardly wait to discover what Hughs had uncovered about his family and their mysterious origins.

"Ah, Tyler," greeted George Hughs when the young man stepped into the professor's office. "It's nice to see you again." He appraised his former student with interest. Tyler Lusk looked the same as he had two years ago—tall and lanky, nearly six and a half feet tall, his dark head shaved clean down to the scalp. The only things that seemed out of place were the suit and tie Tyler wore. Hughs was more accustomed to seeing the former basketball player dressed in a letterman jacket, stonewashed jeans, and Air Jordans.

Tyler reached across Hughs's desk and shook his hand. "Nice seeing you, too, Professor," he said with a nervous smile. "It's been a while."

"Yes, it has," agreed the professor. "Have a seat. The sandwiches arrived ten minutes ago. I ordered coffee, too. I believe you take yours black, don't you?"

"Right again," said Tyler. He took a chair opposite Hughs's desk, looking fit to bust. "Uh, Professor . . . could I take a look at what you found before we chow down? My stomach is tied in knots as it it."

George Hughs chuckled and took a sip of his coffee. "All right. I suppose you've endured enough suspense during the past few years. It would be unfair, even a little sadistic, of me to keep you hanging for even a few minutes longer." The rotund black man with the kinky gray beard winked at his former student and handed him a single sheet of paper.

Tyler felt a twinge of disappointment. "Only one page? That's it?"

Professor Hughs nodded. "Only one. But it contains the clue that we've been searching for." He set his coffee aside and leaned forward. "True, it doesn't tell the entire story. There is much more to be learned yet. But hopefully, this bit of information will lead to the end result."

Tyler studied the sheet of paper. It was a photocopy of an antiquated page of someone's diary or journal. The handwriting was elegant and at least more legible than the letters Tyler had found in his grandmother's attic. "Exactly what is this, Professor?"

"It is from the journal of Robert Edward Millenton, a Quaker clergyman who lived in Lexington, Kentucky, until his death in 1885." When Hughs saw the puzzled expression on Tyler's face, he elaborated. "Millenton was a strong abolitionist who participated in the Underground Railroad. This journal was recently discovered by some of Millenton's descendents during some remodeling that was being done at their family home."

"So my great aunt Josephine and her mother Allie escaped north from wherever they originated by using the services of the Underground Railroad?" asked Tyler, beginning to see the importance of the photocopied page.

"That's correct," said Professor Hughs. "Go ahead and read it."

Nervously, Tyler Lusk began to read the handwriting at the head of the page.

> *December 29th, 1864—We received perhaps two dozen Negroes tonight. Most of them were men, but several were women and small children. My wife and I fed them what little bread and beans we had, as well as water from the well. Most were quiet and well behaved, probably frightened more than anything else. My sympathies were drawn most by a pathetic child of two or three years who constantly wept for her father and grandmother. When I went to comfort the youngster, whose name was Josephine, her mother told me the cause of her grief. Like most Negroes that night, she and her daughter hailed from Tennessee, from the township of Franklin. From what I could gather from her mother, her husband, Samuel, had been brutally murdered by federal troops during the Battle of Franklin in late November of this year. The child's paternal grandmother, Sassy, had also suffered at the hands of the Northerners. The elderly woman had sustained a crippling wound from the sabre of a federal colonel and unfortunately had to be left behind due to her injury while the others fled to freedom. I said a prayer for those who had been lost, comforted the child the best that I could, then continued to attend to the others before making preparations for their journey northward.*

"Tennessee," said Tyler after finishing the page from Reverend Millenton's private journal. "So that's where my family comes from."

"So it seems," agreed Hughs. The professor studied his

former student from the opposite side of his desk. "I assume that you intend to pursue this lead further."

"Certainly," was all Tyler said in reply.

This reaction to the new information puzzled Hughs a bit. At first, the young man seemed ecstatic and full of wonder. Then his brow creased and a frown crossed his lips. "What's the matter?" asked Hughs. "I thought you'd be pleased."

"I am," replied Tyler. "But Tennessee is so far away. More than anything else, I feel like going down there right now and checking the rest of it out, maybe try to find the location of the plantation where Sassy and Samuel lived."

"What is the problem?" asked Hughs. "Can't you take a few weeks off from your job at the bowling alley?"

"No problem there," admitted Tyler. "I've got several weeks of vacation time owed me. I'll probably have to stick around a couple of weeks to help set up the winter leagues for this season, but I ought to be in the clear by the second week of November."

"Then something else is bothering you," surmised Professor Hughs. "Is it a matter of money?"

Tyler seemed a little embarrassed. "Yes, sir, I'm afraid so. I'm making a good salary managing the alley, but my mother's been sick a lot during the past year and I'm afraid my finances aren't in the best shape."

George Hughs regarded the young man thoughtfully and leaned back in his swivel chair. "Well, now, perhaps something might be arranged."

Tyler eyed his former teacher suspiciously. "Exactly what have you got up your sleeve, Professor?"

"What if I were to finance this little fact-finding mission of yours?" asked Hughs with a grin. "You know, pay for your airline tickets out of my own pocket, as well as your hotel and eating expenses."

Tyler was shocked by the man's offer. "I couldn't allow you to do that, Professor."

"Nonsense!" thundered Hughs. "Remember, I'm a lifelong bachelor who has put the lion's share of his earnings into the bank for thirty years. I could send half of the enrollment of this university to Hawaii and back, if I had a mind to. But believe me, Tyler, this is not solely a matter of money—this is a matter of realizing a dream. I recall how I felt when I discovered the facts of my own heritage twelve years ago. I remember how wonderful it was to finally put the mystery of my ancestry behind me. It was like lifting a great weight off my shoulders. Now I have the chance to experience that excitement once again, through you. So please, don't offend me by refusing my offer."

Tyler was nearly speechless. "I don't know quite how to thank you, Professor Hughs."

"Then don't," said the history teacher. "Just make your plans and keep me informed as to when you will be leaving, so I can do my part." He opened the center drawer of his desk and took out a single index card. He handed it to Tyler. "You might have thought that you would be on your own when you arrive in Tennessee, but that won't be the case. When you reach Franklin, get in touch with the people on this card."

Tyler read the names. "Archie and Alma Gant?"

"Yes," said Hughs. "They are considered to be the resident historians of the town of Franklin. I've never actually met them, but several of my colleagues have, and they have the highest of reputations, particularly in the study of Civil War history. Archie was the head of the history department at Vanderbilt University for forty years, and his wife, Alma, was a celebrated professor of archaeology, with a number of important historical finds to her credit. They both retired from teaching in 1985 and currently run a rare and used bookstore in the town square. They shouldn't be difficult to find at all."

"Thanks for the tip," said Tyler sincerely. "And for everything else as well."

"You're more than welcome," said Hughs with a smile. "I honestly don't believe you realize just how much personal satisfaction this discovery has given me. And if you agree to write a brief paper detailing your genealogical findings for publication, it would certainly help secure the network's funding grant for the forthcoming year."

"You've got it, Professor," promised Tyler, shaking his hand again.

"Good," said Hughs. "Now, why don't we get to work on these sandwiches? I'm absolutely famished."

Tyler was suddenly aware that his appetite had returned in full force. "So am I."

As they ate, Tyler Lusk relished his sudden turn of good fortune. There had been times during the last three years when he'd truthfully thought he would never know the whereabouts of his ancestral home. He still had a way to go before the full extent of that knowledge became clear to him, but somehow he knew that it would be revealed in time. And then all the uncertainty and frustration would give way to revelation, as well as the distinct pride of knowing from whom and where he had come.

Chapter Four

Three days of careful unpacking and steady work passed before Laura and Rick began to see the stately manor of Magnolia slowly transform into the comfortable home they'd always dreamed of. Furniture was arranged and rearranged, pictures were hung upon the walls, and rugs were laid across the polished surface of the hardwood floors. One by one, cardboard boxes and their packing of crumpled newspaper were discarded, while the possessions brought from Knoxville found permanent spots in the spacious rooms and corridors of the antebellum mansion.

The last two rooms to be completed were Laura's study and Rick's studio. They had agreed to locate their work areas at opposite ends of the second floor, more for privacy and lack of distraction than anything else. Since the start of their marriage, Laura and Rick had worked that way completely isolated from one another. There were several reasons for this, but the most practical had to do with the type of music each preferred to listen to while working on their individual projects. Laura was a big country music fan, while Rick was a diehard rock-and-roller. Garth Brooks and Reba McEntire didn't mix well with Led Zepplin and ZZ Top, so they decided it would be best to situate their bases of operation as far from each other as possible. That way there would be at least two or three rooms between study and studio to serve as a buffer against their individual stereos.

Laura turned a large bedroom at the western end of the

house into the place where she would write her books. They set up her computer desk, along with its word processor, disk drive, and laser printer, as well a dozen or so potted and hanging plants and several oaken bookcases. Hundreds of hardcover and paperback books were placed in their rightful spots upon the shelves. On the walls, Laura hung vintage movie posters of *Gone With The Wind, Casablanca,* and *The Wizard of Oz,* and of course, the framed covers of all her published novels, from the very first to the most recent.

After her study was completed, they went to work on Rick's studio. He had chosen the bedroom at the eastern end of the house, mainly because the light of the morning sun shone through the chamber's two windows and Rick did a good portion of his work between the hours of seven and eleven A.M. Compared to Laura's study, there was very little furniture here. Most of the room's space was taken up by a couple of large art tables and several standing easels made of seasoned hickory. Two tall metal lockers stood against one wall. One held the tools of Rick's trade: tubes of oil and acrylic paint, brushes, cleaning solutions, and racks of clean, white canvas waiting to serve as the landscape for the artist's rich imagination. The other locker held photo prints of Rick's best work, which he carried with him to art shows and conventions, and sometimes sold to fans and collectors. Along the other walls of the studio hung several of his original canvases, all of which had graced the covers of major magazines and best selling books over the years.

It was around noon of October 28th when Laura and Rick put the finishing touches on the studio and stepped back, satisfied with the work they had done that morning. "I believe this calls for a celebration," said Laura.

Rick put his arm around his wife's shoulders and pulled her closer. "What have you got in mind?" he asked.

"How about a picnic in the garden?" proposed Laura. "It's absolutely gorgeous outside. I'll fix some of my famous egg salad and we'll have lunch beneath that big oak out back. How does that sound?"

"Throw in a bag of potato chips and a pitcher of iced tea, and you're got yourself a deal," said Rick.

The two kissed, and then, hand in hand, made their way down the back stairway to the kitchen downstairs.

A half hour later, they had spread a blanket across the dead leaves that surrounded the base of the towering oak and set out the items of their picnic lunch. The afternoon was brilliant and colorful with the fiery hues of autumn. The temperature depended on where you sat: it was warm where the sun shone and nippy in the shade. Laura and Rick chose the sun-speckled shadows at the outermost reaches of the oak's overhead foliage, where the temperature felt just right.

"I'm certainly glad to get that business over with," said Laura. She spread egg salad generously between two slices of wheat bread and handed the sandwich to her husband.

In return, Rick poured a glass of tea and passed it to her. "I'll say," he replied. He crammed a couple of salty chips into his mouth. "It's always a pain in the ass getting everything situated just the way you want it. But I think we did a damn good job, if I do say so myself."

"I agree," said Laura. She made her own sandwich and took a bite. "Did I use enough mayonnaise in this?" she asked, searching Rick's face for the truth.

Rick took an experimental bite of sandwich and smiled. "It's perfect," he assured her.

"Good." Laura sipped her tea, then went to work on her sandwich, first peeling off the crust as she had always done since childhood. "So, when are you planning on getting back to work?"

"As soon as possible," he told her. "I'm nearly two weeks behind on all of my projects. I've got two book covers and a couple dozen ink-wash illustrations I have to finish before Christmas rolls around. I've got to run into town tomorrow for some tubes of titanium white and yellow ochre, but I hope to be back by eleven or twelve to work up some preliminary sketches, at least. How about you? Are you going to start back on that new book you were working on before we began this wild exodus across the state of Tennessee?"

"Yes," replied Laura. "The one about the Mississippi riverboat gambler and the bordello whore running from her past. I'm going to call it *Raging River.*"

"Good title," said Rick with a nod. "Sounds like it's going to be a steamy one. How much have you written so far?"

"Only the first three chapters, but it's coming along extremely well. I do believe this one is going to be my best book yet."

Rick chuckled. "You say that about them all . . . and, of course, you're usually right."

As the picnic progressed, their conversation slacked off. Rick concentrated on eating, while Laura turned an appreciative eye on the brick walkway of the barren garden and the great white house that stood only a few yards away. It looked nothing like it had when she was a gangly girl of twelve. All traces of age and deterioration had been concealed beneath new wood, mortar, and paint.

She recalled that Halloween night when the old Heller place had made such a lasting impression on her. She looked over at her husband and felt a little guilty about keeping the secret of that night from him, even after five years of marriage.

"Uh, Rick," she began. At first, Laura had debated over whether she should tell him; then she'd decided it couldn't hurt. "Do you remember me telling you that I've had a strange attraction to this place since I was a kid?"

"Sure," said Rick. "That's the whole reason for us moving back here to Franklin in the first place, isn't it?"

"Well, there is something I left out about the first time I came here . . . something I neglected to tell you."

"Oh, yeah?" Rick seemed intrigued. "What's that?"

"You may think I'm crazy, but here goes," said Laura. "Magnolia—the house, the grove, and most of the land around it—well, it's supposed to be haunted."

Rick stared at her for a moment, then burst out laughing. "Yeah, sure!"

"No, it's true," said Laura. Her lovely face grew red with embarrassment. "I know, because I've seen it with my own eyes."

Her husband's laughter died as he noted the grim look on Laura's face. "You're serious, aren't you?"

"Yes, I am," she said. "I saw a ghost, Rick. I really did."

In detail, Laura continued. She told Rick about her nocturnal visit to the Heller plantation on a Halloween night twenty years ago, as well as her sighting of the woman on the mansion's front balcony.

After she had finished her story, Rick sat there with a thoughtful frown on his face. "And you honestly believe this thing you saw was the ghost of Jessica Heller?"

"Yes, I do," said Laura. It was the first time she'd told anyone of the apparition she'd seen and, now that she had, she could not help but feel a little foolish. Such things as ghosts and UFOs seemed almost acceptable in the private realm of one's imagination, but when they are taken from that realm and put into words, they seemed totally childish and unbelievable.

"Are you sure it wasn't just a stupid prank?" asked Rick skeptically. "Maybe one of the other children rigged a bed sheet up there, hoping to scare you."

"It wasn't a sheet, Rick!" Laura snapped defensively. "It was something more than that. I really do think it was some sort of spirit."

"You didn't happen to see Count Dracula or Frankenstein lurking around the place, too, did you?" asked Rick with a little grin.

A hurt look crossed Laura's face. "You don't have to believe it, Rick, but it would be nice if you wouldn't make fun of me,"

Rick reached out and took her hand. "I'm sorry, sweetheart," he said sincerely. "You would think someone who deals with science-fiction and horror on a regular basis would believe in such things. But to tell you the truth, I'm a born skeptic when it comes to parapsychology and the occult. I might spend my days painting spooks and monsters, but I don't actually believe in them."

"Well, I do," said Laura. "At least, in this case." She looked toward the house and suddenly felt a chill overcome here. "I believe there is something here, Rick. Here in Magnolia."

"The ghost of Jessica Heller?" asked Rick.

"Yes," she replied. "And maybe even more than that."

Rick shook his head. "I'm sorry, darling, but we've been living in this house for several days and I haven't seen anything to suggest that this place is haunted. Now, tell me truthfully . . . have you?"

Laura thought about it for a moment. "No, I guess not."

"See? I thought so," said Rick. He leaned over and gave her a loving peck on the cheek. "I know you would like to *think* this place is inhabited by the lost souls of the Hellers. It's only natural that someone as imaginative and romantic as you would have such a fantasy. But the truth of the matter is, there are no such things as ghosts. Wouldn't you agree?"

Laura shrugged. "I suppose so."

"Good. That takes care of that. Now, why don't we finish our picnic, and afterward, we'll load all those empty boxes into the back of my pickup and haul them off to the county dump. Then we'll come back and have a candlelit supper, maybe watch a movie on the VCR or something. How does that sound?"

"Okay," allowed Laura, before returning to her sandwich and tea.

Later, after their picnic was over and they were cleaning up, Laura felt a little angry over their discussion about the ghost she claimed to have seen when she was twelve. Partly, she regretted sharing her childhood secret with someone else, but mostly she was upset over Rick's reaction. She recalled the patronizing way he'd talked to her, as if she were a naive six-year-old instead of an intelligent adult.

The very thought of Rick's smug attitude enraged her. She *had* seen something on the front balcony of the plantation house, and whether Rick believed her or not, Laura was certain that it had been the wandering spirit of Jessica Heller. And no amount of cynical persuasion on her husband's part was going to convince her otherwise.

That night, Rick Gardner found himself caught in the midst of a dream. Or, more precisely, the clutches of a disturbing nightmare.

He found himself standing in the center of a dark thicket, surrounded by rampant brush and bramble, as well as inky patches of dark shadow. Overhead, a full moon hung high in the autumn sky, casting an eerie glow upon the leathery leaves of the trees that stood around him. At first, Rick could not identify his surroundings. They seemed totally alien to him. But then, as he left the magnolia grove and halted before the crumbling structure of an ancient mansion, he realized where he was. He stood on the overgrown plantation grounds of Magnolia, years before its recent revitalization.

Something else puzzled Rick: He was no longer an adult, but a child, perhaps eleven or twelve years of age. Also, he was dressed in the costume he had worn on that Halloween of his childhood: the dark cowl and cape of Batman. Rick looked around, but found himself to be alone. As he started toward the empty ruins of the old house, he could not understand why he was there. He had lived in the city of Knoxville when he was that age and had known absolutely nothing about the Heller plantation or the nearby town of Franklin. Nevertheless, he accepted the fact that he was there, standing before the tall limestone columns and the fire-burnished walls that reared beyond them.

Rick approached the old mansion cautiously, aware of the dense shadows that clung to the dark structure, as well as the unnerving sounds of the night creatures that crept through the thicket around him. He was nearly to the front porch of the house when a forlorn sound drew his attention. It was the sound of mournful weeping, and it came from the balcony directly overhead, a balcony whose boards had burned away long ago.

Terrified, he looked upward and, above him, saw a ghostly figure standing where no one could possibly stand. At first, the weeping woman seemed unfamiliar. She was beautiful, small and petite. Her long hair was dark auburn in color, and her nightgown was made of the sheerest peach silk. The only unlovely thing about the woman was the expression on her face. She seemed to be in the painful throes of some horrid emotion, torn between grief and absolute terror.

Then, without warning, Rick's perspective abruptly changed. He was a grown man again, standing there, barefoot in his striped pajamas. And the wailing woman on the balcony was no longer a stranger. Instead, it was Laura who stood there, clutching the ornate railing with frantic fingers. Her face held an expression he had never witnessed there before, an agonizing mixture of intense fear and suffering. The familiar negligee of delicate lace and peach silk was filthy and nearly torn from her pale body. Even from where he stood, he could distinctly see the inflamed marks of fingerprints of the slim column of her neck, as well as ugly bruises and welts on the mounds of her breasts.

"Laura!" he called out. He wanted to rush forward . . . to make his way up to the balcony and take his frightened wife in his arms. But he could not. He was rooted helplessly to the spot where he stood. He could only watch in horror as the French doors opened behind Laura and a dark, indistinct form emerged. Rasping laughter as evil as that of the Devil himself assaulted Rick's ears as the wraith reached out and, pulling his screaming wife into its shadowy fold, retreated back into the empty hull of the old plantation house.

That was when he awoke, emerging from his troubled sleep like a drowning man struggling for a precious breath of lifegiving air. As he sat upright in the bed, trying to slow the pounding of his heart, Rick was aware that the interior of the room was lit with an odd glow. At first, he thought that he had fallen asleep without turning off the lamp next to the bed. But a second later he knew that wasn't the case. The yellowish light reflecting on the bedroom walls from the panes of the French doors leapt and danced as if alive.

"Oh, my God!" he cried out. He reached over and shook his wife roughly. "Wake up, Laura! Hurry!"

Rick sprang from the bed and swiftly crossed the master bedroom. As he approached the French doors and laid his hand upon the decorative handle, he could think of only one reason for the commotion outside. The magnolia grove that stretched from the main highway to the house was on fire. Beyond the glass of the doors leapt tongues of bright flame, and Rick could even feel the heat of the blaze radiating from the other side.

Afraid of what he might find, Rick took a bracing breath, then wrenched the doors inward. But what he actually experienced when he stepped onto the balcony instantly changed his fearful dread into total bewilderment.

The October night was cool, dark, and silent. He walked to the railing of the balcony and stared down at the heavy foliage of the magnolia grove. There was no raging fire there, only dewy leaves and dense shadow.

"Rick?" came the voice of Laura behind him. He turned to find his wife standing in the doorway, still half asleep. "Honey, what's the matter?"

Rick looked back out over the grove, searching hard for the least flicker of fiery light. He found none. "Uh, nothing, I guess. I just thought I saw something out there."

"What?" asked Laura. She joined her husband on the balcony and followed his gaze. All she could see was the dark grove that stretched below.

"Nothing," Rick finally said. "Just forget it."

"The way you woke me up, I thought the house was on fire," joked Laura. She slipped an arm around his waist and sleepily laid her head on his shoulder.

Rick said nothing. He thought of telling her about his nightmare, but decided not to. He didn't want her to know that their earlier discussion about ghosts had spooked him into having such a frightening dream.

As they stood there in the cool night air, Rick breathed in deeply. As he did, he caught a strong whiff of a peculiar odor. "Do you smell that?" he asked his wife, struggling to identify the sharp scent. "What is it?"

Laura took a breath and nodded to herself. "Burnt magnolia," she told him. "My father used to clear the land around our farm, and he burned his share of magnolia leaves. I remember how they smelled, both sweet and sour, like nothing I'd ever smelled before."

"Are you sure that's what it is?" asked Rick.

"I'm certain," said Laura. "I'd know that smell anywhere."

"But where is it coming from?"

Laura shrugged. "I don't know. Maybe one of our neighbors burned some leaves this evening and the smoke has just now drifted over here."

They stood there for a moment longer, staring out into the midst of the shadowy grove. Then Laura tugged on her husband's arm. "Come on, baby. Let's get back to bed."

"All right," he agreed. Together they walked back into the bedroom and closed the French doors behind them.

A short time later, Laura was already bundled up beneath the patchwork quilt, fast asleep. Rick remained awake a while longer, however. He stared at the walls and ceiling of the bedroom, thinking of the flickering glow of rampant flames. He was certain that what he had seen had not been a part of his nightmare. He knew that he'd been wide awake when he'd seen the light of the blaze and heard its destructive crackle. But there was no evidence that such a thing had actually happened.

He plumped his pillow, turned over on his side, and attempted to drive all thoughts of the puzzling illusion from his mind. Soon, he, too, was falling asleep. As he drifted off, the faint scent of burnt magnolia lingered in his nostrils.

Chapter Five

Laura was washing the breakfast dishes the following morning when her chore was interrupted by the sound of footsteps overhead.

She stood there at the kitchen sink for a long moment and listened. At first, there was only silence. Then the noise came again, the distinct creaking of floorboards directly overhead. Laura held her breath and heard the footsteps cross the ceiling from one end of the kitchen to the other.

Setting her washrag aside and rinsing the suds from her hands, Laura glanced over at the antique clock that sat on the mantel of the stone hearth. It gave the time as 9:47. Initially, she figured that maybe her husband had returned home from his errands in Franklin and entered the house without her knowing it. But Rick had left only a little after nine, and there was no way he could have finished what he had to do in such a brief period of time. No, whoever was causing the racket upstairs, it was not her spouse.

The thought of an intruder crossed her mind, sending a thrill of panic through her. She looked toward the phone on the wall. It would have been wise to simply cross the kitchen and dial 911, just to be on the safe side. Either that, or leave the house until Rick returned home.

But she hesitated: what if she called the local police and it turned out to be a false alarm? What if it was only the house settling and nothing more? She would only end up feeling foolish, and she certainly didn't want that to happen, especially after Rick's reaction to her admitting she believed in ghosts the previous afternoon. If he came home and found out that Franklin's finest had been there on a wild-goose chase, she would only have to endure more of his "you-are-letting-your-imagination-get-the-better-of-you" attitude.

Laura decided it would be best to investigate the puzzling noise on her own. She took a heavy cast-iron skillet from a hook over the gas range and hefted it in her hand. It weighed close to five pounds and was surely capable of knocking an assailant cold, if she had to resort to such measures. She thought again about calling the police, then pushed the idea away and started up the adjoining staircase toward the upper floor.

Halfway up the stairs, she heard the creaking again, this time accompanied by the crisp clack of shoes against the waxed surface of the hardwood floor. It sounded both authentic and strangely surreal at the same time. Laura could not put her finger on it at first, then came to the conclusion that the steady rhythm of the footsteps sounded more like a distant echo than anything else. It was like a noise that was rooted both in the present and the past, if such a description made any sense.

She paused there, midway on the staircase, listening as the sound of walking traveled from the western end of the house, moving slowly down the hall toward the east. Laura tightened her hold on the skillet, then took a couple more steps further up the stairway. As she neared the second floor, she could hear the footsteps coming closer. All she had to do was ascend the rest of the steps and she and the intruder would likely meet in the upstairs hallway at the same time. Laura experienced a moment's hesitation, but that was all. She took a deep breath, raised the frying pan threateningly overhead, then raced up the staircase and stepped into the open corridor.

The mysterious sound stopped the instant she entered the hallway. Adrenaline pumped through Laura as she checked one end of the corridor, then whirled and checked the other. The passageway was completely empty. She took a few cautious steps toward the center of the hall, but there seemed to be no sign of anyone having even been there.

Yet on closer inspection, she found that first assumption to be untrue. The door to her study stood halfway open. Laura was absolutely certain that she had closed it that morning before going downstairs to cook breakfast.

As she started toward the western end of the corridor, she felt her sense of alarm return. At that moment, she'd have preferred holding a gun in her hand instead of an iron skillet. There was no chance of that happening, however. Raised in the country, Laura had grown up with rifles and shotguns, but Rick was a different story entirely. He had grown up in a liberal household in the suburbs of Knoxville and he was staunchly anti-gun, anti-hunting, and anti-self-defense. Before he had made it big in fantasy art, he had even done a few brochure illustrations for some of the more vocal gun-control organizations, characterizing the National Rifle Association as ignorant, gun-toting rednecks. Laura had seen the cartoons and considered them heavily biased and even a little cruel, but she had not told Rick that. She also had known better than to ask Rick to buy a gun for home protection. If she had, he'd probably have given her a lengthy lecture on why it would be safer not to have a firearm in the house. But at that moment, Laura would have felt much more confident if she'd been carrying something more substantial than a cooking utensil into battle.

As it turned out, there was no battle to be fought. She entered her study only to find it empty, too. She looked around the room, but found nothing out of place. Everything seemed to be untouched. Everything, that was, except for her word processor. She caught a glimpse of the red light on the six-outlet power surge suppressor underneath her computer desk and couldn't figure out why it was on. She knew she had turned it off the day before yesterday, when she and Rick had finished hooking up her system. Yet oddly enough, the power was on now.

Laura crossed the room and turned on the disk drive and monitor of her word processor. The second puzzling thing she discovered upon entering the study was that there was a disk in one slot of the duel drive, one that was not supposed to be there.

"What's this doing in here?" she wondered aloud as she pressed the release button and ejected the 3½-inch microdisk. She was even more perplexed when she found it to be the disk that she had stored the first three chapters of her novel on.

A sudden sensation of dread gripped Laura. She slapped the disk back into the drive and punched the keyboard, calling up the disk's menu. Laura expected a listing of the title page and the first three chapters of *Raging River* to appear on the monitor in bright amber letters, but the data failed to materialize. The usual border and character memory count showed up, but the rest of the screen remained completely blank.

"Oh, no," she said beneath her breath. She experienced the fear that strikes every writer at least once during his or her career: the irretrievable loss of a significant amount of work. In her case, it was equivalent to several weeks' worth, counting rewriting and editing.

"No, damn it, no!" she cursed. Laura ejected the disk, blew into the slot of the drive to dislodge any dust or oxidation that might hamper its functioning, then inserted the disk again. And once again, the system came up totally empty. Close to sixty pages worth of carefully calculated prose had somehow been totally erased from the microdisk. And she had carelessly neglected to make a duplicate copy of the text on a backup disk.

"Shit!" was all she could think of to say in response to the disaster. She sat down in her typing chair and stared at the empty screen, feeling close to tears. True, she could probably rewrite the lost chapters, but she would never be able to duplicate them precisely, either in content or fluidity of style. She'd been on a rare roll when she began *Raging River;* as she had told Rick, she had written with an ease she'd never experienced before. But now, with every word of that work lost, tackling the rewrite of the novel seemed more like an unwelcome chore than anything else.

Laura sat there for a long while, staring at the blank monitor, as if attempting to mentally will the lost chapters back into existence. Then, as her anger and frustration began to diminish, Laura felt a sudden tug of inspiration. Usually, the empty screen was intimidating to her, but at that moment it seemed to challenge her, practically beckon her to put something on that black field . . . anything, even if it was only a word or two.

As she sat there, she began to smile to herself. She recalled the rude awakening that Rick had subjected her to the night before and the brief period of time she'd stood on the balcony, overlooking the dark acres of the magnolia grove. She recalled the bittersweet odor, the smell of charred leaves, and it almost seemed to fill her nasal passages again. It wasn't only the smell of fire-blackened vegetation, it was the smell of tragedy and needless ruin, a scent that had tainted the landscape of both South and North during the hellacious War Between the States. She closed her eyes and imagined how the Heller plantation had been before the conflict, a literal paradise on earth, and afterward, a graveyard of lost hopes and deserted dreams.

Laura Locke thought of all those things and a single germ of an idea began to slowly blossom in her mind. She laid her fingers upon the keyboard and slowly typed two words. They blazed from the black screen in bright amber, like the flames of a distant fire.

Burnt Magnolia.

"Yes," said Laura in amazement. "Why didn't I think of it before?"

She quickly entered the title in the disk's memory, afraid that it, too, might escape and become lost. Laura knew that she had things to do that morning: finishing the dishes and washing a few loads of clothes, among other chores. But she simply could not pull herself away from the allure of the word processor and the storyline that was practically writing itself inside her head.

Afraid that she might lose track of the images that her imagination was conjuring, she wheeled her chair closer to the desk and went to work. She typed *Chapter One* across the screen, then let the tragic story of love and war unfold, word after powerful word.

The town of Franklin, Tennessee was fifteen miles south of Nashville. Besides the fact that it was the seat of Williamson County and the site of a number of industries, Franklin's main claim to fame was the part it had played during the Civil War. During Confederate General John Bell Hood's attempt to take back Nashville from the Union, Major General John M. Schofield's 23rd Corps under the command of General George H. Thomas dug in at the small town of Franklin, blocking the way north. On November 30, 1864, they clashed with the forces of Hood's mighty Army of Tennessee. What ensued was one of the most sanguine and violent battles of the entire war. Six hours after the first shot was fired, the fighting finally lost its momentum, both armies past exhaustion. Schofield's forces suffered 2,326 casualties, while Hood's losses totaled a crippling 6,300 men. The surviving soldiers of both North and South moved on to battle once again in Nashville, leaving the town of Franklin shaken and battle scarred, but still intact.

Nearly a hundred and thirty years after the day of that devastating battle, the heart of Franklin remained much as it was back then. The circular hub of Public Square revolved around a tall limestone monument to those who had died there in battle on that thirtieth day of November in 1864. East to west stretched the main street, and along the quaint thoroughfare, stood the buildings of the commercial district, some relatively new, but most as old as the township itself. Further along its outskirts lay the residential sections, boasting some of the finest antebellum homes in the state of Tennessee. The residents of Franklin resided within its scenic boundaries, living the routine lives of ordinary Southern folk, but beneath the veneer of modern times remained a rich history that would never be overshadowed by progress.

On that morning of the 30th, Rick Gardner was just finishing up his errands around noon, when he was walking past the Choices Restaurant on the corner of Fourth and Main. He had bought his art supplies at a Tru-Value hardware store, then stopped at Gray's Drugs across the street to pick up a couple of bags of Halloween candy, just in case the youth of Franklin decided to pay Magnolia a visit two nights later. He was loading the purchases into the cab of his pickup truck when someone called to him from the doorway of the restaurant.

"Uh, pardon me, sir," came a voice harsh with age. "But would you be the husband of that lady writer? The one who just bought the old plantation house out on Highway 31?"

Rick turned and regarded the gentleman. He was short and lean, but seemed uncommonly spry for someone who was obviously in his mid-seventies. He wore wire-rimmed spectacles and sported a bushy mustache that was a shade or two lighter than his full head of iron-gray hair. There was a degree of sharp intelligence in the fellow's eyes that seemed to be a cut above that of a lot of the old-timers who Rick had seen hanging around Public Square or playing checkers on the steps of the Williamson County courthouse.

"Yes, I am," replied Rick. "My name is Rick Gardner."

The old man nodded. "I've heard the name before. You're an artist, aren't you? Did some cover work for a couple books put out by Rutledge Hill a few years back."

Rick was surprised that the gentleman was familiar with such work, since it was done for a small regional press instead of one of the major publishing houses. "That's right, but that was a pretty good while ago. I'm into fantasy illustration now."

"Yep," the old-timer said. "I've seen your work on a couple of the new Stephen King and Piers Anthony hardcovers. You're good. Got a fine eye for detail and bringing out emotion through visual image."

As usual, Rick felt a tad uncomfortable in the face of such high praise. "I don't believe I caught your name, Mister . . .?"

"Gant," said the old man. "Archie Gant. My wife, Alma, and I own the bookshop across the street. We specialize in rare and out-of-print books, as well as reference material and artifacts concerning the Civil War, particularly the battle that was fought here in Franklin." Archie Gant eyed the young artist curiously. "Alma and I were just sitting down for a bite of lunch. Won't you join us? I know Alma would enjoy meeting you."

Rick glanced at his wristwatch. "Well, I really do need to be getting back . . ."

"We won't keep you long, honest," promised Archie. "Just have a cup of coffee and chew the fat for five or ten minutes. That won't hurt, will it?"

"I guess not," agreed Rick.

He followed the man into the restaurant. A moment later, they were sitting down at a table next to the plate glass window. Archie introduced his wife to Rick and they exchanged pleasantries. Alma Gant was also in her seventies, as bone-thin as her husband, but a good head taller. Her blondish-gray hair was pulled up into a bun, and she had a rugged look about her, like someone who had spent the better part of her life outdoors, toiling in the earth.

"I used to be head of the history department at Vanderbilt in Nashville," offered Archie. "Alma here was a professor of archeology, and a damn good one, if I do say so myself."

"Seems like I've heard of you two before," said Rick in dawning recognition. "Didn't *Life* do an article on you a couple of years ago?"

"That's right," said Alma. "Didn't care much for it, though. Hated the photograph they used. It made me look like a shriveled-up old biddy."

"Well, you know what they say, sweetheart . . . the camera doesn't lie," said Archie playfully. He noted the expression of mock hurt on his wife's face and took her wrinkled hand in his own. The old man winked at Rick. "We always kid around with one another. We've been married for going on fifty years. If we didn't both have a great sense of humor, we couldn't have stomached each other's company for so dadblamed long."

Rick laughed. A waitress set a cup of coffee in front of him and he took a sip. "I hope Laura and I end up having the track record you two have."

"I don't know if you're aware of it or not, but Franklin is mighty proud of your wife," Archie told him. "It's not often that a resident here has a novel or two on the bestseller list. Maybe we could talk her into having a book signing at the shop when her next one comes out."

"I'm sure she'd enjoy that," said Rick. "And she'd go absolutely nuts over what you deal in. She's a Civil War buff from way back and uses that era in a lot of her storylines."

"I know," said Alma. "I've read a couple of Laura's novels. She always hits the nail smack on the head as far as historical accuracy goes. Don't care much for the sex scenes, though. They seem kind of trashy to me, but I reckon that's what sells today."

"She pretty much has to give the public what they want," said Rick, hiding a grin of amusement behind the lip of his coffee cup.

"Aw, don't mind her. She's just being a prude," said Archie. "So, how do you like living at Magnolia so far? I've heard tell that you folks really fixed the place up nice."

"We love it," Rick replied. "You'll have to come out and take a tour sometime."

Archie and Alma exchanged enthusiastic glances. "We'd love to. To be honest, we were always a little peeved that the state didn't buy Magnolia, restore it, and make it a historical landmark, like they did the Carter House and Carnton. I reckon you and Laura don't have any intention of opening it up to the general public, though, do you?"

"Not really," said Rick. "But I think Laura would jump at the chance to show the place off to anyone who might be interested in seeing it."

A brief stretch of silence halted their conversation momentarily, as if the Gants wanted to ask Rick something, but did not know quite how to. Then Archie came right out and asked the question. "Rick, have you or Laura experienced anything out of the ordinary since moving to Magnolia?"

"What do you mean?" asked Rick, although he had a good idea what the elderly man was driving at.

"Anything of a supernatural nature?" clarified Alma.

"You mean ghosts?" replied Rick, a little irritated.

"Yes," said Archie. "Have you noticed anything?"

Rick shook his head. "Absolutely not. It's just an old house, that's all. I didn't even know about those silly rumors about it being haunted until Laura told me yesterday."

"I can tell that you don't hold much to the idea of Magnolia being inhabited, do you?" asked Archie. "Well, I'll let you in on one thing, Rick. There are a lot of folks here in Franklin who *do* believe the place is haunted."

"And I take it that both of you believe it, too."

"That's right, we do," said Alma. "In my case, I was a practicing archaeologist for over forty years. I've excavated my share of Civil War sites and Indian burial mounds here in Tennessee, and believe me, I've experienced some things that would set your hair on end."

"Alma's right," said Archie. "There's so many documented cases of spiritual phenomenon around these parts that it's difficult *not* to believe in such things. Take the ghostly light at Chapel Hill, or the Bell Witch Cave up in Adams. And the battlefields at Stones River and Shiloh have their fair share of hauntings, too. Alma and I aren't ignorant by a long shot. Between the two of us, we've got enough degrees and doctorates to fill a good-sized file cabinet. But we believe in spooks, mostly because we've experienced such phenomena first-hand."

"Well, I'm sorry, but I won't believe it until I see it with my own eyes," said Rick, dismissing the idea that he ever would.

Archie shrugged. "Everyone has his own opinion. But if something does happen, if you do encounter something that you can't explain, we'd be obliged if you'd give us a call. We know of a guy by the name of Monroe who specializes in investigating such things."

"If anything happens, I'll give you a call," said Rick, finishing his coffee. "But I wouldn't hold my breath, if I were you."

Alma smiled in the face of the artist's cynicism. "Don't be cocksure, Rick. Magnolia has a long history of spectral activity. You'll be witness to it sooner or later."

The conversation moved on to other subjects concerning the town of Franklin, then Rick politely excused himself. As he left the restaurant and walked to his truck, he found himself feeling a little uneasy. The recurring theme of ghosts was beginning to bother him. The fact of the matter was, he wasn't all too sure he really dismissed such phenomena as much as he let others believe. He recalled the dream he'd experienced the night before, as well as the puzzling illusion of firelight on the walls of the master bedroom. He'd been trying to solve that mystery all morning, trying to work out a plausible explanation in his head, but had come up with nothing. Either he'd actually seen the brilliant cast of a runaway fire reflected through the panes of the French doors or his imagination had played one hell of a practical joke on him.

Chapter Six

It was two o'clock in the afternoon on the thirty-first of October when a Winnebago cruised down a dusty rural road ten miles north of Lawrence, Kansas, and pulled into the gravel driveway of the Applegate farm. The thirty-foot camper braked to a halt behind several parked cars, idled for a moment, then grew silent.

Five people stood on the long front porch of the Applegates' two-story farmhouse, each regarding the vehicle with expectation. "This must be the man we've been waiting for," said a squat, bespectacled man with a salt-and-pepper beard. He chewed anxiously on the stem of his briar pipe, blue clouds of Borkum Riff surrounding his balding head like a vaporous halo.

A moment later, two men left the cab of the Winnebago. One was unremarkable in appearance, just another face in a crowd of average people. He was lean in build, and had mousy brown hair and a moustache, as well as tinted eyeglasses. The occupants of the porch turned their eyes from him and directed their attention to the other man, who rounded the front of the camper and walked toward the farmhouse with quiet confidence.

He was tall, perhaps six foot three, and his autumn clothing did little to conceal his muscular physique. He was obviously a man who cared about his health and adhered to a strict regiment of diet and exercise. He was tanned, his hair was blond almost to the point of being platinum, and his eyes were a brilliant emerald green. To the two women who stood on the porch, the word "Adonis" instantly sprang into mind, while the three men present simply saw the good looks and charisma that were usually possessed by movie stars and young politicians. But all five knew there was much more to the man than that.

The bearded man stepped down off the porch and extended his hand as the blond stranger approached. "You must be Wade Monroe," he said, smiling broadly around the stem of his pipe.

"Yes, sir," replied the tall fellow, flashing a perfect smile in return. He took the elderly man's hand, exhibiting a firm grip that was certainly to be expected. He turned and indicated the young man with the glasses. "And this is my assistant, Bret Nelson. He will be helping me with the investigation."

"I'm Dr. Jonas Haynes," the man introduced himself. "The one who brought this matter to your attention."

Wade Monroe nodded. "The head of the Kansas Society for Paranormal Research. It's a pleasure meeting you, Doctor."

"The pleasure is all mine, Mr. Monroe," said Haynes. "My colleagues and I have heard a lot of good things about your success in solving such, shall we say, otherwordly mysteries?"

"I've had my share of successes as well as failures," Wade told him truthfully. "Let's just hope that this one will turn out satisfactorily."

"I'm hopeful that it will," said the elderly doctor. "Come and let me introduce you to the others."

Jonas Haynes introduced the four on the porch to Monroe and Nelson. Emily Jackson was a representative of the Kansas Historical Society, while Phillip Thomas was a professor of American history at the University of Kansas in nearby Lawrence. The other two, a rustic couple in their mid-forties, were introduced as Joe and Tammy Applegate, the owners of the rural farmstead.

Wade Monroe, on the other hand, needed no introduction to those who greeted him on the front porch. Dr. Haynes had filled them in at length on Monroe's credentials and reputation several weeks before the present meeting had been scheduled. Wade Monroe was known throughout the country as a pioneer in the field of parapsychology and spiritual phenomena. Seven years ago, Monroe had left a prestigious position as a respected historian at Harvard University and shocked his peers by abandoning his normal line of work to pursue "ghost-hunting" as a full-time profession. There had been plenty of skeptics at first. Many had claimed him to be a fake and refused to accept his victories in the strange field of psychic research. Then he'd gained notoriety and acceptance when the President had invited him to the White House to investigate the apparent haunting of the Lincoln bedroom. Monroe and his assistant had successfully documented the spectral presence of Abraham Lincoln in the celebrated bedroom and the hallway beyond, recording the gaunt and bearded image of the sixteenth president using high-speed photography and videotaping. The irrefutable proof of Lincoln's ghost had graced the pages of *Life* and *Time*, as well as countless academic publications, and had thrown the shadow of doubt off Wade Monroe, turning him into America's premier parapsychologist virtually overnight.

There was one interesting aspect to Monroe's selection of investigations, however. The thirty-six-year-old man from Massachusetts accepted only cases that had a definite link to the American Civil War. Monroe had performed numerous investigations of the country's military parks, such as Gettysburg, Stones River, and Shiloh, and had been successful in documenting, and in some case exorcising, the sources of the haunting from those sites of mass destruction and violent death. He had also investigated many private residences, stately mansions and humble farmhouses alike. Monroe laid no claim to possessing clairvoyance or any other psychic abilities in his "cleansing" of the site of a haunting. Rather, he depended solely on scientific means and simple common sense to perform his work. As of that day in late October, Wade Monroe had successfully investigated seventy-four cases of psychic phenomena throughout the United States, with only three known failures during the course of his stellar career.

After all had been introduced on the porch of the Applegate house, they went inside to the front parlor. When everyone had been seated and Tammy Applegate had gone to the kitchen to prepare coffee, Wade Monroe turned to Dr. Haynes. "I studied the information you sent me," he told the elderly man. "Quite a remarkable history . . . almost as remarkable as the phenomena is unique. I'm looking forward to getting to work as soon as possible."

"I assure you, Mr. Monroe, you have plenty of time to set up whatever equipment you brought to record this spiritual occurrence," said Haynes. "Mr. Applegate here claims that the haunting takes place only on the thirty-first of each month, and then for only a few minutes past the hour of eight o'clock P.M."

"That's right," said Joe Applegate, shaking his head. "And it's a grisly sight to behold, I'm telling you. Me and Tammy would've moved out of this place years ago, if we hadn't had so much money tied up in the farm. Usually, we just check into a motel or stay overnight with relatives on the thirty-first of the month, just to stay clear of what goes on in that upstairs bedroom."

Wade nodded. Tammy Applegate entered the parlor with a tray of steaming coffee mugs and the parapsychologist graciously accepted one. Wade took a long sip from his cup, his green eyes roaming the walls and ceiling of the parlor, studying the dimensions of the room and authenticity of its nineteenth-century architecture. Finally, he set his mug aside and looked at Jonas Haynes. "May we review the history of this house, Doctor? I believe it would benefit us all if we kept the tragedy of this place foremost in our minds during the course of tonight's investigation."

"I agree," said Haynes. "I'll leave that to Ms. Jackson. After all, she was the one who compiled the historical profile of the Applegates' home."

Emily Jackson held her cup in both hands, looking more like a spinster librarian than a representative from the state's historical society. "This property was claimed by an Illinois farmer named Elmer Saxton in 1850. The house and several of the remaining outbuildings were constructed by Saxton when he moved his family to Kansas in 1852. Saxton and his wife, Elizabeth, lived a fairly normal existence here for nine years, raising wheat and barley, as well as two beautiful twin daughters named Suzanne and Sarah, who were born in 1858. Then the Civil War broke out in July of 1861 and their idyllic life gradually came to a halt. In the spring of 1862, Elmer Saxton left his family behind and joined the Union Army, intending to help fight some of the guerilla forces that originated from the neighboring state of Missouri. It was a frightening time here in Kansas. The rebel forces of William Quantrill and Bloody Bill Anderson were terrorizing the territory: looting, raping, and murdering with impunity. The worst happened in August of 1863 when Quantrill and his guerillas raided the town of Lawrence. They slaughtered one hundred and fifty men and boys, set numerous houses on fire, then got drunk amid the ruins. It was just the type of bloodthirsty behavior that Elmer Saxton had gone to war to put an end to.

"Then, on a stormy night in March of 1864, Major Saxton and his cavalry were returning to Lawrence after unsuccessfully tracking a band of renegade Redlegs when Saxton decided to stop at his farm and visit his family, whom he hadn't seen in five long months. Saxton was riding onto the property, when over the gale of the thunderstorm, he heard a shrill scream come from the farmhouse. He gazed up at the top floor of the house in time to see his wife, Elizabeth, leap through an upstairs window and plunge to her death almost at his feet. Saxton was horrified by his wife's actions, but had the presence of mind to look for his children. He found the twins, Suzanne and Sarah, in the bedroom from which Elizabeth had jumped. Both were dead . . . drowned by their own mother in a washing tub that she used for giving them a bath."

"And did Elmer Saxton ever discover the reason for the

murder of his children or the suicide of his wife?" asked Wade Monroe.

"No," said Phillip Thomas. "We have the private journal of Elmer Saxton at the university, and even to the day of his death in 1892, the poor man still had no clue as to why Elizabeth Saxton performed the grisly deed that she did." The history professor took a long swallow of coffee and glanced overhead toward the upper floor and the spot where the heinous crime had taken place over a hundred and thirty years before. "I was never a believer in ghosts, Mr. Monroe. I was probably the most stringent skeptic you could find in the entire state of Kansas. But that was before I came here a couple of months ago and saw for myself what takes place in that bedroom on the thirty-first of each month. And, take it from me, it is like nothing you have ever been witness to before."

"Is the display of the phenomenon particularly violent?" asked Bret Nelson out of curiosity.

"Yes," said Professor Thomas uncomfortably. "Extremely violent."

The occupants of the parlor sat in awkward silence for a few minutes. Then Wade Monroe finished his coffee and, setting his mug aside, stood. "I would prefer that you all stayed here while my assistant and I set up our equipment upstairs. Some of the sensors and cameras are extremely delicate, and it takes several hours on our part to make sure that everything goes according to plan."

"Do whatever you need to, Mr. Monroe," said Dr. Haynes. "Just let us know when you're ready to start. We certainly don't want to miss anything."

"We ought to be finished by seven o'clock," Wade assured Haynes and the others. "That should give us sufficient time to take our places before the phenomenon begins."

Joe Applegate regarded the parapsychologist hopefully. "Do you think you can stop it, Mr. Monroe? Do you think you can keep it from happening again after tonight?"

Wade answered the farmer truthfully. "I don't know, Mr. Applegate. But we will certainly do our best to solve whatever mystery lies behind this haunting and try to rectify the solution if it's in our power to do so."

"May I have the time, please?" Wade Monroe asked his assistant.

Bret Nelson sat in a chair at the far side of the upstairs bedroom, surrounded by several banks of electronic monitors. "Seven-fifty-nine and twenty seconds."

The parapsychologist grew silent once again, his eyes centered on the middle of the room's hardwood floor. He waited as the others did: quietly, motionlessly, anticipating the appearance of the phenomenon. A variety of highly sophisticated equipment lined the bedroom walls. Video cameras, audio mikes, and sensors capable of detecting the most subtle changes in the room's temperature and atmosphere were directed at a single spot in the center of the floor. The emotional tension that built in the room was nearly unbearable. Wade knew that some of it was the excitement generated by the living beings who stood in the far corner, out of the range of the cameras and sensors. But he was also experienced enough to know that a lot of it originated from some unknown source, more than likely the specter that was only moments away from making its scheduled appearance.

"Ten-degree drop in room temperature," Bret said suddenly. "Twenty."

"I feel it," whispered Wade. The room had originally been sixty degrees, due to the coolness of the autumn night, but now it had abruptly dropped to forty. Wade waited a few seconds more, then exhaled a deep breath. It exited his lungs in a frosty plume of mist. "Thirty degrees and holding," Bret informed him.

Wade glanced over at Dr. Haynes and the others. They huddled together in the cramped confines of the corner, clutching themselves against the cold, but even more alert than they had been before. He turned his eyes back to the center of the room just as a brilliant flash shined through the chamber's three windows. A moment later a deep rumble like the approach of distant thunder sounded, sending vibrations through the floor beneath their feet. He looked over at his assistant, his eyes questioning. The Kansas sky had been clear and cloudless all day, with no forecast for thunderstorms.

Bret seemed just as puzzled. "The sensors outside show no change in barometric pressure." He sniffed at the air, then checked a reading on one of the monitors. "Olfactory sensors detect the definite presence of ozone."

Wade nodded. He also noticed the sharp scent of raw electricity.

They waited a full two minutes more, listening to the mysterious thunderstorm grow in intensity outside the perimeter of the bedroom. The fury of the gale rattled the windows and sent mild shock waves through the timbers of the floor, but still the sensors outside the house failed to confirm the presence of such a storm. Then another sound echoed just beneath the roar of thunder. At first, Wade could not place it. Then, suddenly, he recognized it as the pounding of shod hooves. It sounded as if a band of horsemen was approaching the farmhouse from the south.

Wade was about to ask for an audio reading when an eerie blue glow blossomed in the center of the bedroom. It was dull at first, then gradually increased in brilliance. The automated video and 35mm still cameras swung immediately toward the source of the light, recording the phenomenon. Wade watched as the light eventually took form. It was indistinct to begin with, then slowly became unnervingly clear.

"Oh, my God," gasped Bret.

Wade's reaction to the phenomenon matched that of his assistant. Very rarely had any of the spirits he'd encountered appeared in such vivid and gruesome detail. Even a veteran like himself was struck speechless for a moment and he felt a cold shiver run down the length of his spine, a reaction that he had not experienced for several years.

The scene that unfolded before them was indeed a grisly sight to behold. A thin, homely woman in a gingham dress and cotton apron knelt before a steel washtub, her bony hands immersed beneath the bubbling surface. An alarming combination of emotions molded the woman's plain face into a mask of hellish torment. Desperation, terror, and intense self-loathing—all were displayed in the woman's tortured features. At first, it was difficult to imagine the source of her anguish. Then her hands rose from the water, driven into the open by the force of those fighting for survival. The woman had the drenched and gasping head of a twin daughter in each hand, her skinny fingers entwined in their golden curls, attempting to press them back into the depths of the huge washtub. Over the roar of the thunderstorm and the sound of approaching horses, the wet screams of the children could be heard, then the awful gurgling noise of their watery suffocation as their mother drove them back beneath the surface.

Wade Monroe and the others watched in shocked silence as the ghost of Elizabeth Saxton completed her heinous act of double murder. The thrashing beneath the soapy water finally subsided, until the liquid within the tub grew still. Then, with the long wail of a woman driven over the brink of insanity, Elizabeth rose and turned toward the tall window in the very center of the bedroom wall. From the story that had been told to him, Wade knew precisely what was on the woman's mind. He watched as she took a couple of faltering steps toward the flashing panes of the window.

But before she could go any further, Wade called out. "Stop!" he yelled as loudly as possible.

The specter halted in mid-step and turned. Her horrified eyes seemed not to see him at first. Then they focused and she gaped at him, appearing to be as surprised to see him standing there as he was to witness her ghostly crime.

"Don't be frightened, Elizabeth Saxton," he said softly, taking a tentative step toward her. "I am here to help you."

A strangled laugh escaped her throat. *"Help me? Oh, sir, it is far too late to help a wretched soul such as I!"*

"No," Wade told her. "I won't accept that." He spoke softly and carefully, yet firmly, well aware that if she neglected to listen to him, she would carry out her act of ghostly suicide and he would not have a chance to converse with her again for another month. "Tell me, Elizabeth. Tell me . . . why did you kill your children?"

"I had to!" she sobbed. *"I had no other choice. They had to be spared . . . at any cost. Even if it was that of their own precious lives."*

"But what sort of horror could their deaths have possibly spared them from?" asked Wade.

Elizabeth Saxton pointed a gaunt finger toward the south. *"Do you hear that? The sound of approaching riders? The fabled horsemen of Revelation's Apocalpyse could have no more of a consequence for my family than they do!"*

"Who do you think they are?"

"Bushwhackers!" moaned Elizabeth. *"Thieving marauders who do as they please and leave pain and death in their wake!"*

"But I don't understand—" began Wade.

"They have darkened my doorway before, a mere six weeks after my Elmer left to fight for the Union," she explained. *"They locked the twins in the root cellar, then took advantage of my helplessness. They raped me! Violated me in every way imaginable, the whole stinking lot of them! They left me half dead and bleeding, then vowed to return before the War's end and do the same to Suzanne and Sarah, whether they be children or not."*

Wade began to see the terrible logic of the woman's ghastly action. "So you spared them the horror of rape by taking their lives."

Elizabeth Saxton wailed, luminous tears rolling down her cheeks.

"*It seemed like the only way at the time. I could not bear the thought of my beloved babies enduring the acts that had been performed on me, as well as the agony and shame of being battered and torn by the lust of those evil bastards. I figured death would be much kinder to them, and so I delivered them into the arms of the Lord Almighty, where Satan's kind could do them no harm."*

Wade said nothing for a long moment; he simply stared at the sobbing spirit. Part of her grief was due to the murdering of her children, but that was not it entirely. There was another part to her grief, a part that had never been revealed . . . until now.

"The riders who visited your farm that night," said Wade softly. "They were not the bushwhackers, were they?"

Elizabeth dropped to her knees, threw back her head, and screamed mournfully. *"No! Merciful God in heaven help me! They were not who I first suspected them to be!"*

"It was your husband, wasn't it? Your husband and his cavalry unit, paying an unexpected visit."

"Yes!" she wailed, wringing her lean hands. *"But how was I to know? Tell me that!"*

"You couldn't have," assured the parapsychologist. He swallowed dryly, then continued. "Listen to me, Elizabeth: it wasn't your fault. Your guilt over what you did has chained you to this realm, trapped you in a place between heaven and earth. You must break free. You must forgive yourself and pass through."

Elizabeth's tearful eyes stared pleadingly at Wade. *"But you don't understand. I cannot go there. I cannot bear the thought of facing him!"*

"Who?"

"My husband! My Elmer. I could never face him after I murdered those two little girls who he cherished so very much! I could never survive the hatred that he must surely hold for me!"

Wade knew that now was the crucial moment. He chose his words carefully. "You are mistaken, Elizabeth. Please, believe me, it would not be like that. Your husband discovered the truth behind your actions the very moment of his own death. He waits on the other side with your two daughters . . . waits for you to come to them. There will be no harsh feelings, no accusation. There will only be joy at the reuniting of your family."

A glimmer of hope emerged in the ghost's tormented eyes. *"Do you really think so? Do you honestly believe that I will be forgiven my sin?"*

"Yes," said Wade, smiling. "I *know* that you will."

Elizabeth Saxton returned the smile. "*Then I will do as you say. And God bless you for delivering me from this long torment.*"

Wade nodded and watched as the ghost turned toward the bedroom's center window. The chaos of the thunderstorm ended abruptly, and beyond the panes of glass, there blazed a light that was nearly blinding in its brilliance. Wade squinted against the glare and caught a fleeting glimpse of three forms standing, hand in hand, amid the white glow—the forms of a man and two small children.

Elizabeth turned back and looked at Wade one last time.

"Go ahead," he urged. "They are waiting for you."

The spirit nodded gratefully, then stepped completely through the window into the light beyond. Instantly the darkness of night returned, sealing whatever portal had opened there temporarily. The upstairs bedroom of the Applegate house also returned to its former state. All that remained was a room full of delicate equipment and seven bewildered people.

Wearily, Wade turned his eyes toward his assistant. "Bret?"

It was a second before Bret could speak. "All monitors show zero readings," he said.

Wade Monroe turned toward the five spectators who stood motionlessly in the far corner. "Ladies and gentlemen . . . this house has been cleansed."

"Bravo," said Jonas Haynes in little more than a whisper. He stared at the parapsychologist with the same emotion that shone in the eyes of the others, a mixture of extreme wonderment and heartfelt admiration.

Two hours after the ghostly incident in the Kansas farmhouse, Wade Monroe and Bret Nelson rested in the main room of the Winnebago.

"You look positively exhausted," said Bret. He poured a generous amount of aged bourbon into a glass and brought it to the man who sat on the camper's sofa.

"I am," said Wade with a sigh. "Physically as well as mentally. You know how trying these investigations can be sometimes. Especially one as tragic as this one was." He took the glass from his companion and took a long sip of the amber liquor.

"I understand," said Bret. He sat on the arm of the couch and stared at Wade with concern. "But this one wasn't so tragic, was it? You saved that poor woman's soul, didn't you? Sent it on the right path?"

"Yes, I suppose so," said Wade. "But the thought of her existing in torment all those years . . . well, it's difficult to fully comprehend."

Bret understood his friend's melancholy. Wade Monroe often suffered a dark mood immediately following an investigation, whether it turned out favorably or not. He knew that Wade laid no claims to any sort of psychic ability, but sometimes Bret wondered. He wondered if perhaps Wade did absorb some of the tragedy and sorrow that the subjects of his investigations endured in their various states of limbo, and that maybe it was that accumulation of raw emotion that affected Monroe so severely.

"Try to loosen up," Bret told him. He set his bottle of Michelob aside and reached out, placing his hands on Wade's shoulders. He kneaded the tight muscles and attempted to work out some of the tension. "Poor baby. You're all knotted up."

Wade turned his head and regarded his companion wearily, his eyes softening. He said nothing at all; their expressions spoke stronger than any words that might be uttered. Their faces grew close, and without the slightest hesitation, their lips meshed in an impassioned kiss.

When the two men drew apart, Wade's smile curled into a sarcastic, almost bitter smirk. "They thought I was a hero in the bedroom of that farmhouse. They thought I was some great champion for lost souls and praised me for releasing Elizabeth Saxton from her ghostly imprisonment." He laughed harshly. "I wonder if Jonas Haynes and the others would still think so very highly of me if they knew the truth? That the man they admired so much was a flaming faggot?"

Bret frowned as he returned his hands to Wade's shoulders and began to massage his lover's muscles once again. "There you go, talking that crap again. I hate it when you get into such a shitty mood."

Wade reached up and patted one of Bret's hands. He knew that it hurt Bret when he spoke of their sexual orientation in such a crude manner. "Sorry," he apologized. "But just consider it for a moment, will you? What do you think would happen to our careers if word got out that Wade Monroe and his skilled assistant, Bret Nelson, were homosexual lovers? Do you honestly think that we would continue to be in the same demand that we are now?"

"No," admitted Bret truthfully. "I suppose not."

"Of course not," said Wade. He took another swallow of his bourbon. "Those stiff-necked conservatives would brand us a couple of perverted queers, and that would be the end of it. No more invitations to investigate the supernatural, no more nationwide exposure in magazines and scholarly journals, and certainly no more government grants. No, Bret, we would be up Shit Creek without a paddle, as my grandfather used to put it so colorfully. Our standing in the field of parapsychology would be forever tarnished."

Bret wanted to assure his lover that the public's discovery of their relationship would not be as severe as he thought it would, but he knew that he would only be lying. Wade was right: if the historic and scientific communities found out about their secret, they had just as soon put a gun to their head and pull the trigger. Professionally, they would be dead men.

"No one will ever find out," said Bret. "Not if we continue to be discreet about it."

Wade sighed. "Maybe. If we're lucky. But everyone's luck runs out eventually. Why should ours be any different?"

Bret stood up and took his bottle of beer. "Come on—it's late. Let's go to bed."

"You go on," Wade said, looking miserable. "I just want to sit here for a while and try to unwind."

Bret ran his fingers gently through Wade's blond hair. "Don't be long."

"I won't," his companion of seven years assured him.

When Bret had disappeared down the narrow hallway of the camper to the rear bedroom, Wade Monroe sat on the couch, slowly sipping his bourbon and thinking of his life. It had been a long time since he'd actually questioned his homosexuality. Upon becoming an adult, he'd grown to accept it. It came to him as naturally as heterosexuality came to most men. But on nights such as this, when the strain of a particularly emotional investigation had come to its conclusion, Wade felt his confidence slip a few notches and he began to wonder whether he was actually a sexual freak or not. The confusion of his adolescence returned in full force. He recalled how he had borrowed his friends' *Playboy* and *Penthouse* magazines, how he had spent hours alone in his bedroom, staring at the pages of naked feminine flesh, attempting to force himself to feel some small twinge of lust at the sight of them, but unable to. He had suffered then, feeling as if there was something horribly wrong with him and feeling dirty and unclean when he was aroused at the sight of his buddies in the locker room shower. During moods of depression like the one he was experiencing tonight, Wade returned to the doubts and self-loathing that he had endured during that difficult time before his college days.

It was three o'clock in the morning and four drinks later when Wade Monroe finally drove away those thoughts of self-doubt and, entering the bedroom, undressed and climbed beneath the sheets, seeking warmth from the young man who slept there silently and hating himself for doubting their love for one another during that brief period of melancholy soul-searching.

Chapter Seven

After the final member of the wedding party had extended their heartfelt congratulations and the last horse-drawn buggy was on its way down the moonlit lane of the magnolia grove, Braxton Heller and his new bride, Jessica, turned to one another. Braxton gazed appreciatively at the lovely, auburn-haired lady in the lacy white wedding gown, while Jessica admired the strapping, mustachioed man in the black dress coat and immaculate white tie.

"Now that our guests are gone," said Braxton, a sly spark glinting in his iron-gray eyes, "the remainder of this night belongs to us and us alone."

Shyly the young bride smiled at her new husband. "Let us go upstairs," she suggested. Behind Jessica's customary air of demure femininity lurked a hint of something wild and untamed. "Now."

Braxton wasted no time. He offered the lady his arm and escorted her through the open doorway of the plantation house. A Negro butler closed the double doors of heavy oak behind them, then awaited further instructions from his master.

"We are not to be disturbed until breakfast tomorrow morning, Josiah," Braxton told him. "Do you understand?"

Josiah nodded sternly. "Yes, sir. I'll see to it that no one bothers you or the mistress."

"Very good," said Braxton. Then the handsome young

planter took his wife's delicate hand and assisted her up the winding staircase to the floor above.

A moment later, they were in the master bedroom. Tension filled the chamber. Most of it was due to the nervousness of their first night together as man and wife, as well as the anticipation of passions that had been honorably suppressed since the first day of their courting, but would soon be wantonly unleashed.

Braxton closed the bedroom door behind him and engaged the latch. He turned toward his bride. Jessica had already taken the pins from her hair and let its coppery locks spill over her porcelain-white shoulders. Braxton reached to his throat and with a single tug pulled away the constricting length of the bow tie. "I've waited so long for this moment, my dear," he told her. "So very long."

"So have I," said Jessica softly. Her petite arms reach around and deftly unfastened the hooks on the back of her wedding gown. The white dress fell away from her body and pooled around her feet. "Take me, Braxton. I am yours now."

Without further hesitation, Braxton stripped off his coat and shirt, then advanced on her. Jessica moaned as his lips meshed with her own and she felt his fingers feverishly working to unfasten the restraints of her foundation garments. She abandoned the prim teachings of her mother and used her own initiative, unbuttoning the front of Braxton's trousers. Soon, both husband and wife were completely naked. Flesh pressed against flesh as Braxton took Jessica in his arms and carried her bodily to the big, canopied bed.

"Gently," whispered Jessica, as the man's weight bore down on her. His steely eyes showed compassion and tenderness as he slowed his pace. The young woman gasped at his entrance, then cried out at the piercing of her maidenhead. A moment later, however, all pain had turned into pleasure. Jessica's low moans accompanied the labor of Braxton's breathing as they clung tightly to one another, abandoning themselves to the passion they had been denied for so long.

Gradually, their coupling became more frantic, growing with needful urgency. They reached the pinnacle of ecstasy at the same instant, then collapsed, exhausted, into the engulfing folds of the big feather mattress.

"I love you, Braxton," whispered Jessica as she lay in the arms of her new husband and rested her head on his hirsute chest.

"And I love you as well, my dear," reciprocated Braxton, pulling her closer. "I love you with all my heart and soul."

After they had rested, the two rose from their marriage bed and stood at the French doors, staring past the panes at the Southern night that stretched beyond. "All this is yours, Jessica," vowed Braxton. "The plantation grounds, the magnolia grove, this fine house . . . it is yours now."

Jessica stared up into her lover's face, her eyes glistening with tears of joy. "All I really need is you, Braxton," she told him. "That is all I could ever hope for."

The two newlyweds embraced and stared out over the richness of the land, both feeling truly blessed by God. They stood there in the shadow of the deepening twilight, dreaming of the life they would share together and the family they would build within the boundaries of the plantation called Magnolia.

Laura sat back in her chair and nodded with approval. Sure, the prose could use a little spit and polish, but it was still an effective opening to her new book. She could not help but feel a little pride at the ease with which the storyline was unfolding. Rarely did she write so effortlessly. The first three chapters of *Raging River* had taken her several weeks to complete, but she had finished the first part of *Burnt Magnolia* in only a few days' time. If she continued at this pace, Laura figured she'd have the novel ready for her publisher at least a couple of months before its scheduled deadline.

She stretched, hearing her back pop from the hours of sitting stationary at her word processor that morning. Laura inserted a microdisk into the drive, recorded the chapter she had just completed, then did the same with a second disk. She had learned her lesson with the loss of *Raging River*. She certainly was not going to make the same stupid mistake with this latest work.

Laura sat there for a moment and contemplated the scene she had just finished. She recalled the images of desire and abandon she had conjured from her imagination and smiled to herself. The writing of such scenes, especially those as potent as the one she had just penned, always put her in a particularly amorous mood. She left her chair and turned off her compact disk player, cutting Sawyer Brown off in mid-lyric. As she stepped out into the hallway, she could hear the distinctive guitar riffs of Stevie Ray Vaughn echoing from the door at the far end of the corridor.

Laura paused for a moment, wondering if she should break the rule that she and Rick had set at the beginning of their marriage. They had agreed that it would be best if both respected each other's periods of creativity and didn't disturb each other needlessly. Laura knew as well as anyone else how difficult it could be to get back on track, even after a brief interruption. But that afternoon, she figured, what the hell, one time out of the five years they had lived together wouldn't hurt.

She walked down the hallway to the door of Rick's studio. She entered the room to find her husband standing with his back to her. He was wearing that funky flannel shirt with the career's-worth of paint on its front and was meticulously putting the finishing touches on a canvas that stood on one of the three wooden easels. As Laura closed the door behind her and moved, unnoticed, toward Rick's stereo system next to one of the steel lockers, she saw that it was a surreal sword and sorcery painting of a beefy barbarian slaying a multiheaded serpent, while a scantly clad woman lay at the hero's feet.

At first, Laura had thought that such paintings were sexist—the woman always depicted as the helpless victim. But on further reflection, she realized her own writing suffered from similar clichés from time to time. The truth of the matter was, in the world of fiction, it was still a predominantly male world, and those who dealt in that business pretty much had to conform to the traditional guidelines, whether they were justifiable or not. There were exceptions, of course, but most genres, be they romance, western, or horror, were still being written the same way they had been written thirty years ago.

Laura crept over to the stereo and without warning cut the power switch on the receiver. The blare of music that rumbled from the big three-way speakers abruptly ceased. In turn, Rick whirled, startled. His frown of confusion turned into one of mild reproach when he saw his wife standing there with a mischievous grin on her face.

"I thought we had an agreement," he said, turning back to his painting. He took a dab of burnt umber from his palate and carefully touched up the tanned biceps of the barbarian's arms.

"Aw, don't give me that," said Laura. She came up behind Rick and ran her hands around his waist, pausing for a second to pinch his sagging love handles. "Why don't we take a break? You've been cooped up in here half the day. I'd say you could use a little exercise."

Rick's brows clinched in concentration as he rolled a dab of yellow on an ultra-fine brush and put a meaner glint in one of the serpent's dozen eyes. "What do you mean, sweetheart?" he asked absently. "A walk around the garden?"

Laura laughed huskily. She kissed Rick softly on the back of the neck and lowered her right hand to the crotch of his jeans at the same time. "No, walking wasn't exactly what I had in mind."

Rick reached down and caught his wife's hand before it could reach its intended destination. "Come on, Laura, cut it out. Really, hon, I have work to do."

"That silly old painting can wait another hour or two, can't it?" asked Laura, continuing to run her lips along the nape of Rick's neck. "Let's take a break, okay? Have a little fun."

Laura had hoped that her aggressive overture would turn Rick on, but it seemed only to annoy him instead. "Please, Laura, not now! I told you, I'm busy, all right?"

She stepped away from him, at first stunned by his harsh tone of voice. Then she became angry. "What the hell is the matter with you?" she asked bluntly.

Rick glanced over his shoulder, then back at his painting. "What do you mean, what's the matter with *me?* You're the one who's acting all hot and bothered."

"What I mean is . . . what the hell is wrong with *us* lately?" she asked. "We used to be so passionate. We used to make love whenever we wanted, wherever we wanted. But now . . . well, our love life just seems to have fizzled out."

"Don't overreact just because I'm not in the mood at the moment," Rick told her "We're fine. We're just going through a slump, that's all. It happens to every couple, sooner or later."

"Maybe," said Laura. "But our slump has been going on for a while now. I swear, Rick, I don't think we've made love more than a dozen times during the past three months."

"Come on, Laura. I think you're exaggerating a little."

"No, I don't think so," replied his wife. "And I know exactly when it began, too—when we started trying to have a baby."

Rick frowned, his male pride on the verge of being wounded. "Uh, let's don't bring that up, okay?"

"Why not?" persisted Laura. "That's the root of our problem, isn't it? We tried so hard to conceive a child that it put a damper on our sex life."

"I'd rather not talk about this right now," said Rick. He moved in closer to his canvas, as if trying to escape into the scene he was painting. "Like I told you, I'm past my deadline on this piece. When I'm done and this cover is on its way to New York, I'll be more than happy to sit down and discuss the matter with you.

"Damn it, Rick, you sound like someone making a blasted business appointment," said Laura. She stared at her husband, her anger flagging, turning into sad confusion. "Honey, what's happening to us?"

Rick set his palate aside and went to his wife. "Nothing, sweetheart. Really," he assured her, as they joined in a tense embrace. "I'm sorry I snapped at you. It's just that I've been under a lot of pressure lately. All these different projects and past-due deadlines turn me into a real Looney Tune sometimes. You know that."

"You're right about that," said Laura. "But that doesn't give you the right to act like such an asshole."

"I apologize," said Rick. He gave Laura a kiss, but found her unwilling to return his affection just yet. "I'll tell you what—I should be done with this canvas by four or five o'clock. After I get through, I'll get cleaned up and take you out to eat, my treat. Just to make up for being such an insufferable grouch. How does that sound?"

"It's going to cost you," Laura warned him. "I've had my sights set on the fancy Italian restaurant just off Public Square. The one with the expensive wine list."

"You've got it," said Rick in total surrender. "Anything you want."

"Okay, you have your cease-fire . . . for now," she said. "But we still have some things to talk about. Don't you agree?"

"Sure," admitted Rick. "But don't worry. We'll straighten everything out."

"I hope so," said Laura. Then she exited the studio and left her husband to finish his work.

As she returned to her own study to polish up the chapter she'd written that day, Laura found herself wondering if everything would truly straighten out between her and Rick. God knew that she loved the man, but sometimes he seemed to totally ignore her and lack a genuine understanding of her feelings. Sometimes he seemed to relate more to the subjects of his illustrations and paintings than he did to his own wife.

Maybe Rick was right—maybe she *was* overreacting. Maybe it was unrealistic to think that their marriage could remain as passionate and spontaneous as it had been five years ago. But whether it was asking too much or not, Laura could not help but wish that her and Rick's love life was as steamy and exciting as that of the characters she wrote about.

Chapter Eight

Later that night, after he and Laura had returned from their supper at Monteleone's Italian restaurant a few blocks north of Franklin's town square, Rick Gardner returned to his studio, anxious to get back to his work.

The sword and sorcery painting was on the brink of completion, but even after that, there would be no rest. He had several more projects looming threateningly toward their respective deadlines. The most challenging would be the cover painting and inside illustrations for a horror-western that would be published in a lavish hardcover edition by a leading small press. There would be a fair amount of research into Old West attire and landscape to be studied in order to match the genuine feel of the book's dark and gritty text, but Rick was looking forward to the diversion from sword-wielding barbarians and toothy space aliens from distant galaxies.

The evening meal he had shared with his wife had gone well, but there had still been some tension between the two, despite the romantic setting of Monteleone's. The checkered tablecloths and soft light of the candles could not hide the fact that there were still unresolved problems between them. The pasta and wine had been excellent, but neither he nor Laura had said very much to each other during the entire evening.

As Rick signed his name to the bottom of his latest canvas and stood back to appraise it, satisfied with what he saw, he could not help but regret the incident that had taken place in the studio earlier that afternoon. Laura had been right; he had acted like an asshole. She had come to him for love and affection, and instead, had received the cold shoulder. Rick could not figure out why he had reacted so negatively. True, he did have a lot of work to catch up on, but he could have easily taken a break. In the past, Rick would have responded passionately to such an amorous advance by his wife, but lately such actions on her part only seemed to irritate him. Or was *threaten* a more appropriate way of putting it?

Rick thought of the reason Laura had given for his sudden disinterest in sex. He had wanted to deny it, but thinking back on it, Rick wondered if maybe she was right. Secretly, he had to admit that he'd become a little defensive when the subject of lovemaking came up. He recalled those difficult days when he and Laura had desperately attempted to conceive a child, but without success. The constant temperature-taking, the nonstop monitoring of Laura's ovulation, and the uncomfortable and unromantic positions the doctors had suggested: all had take the normalcy out of sex and made it all too clinical. Although he had never said anything to Laura, Rick had felt more like a sperm bank than a husband during that period. When, after five long months of trying, they still had not succeeded in getting Laura pregnant, Rick had felt like a failure. Tests had shown that they were both fertile, but something stood in their way of becoming parents and that unknown factor had definitely put a strain on their relationship, whether either one of them wanted to admit it or not.

Finished with his work for the night, Rick went to the adjoining half-bath and washed his palate and brushes in the sink. He then turned off the studio's track lighting and left the darkened room. As he walked down the hallway toward the master bedroom, he glanced at the Westminster clock that hung at the far end of the corridor. The ornate hands showed it was nearly half past midnight.

Rick entered the bedroom. He smiled warmly at the sight of his wife. Laura snoozed peacefully in the big king-sized bed. The nightstand light was still on and a copy of a Judith Krantz novel lay open in her lap. Rick walked over and, slipping her butterfly bookmark between the correct pages, laid Laura's book on the nightstand and turned off the lamp. He kissed his wife gently on the forehead, drawing only a low mumble and a slight stirring from the sleeping woman. Rick tucked the patchwork quilt around her, then made his way to the opposite side of the canopy bed, intending to undress and go to sleep himself.

He was opening the cherrywood armoire to get his pajamas when something drew his attention from the direction of the French doors.

He walked to the twin doors and stared through the panes at the autumn night. "What the hell is that?" he whispered, then opened one of the doors to get a better look. He stepped out onto the balcony and peered over the railing at the dark grove of magnolias that grew in abundance below.

It was a light, but not the flickering of rampant fire he had experienced several nights before. No, this time there was only a single light, the muted glow of a solitary lantern drifting slowly through the close-grown stand of leafy magnolias. Rick came to an instant conclusion: someone was down there, trespassing on their property.

The very thought angered him. They had lived there less than two weeks and already somebody was lurking on the plantation grounds. Although he did feel a little apprehension and considered calling the county sheriff, Rick thought better of it and decided to confront the intruder himself. Whoever it was, Rick wanted to scare them off and let them know that they were not welcome at Magnolia, uninvited and in the dead of night.

Rick decided not to wake Laura. He left her asleep in the big bed as he stepped out of the master bedroom. He walked to a hall closet and rummaged through the clutter for a moment. He eventually found what he was looking for: a bat of seasoned hickory left over from when Rick played on an adult baseball team a few years before. He hefted the Louisville Slugger in one hand, then made his way down the main staircase to the foyer.

He stepped through one of the front doors and closed it behind him. Rick stood on the porch and stared across the circular driveway, searching for a sign of the light he had witnessed upstairs. He spotted it a moment later, close to the center of the grove. The light waxed and waned in the cool night breeze, but no longer moved; it remained in a single spot. From the location, Rick knew where it was, too. It was a small clearing midway between the house and the highway. Rick recalled Laura mentioning that it would be the perfect place to build a gazebo, there amid the picturesque stand of tall magnolias.

Cautiously, Rick left the front porch and made his way across the driveway, toward the edge of the grove. The night air was crisp. Halloween had already passed and it was now the beginning of November. Rick recalled Halloween night and the meager turnout of local children who had visited Magnolia. He and Laura had greeted only a handful of trick-or-treaters, and even those had seemed nervous about including the old mansion on their list of stops. Obviously, the old ghost stories concerning Magnolia remained as strong and effective in Franklin as they had for generations past.

Rick picked his way through the magnolia grove, careful to make no sound as he made his way through the darkness toward the solitary light. He choked the taped handle of the baseball bat in both hands, wondering exactly what he would do when he confronted the trespasser. He originally intended to surprise the intruder, waving his bat threateningly and warning them to get the hell off his property. But now he wasn't so sure if that was the right move to make. He could not figure out what rcason someone would have for prowling through the dark grove. The only thing that sprang to mind was that the trespasser was a treasure-hunter. Rick recalled reading about scavengers sneaking into Civil War graveyards and battlegrounds late at night, armed with metal-detectors and shovels. Without a shred of decency or conscience, the looters would locate the graves of buried soldiers and exhume their remains, looking for uniform buttons and belt buckles, or even the rings or gold teeth that those unfortunate fighting men had been buried with. Perhaps that was the motive of this nocturnal prowler. Perhaps he was covering the acres of the magnolia grove, foot by foot, waiting for his metal-detector to reveal some hidden cache of Civil War artifacts. It seemed more logical than any other explanation Rick could come up with.

As he drew nearer, Rick's suspicions appeared to become valid. He heard noises echo from the lantern-lit clearing ahead—the distinct sounds of a shovel burrowing into the earth and then tossing the loose soil aside. That and the sound of hoarse coughing. Whoever the trespasser was, he had a bad case of bronchitis.

Rick's heart thundered in his chest as the adrenaline of mounting fear pumped through his veins. He had never considered himself to be a confrontational person, he'd avoided conflicts and fights since he was a small child. Even in business, Rick relied on an agent to perform the unsavory task of negotiating contracts and collecting monies due for his work. Rick had always seen himself as a very mellow and nonthreatening man, and he had consciously tried to avoid the macho attitudes adopted by many men in the South. That was one reason why he had shunned firearms and the sport of hunting since his high school days. He considered such manly things backward and uncivilized.

But as he approached the clearing in the magnolia grove, Rick began to feel his resolve slip away and he wondered why he had chosen to confront the trespasser, instead of simply calling the police. He also began to wish, quite uncharacteristically, that he was carrying more than a length of seasoned hickory in his hands.

Only a few more yards of grove lay between him and the open clearing. Through the dense leaves, he could make out the form of a man in the pale glow of the lantern light. The fellow was tall and as gaunt as a skeleton, and wore a wide-brimmed slouch hat. That was all that Rick could make out. The rest of the scavenger's features were obscured in shadowy silhouette.

A single magnolia tree stood between Rick and the clearing when he halted his advance. He stood there, the heavy boughs of the magnolia obscuring his view as he clutched the bat tighter and held his breath. He listened intently. The man on the far side of the tree grunted in exertion, his breath wheezing from his lungs with a harsh, wet rattling. Rick could not help but sense some great urgency in the digger's frantic excavation of the clearing, as if he was possessed by some inner frenzy and was racing against time to find something he was searching for.

Don't just stand here, Rick told himself. *Get it over and done with!*

Summoning his courage, the artist lifted the bat over his right shoulder, ready to swing at the first sign of provocation on the scavenger's part. Then he stepped around the tree.

Abruptly, the lantern light was gone. Rick found himself standing in the clearing . . . an empty clearing pitch black with shadow. He was completely alone. The figure of the digging man he had spied from a distance was gone. The sound of spade against earth, as well as that of ragged breathing, had also vanished. In its place were the customary noises of night: the whistle of the wind through the magnolia leaves and the singing of unseen crickets.

"No," muttered Rick, as he took a couple of steps into the clearing. "No, damn it, I saw it for sure this time!"

He loosened his grip on the bat and stooped to study the ground. A thick scattering of dead leaves covered the earth. It seemed completely undisturbed. There was no sign whatsoever that anyone had stirred the leaves lately, let alone that the ground underneath had been broken by the sharp edge of a shovel.

As he crouched there, Rick wondered if he was going crazy. He had not imagined it this time. He had seen the yellow glow of the lantern, as well as the gaunt figure of a man digging frantically in the grove. The puzzling flickering of firelight that he had seen on the walls of his bedroom might have been the lingering aftereffects of a nightmare, but there was absolutely no explanation for this latest occurrence. Either he had indeed seen the lamp-lit scavenger in the clearing, or else his mind had conjured a particularly realistic delusion.

Rick stood back up and took a couple more steps forward, walking to the very center of the clearing. When he reached the spot where the man had labored, he felt as if he had stepped into the frigid depths of a meat locker. An intense cold like he had never experienced before engulfed him. It cut past his clothing and sank into his skin and muscle, causing his very bones to ache. A fit of coughing gripped him, wracking his entire body, and great gusts of frosty breath rolled from his mouth and nostrils. It was almost as if the fifty-degree weather of early November had suddenly dropped twenty or thirty degrees in temperature.

That was not all that affected Rick, either. He began to feel physically ill, both feverishly hot and deathly cold at the same time. His lungs felt heavy and full, and he found it difficult to breathe. He was also aware that he was suffering mentally. He felt a great sense of sadness and grief possess him, as if everything that he held dear in his life had been irretrievably lost.

"What's happening to me?" he said out loud. As another fit of coughing shook him, he stared at the earth beneath his feet. Strangely enough, it was no longer blanketed with the shriveled husks of autumn leaves. Rather, it was covered with scattered patches of dirty snow, the grass and dirt inbetween charred and black. That odd scent of burnt magnolia curled through his nostrils. It seemed to infiltrate his nasal passages and open some dark gateway to his brain. Outrage blossomed in his mind and he felt as if he wanted to scream at the top of his lungs.

Stunned by the flood of sensations and emotions that gripped him, Rick staggered back a few steps. Almost immediately, the confusing phenomenon ended. Both the physical sickness and the mental anguish vanished, leaving him dazed and disoriented. He breathed freely, his lungs unburdened like they had been a moment ago, and he felt his goosebumps recede as the temperature rose to the mid-fifties once again.

Rick took a couple more steps backward, then stood there, attempting to gather his wits. "Damn," he said. "What *was* that?"

Staring into the pitch darkness of the clearing, Rick could find no answer to his question. There was nothing out of the ordinary there. It was simply a small patch of clear land amid a dense grove of towering magnolias. He considered walking to its center again, then thought better of the idea. He recalled the feeling of creeping death that had gripped his body as well as the dark emotions of grief and lunacy that had infected his mind like an expanding cancer. Rick did not want to chance experiencing those sensations . . . not ever again.

He turned, and, still dazed, made his way back through the grove to the plantation house. When he finally stepped onto the familiar hardness of the paved driveway, Rick released a sigh of relief. He stared up at the tall structure of wood, brick, and limestone, lit brilliantly by the glare of security lights, and felt as if he were back home again. He glanced back at the grove one more time, expecting to see the light of that ghostly lantern hovering amid the tree boughs, but it was not there. There was only darkness as far as the eye could see.

As he crossed the front porch of the house and bolted the main doors behind him, Rick Gardner could not help but recall the things Laura and the Gants had told him. And as he stood there alone in the foyer, he wondered, if only for a moment, whether what he had experienced in the center of the magnolia grove had originated purely from his imagination . . . or from some source that was totally beyond his ability to analyze or explain.

Chapter Nine

A few days after their argument in the upstairs studio, married life was back to normal for Laura and Rick. They had kept their distance for a while, each concentrating on their individual projects and hoping that time would alleviate the tension between them. Fortunately, the old adage of "absence makes the heart grow fonder" seemed to have some truth to it. Like most couples, they made up and put their problems on the shelf for the time being.

On the sunny November morning of the sixth, Laura and Rick took a short break from their work and decided to run into town to have lunch and pick up a few supplies. They had a lunch of roast beef and mashed potatoes at the Choices Restaurant on Main Street, then separated to do their individual shopping. Laura needed a couple of reams of typing paper, a pack of computer disks, and a new cartridge for her personal copier, while Rick needed some new brushes and a few bottles of India ink for the black and white illustrations he was about to start on.

Thirty minutes after their parting, Laura arrived back at her burgundy Saturn, struggling to carry her purchases. She popped the lid on the trunk and loaded the office supplies inside, then locked it back. Laura was considering walking down to the hardware store where Rick had began to buy all his art supplies when she spotted an intriguing shop across the busy street. It was set in the center of one of Franklin's oldest commercial buildings and its ornamental bay window was filled with hardcover and paperback books. The dignified sign over the window—polished brass letters against a background of hunter's green—proclaimed GANT'S BOOKSHOP.

Figuring that she had a few minutes to spare, Laura slipped her car keys into her purse and made her way across the street to the opposite sidewalk. When she stepped into the shadowy interior of the shop, one of Laura's favorite smells greeted her: the musky odor of old books. She looked around and found that there were a couple of aisles of bookshelves on each side of the establishment, and that every available square foot of wall space was lined with shelves as well, reaching from floor to ceiling. Laura was amazed at the amount of printed material that could be crowded into such a limited area. Expensive leatherbound books stood shoulder-to-shoulder with humble clothback and paperback editions.

Laura started slowly through the center of the bookstore, studying the tables of stacked books and locked display cases that stretched from the front door to the walnut counter at the far end of the long room. Most of the books that graced the tables specialized in three particular subjects: the history of the state of Tennessee, the heritage of the town of Franklin, and the American Civil War. Likewise, the items in the display cases also were linked to that bloody four-year period when the North and South clashed over the explosive issue of slavery. As Laura went from one case to the next, she studied the collected artifacts of the tragic War Between the States: bayonets, sabres, old miniballs, and fragments of cannon balls, as well as the tarnished buttons and buckles of the uniforms those proud men of blue and gray had worn a hundred and thirty years ago.

"May I help you with something, ma'am?" asked a gravelly but polite voice from the direction of the sales counter.

Laura looked up at the one who spoke. Sitting before a framed painting of the historic Battle of Franklin sat a small, silver-haired man in his mid-seventies. He was hunched over a ledger, his pen poised over a page while his sharp eyes peered inquisitively at her over the top of his wire-rimmed spectacles.

"This is quite a collection you have here," said Laura. "It must have taken a lot of time to gather all these things."

"Nearly fifty years," replied the bookseller. An expression of dawning recognition began to bloom in his aged eyes. "Now, I know pretty much everyone in Williamson County, but you're a total stranger to me. That could only mean two things—either you're a tourist or a visitor from Nashville, or you just moved to Franklin recently." A slight smile curled beneath his bushy mustache. "You wouldn't happen to be a certain lady romance writer who moved into the mansion out on Highway 31, would you?"

"You'd put Sherlock Holmes to shame with that deduction," said Laura with a laugh. She stepped up to the counter and extended her hand. "I'm Laura Locke. And I assume that you're Mr. Gant."

"To hell with that 'mister' business!" balked the old man. "Just call me Archie." He took her slender hand in his own wrinkled one. "It's nice to finally meet you. Did your husband mention that we met the other day?"

"Yes, he did," admitted Laura. "That's why I decided to stop by. I'm utterly fascinated with anything having to do with the Civil War. I've been a student of the period most of my life and done a lot of research on the subject for my books. I know they're only romance novels, but I try to put as much realism and historical accuracy in my work as I possibly can."

"So my wife has told me," said Archie Gant. "She's quite a fan of yours, although she isn't too keen on the love scenes. But, then, Alma always was a stick-in-the-mud as far as the sexual revolution was concerned."

"Don't believe anything this old jackass tells you," came a voice from the adjoining office. A tall, elderly woman stepped through the doorway and elbowed her husband sharply in the shoulder, drawing a scowl of mock pain. "He just jabbers to hear himself talk most of the time. I'm Alma Gant, Miss Locke."

"Please . . . call me Laura." The romance writer surveyed the cramped surroundings of the little bookstore. "Great place you have here. Looks like you have most everything covered here—history, science, philosophy, fiction."

"Yep," replied Alma. "The shop is a little cramped for space, but what good bookstore isn't? We try to carry as large an inventory as possible, the good as well as the bad. We're not stiff-necked purists, like some bookstore owners. We figure pulp and genre writers deserve a place right alongside Shakespeare and Faulkner. Like Archie told you, I have a weakness for romances, particularly the historical variety. And the old coot here would just as soon read Louis L'Amour or Zane Grey than any of the classics." Alma looked a little worried. "Not that I'm calling you a pulp writer, Laura. Lord have mercy, no! You can write circles around most of the romance writers who are published these days."

"Thanks," said Laura. "I certainly try to do the best I can."

"Tell me, what are you working on now?"

"Well, interestingly enough, I've just began a new novel and it's set here in Franklin," Laura told her. She cast a curious glance at the rows of ancient books. "In fact, that was one reason I decided to stop in. I'm a little rusty on my knowledge of Franklin history, and I was wondering if you could suggest some material on the subject."

Both Archie and Alma's eyes lit up at the mention of providing such assistance. "Are you kidding?" chuckled Archie. "We've got everything under the sun. Alma would be glad to gather up some of the best histories, wouldn't you, dear?"

"Why, I'd be tickled pink!" said Alma sincerely.

"And I'm guessing that you'll be including the Battle of Franklin during the course of your story, too, won't you?" asked Archie.

"I plan to," said Laura. She was pleasantly surprised by the enthusiasm the Gants seemed to have for her new project.

"Well, we've got plenty of that around here, too," said Archie. He left his place behind the counter and went to a wall of old books. He fingered the faded spines, choosing those he thought would suit her best. When he returned to the counter, he had a half-dozen volumes dedicated solely to the subject of the violent skirmish in Franklin. "No need to pay us for these, Laura. You just keep them as long as you need and bring them back whenever you get through."

"I appreciate that, Archie," said Laura. Soon, Alma also returned to the counter. She set four good-sized volumes on the history of the township next to the other books.

"There's only one thing that we ask for in return," said Archie. "Invite us to supper one night and give us a private tour of Magnolia."

"We really would like to see how you've fixed up the place," added Alma. "The last time Archie and I went out there, it was no more than barren ruins."

"You've got a deal," agreed Laura. "I've been wanting to show Magnolia off to someone and it would be a pleasure to give the first tour to people who are genuinely interested in its history." Laura wondered if she should ask for any more favors, especially considering the wealth of material the Gants had already provided. But somehow, she knew that Archie and Alma wouldn't mind. "Speaking of Magnolia's history, I was wondering if you might know where I could find a book on the Heller family. I've searched all the historical nonfiction catalogs, both mainstream and collegiate, but I've never been able to find anything on the subject."

"As far as I know, there's never been anything published concerning Magnolia and its history," said Archie regretfully. "I'm afraid that very little is known about the Hellers and their plantation, or what happened there on the night of November 30, 1864. Oh, there's been plenty of tall tales and folk stories. Or perhaps 'ghost stories' might be more precise."

Alma was silent for a moment, then she spoke. "There *is* the diary," she said.

Archie rolled his eyes and shook his head in annoyance. "Confound me! Why didn't I think of that in the first place? I swear, I'm getting flat-out senile in my old age!"

"What diary?" asked Laura, out of curiosity.

"The diary of John Herbert Ashworth," explained Archie. "He was a neighbor of the Hellers and owned the tobacco plantation adjoining their property. In fact, it was Ashworth who buried Braxton Heller after he succumbed to pneumonia and the heartbreak of failing to locate the body of his wife."

"Did anyone ever find out exactly where she was buried?" asked Laura.

"No," said Alma. "Braxton is buried in the family plot on the southern edge of the property, but no one has a clue as to where poor Jessica was laid to rest."

"That's strange," said Laura. "And a little creepy, too, if you think about it."

"Yes, it is," said Archie. "But I reckon that's just a part of the mystery of Magnolia, though." He closed the ledger he had been writing in and hopped down off his stool. "Give me a minute and I'll get that diary for you."

Laura waited at the front counter, while Archie Gant entered the office and passed a couple of desks cluttered with old books and stacks of purchasing invoices. The elderly man crouched next to a sturdy iron safe that looked as if it had been manufactured in the 1800's. He fiddled with the combination dial for a moment, then, grasping the brass handle, disengaged the lock. A moment later, he was back at the counter with a small, but thick book in his hand. Its black leather cover was cracked and its pages were stained brown with age.

"Be careful," warned Archie as he handed the diary to Laura. "It's mighty fragile. I'm afraid I can't allow you to take this one home with you, but you're certainly welcome to come in here anytime and read it to your heart's content."

Gently, Laura took the book, laid it on the countertop, and opened the front cover. The handwriting was heavy and masculine, but legible enough to read without any trouble. The inscription on the first page simply read: *The Journal of John Herbert Ashworth; Township of Franklin, State of Tennessee.*

As Laura carefully turned one page after another, she found that most of the entries had to do with Ashworth, his family, and the business of their tobacco plantation. "Where in the diary does Ashworth refer to the Hellers?" asked Laura. "The reason I ask is that I'm using Jessica and Braxton as actual characters in my novel, and I was wondering if he gave any description of his neighbors."

"Now that you mention it, I believe that he does," said Archie. He took the book and flipped through the brittle pages until he was halfway through the diary. "Here you go. This entry right here."

Laura took the journal and read the passage Archie had located. It was dated June 12th, 1859.

> *Tonight I visited the neighboring plantation of Magnolia for the first time since Augustus Heller's death nearly seven years ago. I know that it is rude and unforgivable that I have not paid my respects to the Heller household in such a lengthy period of time, but I have been busy with my own affairs, and so has the current master of Magnolia, young Braxton. Directly after his father's death, Braxton attended a Northern university and then went on to West Point in hopes of building a future in the military. However, Braxton left the school and returned home to Magnolia when the threat of abolition swept the country. I take it that Braxton Heller felt it necessary to return to Franklin and make sure that the business of his father's plantation continues to run as smoothly as it has for the past fifty years.*
>
> *The purpose for my visit this evening was the wedding of Braxton to one Jessica Prentiss, formerly of the affluent Prentiss family of Richmond, Virginia. The ceremony and reception afterward were joyous and extravagant. From what Braxton told me, he had met young Jessica at a society ball when he attended the Point. Only a few months after their initial meeting, Braxton asked Jessica's parents for their daughter's hand in marriage and they gladly consented. All in all, the decorations, the music, and the food and drink made the entire event one of the most lavish and memorable of any I have attended here in Franklin for many years.*
>
> *Man and wife are an impressive pair, to be sure. Braxton is tall and handsome, having inherited the coal-*

black hair and gray eyes of his late father. He is a brash and outspoken young man, but one certainly deserving of any man's trust and respect. Braxton was quite dapper tonight; mustachioed, straight as a fence post, and dressed in tails and white tie. But the vision of the night's celebration was most certainly the new Lady Heller. Young Jessica, herself only eighteen years of age, was the picture of pure loveliness. She is a small woman, as petite and delicate as one of my daughter's china dolls. The lady's hair is long and of a shade of coppery auburn that I truly do not believe I have ever seen before. Her eyes are blue and her skin as pale as fine porcelain. She was dressed in a long wedding gown of the most lavish silk and lace, which included a train a good eight feet in length, carried by the children of the Heller slaves. Jessica is the complete opposite of her husband. She is shy and demure, and exhibits the most engaging personality and manners. As my family and I witnessed the exchanging of the vows, I could not help but hope that Jessica would have a positive influence on young Braxton. Perhaps she will be able to polish away some of her husband's rough edges and tame a little of the fire that he has possessed since his childhood.

Laura finished the entry and felt a sudden chill run down her spine.

Alma noticed her reaction. "What's the matter, girl? Did a possum just run over your grave?"

"It's strange," Laura told Alma and her husband. "The descriptions that John Ashworth gives of Braxton and Jessica Heller are almost identical, word for word to the ones I came up with for my book."

"A coincidence, maybe?" offered Archie.

"It could be," agreed Laura. "But there's something else. I had the scene of their wedding take place in mid-June, and it turns out that it actually happened then."

"That does seem odd," said Alma. "But you have a very

vivid imagination, Laura. I'm sure it isn't really as bizarre as you seem to think it is."

"No, I suppose not," replied Laura. But she could not shake the feeling that the writing of the first part of her novel had not involved coincidence, but had been unwittingly influenced by some source other than her own imagination.

Rick stood in front of the gun shop on Third Street, hesitant about setting foot inside. He nervously scratched at the stubble on his upper lip and peered through the front window at the racks of rifles and shotguns that lined the inner walls of the store. Normally, the idea of actually becoming a patron of such a business would have been unthinkable, given Rick's staunch opinion of gun control. But the authenticity of his craft forced him to abandon his principles, if only for that one project he was about to start on.

The western-horror book he was illustrating involved a character who was a gunslinger. But, unlike the protagonists of most western literature, this one failed to carry the classic Peacemaker revolver. Instead, he toted an 1851 Colt Navy pistol. Rick was embarrassed to admit it, but he had no earthly idea what that particular model looked like. It was necessary, however, that the cover painting and inside illustrations be true to the text of the novel, so, like it or not, Rick was forced to find a Colt Navy, just so he would be able to render the likeness of the cap-and-ball revolver correctly.

Despite his reluctance, he walked into the gun shop and closed the door behind him. Instantly, he smelled the sweet scent of gun oil and the bitter tang of gunpowder in the air. He was surprised to find that the odors were not nearly as offensive as he would have thought.

"Can I help you?" asked a bearded man behind the long glass display counter, which held every brand and model of handgun imaginable. He was heavyset and dressed in jeans and a red-and-black checkered lumberjack shirt.

"Uh, well, what I'm looking for is a Colt Navy revolver,"

said Rick, feeling a little out of his element. "You know, the old cap-and-ball type."

"Model 1851?" asked the salesman.

Rick simply nodded as he stared at the rolls of blued and nickel-plated revolvers and semiautomatic pistols that lay on red velvet behind the glass of the display case.

"I have two I can show you," said the big fellow. "One is a bona fide item, an original .36 Navy pistol straight from Sam Colt's munitions factory. The other is an Italian-made replica, but it shoots as well as any of the other black powder revolvers put out during the mid-1800s. I reckon it just depends on whether you want a collector's item or a gun you can have fun shooting bottles and tin cans with."

"How much is the original?" asked Rick.

"It's in excellent condition, which is rare for a firearm with so many years on it," replied the salesman. "I'm asking $1,200 for it."

"That's kind of expensive, isn't it?"

The bearded man shrugged his broad shoulders. "Not really. I could cut the price down a couple hundred, but not much further."

"How about the replica?" asked Rick.

"Two hundred," the salesman told him. "Three hundred with the custom case, powder flask, and brass bullet mold."

"Can I see it?"

The salesman crouched behind the counter and unlocked a door set underneath the display case. He set a rectangular case with brass hinges and slide-lock on the counter and pushed it toward Rick. "Be my guest."

Rick fumbled with the lock for a moment before he finally lifted the hinged lid of the guncase. Inside, cradled in their individual compartments, were a copper powder flask, a heavy brass bullet mold, and the .36-caliber cap-and-ball revolver. The Colt Navy's octagonal barrel and engraved cylinder were a deep black-blue, while the frame, triggerguard, and loading lever were case-hardened a mottled gray color. The walnut grip was dark brown and polished to a smooth, high sheen.

Rick never thought that he would consider a gun beautiful.

Before, he had always viewed firearms as ugly devices of violence. But despite his prejudices, he could not help but admit that the Colt Navy was indeed an object of beauty. The length of oiled gunmetal and polished walnut was much like a piece of fine art, meticulously designed and painstakingly constructed, one piece at a time.

"May I?" he asked, almost breathlessly. He was a little peeved at himself for even wanting to pick up the gun, but he couldn't seem to help it. He was captivated by the Civil War replica.

"Sure, go ahead," invited the salesman.

Rick reached out and carefully withdrew the revolver from its compartment. The pistol was heavy, mostly because it was constructed of tooled steel and not the lighter alloy metals used in most of today's modern firearms. His fingers entwined the curve of the pistol butt and, oddly enough, it appeared to be a perfect fit. Rick lifted the Colt Navy, turned, and extended it at arm's length. He laid his thumb upon the spur of the hammer and cocked it back, working the cycle of the cylinder and positioning a capless nipple in line. Slowly, he eased the hammer into the half cocked position, then manually gave the cylinder a spin with his free hand. The six-chambered cylinder spun with the ease of a greased top. He then took the revolver in both hands, disengaged the wedge, and separated the barrel from the central frame. He examined the cylinder, as well as peered down the barrel, checking the twist of the rifling. Then, just as quickly, he reassembled the gun.

The salesman was impressed. "Looks like you know how to handle one of those."

Rick stared at the gun in his hand, confused over what he had just done. "No, I've never seen one until now. In fact, I've never held a gun before in my life."

"Well, you sure could've fooled me," said the man. "Looked like you knew every last inch of it, the way you aimed and disassembled it."

The artist stared at the black powder revolver in his hand. "Three hundred for the entire set-up, eh?"

"That's right," he replied. "I'll even throw in a can of black powder, a hundred lead balls, and a tin of percussion caps . . . free of charge."

Rick shook his head. "I really don't intend to actually fire the thing. I just need to use it as a model for some illustrations I have to do."

The man chuckled. "Yeah, sure. I get that all the time. People come in here just looking for something to hang on the wall or over the fireplace mantel. But sooner or later, the temptation to load it up gets to them. Believe me, it won't be long before you're out in your backyard, firing away."

"No, I don't think so," said Rick. "Not me, of all people. But I will take the gun. If only because I need to make these illustrations as authentic as possible."

The gunshop owner wrote out a sales receipt on the cased gun, took Rick's American Express card, and finalized the deal. He slipped the rectangular guncase into a cardboard sleeve, sacked the powder, balls, and caps, then thanked Rick for his business.

Rick left the gun shop almost in a daze. He could not believe that he had actually bought a gun. And what was more, he could not understand why he felt so pleased about the purchase. Instead of abhorring the thing in his possession, he felt an odd thrill at having it near. For the first time in his life, Rick understood the attraction that firearms held for hunters and gun collectors.

Fortunately, he reached his wife's Saturn unnoticed. He took the spare set of keys that he always carried in his wallet and opened the trunk. Secretively, Rick stuck the paper sack beneath an old blanket Laura always kept in the trunk. But before he concealed the guncase there as well, he was overcome by the urge to see the Colt Navy once again. He slipped the case from the cardboard sleeve and opened the lid. Almost reverently, he took the revolver in his hand. It felt less heavy now, more like a natural extension of himself. And he experienced another sensation that was totally alien to him—a sense of power. Holding the Colt Navy in his hand, Rick felt like he could do anything. He almost felt invincible.

Frightened by the feeling, he returned the gun to its compartment, then quickly placed the case next to the sack of shooting supplies. He glanced up and saw Laura leaving the Gants' shop with a stack of books in her arms. Not wanting her to know what he had bought, he pulled the blanket over his purchase and set his bag of art supplies on top of it. Then he slammed the lid of the trunk shut.

"You were right," Laura told him, as he helped her pile the books onto the back seat of the car. "The Gants really are nice. And they're certainly helpful. Look at all these reference books they let me borrow. My research should go smoothly now. They even showed me the diary of the Hellers' neighbor, John Herbert Ashworth. It'll be an invaluable source of information, too."

"It looks like they made quite an impression on you," said Rick. He climbed into the passenger seat and buckled up, while his wife did the same behind the steering wheel.

"They certainly did," agreed Laura. She glanced curiously at her husband. "What about you? What were you up to while I was in the bookstore?"

He shrugged innocently. "Nothing. I just picked up those art supplies and came back here, that's all."

As they left the heart of Franklin and started back down Highway 31 for Magnolia, Rick could not help but feel a little guilty for lying to Laura. But for some reason, he decided it would be best to keep the purchase of the Colt Navy from his wife for the time being. At least for a while, he wanted to keep the presence of the black-powder gun his own personal secret.

Chapter Ten

Tyler Lusk found himself alone in the bowling alley. He had no idea exactly why he was there at such a late hour. All he knew was that it was well after dark; the blackness of night shined through the plate glass of the entrance doors and most of the building's lights were off. Only the multicolored glow of the neon beer signs at the snack bar and the bank of lights over the main counter were on.

The silence in the alley was almost oppressive. The usual noises—the laughter of bowlers, the thunderous rolling of balls on the lanes of oiled hardwood, and the brittle crack of colliding pins—were absent. The place was as quiet as a tomb.

Tyler moved past the counter and stood on the carpeted floor that lay between the foyer and the roll of dark lanes. Each pit was unoccupied; the ball returns and pedestals of the Accu-Score consoles stood in shadow. Tyler stared out over the darkened alley, feeling as if he had come here to perform some particular deed, but unable to remember what it could possibly be.

He was turning to leave when a shrill scream echoed from the direction of the rear of the building. Tyler stood there, rooted indecisively to the spot for a moment. Then the scream came again, more fearful and urgent than it had been before. He found himself moving at a brisk walk at first, then accelerating into a dead run. Tyler made his way to the side wall and the walkway that led to the back. Beyond a single access door lay the computer-driven machinery that worked the pin-setters and ball returns. He reached the door, turned the knob, and stepped through the doorway.

But strangely enough, instead of entering the rear of the building, Tyler found himself standing outside. But it was not the cluttered rear alleyway that normally stretched behind the bowling alley. Rather, he found himself standing in a winter landscape. The air around him was bitterly cold, well past the point of freezing. The moon overhead cast pale light upon the snow-covered earth and the icy branches of leafless fruit trees.

Confused by his surroundings, Tyler Lusk took a cautious step forward. He stared ahead and saw the lighted windows of a tall mansion gleaming in the distance. Then, again, there came the shrill shriek of a woman in distress. He started toward the cry for help, but halted when someone called out to him from behind.

"Samuel!" came a terrified voice that sounded somehow familiar, even though he knew he had never heard it before in his life. "Please, son, don't go! Yo only gonna get yo'self kilt!"

Tyler turned and glanced back at the source of the warning. It came from the open door of a small cabin. Inside, he saw a number of people, all black and dressed in shabby clothing, standing around a crude bed. On that bed lay a large woman whose eyes were bright with pain. She had been severely wounded. It looked as if her left leg had been cut clean in half just below the knee. The cloth linen of her simple cornhusk bed was completely saturated with blood.

He almost turned around and went back to the cabin, but his attention returned to the plantation house when the sound of screaming cut through the winter air. This time the tone of it was different. There was less fear, but more agony and indignation. Tyler was stunned by the emotion that the woman's screams conjured within him. He felt rage . . . as well as a distinctive sense of honor and undying obedience toward that helpless victim.

Tyler ran through the snowy orchard until he reached the

weathered structure of a smokehouse. He paused next to a chopping stump and, grasping the frosty handle of a broad ax, wrenched its blade from the wood. Tightening his dark fingers around the length of seasoned hickory, Tyler stalked toward the main house.

Soon, he was approaching the circular thicket of a flower garden. The colorful flowers of spring and summer were gone now. Only dead brush and accumulated snow blanketed the earth. Tyler stopped next to a leafless hedge and stared through its naked branches at the ugly scene that unfolded before him.

A roaring bonfire blazed beneath a towering oak tree. Around that fire—which appeared to be fueled by the smashed furniture of the great house—stood twenty or thirty soldiers, all dressed in uniforms of navy blue. Some drank freely from crystal decanters confiscated from the mansion, cheering loudly, while others simply stood there, looking pale and sick to their stomachs. Tyler could not understand what was causing such different reactions in the troop of soldiers, until he cast his gaze toward the far side of the bonfire.

There, on the frozen earth, lay two writhing bodies . . . one male and one female. Tyler drew closer, stepping through the brush. Immediately, he knew what horrible act was being committed forcefully and violently upon the fairer sex. The woman screamed out once more, but this time her cry was cut abruptly short. Laughing, the man on top of her tightened the hold he had on her slender throat. The tendons of his fingers and hands flexed powerfully in the firelight, then the woman grew strangely silent.

A shout of moral outrage ripped from Tyler's throat, and before he could stop himself, he leaped over the crackling mound of the bonfire. The flames licked at his flesh and clothing, but he was oblivious to the heat and agony that engulfed him. He landed on the other side and stood above the tangle of bodies—one still, the other shuddering with the ecstasy of spent lust. He stared down contemptuously at the one who remained alive. The man's face was sheened in sweat, his eyes sparkling with sadistic pleasure. Tyler had never seen such an evil face before, but then, he had never laid eyes on the face of Satan, either . . . and he knew in his heart that they must bear an uncanny resemblance to one another.

A rage unlike any Tyler had ever experienced shook his tall frame uncontrollably. Without hesitation, he found himself lifting the heavy ax over his right shoulder. He glared at the Devil beneath him for only a second longer. Then he unleashed his rage both in voice and in action as he screamed at the top of his lungs and brought the blade of the broad ax downward.

Tyler sat up in bed, a great roar of anger rising up out of his throat. His yell filled the darkened bedroom, then faded as he was jolted awake.

"Damn!" he whispered. He pulled down the bedcovers and swung his legs over the edge of the mattress. His hands ached, as if he had been gripping something much too tightly.

Behind his eyelids, the faint impressions of the images of his nightmare lurked, then retreated rapidly. By the time he reached over and snapped on the nightstand lamp, whatever had lingered of the dream was gone. He tried hard to recall the details of the nightmare, but most of them eluded him. All he could remember was the name of Samuel, the frantic screams of a woman, and the leering face of a demon.

Shaken, Tyler rose from his bed and padded barefoot from the bedroom. He walked down the hallway of his apartment to the kitchen and sluggishly made himself a cup of hot chocolate in the microwave. He then went to the living room and settled into his reclining chair. A few sips of the cocoa seemed to relax him and clear his mind a little.

He sat there for a long time, trying to analyze the dream and exactly why he had experienced it. That he had been referred to as Samuel in the dream was probably due to the information that had preyed on his mind for the last week or two, the knowledge that he had descended from a Southern slave with that same name. But the rest of the nightmare, what little of it he could recall, made no sense to him. Had it been a dreamscape manufactured solely by his imagination? Or had it been something more?

Tyler finished his cocoa, but continued to sit in the recliner, a little hesitant about returning to his bed. He glanced over at the coffee table. Next to copies of *Newsweek* and *Sports Illustrated* lay an envelope with the emblem of Delta Airlines printed across the front. Inside was his round-trip ticket from Detroit to Nashville. His flight was scheduled for the following weekend. After two weeks of catching up on his workload at the bowling alley, Tyler was finally on the verge of taking a three-week vacation to explore the circumstances of his family history in Tennessee. Professor Hughs had made good on his promise, arranging his plane and hotel reservations, as well as providing him with more than enough money for any other expenses he might have.

More than ever, the dream increased Tyler Lusk's desire to search out the truth concerning his ancestors. What he had just experienced subconsciously might have had nothing to do with what he would find in the town of Franklin. But for some strange reason, Tyler could not bring himself to believe that. The gruesome incident that had taken place on the snowy grounds of the mystery plantation seemed, to him, to be cut more from the cloth of reality than from mere imagination.

Chapter Eleven

"A fabulous meal, Laura!" smiled Archie Gant. He wiped his mouth with a napkin and scooted his chair back a few inches from the dining room table, allowing his swollen belly a little more room. "I declare, it's been a while since I've had fried chicken quite as good as that."

Alma frowned at her husband from across the table. "I just fixed you chicken for supper three days ago," she reminded him.

Archie gave Laura a playful wink. "Like I said before . . . it's been a while since I've had chicken as good as that."

Alma ignored the comment on her cooking and rewarded Laura with a nod of approval. "I must admit, it was tasty. And that sweet potato casserole . . . why, I wouldn't mind having the recipe for that myself."

"I'll be happy to write it down for you before you leave," promised Laura.

As she took one final sip of iced tea, Laura looked toward the opposite end of the dining room table to where Rick sat. He crammed the last bite of a buttered roll in his mouth and gave a "thumb's up." Secretly, Laura knew that the meal had indeed been a success, but one that had been proceeded by a fair amount of nervousness and uncertainty.

To tell the truth, Laura and Rick had never given a dinner party of any kind. In fact, neither was particularly skilled when it came to cooking. They had never been gourmet chefs or fussy eaters during the five years they'd been married. Nine times out of ten, they'd chosen to forgo the time-consuming task of cooking, instead frequenting restaurants, or when they had been particularly lazy, ordering out for pizza. It had been several years since Laura had cooked a multicourse meal or entertained guests, and as Sunday night had approached, she'd wondered if she could pull it off without embarrassment. She'd even resorted to leafing through some of her mother's old cookbooks, looking for dishes that would appeal to the appetites of her down-to-earth guests. Laura had finally settled on a menu of fried chicken, green beans, sweet-potato casserole, fluffy yeast rolls, and, of course, the traditional Southern beverage of cold iced tea to wash it all down with. Later, in the parlor, Laura would serve coffee, as well as a rich but scrumptiously delicious chocolate-pecan pie, a dessert that had been a specialty of the Locke women since the days of her great-grandmother, Stella Mae.

Alma Gant looked around the huge dining room. It was decorated with table and chairs, china cabinet, and sideboard, all constructed of fine white oak, while the ceiling boasted a modest chandelier and the walls were papered with a delicate floral print. "I'm very impressed with what you've done with the house, Laura. I never thought I'd live to see the day when this old place looked like anything other than burned-out ruins."

Archie agreed wholeheartedly. "I'm sure the Hellers would have been extremely pleased."

"Well, I'd like to think so," said Laura, a little flustered by the praise. "Would you like to have coffee and pie in the parlor now . . . or take that tour that I promised you?"

Archie and Alma exchanged a mutual glance of anticipation, causing them to look like excited children on Christmas Eve. "To tell the truth, we're chomping at the bit to see the rest of the house," said Archie. He patted his swollen stomach. "Anyway, I'm going to have to let this bellyful settle a while before I can find room enough for coffee and dessert."

"Then follow me," invited Laura. "I'll show you what we've done."

All four left the dining room and moved on to the kitchen. A round table of polished walnut with four Windsor chairs sat in the bay-windowed breakfast nook with a stain-glassed pendant light dangling from the ceiling overhead. The kitchen, with its hand-made oak cabinets and butcher-block counters, complimented the old-fashioned walk-in pantry and gray stone hearth. An authentic antique bellows and iron poker set graced the left side of the fireplace, while a brass replica of an Early American bedwarmer hung on the wall to the right. On the heavy oak mantel were arrangements of dried flowers and several Blue Willow plates on brass stands.

They ascended the narrow passageway of the kitchen stairway to the floor above. A carpeted runner bearing a delicate Oriental pattern stretched the entire length of the upstairs hallway. Laura showed them her study, then took them from one bedroom to another. There were only four of the original eight that now served that function. Each was fully furnished, two with bedroom suites of light oak, one with curly maple, and the master bedroom with its suite of dark cherrywood. Plush carpeting of light beige accented each room, and custom-made ruffled curtains bordered the windows. One of the other two rooms had been turned into a combination reading parlor and sewing room, while the other had been fashioned into a spacious bathroom, something Magnolia had lacked in its heyday in the mid-1800s. The bathroom glistened with new porcelain and polished brass fixtures, and the window and shower curtains were pale blue and simple in design.

They took a moment to take a detour through the master bedroom to the balcony that overlooked the front grounds. As they stood there in the cool November twilight, Archie told them about the Battle of Franklin. He pointed across the dark grove, showing them the general direction where Union forces had clashed with those of the Confederacy on the two-mile stretch of Winstead Hills. He also explained that, just before the fuse of the battle had ignited, a brigade of cavalry from Wagner's Division, led by Union Colonel Fredrick Bates, stormed the plantation of Magnolia and seized the main house for use as a temporary command post. But just after the skirmish began along the Franklin Turnpike, something went wrong at Magnolia. The drunken troops of the brigade left the plantation in flames, unaccompanied by the colonel who had originally led them.

Laura's tour of the house progressed on down the corridor to Rick's studio, then they descended the graceful curve of the main staircase to the first-floor foyer. The only two rooms downstairs that the Gants had not yet seen were the living room and the parlor at the rear of the house. It was in the latter that they settled in for coffee and pie. The chamber was decorated with Victorian furniture—all inexpensive but convincing reproductions—and the walls held the framed covers of Laura's books, as well as some striking landscapes that Rick had painted in his younger days, before the demand for his fantasy artwork had deprived him of the time for such simple pleasures.

Archie Gant was starting on his third cup of coffee and his second slice of pie when he indicated the spot where he was sitting. "You know, it's funny that you should place this couch where you did," he told Laura.

"Oh?" She took a sip of coffee, her eyes questioning. "And why is that?"

"Well, according to Ashworth's diary, this rear parlor was where he found Braxton Heller, consumed with pneumonia and on the brink of death," he informed her. "And the scorched sofa he was lying on was located in front of the window, closet to the western corner of the house . . . precisely where you chose to put this couch."

"What a creepy coincidence," said Rick with a chuckle. His laughter was deeper tonight, more resonant than Laura had ever heard it before. She glanced over at her husband, who sat in a wingbacked chair next to the fireplace. Laura wondered, for the second time that day, exactly what it was about Rick that struck her differently. One thing was obvious, and that was the addition of the stubble that peppered Rick's upper lip. He had neglected to shave for the past several days and was, apparently, attempting to grow a full mustache.

Laura had not said anything to discourage him, though. In fact, the addition of the new facial hair was appealing to her. It somehow seemed to strengthen his face. His jawline did not look quite so soft and flabby as it usually did, and strangely enough, his eyes appeared darker and more piercing, and less washed-out and disinterested.

"Maybe," said Archie. "Or maybe it was like Laura using the precise description of the Hellers in her new book when she had no earthly idea how they looked."

"I know what you're driving at, Archie," said Rick. "You're saying that something influenced Laura. Ghosts, perhaps?"

Archie shrugged. "I don't know what to call it, but it is strange, don't you admit?" The elderly man regarded his hostess. "What about it, Laura? What do you think?"

"I really don't know what to think," said Laura. "I agree it is a little odd, but that's all. It's ludicrous to think that some spirit subconsciously influenced me to write this book and place my furniture in one particular spot."

"So I take it that neither of you has experienced any type of inexplicable phenomenon since moving here?" asked Alma. "Nothing out of the ordinary?"

"Certainly not," Rick assured them. He thought of the weird illusion of flamelight on the bedroom wall, as well as the shadowy form of the digging man in the magnolia grove, but mentioned neither one. He thought it would be best to keep the two incidents to himself for the time being, although he really did not understand why he would want to keep them a secret from his wife or the Gants.

"No, I haven't really experienced anything unusual lately," said Laura. "Except for the morning I heard footsteps coming from upstairs when there was no one else in the house but myself."

"Hmmm," said Archie, his eyes gleaming with sudden interest. "And was that all there was to it?"

Laura smiled. "I'm afraid so. I went upstairs to investigate, but found nothing."

"Why don't you tell them about what you saw when you

were a child," urged Rick, his eyes amused. "You know, the ghostly woman on the balcony."

Laura had a feeling that Rick was making fun of her a little, but ignored him. She told Archie and Alma about the Halloween night when she was twelve years old, and her encounter with the grief-stricken apparition who stood on the dilapidated balcony of the plantation house. She expected to see the same looks of skepticism on their aged faces that showed in Rick's. But to the contrary, they seemed genuinely interested in the story of her first visit to Magnolia.

"It sounds like the spirit of Jessica Heller to me," said Archie. He took his briar pipe and a leather tobacco pouch from his jacket pocket. "Mind if I smoke?"

"No," said Laura. "Go right ahead." She looked from Archie to his wife. "What about it, Alma? Do you think it was just my childish imagination playing tricks on me?"

Alma shook her head. "If that's the case, then I've had tricks played on me well into my seventies," she told her firmly. "I don't care what Rick here believes, but I've seen proof of ghosts on several occasions. There is existence after death. Whether it's only a remnant of an emotional occurrence being played over and over again like some psychic instant-replay, or the actual lost soul of someone who died decades, even centuries ago . . . there is one thing for sure. The phenomenon is real, and not a load of bullshit . . . pardon my French."

"You won't convince me of that until you march me right up to one of those spooks and let me look it straight in the face," Rick said smugly.

Archie stared at the artist, as if detecting a false note beneath Rick's undaunted skepticism. "Are you certain that *you* haven't encountered something, Rick? It wouldn't have to be an actual apparition. Maybe only a sound or scent. Something as innocent as that."

"I'm afraid not, Archie," lied Rick. "Besides, it seems a little strange that educated folks like you and Alma would even believe in such hogwash."

"It is because of the fields we specialized in that we *do* believe in the paranormal," Alma told him flatly. "Between Archie and me, we've visited more graveyards, burial mounds, and battlefields than perhaps any other two people in the state of Tennessee. And at a few particular spots, we experienced what most folks would refer to as 'ghosts.' We spent the night in the Bell Witch Cave up in Adams, as well as haunted locations at the Stones River, Shiloh, and Chattanooga battlefields. In all those places, we encountered things that no man of science and learning, no matter how intelligent he might be, could rightfully explain. We're not senile old farts, Rick. Our minds are as sharp as they were when we were your age."

"I didn't mean to offend you," Rick said, sensing a little resentment in Alma's statement. "I simply don't believe in that sort of stuff."

"Come on, now," laughed Archie. "Let's change the subject before the two of you end up going a couple of rounds right here in the parlor." The old man arched his bushy eyebrows at Rick. "I must warn you, sir, Alma's as skinny as a beanpole, but she has a helluva right hook."

Rick smiled. "Okay, I get the idea. I apologize if I spoke out of turn, Mrs. Gant," he said graciously.

Alma's stern features softened a degree. "Apology accepted, Mr. Gardner."

As Laura poured more coffee, something came to mind. "There is one thing I'd like to discuss," she said. "It seems like most folks around here know about the tragedy of Braxton and Jessica Heller, whether historically or through tall tales. But does anyone know anything about the man who was directly responsible for it all?"

"You mean the Union colonel?" asked Archie, intrigued. "Fredrick Bates?"

"Yes."

"Alma and I have done some research on Bates, so I'll fill you in on what we found out about him," said Archie. "He was born Fredrick Daniel Bates in Albany, New York, in 1827, the product of a pompous and wealthy family who had immigrated from Great Britian a hundred years before. He shocked his parents when he snubbed their desire that he study to become an attorney, instead enrolling at West Point. In fact, he was in the same class as George Armstrong Custer, another Union officer who had a particularly grandiose opinion of himself.

"When the War Between the States followed the secession of the South, Bates was immediately commissioned to McClellan's army. Bestowed the rank of major, he led cavalry troops at Antietam, Chancellorsville, and the bloodbath at Gettysburg. By the skirmish of Spotsylvania, Bates had risen to the commanding rank of full-fledged colonel. Battle after battle, the brigades that he led became known as undefeatable fighting machines. And there was really only one reason why they succeeded under the command of Bates where they would have probably failed under any other leader."

"And what was that?" asked Rick. Much to Laura's surprise, her husband leaned forward in his chair, looking genuinely interested.

"Mostly it was due to Bates's own personal lack of honor or ethics," explained Archie. "He would stop at nothing to win a fight, even if it meant creeping up behind an unsuspecting soldier and shooting him square in the back. He was not a particularly brilliant strategist, that's for sure. He depended more on ambushes and dirty tricks than anything else. And for the most part, the soldiers he drafted into his brigades were not exactly the cream of the crop. Many of them came from prisons and insane asylums. When it came to the cold-blooded disregard for human life, Bates's crew made Quantrill's guerrilla fighters look like saintly choirboys by comparison."

Archie looked around, and satisfied that he had his audience completely enthralled, puffed on his pipe and continued his story. "The threat of Bates's 'Bloody Brigade' was nearly legendary by the time the Union had control of such Southern cities as Atlanta, Chattanooga, and Nashville. The acts of wanton killing and sadistic cruelty that Bates and his soldiers became famous for began to make the military hiarchy a little nervous. The man who Bates received his basic orders from,

General George H. Thomas, decided that it would be best if the 'Bloody Brigade' was prohibited from fighting in the approaching skirmish against Hood's army. When the Union entered Franklin, intending to stop Hood's march to Nashville, Thomas ordered Bates to set up a command post outside the city limits and stay there throughout the duration of the battle.

"Naturally, being the egomaniac he was, Bates was furious. He had looked forward to participating in the battle, certain that he could up his rank to brigadier general if he played his cards right. But Thomas's decision turned Bates's winning hand into a game of solitaire and dashed his hopes for an instant promotion. Therefore, when he did come to the first plantation and put it under siege, he was quite simply 'pissed off.' And he put Magnolia and its residents through a living hell, although there is no accurate record of what atrocities took place here. At least, none that we have been able to lay our hands on, as of yet."

"What do you mean?" asked Laura.

"There is a source of information that could very well shed some valuable light on the mystery of Bates's time here at Magnolia," said Alma. "It is the private journal of Bates's second-in-command, Major Alexander Hudson. It has been auctioned several times during the last fifty years, making its way from one collector to another. In fact, it is scheduled to be auctioned off again three weeks from now, in St. Louis. Archie and I plan to attend the auction and acquire the journal for ourselves, although the bidding is certain to be rather high. We don't mind, though. If we could get our hands on Hudson's journal and solve the mystery of Magnolia, it would be well worth our effort and expense."

"It would help me out a lot, too," said Laura. "After all, I do need an ending for my novel."

Conversation turned toward other subjects, but Laura could not help but feel excited over the prospect of finding out exactly what had taken place at Magnolia on that snowy November night in 1864, and particularly, what had happened to Jessica Heller. Growing up with the legend of Magnolia when she was a child, Laura had known Jessica only as a tragically romantic figure, a Southern heroine who had perished in the clutches of the enemy. But now, Laura had a rare chance to discover the true facts concerning the burning of Magnolia. And if she was honored with such knowledge, she hoped to find out that the Jessica Heller of folklore was every bit as vulnerable and human as Laura herself.

Chapter Twelve

On the night of November 8th, Wade Monroe was subjected to the most grisly nightmare of his life.

He found himself on horseback, riding cautiously through a stretch of dense woods. The animal beneath him was a sturdy chestnut gelding, and the bridle and saddle were that common of the federal cavalry in the mid-1800s. Wade surveyed his surroundings. It was spring. The forest was lush and green with new leaves, and the white blossoms of dogwood were in bloom. He stared up through the foliage above him. The sun hung high in the sky; it was early afternoon. But for some reason, time had no bearing on why he was there, deep in the backwoods. No, something more basic was the catalyst for bringing him there that day.

He rode onward for a while, finally reaching a small stream. Clear water trickled over smooth creek stones, playing a gentle symphony of nature. But, strangely enough, Wade found no beauty in the sound of the brook nor in the greenery around him. He shucked a Spencer repeating rifle from a saddle boot and dismounted. He tethered the horse to the trunk of a birch tree, then knelt next to the stream to fill his canteen. The container was made of tin and had a bold U.S. symbol emblazoned across the side. As he submerged the canteen beneath the cool water, he stared down at the shimmering surface of the creek. The reflection that stared back at him was his own, yet not entirely. There were confusing differences, like the battle-worn uniform of a Union colonel that clothed his powerful form and the bushy muttonchop sideburns that graced both cheeks.

He gave no further thought to his appearance as a sound echoed from further down the creekbed. Wade took the canteen from the water, returned the cork to the spout, and slung it over his shoulder. He stood and strained to hear the sound again, channeling out the babble of the brook and the cheerful chirping of spring birds. It came to him a moment later: someone fifty yards or so down the stream was singing happily. He recognized the hymn they sang as being an old Negro spiritual.

Wade could not understand the emotion that filled him when he heard the chorus of that hymn. He was suddenly blinded by such a feeling of hatred and contempt that the very strength of it threatened to consume him. A cruel smile crossed his face and he worked the lever of the Spencer, jacking a fresh cartridge into the breech. Then he left his horse where it was and started stealthfully through the underbrush along the creekbank, toward the source of the singing.

He found her a moment later. It was a young Negro girl, perhaps sixteen or seventeen years of age. She was dressed in the ragged, threadbare clothes of a slave, but did not exhibit the air of the oppressed like many he had come across since the beginning of the War Between the States. No, the girl seemed content in her chore of washing a basket of fine clothing against the smooth stones of the stream, singing praises to the Lord as she worked. Again, Wade felt himself bristle at the words that rose musically from her throat. They seemed to awaken something ugly inside him, something sadistic and ungodly. And, as he stared at the black girl herself, something else surfaced within him, something that had never been conjured by the sight of a woman before: lust, pure and unbridled. But it was a lust born not of love, but of cruel power and control.

Wade took another step forward, the sole of his cavalry boot bearing down on a twig. The length of wood snapped brittlely, drawing the slave's attention from her washing. Her singing ended and her eyes widened with alarm at the sight of the tall

Union colonel with the muttonchop whiskers. The girl cried out in alarm and fled, leaving her master's clothes behind. Wade waited until she got a few yards along the creekbed, then, without hesitation, lifted the stock of the Spencer to his shoulder and snapped off a single shot. The bullet hit the young woman squarely in the center of the lower back. Her spine shattered by the 52-caliber slug, she collapsed, falling facedown onto the moss of the creekbank.

As he advanced toward the wounded girl, Wade Monroe tried to feel outrage and revulsion at what he had just done, but there was no place for such emotions within him. He walked toward the whimpering woman slowly, his gait almost predatory in its leisure. When he reached the spot where she lay, he stared at the bloody hole in her back with satisfaction, relishing the skill of his aim. Wade could conjure no degree of pity for his victim, only contempt and that awful sensation of mounting desire.

As if she were no more than a sack of flour, he slipped the toe of his boot beneath her body and flipped her over on her back. The look of horror and searing agony that contorted her dark face only seemed to fire his carnal hunger. He lowered the warm barrel of the rifle toward her gingham skirt and hooked its muzzle in the helm. He pulled the skirt upward, until it was around her waist. She wore no undergarments.

"No, suh," she pleaded, tears coursing down her dark cheeks. "Please, suh, don't . . ."

He ignored her feeble protests. He laughed loudly, savagely, then tossed the Spencer aside and began to unbuckle the brass buckle of his belt . . .

Wade Monroe cried out as he sat up in bed. He sat there amid a tangle of sweaty sheets, gasping for air, trying to drive the awful nightmare from his mind. He reached up and turned on the light over the bed, his fingers trembling as he did so.

"Wade?" came the drowsy voice of Bret beside him. "What's wrong?"

"Nothing," said Wade. "Really, it was only a dream."

Sleepily, Bret sat up in bed. He noticed the bulge of Wade's crotch straining against the linen of the bedsheet and smiled slyly. "Oh, dreaming about Mel Gibson again, were we?"

Wade was shaken by his erection, for he knew that it was a direct result of the sordid nightmare he had just experienced. He felt the hot sting of bile rise swiftly into his throat. "I think," he sputtered, "I think I'm going to be sick."

A moment later, he was in the bathroom, puking his guts up. As he voided that evening's supper into the commode, lurid flashes of his nightmare came back to him: the brutal shooting of the slave girl and his intention of rape as she lay there on the creekbed, helpless and dying. Both acts had been performed by him, and he had done them unwillingly and without control, like a Shakespearean actor forced to star in some wretched porn flick.

"Wade?" asked Bret from the opposite side of the bathroom door. His voice was soft with concern. "Love . . . are you all right?"

"Yes," sighed Wade. He stepped weakly to the sink, ran the water, and washed the remnants of sickness from around his mouth. "Go back to bed. I'll be out in a few minutes."

Wade listened as he heard Bret walk across the bedroom and crawl back into bed. His lover's concern comforted him, but for some reason, he simply could not seem to drive away the ugly afterimages of that terrible nightmare he'd just awakened from.

It was half past eleven when Laura finally finished the last of the supper dishes. The Gants had left around eleven, grateful for the meal and the tour of Magnolia's plantation house, as well as the discussion of subjects that were so dear to them. All in all, the dinner party had gone much better than Laura had expected, much to her relief. She had invited them to come back during the daylight hours to take an extended tour of the magnolia grove, the rear garden, and the overgrown ruins of the slave cabins that still stood in the orchard out back. In turn, Archie and Alma had promised to let Laura be one of the first to read the journal of Major Hudson. That was, if they succeeded in acquiring the item at the auction in St. Louis.

Laura was rinsing the last cup and saucer, and setting them in the rack of the dish drainer, when a pair of hands grasped her firmly by the waist. She was startled, because at first, she did not recognize the touch of the one behind her. It was stronger, more electrifying than that of her husband. But when she felt his lips on the side of her neck and the prickle of his new mustache against her skin, Laura knew that it was, surprisingly enough, Rick, after all.

"What's gotten into you?" she asked. Not that she objected to his sudden show of affection . . . instead, she was pleasantly pleased. She closed her eyes and relaxed, enjoying the sensation of Rick's teeth and tongue as they traveled from the left side of her neck, across the nape, and on to the other side.

"I'm not sure," said Rick, although the tone of his voice told her that he really did not care what his motivation was. "I suppose it could be several things. The meal, the conversation, that wickedly delicious chocolate-pecan pie. You were the perfect hostess, Laura. The combination of it all . . . well, it just made me hornier than hell!"

His words were crude and uttered without restraint, two things that were uncommon for someone like her Rick. But she decided not to say anything about the refreshing change. Laura did not want to do anything to ruin that rare act of spontaneity on his part. Instead, she gently urged him on. She took one of his hands and raised it to her right breast. His fingers went to work immediately, kneading the mound of flesh through the sheer barriers of her dress and bra. His thumb stroked hard against the button of her nipple, causing her to gasp out loud.

"I want . . ." she began.

"What?" demanded Rick, his breath hot in her ear. "Tell me . . . *what* do you want?"

"I want to make love," she finished, leaning back into him.

She could feel the hardness of Rick against her. "I want to . . . now."

Rick embraced his wife hungrily, as if intending to consume her body with his own. He said nothing in reply. He simply turned her around and, cupping her face gently in his hands, kissed her. It was not a tame kiss; it was full of fire and fury, a melding of yearning lips and probing tongues. Laura did not surrender to the act of passion. Rather, she acted on it, grasping the hair of Rick's head and pulling his face closer, if such a thing were physically possible.

Then, suddenly, she was literally swept off her feet by Rick. Arms she had never really considered powerful lifted her easily into their cradle. Their kiss ended and their lips parted as Rick carried her across the kitchen to the narrow staircase that led upstairs. As he mounted the steps, Laura stared into his eyes. What she saw there both frightened and fascinated her. The dull, washed-out expression that usually occupied her husband's gaze was no longer present. Instead, his eyes held a boldness she had never seen there before. Uncharacteristically, he appeared to be a man brimming with life and passion, a man devoid of distractions and focused solely on one thing and one thing only . . . the woman he loved.

Together, they ascended the stairway to the upper floor and the firm bed that awaited them two doorways down the hall. During that maddening journey between kitchen and bedroom, Laura was again gifted with the touch of Rick's mouth. This time the hot, wet tip of his tongue probed into the curve of her ear, sending wild thrills of delight down her back, to the base of her spine and beyond. And she began to think that she had been wrong several days ago. Perhaps, on rare occasions such as this, love was as exciting and unpredictable as the passion she bestowed on the characters in her romance novels.

Chapter Thirteen

He awoke.

For well over a century he had lain dormant beneath the cold earth, condemned to remain there, inactive, while others of his kind roamed freely within the realm of the living. But now he had been remembered. His name had been spoken aloud and he had been roused from the dark sleep of the dead. After nearly a hundred and thirty years, the chains of limbo had been cast away and he was, once again, free to do as he pleased.

His essence wasted no time in leaving its resting place. It rose past the oppressive weight of dense earth and rock, sending a blanket of dead leaves fluttering as he met the air above. The night air was crisp and cool, and he could detect the sharp tang of woodsmoke in the air. He sensed a changing of seasons. Autumn was swiftly turning to winter. The weather conjured memories from the time when he walked the earth as a flesh-and-blood man, and not an entity of the soul. He had memories of fury and carnage; the thunderous roar of cannonfire, the flash of sabre blades in sunlight, and the countless torments he himself had inflicted before the final act of death was administered.

The plantation house stood where it had during the violent instant of his own demise, but it was not the same. It appeared different than it had before. He could smell the stench of chemicals and materials that were not known to him during his time. He rose upward, past the boughs of trees, spiral-

ing toward the dark sky. He rested on the peak of the mansion for a while, exhausted by the effort of his flight. His period of confinement had weakened his spirit, but he knew that it would eventually grow stronger, much stronger. But for the time being, he would have to content himself with watching, rather than acting.

He stared down at the circular drive that stretched in front of the big house. He puzzled over two vehicles that were parked there. One appeared to be a horseless buckboard, while the other seemed to be a strange buggy of some sort. Curiously, he descended and studied them. He detected the stench of rubber and the metallic tang of steel, as well as a noxious odor that was similar to coal oil, yet was still alien to him. The vehicles of this time fascinated him. Oh, what havoc he could have wreaked if only he had been blessed with armored wagons such as these!

He then turned and regarded the front of the plantation house. The structure was dark, except for a faint light emanating from the upper story. Soon, he was there, on the balcony, staring through the panes of the French doors. He laughed softly to himself at the sight of two forms lying naked upon a bed, engaged in a feverish act of copulation. That old, familiar urge nagged at him, even though he was no longer a physical being—the maddening desire that had led to the carnal invasion of countless women, and sometimes even children, if the opportunity arose.

As the passionate rutting grew faster in its urgency, he felt like bursting through the double doors, flinging the man aside, and partaking of the pleasures of the flesh, forcefully and without invitation, as he had done so many years ago. But it was impossible. He was weak and without the solidity of mortal muscle and bone. His power in the scheme of this realm would be severely limited, at least until he regained his energy. And even then, he would be denied the sadistic pleasures he had once taken in conquest.

That was, unless he found a host to inhabit. Then he would be able to live as a man again. He would be able to perform the atrocities he had once implemented with relish and abandon.

Again, he rose skyward and contemplated the place known to him as Magnolia. He sensed the approach of an anniversary: the anniversary of the plantation's fiery destruction, an incident he had missed out on due to his unexpected death. He could sense the coming of the cold and snow, as well as a confrontation. A confrontation of destructive consequence between himself and the master of Magnolia.

But even he knew that it could not take place on the spectral plane he now occupied. Rather, it would have to take place in the land of the living, between men who could clash, tooth and nail. Men who could fight and bleed . . . and even die, if it came to such an extreme.

And if it was up to the spirit of Fredrick Bates, it most certainly would.

PART TWO

UNWILLING HOSTS

Chapter Fourteen

Rick Gardner stepped back from his canvas and scrutinized his work in the bright morning light.

He had originally intended to do the ink illustrations for the horror-western book before he tackled the task of doing the cover painting. But for some inexplicable reason, he had awakened before six that morning with the image of the novel's main character etched firmly in his mind. He was rarely blessed with such a bolt of inspiration, so he had acted quickly, rising two hours earlier than Laura and entering his studio while the darkness of dawn still pressed at the upstairs windows. By the time the first rays of the sun broke the hilly Tennessee horizon and gave him the natural light that he preferred to paint by, Rick had already set up his canvas, done the preliminary pencil sketch directly on the blank surface, and prepared his paint and brushes. He had started work the moment sunlight hit the canvas and had not stopped until Laura poked her head sleepily through the study door a little after eight. He left the canvas just long enough for a quick breakfast of orange juice and French toast, but even then, being away from the canvas for even that brief amount of time had seemed almost maddening. Soon he was back upstairs, finishing the muted golden-orange background of the landscape and starting on the form of the novel's hero.

Now, five hours later, he was nearly a third of the way done with the painting. Rick studied the balance and power that the male on the canvas exhibited, and smiled in approval.

Just like in the book, the protagonist came across visually as a man not to be messed with. He was not the clean-cut cowboy that many western novels depicted. Rather, he was more of a gritty antihero, the kind who survived by whatever means he deemed necessary, whether honorable or otherwise. He was dark and brooding, his shaggy hair and untrimmed mustache the oily blackness of a crow's feathers, and his piercing gray eyes, hardened and cynical from years of gunfighting, held an almost hidden quality of goodness and compassion. His stained silverbelly Stetson and frayed duster gave him the appearance of a man who spent a lot of time on the trail, rambling aimlessly from one town to another. Rick checked the upper half of the gunfighter for any sign of inconsistency, either historically or stylewise, but was pleased to find that the rendering was coming along exactly as he'd hoped it would.

Rick's gaze shifted down to the outstretched hand of the gunslinger . . . a hand still crudely sketched in number-two pencil. He had dreaded reaching that point in the painting, for it was the hand that would hold the Colt Navy revolver. He had to admit he was a little intimidated by the challenge of painting the cap-and-ball revolver. Thinking back, he realized that he'd never included a firearm in any of the work he had done prior to this painting. This particular work demanded that the revolver be shown at a particularly sharp angle, the muzzle pointing directly at the viewer.

True, Rick had done some work as a draftsman before entering the field of commercial illustration, and he was no stranger to using a T-square or compass when a particular project demanded it. But he knew that he would be unable to implement such tools of the trade on this work of art. If he did, the gun would come across as too precise and cleanly drawn. It would contrast with the gritty look and feel of the rest of the painting. Therefore, he would have to resort to the difficult task of drawing the gun free-hand, and he was not at all sure that he could pull it off convincingly enough.

Rick sighed at the prospect of his next step, but he knew he could not let up now, not after his work had gone so effortlessly all morning long. He made sure the door to his study was closed, then walked to one of the tall storage lockers. He unlocked it with a key from his pocket, then rummaged through a cardboard box of cleaning rags until he found what he'd hidden there. He tucked the rectangular guncase beneath his arm and walked back to the easel and the table that stood next to it. There his paint-laden palette and a mason jar of spare brushes sat easily within reach.

He did not know exactly why he thought it necessary to hide the gun from Laura. He could just as easily have explained his reason for purchasing it to her: that he had found it necessary to have an actual model of the handgun to make the painting as authentic as possible. She might have kidded him a little about buying it, but she'd have certainly understood. After all, one's imagination can do only so much. Sometimes it needed a little boost in the right direction, whether it be a prop for an artist to refer to, or research material for a writer's body of work.

Rick set the case on the table and opened the lid. The smell of gun oil drifted up from the instrument of blued steel and polished walnut, and he breathed it in eagerly. He took the gun from its compartment and hefted it in his right hand. He had handled the gun numerous times since buying it nearly a week ago, and just like all the other times, simply holding it affected him in a way that he could only describe as oddly satisfying. He again experienced that sense of overwhelming power. He glanced at the man in the painting and wondered if the expression of cold confidence that shone in the gunfighter's gaze was present in his own eyes.

He propped the Colt Navy on the table, using the brush jar and the tackle box he stored most of his acrylic paints in. It took a few minutes of adjusting the gun from one degree to another, but finally he found the proper angle. He then stepped back to the canvas and with a pencil carefully began to sketch the basic framework of a black-powder gun in the shootist's right hand. A few minutes later, Rick stepped back and studied the sketch, a little surprised at how well he had done. Satisfied enough to proceed, he took up his palette and a fistful of brushes, mixed Mars black with Payne gray and a little white, then went to work.

A half hour later the task was completed. Rick stepped back and was pleased at how authentic the gun looked. It appeared as though the viewer was actually peering down the dark and deadly muzzle of a 36-caliber revolver. He studied the painting closely, looking for spots that needed to be touched up, but he could find none.

"Nice work, buddy," he told himself in congratulation. He set the palette and brushes aside, wiped the excess paint off his hands, then picked up the Navy pistol once again. He extended the gun at arm's length and cocked the hammer several times, turning the engraved cylinder from one empty chamber to the next.

Suddenly, the temptation grew to be too much for him. He had thought about loading the gun a couple of times before, but he'd never gathered the nerve to actually go through with it. But that morning, he did not shy away from the impulse. He took the copper flask from its compartment and tipped its brass spout over the first of the cylinder's chambers. It was heavy with the black powder he had filled it with several days ago. He slid the release switch to the side with his thumb, letting an ample charge of grainy powder fill the chamber halfway. Then he did the same with the remaining five chambers. After that, Rick seated a 36-caliber round ball of cast lead onto the mouth of each chamber and packed it firmly atop the powder with the loading lever that was hinged underneath the octagonal barrel. The final step came with the capping of the firing nipples.

Rick's stomach fluttered a little. A heightened sense of nervousness and underlying bravado filled him as he held the loaded gun in his hand. The simple knowledge that the gun was no longer a showpiece, but a deadly weapon, loaded and ready for firing, sent a thrill through him. It also increased his strange sense of power tenfold. He now knew how a Civil War cavalryman might have felt riding toward the enemy, pistols blazing, or how Wild Bill Hickock had felt facing a rowdy upstart, his hands poised over ivory-handled Colts the same make and design as the one Rick now held in his grasp.

Finally, the tension of holding such a potentially explosive object in his hand got to him. He decided to place the Colt Navy back in its walnut case and return it to the metal cabinet. He toyed with the idea of unloading the gun, but decided against it. Knowing his luck, he would probably end up shooting himself if he took on such a tedious task. Instead, he laid the revolver in its compartment and closed the lid.

A moment later, the guncase was back beneath the concealment of the cleaning rags and locked behind the metal door of the cabinet. The tension that had filled Rick during his handling of the loaded gun now drained away. He felt oddly exhausted and a little let down, although he could not understand why. After all, that morning's work had been a complete success. He still had a few more days' worth of work to do on the painting, but it would be a piece of cake compared to what he had done today.

Rick returned to the canvas and studied it again. This time, something peculiar struck him about the face of the gunfighter that had not bothered him before. He stood there for a long time, trying to identify the mood of déjà vu that had suddenly hit him, but he simply could not put his finger on it.

It was not until he went into the half-bath to wash up for lunch that he looked into the mirror and realized the source of the nagging feeling: his face stared back at him, his hair a little longer and shaggier than usual, his eyes strangely darker and more cloaked in shadow, and his new mustache much fuller than it had been several days ago.

It was only now that Rick Gardner realized that the face of the gunfighter was his own. Strangely enough, he had unconsciously used himself as a model for the subject of his painting, although he could not understand what had possessed him to do so.

For Jessica Heller, life at Magnolia was pure paradise. To say that her time there at the plantation had been idyllic would be putting it mildly. Since marrying Braxton a year before, Jessica had been treated with an honor reserved for royalty. The Heller slaves had taken to her directly from the start, particularly the cook, Sadie, and her son, a strapping fieldhand named Sebastian. In fact, the young lady would have gone so far as to say that they were more like good friends than servants. They constantly went out of their way to look after her and make sure she received the attention befitting a belle of the South.

Not that she spent all her time reading in the parlor and acting like the perfectly genteel woman that the citizens of Franklin expected her to be. No—sometimes, when she became particularly bored, she would saddle her finest horse and ride like the wind along the dirt stretch of the main road to town and back again. This act in itself raised some eyebrows and caused some gossiping tongues to wag in displeasure. But Jessica was not one to put stock in the opinions of others. The more she grew to understand the workings of plantation life, the stronger she became in spirit. Her former air of shy demureness slowly vanished as she grew from a flighty girl into a sure and capable woman. There were even times when she changed into some of her less elegant clothes and helped the Negroes pick apples and peaches in the fruit orchard near the slave quarters. But she did that only when Braxton was away on business. He'd have thrown a fit if he'd known she was out there laboring, side by side, with the slaves.

Her life at Magnolia was much different than it had been in Richmond. Here, there were no crowds, no noise of clattering wagons or roaring trains. Compared to the bustling metropolis where she had resided before, Magnolia was pleasantly isolated. Never in her life had she felt such peace and tranquillity. True, she missed some of the social functions she had once attended, as well the convenience of shopping in Richmond, but for the most part, those yearnings seemed unimportant. Before marrying Braxton and sharing his Tennessee home, Jessica had never smelled magnolia blossoms on a warm summer night, nor taken a cheerful sleighride along a snowy rural road. No, even if she were given the chance, she would not trade her life at Magnolia for all the riches in the world.

If anything cast a pall over her happiness, it was the trouble brewing among the slaveholders and the federal government. Plantation owners across the South were bristling with indignation over the North's support of the abolitionists. Personally, Jessica believed it morally wrong to hold the deed to another's body and soul, but that was not the entire gist of the conflict. Rather, it was the power of the Northern states to dictate to the Southern states what they could and could not do. Jessica knew that the debate over slavery was putting a strain on her husband. Lately, Braxton no longer seemed like the bold and spirited man she had first met at a society ball in Richmond. These days, he seemed pensive and troubled. She knew that he was frightened, even though he'd never have admitted such an emotion existed within him. He was secretly frightened of losing everything that his late father had built during his lifetime. There had even been talk of seceding from the Union and forming the Southern states into a separate government unto itself. That way, the South could dictate its own laws and policy without any interference from the North.

Jessica attempted to ignore such talk. As her lady-friends on the neighboring plantations told her, such matters were the concern of menfolk. She knew that she should do as the other belles in Franklin: cast the troubles of plantation business aside and concentrate on the genteel pleasures of being a well-to-do lady of the South. But still she could not help but share Braxton's concern and hope that the storm that was brewing dissipated before it grew into something that neither North or South could control.

Laura stored her latest chapter on microdisk, then turned off her word processor. She sat there at her desk for a moment and listened. The house was completely silent. There was no clashing of stereos, no battle between hard rock and soft country. Both she and Rick had been working at a steady pace all day, but neither had even bothered to turn on some music. Normally, they used music to stimulate their creativity and set a rhythm to their writing and painting. But lately, they had chosen to work in complete silence.

Like the heroine of her novel, Laura could not help but feel a little uneasy these days. She could not quite understand why, but things had changed since they'd first moved to Magnolia. Subtle things, to be sure, but it was still significant enough to put Laura a little more on edge than usual.

One thing was the transformation her husband seemed to be undergoing. He no longer seemed like the cuddly teddy bear of a guy she had met and fallen in love with at a Southern convention five years ago. Instead, he seemed to have become bolder and more self-assured since their arrival in Franklin. At first glance, all the changes seemed to be to Laura's advantage. He had grown the mustache and had even begun working out more frequently, performing a regimen of push-ups and sit-ups every morning after getting out of bed. And he'd certainly grown more passionate and spontaneous during the last week or two. Without warning, he would appear out of nowhere and make love to her, right then and there. Come to think of it, every room in the big house had been christened by their growing passion for one another, including such unlikely places as the kitchen and the staircase of the main entrance hall.

No, such behavior on Rick's part was not what concerned Laura, not by a long shot. Rather, it was an underlying attitude that lurked just beneath the surface of her husband's personality that frightened her a little. Previously, she had always considered Rick to be an extremely safe and even bland person to be around. He had been totally predictable and had adhered staunchly to a set of principles he had held since high school. But now, he seemed different somehow. Sometimes, when he made love to her, he did not seem like the same Rick. He was brasher and more impulsive, acting more on his instincts than on his intellect. Laura had also detected a hint of genuine danger in the man, something she would never have connected with the old Rick. That was what disturbed her the most. Before, she could safely have said that her husband would not harm a fly, let alone a human being. But lately, she had begun to wonder about that.

Rick's changing behavior was not the only thing that bothered her. She began to notice more and more that something strange was taking place at Magnolia, something more subtle than obvious.

It had started only a few days ago, with the odd sensation that she and Rick were not the only ones present in the house. Several times, while she was writing in her study or doing her chores in the kitchen or the laundry room, Laura had gotten the overwhelming feeling that she was being watched. Then there was the matter of items that had mysteriously moved to other places in the house or even vanished completely. At first, Laura thought it had been due to an act of forgetfulness on her part. But as the incidents grew in number and frequency, she began to sense that something else was responsible.

Initially, Laura thought back to her youthful encounter with Jessica Heller and wondered if it might possibly be the ghost of the Southern belle who was pulling such pranks. The very thought of it excited her at first. But as the incidents increased, more mischievously than before, she began to doubt that theory. If there was, indeed, a spirit causing such things to happen, it was not that of Jessica Heller. No, this ghost was proving to possess a decidedly cruel streak in its shenanigans. One such example had taken place only the day before. A can of Laura's hairspray had turned up missing from her vanity yesterday morning. It had reappeared later that afternoon . . . on one of the upper steps of the main staircase. If Laura had not glanced down and spotted the can in time, it would have surely caused her to lose her footing. More than likely, she'd have tumbled down the stairway and seriously injured herself.

That was what disturbed her most of all. She began to become more and more convinced that there was a presence in the house, a presence that was up to no good and, in time, could prove to be more dangerous than it was playful.

Chapter Fifteen

On the morning of November 10, Tyler Lusk arrived in the town of Franklin.

He had landed at Nashville's Metro Airport at ten o'clock, rented a white Ford Tempo from Avis, then driven fifteen miles southward to his intended destination. The day was cool but sunny, and his trip to Franklin was a pleasant one. As he made his way along the rural stretch of Highway 31, he passed both wooded hill country and rolling pastureland, as well as several horse farms. The grass of the fields was brown with lingering patches of green and the trees were completely bare, the last of their leaves having fallen around the first of November. But those things did nothing to take away from the natural beauty of the Tennessee landscape.

Soon, Tyler was past the town limits and circling Public Square. As he made his way down Main Street, he kept his eyes peeled for the place of business Professor Hughs had suggested he visit upon his arrival. He spotted a brass-lettered sign that read GANT'S BOOKSHOP a moment later, and finding a parking spot out front, pulled his car into the empty space.

He took the index card out of his jacket pocket and reviewed its contents before leaving the car. Then he opened the door to the bookstore and walked in.

"May I help you, young man?" came a voice, strangely enough from overhead.

Tyler glanced over at a far wall and saw a tall, elderly woman on top of a sliding ladder. She was perched on the top rungs, placing an armload of ancient books into their proper places on an upper shelf.

"Yes," replied Tyler. "I'm looking for Archie and Alma Gant."

The woman climbed down off the ladder. "Well, you've found half of the pair. Now, let's see if we can stir up the other half." She turned toward the doorway leading to the rear office. "Archie? Where in tarnation are you, old man?"

"Just hold your dadblamed horses, woman," came a gravelly voice from the back of the building. "I'm a little busy at the moment."

Tyler heard the muted flush of a toilet. Then, a moment later, Archie Gant appeared in the doorway, double-checking his zipper. Satisfied that it was secure, he walked out into the main room of the bookstore.

"We've got a customer here," Alma told him.

"Not exactly a customer," corrected Tyler. "My name is Tyler Lusk, and I just flew in from Michigan. I was hoping maybe you could help me with a little research. Professor George Hughs at the University of Michigan recommended I look you up when I got here."

"I know of Professor Hughs," said Archie with a nod. "I hear he's a fine man and one helluva history teacher. Exactly what sort of research can we help you with, Tyler?"

"Well, my purpose for coming to Franklin is to find out where my ancestors originated from." He took the photocopy of the page from Reverend Millenton's private journal from his pocket, unfolded it, and handed it to Archie.

Both Gants studied the brief page, their interest growing with each line they read. When they had finished, they handed the paper back to the young black man. "So your search for your roots has led you here to Franklin?" asked Alma.

"That's right."

"How long did it take you to find that one bit of information?" asked Archie out of curiosity.

"Three years," Tyler told him. "Three very *long* years."

The old man arched his bushy eyebrows. "I suppose it felt even longer than that to you, didn't it?"

"You got that right." Tyler regarded the elderly couple. "So, will you help me?"

"Of course!" said Alma. "It's challenges like this that keep Archie and me alive and kicking. Right, old man?"

"Right as rain," replied Archie. His brow grew even more wrinkled in thought. "Let's see . . . we'll need to find out if any of the plantations in the area had any slaves named Sassy, Samuel, Allie, or Josephine."

"I'll get to work on it right now," said Alma. Her eyes were stern with determination as she headed toward the section on Franklin history.

"Alma really gets a bee in her bonnet when it comes to tracking down someone's family history," Archie assured Tyler. "We'll do everything we possibly can to help you out."

Tyler was pleasantly surprised with the cooperation he was receiving, considering that he was a complete stranger. "Really, Mr. Gant, I'll be more than happy to pay you for your assistance."

"Nonsense!" scoffed the elderly man. "And just call me Archie, okay?"

"Yes, sir . . . Archie," Tyler said with a smile.

While Alma slid the wall ladder back and forth on its rail, meticulously searching for one worn volume after another, Archie and Tyler discussed their backgrounds a little. Archie told Tyler of his and Alma's days at Vanderbilt University, and Tyler related his long search to discover his heritage. When the conversation turned to the subject of college sports, Archie eyed Tyler curiously. "Tell me, did you ever play any basketball at the university?"

Tyler hid a grin of amusement. Since he was black and overly tall, Tyler had been asked the basketball question a thousand times. This time, as always, he simply smiled and nodded politely. "Yes, sir. My freshman year. But I hurt my knee and had to bail out after one season."

"That's a shame. I bet you were a whiz on the court. You've certainly got the height and reach for the game." Archie stared at the young man for a moment, then frowned. "Am I coming across like typical white folks?"

"Yes, sir," replied Tyler with a laugh. "I believe so."

"I was afraid of that," said Archie. He glanced over and was relieved to see Alma returning with a stack of books up to her chin. "Ah, here's the little woman, just in time to save me from further embarrassment."

Alma deposited the books on the sales counter. There seemed to be ten or twelve volumes in all, most of them clothbound, with yellowed pages and threadbare covers. "This ought to give us a good enough start. We'll search through these, and if we come up empty-handed, we can always try the county courthouse. A good portion of the slaveholder records were destroyed during the Battle of Franklin, but there are still a few left. Who knows, they might be the very ones we need."

"Good idea," agreed Archie. "And if that doesn't pan out, we'll visit some of the old plantation grounds here in the area. Some have slave cemeteries. We might find the names you're looking for on some of the tombstones."

"Looks like I came to the right people," said Tyler. "I really do appreciate this."

"Don't mention it," said Alma. "Things were getting kind of boring around here. You just walked in and livened it up for us a bit."

Archie fished a gold pocketwatch from his vest and snapped the lid open with his thumb. It was a quarter till twelve. "I suggest we go across the street and grab us a bite of lunch. Then we'll come back here and tackle those books. What do you think?"

"Sounds good to me," agreed Tyler.

As he and the Gants left the cluttered confines of the rare and used bookstore, Tyler felt all the nervousness and uncertainty he'd experienced during the flight to Tennessee suddenly vanish. He knew now that if anyone in the town of Franklin could help him locate his ancestral home, it was Archie and Alma Gant.

Chapter Sixteen

About the same time that Tyler Lusk arrived in the town of Franklin, Laura and Rick, having eaten breakfast several hours before, were in the process of working off the excess calories. For years, Laura had wanted her husband to take more interest in physical fitness, but her suggestions had always fallen on deaf ears. But for the past week, she had been completely amazed at his sudden change of attitude. He was watching what he ate and exercising much more frequently.

That morning, Laura had been dressing in her silk jogging outfit in the bedroom, preparing for her daily run, when Rick had appeared in the doorway and asked if he could join her. Needless to say, she was flabbergasted. He had found himself an old pair of sweats he usually wore when cleaning around the house or washing his truck, and put them on. Soon, they were outside and heading along Laura's normal route—down the paved drive through the magnolia grove and then along a wooded pathway that encircled the entire boundary of the property.

Laura started out at a slow pace at first, suspecting that Rick would grow tired and run out of steam pretty fast. But as they left the driveway and jogged along the shaded path of the grove, her husband had surprised her. He turned out to be the one who picked up the pace. It was not long before they were running along the wooded trail at an even speed. Laura glanced over at Rick every so often, expecting to see his face red with exertion. But he simply smiled back at her, looking the picture of health, his breathing steady. In fact, he looked more like a seasoned marathon runner than someone who was basically out of shape and unaccustomed to strenuous exercise.

They paused to rest a third of the way around the plantation grounds. Oddly enough, the spot where they stopped was the Heller family burial plot. The ornate fence of wrought iron was corroded and choked with weeds and honeysuckle vine, but it still stood sturdily enough. The latch of the gate was fused together with rust, so they had to climb over the waist-high barrier. The area was relatively small for a cemetery, fifty feet in width by fifty in length. From the dozen or so gravestones that stood shoulder to shoulder, they surmised that three generations of Hellers had been interred there. They found the headstones of Joshua Heller, patriarch of the Heller clan, and his wife, Harriet. Next to them were buried Braxton's father, Augustus, and his mother, Sarah, who had died giving birth to her only child. The only other stone there, and the last one erected, from what they could tell, belonged to Braxton Heller himself. It was simple and not nearly as lavish as the others, but it served its purpose well. The inscription had nearly been worn away by time and harsh weather, but it was still legible. It read: *Braxton Heller, 1832–1864. Respectful Son, Loving Husband, & Gallant Soldier.*

There were several plots to the right of Braxton's grave, obviously reserved for his wife and the family he'd never been given the opportunity to sire. Laura stared at the earth next to Braxton's headstone and knew that Jessica should be there, beside her husband in death, as she had been in life. She turned her gaze across the vast expanse of the plantation grounds and wondered exactly where the woman's remains were buried. It saddened Laura a little just thinking about it.

When they had rested up sufficiently, they were back on the trail again. They passed the broad stretch of land that had once flourished richly with cotton and tobacco. Its divided acreage now lay barren, their crops of tobacco and soybean having been harvested several months ago. By springtime they would be plowed and planted for the new crop, and by summer, the earth would be lush with greenery once again.

They reached the halfway mark when they came to the overgrown structures of the old slave quarters. Only a couple of the cabins remained standing, and even they were nearly in ruin. Their roofs had caved in and the red clay chinking between the dovetailed logs had crumbled and fallen away over the years. The others were no more than piles of rubble. Laura and Rick explored one of the cabins for a moment, but found only debris and the rusted hull of a kerosene lantern. Anything else that had been there had either been pilfered by curious children or had simply rotted away to dust.

The two began to jog again, but they did not get far. They were taking a shortcut through the fruit orchard and approaching the ramshackle structures of the old barn and smokehouse when Laura noticed that Rick was no longer beside her. She smiled to herself, figuring he had finally lost his wind. But when she turned, expecting to see him stumbling behind her in complete exhaustion, Laura found him almost upon her, a mischievous gleam in his blue eyes. Before she knew it, he grabbed her around the waist in a playful tackle. Laughing, they both landed in a bed of dead leaves beneath the naked branches of a peach tree.

"Stop it!" giggled Laura shrilly, as her husband placed his hands beneath her silk top and began to tickle her. A second later, she realized that he had another motive for his action. He grabbed a breast in each hand and squeezed them roughly.

Laura's heart began to pound as his fingers kneaded her flesh, the thumbs stroking the buds of her nipples. Her laughter faded as she strained up to meet his lips. Their mouths clashed hungrily.

"I want you," Rick told her. Laura was thrilled to hear it more as a demand than a request. "Right now."

"You mean, right here out in the open?" asked Laura incredulously. "You've got to be kidding me."

Rick answered by slipping his hands along her abdomen to her hips. He hooked his fingers in the elastic waistband of her jogging pants and tugged, both them and the bikini panties she wore underneath, down to her knees. "Do you think I'm kidding now?"

"No, I guess not," gasped Laura. She reached down to help him off with his own pants, but he had beat her to it. A moment later, he was pressing her down into the bed of soft leaves with the thrust of his hips. Laura cried out, not in pain, but in pleasure. Never had he taken her with such force and abandon. She looked up into his eyes and saw a passion burning there that she had never witnessed before, even during their honeymoon.

The act of lovemaking was short, but exquisitely sweet. Laura grabbed fistfuls of his sweatshirt and pulled him into her as she felt her arousal build toward ecstasy. He was on the verge of release also, and a moment later their cries mingled in the fresh country air. When the last spasm of pleasure had faded and the last tightened muscle grew relaxed, man and woman lay beneath the apple tree contentedly, holding each other in a tender embrace.

"I love you, Laura," Rick told her softly.

Laura smiled dreamily up at her husband. "I love you, too. I love you so very much."

After they had rested a few minutes, they got to their feet, dressed, and walked hand in hand back in the direction of the main house. All thoughts of finishing their run had vanished. They had certainly exerted themselves enough in the orchard to make up for another mile or two of steady jogging.

They were entering the flower garden at the rear of the house when a noise echoed from the opposite side. It was a peculiar noise, a brittle *crunch.*

"What was that?" asked Laura. There had been something sinister about the sound.

Rick seemed to think along the same lines. "Stay here," he told her.

"The hell I will," said Laura. "I want to see what it was."

"I said . . . *stay here,*" repeated Rick.

Laura opened her mouth to argue the point, but something in Rick's eyes stopped her. She could not identify his expression at first, then decided it was just plain old male overprotectiveness. She was a little taken back, for Rick had always allowed her to do as she wished, secure in the knowledge that she was a confident and capable woman. But this time, his eyes clearly said "stand back and let a man handle this." This new trait in him drew a mixed reaction from Laura. In one way, she was turned on by his show of macho aggressiveness, while in another she was a little irritated that he was telling her what she could and could not do.

In any case, she decided to let him play the protective studmuffin, if only this one time. She watched as he picked up a fallen tree branch and cautiously started around the western end of the house. Laura waited until he was out of sight, then took a few steps toward the corner of the house herself.

She was almost there when she heard Rick speak out in disbelief. "Well, I'll be damned," he said, sounding both shocked and more than a little angry.

Laura dropped the timid female act and joined her husband in the circular driveway in front of the plantation house. "What is it, hon?" she asked.

"*That's* what," said Rick, pointing toward his pickup truck.

"I can't rightly say I've ever seen anything like this before," said the deputy named Craven. He jotted a few things down on a report form, then approached the truck again, studying it more carefully, as if afraid that he might have missed something of importance.

Rick was a little annoyed by the lawman's reaction to the damage that had been inflicted on his vehicle. He had expected more from the man. He was certainly no wet-behind-the-ears deputy, having served in the Williamson County Sheriff's Department for ten years. Rick walked up next to him and waved toward the fist-sized hole in the center of the windshield. "I really don't know what you're so perplexed about," he told him. "It's simple enough what happened here. Someone vandalized my truck. They threw a damned rock through the windshield."

Deputy Craven picked up a plastic evidence bag from off

the hood of the truck. Inside, ready to be dusted for prints, was a stone roughly the size of a golfball. It had been found lying on the front seat of the cab, surrounded by tiny fragments of safety glass.

"Well, you're right," allowed Craven. "That's certainly the way it *looks*. I'm not sure if that's actually the way it happened, though."

"And why is that?" asked Rick.

Craven seemed to sense Rick's impatience. "Despite what you think, Mr. Gardner, I'm not some hick-town law officer. I've seen my share of vandalism since I joined the force back in '83. And this just doesn't fit the bill." He pointed at the ragged hole with the end of his pen. "Take it from me, these modern windshields are pretty damned tough. If someone were to throw a little rock this size at it, the most you would get would be a ugly crack . . . not a hole big enough to stick your fist through."

"What do you mean?"

"What I'm saying is that a helluva lot of force was put behind that rock," said Craven. "Either somebody had a pitching arm three times stronger than Nolan Ryan's, or it was shot out of the barrel of a dadblamed cannon."

Rick snorted at the deputy's opinion. "Very funny."

The deputy stared at him, his face serious. "Now, you don't see me laughing do you, Mr. Gardner?" He wrote a couple more things on the report, then handed Rick a carbon copy. "We'll certainly look into it, but I doubt if we'll find out anything. Not anything of a criminal nature."

Rick noticed how the deputy kept glancing at the front of the manor house and the shadowy expanse of the magnolia grove. "Oh, I see," said Rick, shaking his head in wonderment. "You're just going to write this off as 'unexplainable,' aren't you? You wouldn't if it happened in the middle of Public Square, but it's a different matter entirely if it happens out here at haunted Magnolia, right?"

Deputy Craven shrugged. "I don't care what you think, Mr. Gardner. All I know is that strange things happen around this place. Believe me, I've been out here on many a wild-goose chase a long time before you and Ms. Locke bought the place—too many for me to even count."

"What do you mean, wild-goose chases?" asked Rick. His irritation gave way to mild curiosity.

"Aw, folks claiming that they heard screaming out here in the dead of night," replied Craven. "Either that, or they saw a lantern floating through the magnolias over yonder. Never amounted to anything, though."

Rick considered telling the deputy about his own sighting of the light in the grove, as well as the figure of the digging man, but decided against it. He still had not come to grips with whether he had actually seen what he thought he had, or merely imagined it.

"Well, thanks for coming out," said Rick. He offered his hand and the lawman shook it with a firm grip.

"No problem," said Craven. "We will dust this rock, in case there are prints on it. I'll give you a call if we find out anything."

"I'd appreciate that," said Rick. He watched as the deputy climbed back into his Williamson County patrol car and then started back up the driveway to the main highway.

Rick was examining the ugly hole in his windshield when Laura appeared on the front porch with a mug of hot coffee in each hand. "Well, what did Joe Friday have to say?" she asked.

Her husband laughed. "Barney Fife was more like it," he told her. "He was of the opinion that this was not a case of vandalism. He seemed to think that there was no way someone could throw a rock that small through a windshield as tough as this one. He said if they tried, it would leave only a crack, if anything."

"Then what was his theory?"

"He didn't give me one," said Rick. "But I knew what he had in mind. He thinks this incident isn't much of a mystery . . . given where we chose to live."

Laura grinned. "You mean, he thinks a *ghost* is responsible?"

"Well, he didn't come right out and say it, but that's the

impression he gave." Rick regarded his wife with mock seriousness. "What do you think? Does the ghost of Jessica Heller have a compulsion for rock-throwing?"

Laura decided to have a little fun with Rick. "How do you know it was Jessica's ghost? Seems to me that Braxton would be more the sort to pull a prank like that."

Rick thought once again about the skeletal man he had seen in the magnolia grove and could not help but shudder a little. "Aw, give me a break, will you?" he said, accepting a steaming mug from Laura.

"No, I think maybe I'm right," she continued. "I think maybe poor old Braxton has given up looking for his long lost Jessica and developed a crush on me instead. Yeah, that's it—he's grown jealous of you, and that's why he threw that rock through your windshield. No telling what he's likely to do next."

"Sounds like your writer's imagination at work to me," said Rick in dismissal. He would never admit it to Laura, but the very mention of some earthbound spirit having a vendetta against him gave him the creeps, whether he actually believed in such things or not.

"Come on, handsome, I was just kidding around with you," laughed Laura. She entwined her arm around the crook of his elbow and ushered him away from his damaged truck and toward the house. "You know that in my eyes, no ghost could hold a candle to you . . . especially after what happened out in the orchard this morning."

Rick smiled broadly. "It did get pretty wild out there, didn't it?"

Laura squeezed his arm and laid her head on his shoulder. "Wild wasn't the word for it," she whispered. Laughing, husband and wife entered the plantation house, all thoughts of jealous spirits and broken windshields temporarily forgotten.

Chapter Seventeen

The dream he found himself in held similarities to the moment before sleep had claimed him. It was a chilly, autumn night, and he found himself encamped on the edge of a battlefield. But that was where the similarities ended. For in this most recent nightmare, he was in another place and another time.

Wade Monroe found himself sitting on a fallen log in front of a crackling campfire. He wore the same blue uniform he had in his previous dream and possessed the same bushy muttonchops along his strong jawline. He drank from a silver flask of liquor—whiskey, from the taste of it—and stared past the immediate circle of the campsite, off into the darkness beyond. There was no moon that night. Rainclouds hung heavily in the Pennsylvania sky, promising a downpour before morning. The only glimmer of light that shined across the dark pastureland was the single glow of a coal oil lamp in a farmhouse window no more than five hundred yards from where he sat.

Something about that solitary light beckoned to him, awakening emotions that lay, dark and temporarily dormant, deep down within him. He took another swig from the flask, then capped it, letting the whiskey burn its way down his throat and into the pit of his belly. As he arose, he unbuckled the brass buckle at his abdomen and left the heavy leather belt, with its holstered Colt Army .44 and cavalry sabre, in a coil on top of the log. He did, however, unsheath a long-bladed

Bowie knife and slid it into the waistband of his military trousers.

He looked over at a young man with a dark brown beard and the stripes of a major on his sleeve, his second-in-command. "I'm going for a walk," he told him. The man simply nodded, an expression of understanding in his hard eyes.

Wade stepped out of the firelight and into the darkness. The night swallowed him like the maw of some monster, but he had nothing to fear. After all, was he not a monster himself? He found humor at this thought, as he picked his way through the undergrowth of a dense forest. Soon, he reached the edge of the thicket. The uneven ground of the pasture stretched before him, its grass brown and brittle from the changing of the season. Wade removed his scuffed cavalry boots, set them beneath a crabapple tree, then, in his stocking feet, began to walk silently across the barren field.

A few minutes later, he was at the farmhouse. It was a simple structure consisting of a single floor with a root cellar underneath. Wade made his way unnoticed to the southern wall of the house and peered through the window. Inside was a modest kitchen. The lantern he had spotted from his camp glowed from the center of a long eating table.

As he crept stealthfully along the side of the house toward the back porch, he was jolted into immobility by the unexpected striking of a match no more than fifteen feet away. He pressed his back to the wall and watched as the lanky form of a man raised the fire to the end of a handrolled cigarette pursed between his lips. In the light of the match, Wade studied the fellow's face. It was a stern face, lined and weathered by years of toiling the earth in the blazing sun. It was the face of a farmer.

The man who leaned against one of the porch's support posts cradled an old flintlock rifle in the crook of his arm and stared off in the direction from which Wade had just come. Wade matched the farmer's gaze and saw what he saw: dozens upon dozens of flickering lights set against the dark horizon like a sea of stars. It was the collective campfires of the Army of the Potomac, awaiting the coming of dawn and the inevitable call of battle. Wade knew that tomorrow he would engage in the skirmish, the same as his fellow Union men. But tonight, whatever blood he let, whatever havoc he wreaked, would be for his own selfish benefit, and not that of the country he supposedly fought for.

Quietly, Wade grasped the wooden haft of the Bowie and withdrew the knife from the waistband of his trousers. He moved with the speed of a hawk, taking the farmer by surprise before he could react. Wade swung upward with all the might he could muster. The heavy blade of the Bowie cleaved the farmer's throat open from collarbone to jaw. With a wet gurgle, the man stumbled forward as Wade withdrew the knife and acted with precision once again. This time the knife went in just underneath the farmer's ribs, burrowing upward and slicing cleanly into his heart. The act of slaughter lasted no more than a few seconds. Then the farmer fell flat on his face into the autumn grass, his body lurching only once before growing still.

Wade should have felt disgust at the stabbing, but instead an incredible rush of adrenaline shot through his veins. Silently he stepped over the dead farmer and entered the farmhouse through the rear door.

He crossed the kitchen to a hallway that led to several bedrooms beyond. Pausing in front of an open door, he surveyed those who slept within. Two small children slumbered in a huge featherbed, unaware of the danger that lurked only steps away. He passed them by, if only for the time being. He would deal with them later.

Wade turned to the opposite side of the hallway and entered another bedroom. A single form slept in the bed there, the distinctive form of a woman. Again, as in his previous nightmare, Wade experienced that strange lust for female flesh trapping him in its steely grasp, refusing to let go. He felt the crotch of his uniform trousers tighten as he crossed the bedroom floor.

His weight creaked against a sagging floorboard and he stopped in his tracks, his heart pounding, the knife poised and ready if he should need it. The woman stirred slightly, but did not awaken. He proceeded with caution. A moment later he was standing next to the bed, staring down at his next victim. She was a lovely woman, perhaps in her mid-twenties, and possessed the flaxen hair and the peaceful face of an angel. Wade found himself smiling at such a comparison, for it would not be very long until she truly became one.

He reached out with his free hand and very softly began to stroke the woman's long, blond hair. His fingers traveled through her locks like a sinister comb. She stirred a little, a slight smile crossing her lips. "Charles?" she muttered drowsily, apparently under the impression that it was her husband who stood over her.

"No," whispered Wade in reply. He laughed softly as he grabbed a fistful of hair and brutally pulled her toward him . . .

A scream jolted Wade Monroe from his nightmare. But strangely enough, he found that it was not his own. Rather, it was the shrill shriek of a woman.

Confused, he stumbled backward, feeling the soft strands of someone's hair leave his fingers. He lost his footing and landed on his butt on the bare earth. As he shook the last remnants of sleep from his mind, Wade was surprised to find himself within the cramped framework of a tent.

"Who is it?" screamed a woman a few feet away. "What do you want?"

"I . . . uh . . ." Wade stuttered, unable to answer. As his eyes grew more accustomed to the gloom, he saw that the woman was little more than a teenager and that her hair was long and dark. She cowered at the rear of her tent, pulling the folds of her thermal sleeping bag up around her chest.

It took Wade a moment, but gradually he remembered exactly who the girl was. It was November the 12th, and he and Bret were on location at the battlefield near Petersburg, Virginia, investigating the strange specter of a ghostly cavalry rider. Their vigil had been an unsuccessful one, and after several hours of waiting, both parapsychologists and spectators had decided to retire for the night. Among those spectators were a group of students from the College of William and Mary in Williamsburg. One of those students was the young lady whose tent he had unconsciously invaded, a pretty brunette history major named Cathy Hunter.

"Get out of here!" demanded the girl, the shock of her rude awakening giving way to indignation. "I swear, I'll scream bloody murder if you don't get out of my tent right now!"

He was about to answer when the flap of the tent was wrenched open. Bret was standing there, dressed only in his boxer shorts. "Wade . . . what the hell are you doing in here?"

The girl's fear seemed to change into confusion at the mention of his name. "Mr. Monroe?" she said, with the bewilderment of someone who has seen an unflattering side of a much respected idol.

"Yes, Ms. Hunter," Wade finally managed. "I'm terribly sorry. I must have been sleepwalking or something like that. In any case, I apologize for scaring you as I did."

Cathy's panic seemed to abate in lieu of his explanation. "Oh, that's okay, Mr. Monroe. No harm done, really."

Bret took hold of Wade's arm and helped him to his feet. "Come on, Wade. Let's get on back to the camper." He flashed the girl an apologetic look, then ushered the befuddled parapsychologist from her tent.

During their walk back to the Winnebago, several people emerged from their tents, wanting to know what the commotion was all about. Bret gave them the same sleepwalking story that Wade had come up with on the spur of the moment. Fortunately, the explanation seemed to appease their curiosity, and they returned to their sleeping bags to finish out their night's rest.

Once they were back inside the camper, with the door firmly shut behind them, Bret turned toward Wade, a questioning look on his face. "Okay, tell me what happened. Why were you out there in that girl's tent?"

Wade sat down heavily on the couch in the camper's main room, still confused by the incident. "It was like I told her . . . I was sleepwalking."

"How come you've never done it before?" asked Bret.

Wade shrugged his muscular shoulders. "How the hell should I know? All I know is that I was having this weird nightmare and I woke up in her tent."

"And that's all there was to it?" Bret demanded to know.

Wade began to grow annoyed at his lover's harsh line of questioning. "Of *course* that's all there was to it. I swear, Bret, you're acting like a jealous asshole."

"Maybe I have good reason to," Bret told him. He grabbed Wade roughly by the wrist, bringing his clenched hand into view. "Explain *this!*"

Wade was stunned to find several strands of brown hair entwined around his fingers. They had apparently been yanked out of Cathy Hunter's head by the roots.

With disgust, Wade let the strands fall to the floor. He stared up at Bret, his eyes frightened. "I can't explain it," he muttered. "Lord help me, what did I go in there for?"

Bret grew less upset as Wade began to shake with a sudden fit of bad nerves. He stepped up to the wet bar and quickly returned with a glass of bourbon. "Calm down, love," he whispered soothingly, as he raised the lip of the shotglass to Wade's lips. "I'm sorry I was so hard on you. I should have known that you didn't do it intentionally."

Wade Monroe took the glass in his trembling hands and took another long sip of the amber liquor. As Bret put his arms around him, Wade could find no comfort in his touch. His mind went back to the nightmare he had experienced. The images had been much more lasting this time, and more difficult to forget. He replayed the murder of the farmer and the invasion of his wife's bedroom, and knew that he had, partially, acted out that disturbing dreamscape. He also found himself wondering what he would have ended up doing if that girl's scream had not awakened him in time.

Chapter Eighteen

They made their second stop of the day, parking on the shoulder of Highway 96, ten miles due west of Franklin. Tyler Lusk and the Gants left the rental car, and crossing a drainage ditch, started across a stretch of wooded property.

It had been three days since Tyler had arrived in Franklin, and so far, they had found out absolutely nothing concerning the whereabouts of his ancestral home. After the volumes on Franklin history had revealed no clues as to which plantation Sassy and Samuel had lived and died on, they had visited the Williamson County courthouse. He and the Gants had spent the better part of six hours poring over the remaining slave-holder files in the cellar archives. After none of the names listed matched those of Tyler's ancestors, they decided to take a breather from the printed word for a while and set out to visit several of the plantations in the area that had been in operation before the Civil War began. They started with the obvious choices at first: the historical sites of Carnton and the brick home of Fountain Branch Carter. But unfortunately, neither shed any light whatsoever. With those two sites out of the picture, Archie and Alma suggested that they visit some of the lesser known plantations in Williamson County.

They had started early that morning, searching the scrubby grounds of a couple of tobacco plantations mentioned in several of the Franklin histories. One had a small slave cemetery on the rear of the property, while the other offered no sign of one. It was now a little past noon and they were on the verge of exploring a plantation called Willowcrest. It had once spanned seven hundred acres and boasted pastures of beef cattle and orchard upon orchard of apple, peach, and pecan trees. But as they picked their way through a thicket of kudzu and blackberry bramble, it resembled nothing more than a stretch of land that had been neglected and forgotten for well over a century.

"Watch your step," Archie warned Tyler. "It's too cool for snakes, but I've heard there's a few sinkholes out here deep enough to twist your ankle, if you don't take care."

Tyler nodded in acknowledgment and kept a close watch on the ground at his feet. He was not accustomed to tramping through the forest like this. He was more at home with his feet planted on solid pavement, surrounded by the noise and bustle of downtown Detroit. He felt like a fish out of water at that moment, stepping high through ivy and ragweed, the quiet of the rural countryside almost as oppressive to him as the blaring of impatient car horns and the rattle and roar of commuter trains. So far, the only sign of life he had spotted other than himself and the Gants was a frightened jackrabbit leaping for cover and a flock of sparrows winging their way southward in the bright Tennessee sky.

"The plantation house is up ahead," called out Alma. "Or, rather, what's left of it."

As it turned out, there was not very much to see. The main house of Willowcrest could no longer even be considered a structure. There were only a couple of crumbling brick walls standing, covered by rampant kudzu and strands of clinging honeysuckle vine. Around the site of the house stood a scraggly semicircle of weeping willow trees, which undoubtedly had given the plantation its name during better days.

They looked through the ruins, but found nothing of interest. "Have you ever been on this particular property before?" Tyler asked the Gants, a little disappointed at what they had failed to uncover so far. When the Gants had suggested visiting some of the plantation sites in the Franklin area, he had invisioned tall white mansions and meticulously manicured grounds. That had been the case with Carnton and the Carter

House, but the others they had visited had been overgrown with thicket and in much the same condition as Willowcrest.

"Yes, but it's been several years," Alma told him. "I do know there is a slave graveyard on the other side of that hollow over yonder." The elderly woman pointed past the jagged ruin of Willowcrest's western wall to where the forest sloped gently down into a shadowy depression.

"Follow me," waved Archie, starting toward the hollow at a quick pace for a man his age. "I know the way."

"You watch where you're going, old man," Alma called out to him. "It's mighty steep down that grade. If you tumble head over ass down into that hollow and break your dad-blamed back, don't expect me to carry you back to the car."

Archie turned his head and grinned at his scolding wife. "Ah, the extent of your love and loyalty never ceases to amaze me, my dear."

"Just be careful, that's all I ask," said Alma.

Fifteen minutes later, they had crossed the broad back-woods hollow and began to struggle up the other side. Mid-way up the hill, they came to a copse of white oak trees. Amid a dense blanket of kudzu protruded a scattering of grave markers. Some were crudely chiseled from limestone, while most were simple crosses constructed of ancient wood, covered with moss and half eaten away by termites and dry rot.

"Doesn't look very encouraging, does it?" remarked Archie, sitting down on the exposed roots of an oak to catch his breath.

"No, it doesn't," said Tyler. He crouched next to one of the limestone markers and swept back the weeds that obscured its front. "Hell, I can't even make out what this one says." He ran his fingers across the smooth surface of the headstone. Once a name and a series of dates had been chiseled there, but they had been scrubbed away long ago by years of harsh weather.

"Same here," said Alma. She knelt beside a small stone that was apparently the marker of an infant or small child. Its surface was covered with green algae and there was a hint of letters across the front, but they looked more like random hen-scratches than anything resembling characters of the alphabet.

"Well, let's don't give up yet," Archie told them. He rose to his feet and from his coat pocket took several folded sheets of typing paper and a eight-count pack of Crayola crayons. "There's still a way to decipher a few of these stones. The naked eye might be blind to the ravages of nature, but a sturdy crayon and a little elbow grease can do wonders."

Archie squatted next to the stone. He laid one of the sheets against the front of the rock, and taking a purple crayon in his other hand, began to color over the paper in broad, hard strokes. Almost magically, the weathered inscription appeared across the white sheet in dark violet. It was faint, but legible, reading *Yancy, Beloved Husband an Pappy, 1803–1857.*

"That's amazing," said Tyler, his spirits lifted a little by Archie's trick of the trade.

"It is, isn't it?" agreed the old man with a smile. "I learned that from my grandpa when I was just a kid. We'd visit all the old graveyards in Williamson County and do dozens of etchings. I even had them hanging on my bedroom walls, until my mother made me take them down. Said it was too morbid a thing for a boy my age."

Archie passed out paper and crayons to Tyler and Alma. One by one, they tackled the weathered headstones of the slave cemetery. Out of thirty-two markers, they came up with eighteen readable etchings. Unfortunately, however, none of them bore the names of Sassy or Samuel.

Alma tossed the stub of her fire-engine-red crayon into the high grass and glanced at her wristwatch. It was already past three in the afternoon. "We might have time to visit one more place before it gets dark," she suggested.

"What's the use?" asked Tyler in disgust. "This is getting us nowhere, just like those books and the records at the courthouse."

"Don't go getting discouraged," Archie told him. "It took you three years to find that page from the Quaker clergyman's journal. We haven't even been at it three days yet.

Trust us, Tyler. We know the best leads to pursue. Who knows, we might hit pay dirt at the very next place we visit."

Tyler nodded, swallowing most of his disappointment. "I appreciate what you're doing for me," he told the elderly couple. "I really do. I guess I'm just being impatient."

"You have good reason to be," said Alma. She walked up and in a rare display of affection laid a comforting hand on Tyler's shoulder. "Tracking down one's family history can be a frustrating process. Rest assured, the answers to your questions are here, somewhere in Williamson County. As for Archie and me, we'll do our level best to dig them up for you."

"Thank you," said Tyler. He looked over to Archie, who was polishing the lenses of his eyeglasses on the front of his flannel shirt. "So, where do you suggest we go next?"

"Well, we have several options to explore," said the elderly bookseller. "There are four or five more plantation sites around Franklin: Simpson Manor, up near Berry's Chapel; Magnolia, out on Highway 31; and Silverpoint, down close to Leiper's Fork, to name only a few. There's the site of a tobacco plantation called Harrison Heights a mile or two further down Highway 96 here. I suggest we check it out, while we still have the daylight to our advantage. If that doesn't pan out, we'll sit down over supper and figure out our next step. Does that sound okay to you?"

"Sure," agreed Tyler, although in his heart, he already knew that their visit to Harrison Heights would end up the same as the one to Willowcrest . . . unproductive and completely pointless.

That night, Laura Locke was awakened by the sound of weeping.

She opened her eyes and listened for a moment. Yes, there was no mistaking the noise. It was the heart-wrenching sobs of a grieving woman.

Gently, Laura lifted the cover off herself and slid out of bed. She considered waking Rick, but he was curled up on the other side of the bed, dead to the world. Besides, if she roused him and it turned out to be nothing but the television in the downstairs parlor that they had forgotten to turn off, it would be just another incident for Rick to kid her about. And in view of how wonderfully they'd gotten along lately, she wanted to do nothing to spoil their renewed affection for one another.

Laura put on her bedroom slippers, then pulled the folds of her terrycloth robe around her and tied the sash. It had been in the lower sixties that day, but the night had grown colder. It felt as though the temperature had dropped to the mid-forties in the span of only a few hours.

Glancing back at her sleeping husband, Laura left the bedroom and crossed the hallway to the combination reading and sewing room. She went to the only window in the room and pulled back the frilly curtains. There were no clouds that night. The sky was clear, and a full moon hung overhead. The glow of that heavenly body cast its pale light down upon the flower garden at the rear of the plantation house, illuminating the bricked walkways and the sturdy column of the big oak in the very center.

At first glance, Laura saw nothing in the garden that might be making the mournful sound that had awakened her. Then, abruptly, she spotted *her,* almost concealed in the shadow of the huge oak, a pale-skinned woman clad only in a silken nightgown. The woman knelt at the base of the tree, her face buried in the palms of her hands, her slender shoulders shuddering with the force of her weeping.

Laura's heart leapt into her throat and she felt as if she was on the verge of fainting. She had seen that woman once before . . . on a Halloween night twenty years ago.

Laura closed her eyes and breathed deeply, fighting off a bout of dizziness. Then she opened her eyes and peered out the window again. The woman was still there, beneath the tree.

It took an effort of sheer willpower on her part, but Laura eventually found the power to move. As if in a dream, she moved across the room and out into the hallway. The thought of returning to bed never crossed her mind. She knew that she had to go downstairs, to the garden, and see the weeping woman up close.

As quietly as possible, Laura took a shortcut down the back stairway to the kitchen. As she reached the lower floor, the sound of weeping grew louder. Laura's heart sank at the agony expressed in those terrible sobs. She wondered if there could ever be a time when she herself might cry so forcefully and without restraint. She knew that only one thing would make her lose such control, and that was if she lost Rick for some unforeseen reason. It was clear to see that this poor woman's heart was broken to its very core.

Laura walked across the kitchen to the back door. She looked through the gilded panes at the garden beyond. Her vantage point here was much clearer. The young woman knelt beneath the tree, facing the back of the plantation house. From this distance, Laura could see that the woman's gown was dirty and torn. The front had been ripped down the middle and one of her small breasts was revealed, its swell marked by angry red welts and shallow cuts. In addition to the soiling of mud, there were other dark splotches on the elegant fabric of her nightdress. Laura studied them by the light of the November moon and realized, in alarm, that they were the stark stains of freshly let blood.

Don't go out there, warned a sensible voice hidden somewhere in the back of her mind. *Just go back upstairs and wake Rick.* But did she listen to that voice? Of course not. She reached out and unlatched the deadbolt of the back door. Then, taking the brass knob in her hand, Laura turned it and stepped out onto the concrete stoop that looked out onto the garden.

A cold wind enveloped Laura as she started along the brick walkway toward the big oak. She ignored the frigid gale, all her attention focused on that pathetic woman who knelt in the shadow of the tree. Her previous sense of panic and uncertainty faded with each step she took. Instead, a calm like none she had ever felt before took over. One thought occupied Laura's mind: she wanted to help the weeping woman.

She wanted to do whatever she could to somehow ease her terrible pain.

A moment later, she was there, standing scarcely six feet from the woman. Close up, Laura could see that she was not a being of flesh and bone, but merely a shadow of one. She could see the dark husks of dead leaves and the rough grain of the oak's bark through the woman's transparent form. So this was how it felt to encounter a ghost up close. Strangely, she felt no fear, only awe. That, and a sympathy much too strong to express in words.

She took another step or two forward, then spoke. "Jessica?"

The weeping woman stopped her sobbing. She lifted her face from the cradle of her small hands and stared straight at Laura. It was a beautiful face, delicately boned, the skin as smooth as the finest of porcelain. But the face was flawed by an expression that never should have been there, an expression of torment that would have been difficult for the average person to even comprehend.

The wind blew coldly against Laura, ruffling the heavy material of her robe. But the breeze seemed to not effect the specter of Jessica Heller. Her long hair of dark auburn lay around her shoulders, unmolested by the wind that rolled across the garden from the north. Laura's eyes were drawn to the woman's slender neck and the cleavage of her chest. Her breasts were marred with ugly teethmarks, and her throat was laced with an appalling necklace of dark bruises. Those were the fingerprints of the hands that had throttled the very life from her and turned her into the creature she now was.

Then Laura turned her gaze to Jessica's tearful eyes. They seemed to plead to her silently, begging for assistance. Laura felt that overpowering urge to help fill her once again, but she was at a loss as to what to do. How could you help a being who was not physically there? How could you offer comfort to someone you could not embrace or even converse with?

As if reading her thoughts, Jessica raised her hands toward Laura. Unable to stop herself, Laura moved closer and extended her own hands outward. Slowly, the space between them grew smaller and smaller, until their fingertips were on the verge of meeting.

When they did, Laura was unprepared for the flood of emotions that rushed through her. Terror, agony, humiliation, and grief . . . they all assaulted her, engulfing her mind like a dark, smothering blanket.

Finally, she could endure it no more. She felt herself falling to the ground, a shrill scream tearing up out of her throat like something alive and desperately eager for escape . . .

Rick was jolted awake, his wife's tremulous cry pushing away the sluggish aftereffects of the deep sleep he had been enjoying. He sat up in bed and moved his left hand to her side of the bed. The space where she normally slept was still warm to the touch, but unoccupied.

He fought with the covers and stumbled from his bed. As his eyes grew accustomed to the dark, Laura's scream came again, as full of terror and agony as it had been upon his awaking. A moment later, he was running down the hallway, to his studio. He took the keyring he had dug from his jeans pocket before leaving the bedroom, found the right key, and hastily unlocked the metal cabinet. He fumbled through the darkness until he found what he was looking for. Soon, the lid of the guncase was flung open and the loaded Colt Navy was fisted firmly in his hand. Then he descended the narrow staircase to the kitchen, heading in the direction Laura's screams came from.

Rick found her in the garden at the rear of the house. She was kneeling at the base of the big oak, her face buried mournfully in her hands. Her soul-rending screams had stopped. She now wept violently, her entire body shaking with the impact of each heaving sob.

"Laura?" Rick called out to her. As he made his way down the cobbled walkway of the flower garden, he held the gun aloft in his hand, the hammer cocked. He searched the moonlit yard for any sign of an attacker, but there was no evidence that anyone other than Laura had even been there that night.

He eased the hammer of the revolver down gently and stuck the gun in the waistband of his pajama pants. Then he approached his wife cautiously. Her sobs had decreased in intensity, having changed into a mournful murmur. Slowly, he reached out and laid his hand on her trembling shoulder.

"Laura?" he asked softly. "Sweetheart, what's wrong?"

His wife let out a startled squeal at his touch and recoiled from him. She lifted her face from her tear-drenched palms and at first stared at Rick as if she did not recognize him. "She was raped!" she moaned. The words were forced from her throat hurtfully, as if they were shards of broken glass instead of mere words. "Murdered!"

Rick could only stand there and gape at her for a moment. "Who?" he asked tenderly. "Who are you talking about?"

The confusion in Laura's eyes seemed to clear a little, and she reached out to her husband, pulling him closer. "Jessica," she whispered as he took her in his arms. "It was Jessica Heller . . . right here . . . beneath this tree."

Rick embraced her. "No, Laura . . . it was only a dream."

Laura reacted explosively, pulling away from him, her eyes angry. "It was *her,* Rick! It wasn't a damned dream! I *saw* her! Lord help me, I even *touched* her!"

Gently he pulled her back into his arms. He refrained from trying to convince her that she had only suffered a nightmare. She was adamant about encountering the spirit of Jessica Heller, and if he tried to tell her otherwise, he was sure that she would only become more and more upset.

"Come on, sweetheart," he urged, helping his wife to her feet. "Let's go inside."

"Yes," muttered Laura. She leaned against him, seemingly exhausted by her nocturnal walk. "It is cold out here."

A few minutes later, they were back in the master bedroom. Rick helped Laura to the canopy bed, wiped the dirt and bits of dead leaves from the soles of her bare feet, then tucked her in. By the time he bent down to kiss her, Laura was already fast asleep.

Rick stood there for a while and stared at his wife with concern. Even in her slumber, her brow creased and her eyelids twitched, as if she were reliving some horrible event deep down in her subconscious mind. He reached around to his lower back and withdrew the black-powder revolver. Fortunately, Laura had not even noticed it during their trip upstairs.

He left the bedroom and again went to his studio at the eastern end of the house. He placed the black-powder revolver in its case, then locked the cabinet securely. Before he returned to bed, he went to a window that looked out onto the rear garden. For a long time, he stared down at the bricked walkways and the towering oak that stood below. The moonlight revealed nothing out of the ordinary; there was only the customary landscaping of bare flowerbeds and encircling shrubbery, partially cloaked in patches of deep shadow.

Rick knew that he had told Laura that she had only experienced a dream, but he was not so sure about that. He recalled his encounter with the digging man in the magnolia grove. He had been certain that had not been a dream or a figment of his imagination, yet like this incident, there was no evidence of it ever having taken place. But he could not deny the fact that something had affected Laura strongly. Just recalling the expression of terror and pain on her face made Rick uncomfortable. For during his own chance meeting with the skeletal scavenger, he was sure that he had worn that same expression of grief and desperation the moment he had unwittingly stepped into the cold spot in the center of the little clearing.

"Something strange is going on here," he told himself. "Something very, very strange." He stood at the window and stared out at the garden, trying hard to identify what that something was. After a few moments, he finally gave up and went back to bed.

Chapter Nineteen

The following morning, Rick again awoke with the sense that something was wrong. This time, however, his fears had more substance to them than they had the night before.

The first strange thing he discovered upon awaking was the change in the positions of the framed photographs that Laura had set on top of the chest of drawers. Oddly enough, all the pictures that included Rick lay facedown. When Rick asked Laura about the photos, she was at as much of a loss for an explanation as her husband was. She recalled very little about her sleepwalking the previous night, but she knew that they had both been up and around. She suggested that perhaps their footsteps had jarred the bureau and caused the pictures to fall flat. Rick agreed that it could have happened, but privately, he still wondered why only photos of him had fallen flat.

The second incident took place in the kitchen. As Rick and Laura prepared a quick breakfast of scrambled eggs and toast, he noticed that the frying pans that hung on the kitchen wall were arranged in the wrong order. Usually, Laura had the cast iron skillets running from largest to smallest, left to right. This morning, however, they ran from right to left instead. Also, the fireplace bellows and the brass bedwarmer had mysteriously switched places on either side of the hearth.

Again, neither Rick or Laura could figure out how the articles had changed positions. Rick asked his wife if she might have done a bit of redecorating, switching the order of the frying pans, as well as the bellows and bedwarmer, on a sudden whim. Laura denied having done that, though. She insisted that she liked where the utensils had hung and had no desire to hang them elsewhere. It was not until they sat down at the table in the breakfast nook that they discovered that something else had been tampered with in the kitchen. The contents of the pewter salt and pepper shakers had, strangely, been switched sometime during the night. Rick was in the process of peppering his eggs when the top came loose and a mount of salt ruined his breakfast. Any other time, it would have seemed more like a sophomoric prank. But given the odd happenings of the last few days, the action seemed more menacing than humorous.

After breakfast, Laura decided to take a break from her writing and drive into Franklin. She had a few groceries to pick up and planned to have her hair styled at a beauty salon called the Dippity Doo on Bridge Street, if they could fit her in at such short notice. Rick kissed her goodbye, then headed up the back stairway to the second floor. He heard her Saturn start up and the hum of the fuel-injected engine as she headed down the driveway toward the highway.

When he reached the upper story, he stepped into the hallway and turned toward the eastern wing. The door to his studio stood partially open. Rick found that odd; he had shut the door securely the night before, after returning the Colt Navy to its walnut case, and he was certain it had been closed when he and Laura had gone down to the kitchen for breakfast that morning. The strange activity of the past few days—the rock through his truck's windshield, the photos of Rick that had been placed facedown, and the switching of the salt and pepper shakers' contents—preyed on his mind, and he felt the same sense of guarded apprehension concerning the open doorway at the end of the hall.

Cautiously Rick approached his studio, prepared to find another hostile act directed toward him. Still, when he entered the room, he did not expect to find exactly what he did.

At first, nothing in the studio seemed to have been disturbed. Then, as Rick turned his eyes to the cover painting that was propped on the hickory wood easel, he felt his heart sink: the canvas had been slashed in several places by the edge of one of his palette knives. Broad splashes of blood red paint splotched the work of art. The heroic gunfighter who stood there, gun drawn, now resembled a victim from some third-rate slasher movie.

"Damn!" was all that Rick could say at first. Then his shock swiftly turned into outrage. "Damn it to hell . . . *why?*"

He stood there for a long moment, staring at the ruined painting, his fists doubled into angry fists. He tried to rationalize the attack on the painting, just as he'd tried to find an answer for why someone would vandalize his pickup truck. Just as before, Rick could think of no one who disliked him enough to terrorize him in such a way. Rick was well liked in his profession; he had no enemies that he could think of. Still, someone had it in for him, that was for certain.

Rick thought about going to the phone in the master bedroom and calling the sheriff's department in Franklin again, but he decided against it. Nothing would come of his reporting the incident. Deputy Craven would show up again and dismiss it as the act of some spirit that haunted Magnolia, just as he had subtly done before. Rick still was not sure if he believed in spectral phenomena, even after his sighting of the digging man in the magnolia grove and Laura's supposed encounter with Jessica Heller the night before. All he knew for sure was that someone—or *something*—had a vendetta against him, a vendetta that was growing more threatening and more violent with each new incident.

All thoughts of working that morning had disappeared with the discovery of the mutilated painting. Rick felt his anger and his fear slowly merge, changing into a steely resolve. He knew that the county law would not be able to help him or Laura against the threat that faced them. If there was some sort of mischievous ghost harassing them, they would have to resort to enlisting outside help to assist them in settling it. But if it turned out to be a threat that was human in nature, Rick new that it would be up to him and him alone to put an end to it.

Without a second thought, Rick walked to the steel cabinet. Unlocking one of the vented doors, he took the guncase from its hiding place. He lifted the wooden lid and removed the 36-caliber revolver from its compartment. The gun felt heavy, yet comforting, in his hand. Before he knew it, he was filling the pockets of his jeans with the powder flask, a handful of lead balls, and the circular tin of extra-hot percussion caps.

Ten minutes later, he was standing in the fruit orchard, facing the chopping stump next to the rickity smokehouse. Two aluminum soda cans and a glass ketchup bottle stood on top of the stump, awaiting his first shot. Rick held the Colt Navy at his side, feeling more than a little nervous. It would be the first time he'd actually fired a gun. He held the pistol at arm's length several times, aiming down the octagonal barrel at the three targets that stood on the stump thirty feet away. But every time he was on the verge of cocking the hammer and pulling the trigger, his hand began to tremble and he ended up chickening out at the last moment.

"Come on, Gardner," he scolded himself. "Quit being such a wimp." He swallowed his nervousness, lifted and cocked the gun, and fired.

The Colt Navy went off like a miniature cannon. The revolver bucked in his hand, its muzzle expelling flame and a cloud of burnt powder. Its report was nearly deafening, causing his ears to ring. Then, an instant later, it was over.

Rick stumbled back a couple of steps, a little shaken by the recoil of the gunshot. He figured that such a reaction would make him toss down the gun in fright and disgust. But instead, he found himself strangely invigorated by the kick of the pistol and the sulfurous odor of gunsmoke that lingered on the autumn air. He walked to the stump, but found that his shot had fallen short of its mark. A divot of grassy earth had been dug up by the slug two feet from the stump, but that was all.

Determined to do better next time, Rick returned to his spot thirty feet away. He laid his thumb upon the spur of the hammer, cocked it, then aimed carefully and fired again. This time the round ball hit the center of the stump, shedding bark and burrowing a hole into the weathered wood. Rick cocked the hammer again, turning the cycle of the cylinder and aligning the next chamber with the barrel. He fired again. This time, the soda can to the left spun off the top of the stump, rising into the air and landing a good eight feet away.

"Now we're getting somewhere," he told himself. He lifted the gun again, cocked, and fired. The aluminum can to the right followed its mate, spinning off into the high grass, nearly torn in half by the impact of the lead bullet. The fifth shot dispatched the ketchup bottle. The slug hit it dead center, shattering it into a dozen fragments of glass.

Amazed, Rick stared at the revolver in his hand. He never thought that he'd have become so proficient with a gun in such a brief period of time, especially not a firearm as primitive as a cap-and-ball revolver. Carefully he reloaded, wondering if the last three shots had merely been a fluke. But when his next six shots unerringly found their targets, he was convinced that he had somehow acquired the skill to put the gun to deadly use, if it should ever come down to it.

The only thing that Rick could not figure out was whether his proficiency with the Colt Navy had come from some natural ability on his part . . . or from some source he was not yet fully aware of.

Around eleven-thirty that morning, Laura sat in the third chair of the Dippity Doo Hair Saloon, located on Franklin's historic Bridge Street. It was her first visit there and she had no appointment, but still she had been welcomed with open arms. Her hairstylist, Pam Stricklin, had finished shampooing her hair and was in the process of trimming and styling it.

Even though Pam was a talkative lady and tried to engage her newest client in her rambling conversation, Laura kept strangely to herself that morning. She thought of her nocturnal visit to the garden the night before and tried to remember exactly what had taken place. She recalled very little—only the sound of weeping, the sight of a despondent woman kneeling beneath the oak tree, and the icy touch of her fingertips against Laura's own. Beyond that, she could remember nothing about the strange experience. She vaguely recalled Rick helping her upstairs and tucking her into bed, but nothing more. When she had questioned her husband about it that morning, he had insisted that she had been walking in her sleep, and that that was all there was to it.

Laura was not so sure that the explanation was as simple as that. Since waking that morning, she had felt strangely depressed and on edge. The inexplicable tampering with the photos on the bureau and with the salt and pepper shakers did not help matters any. The mystery of those incidents scared her a little. Once again, she felt as if there was some unwelcome presence in the plantation house . . . a presence that was only toying with her and Rick right now, but would eventually resort to more perilous pranks as time went on . . .

Her train of thought was disturbed when Pam began to comb and blow-dry her shoulder-length hair. "So, Laura, how long have you been a blonde, if you don't mind me asking?"

Laura was puzzled by the hairstylist's question, as well as a little offended by it. "I'll have you know that I'm a natural blonde," she told her.

Pam smiled smugly and laid the blowdryer aside. "Okay, if you say so," she said, picking up a brush. "True, no one would know the difference . . . until they got down to the *root* of the matter."

Laura was becoming annoyed at the woman's insinuation. "I don't know what you're talking about."

"Come on, dear, you can't hide it from me, of all people," said Pam. "Besides, I don't know why you would want to dye your hair blonde. It would look so pretty its natural color."

"Natural color?"

"Why, of course," replied the hairstylist. "I do believe that's the prettiest shade of dark red I've ever seen. It's a shame you wanted to change it."

Laura's initial feeling of irritation suddenly changed into an odd sensation of foreboding. "Red? What in the world are you talking about?"

Pam stared at her newest customer as if she were touched in the head. "Just like I said . . . see?" She pulled one of Laura's stray hairs from the brush she had been using and handed it to her.

Laura held the hair to the lighted mirror she sat in front of and inspected it closely. Two-thirds of the strand was Laura's normal hue of honey-blond. But surprisingly, the other third and the root at the very end was of a completely different color.

It was not blond at all, but a coppery shade of pure auburn.

Chapter Twenty

Again Tyler Lusk found himself on the snowy plantation grounds that he had visited in a similar dream a week ago. As before, he found himself running through the cold darkness toward the flickering glow of a bonfire, the shrill screams of a terrified woman spurring him onward. He heard the calling of a name—Samuel—and looked back at where the voice originated from. Again he saw the slave cabin and the injured woman lying on the blood-drenched bed within the frame of the doorway. His heart was torn between the woman in the cabin and the one who shrieked for help beyond the reach of the fruit orchard. Finally, he made his choice, vaguely recalling a request from someone who he admired and respected a great deal, a request that he should look after the woman in distress, no matter what peril might befall her.

That familiar sensation of rage pumped through him, sending him at a mad dash toward the edge of the orchard and the big plantation house that stood a good acre and a half beyond. He paused next to the smokehouse only long enough to wrap his fists around the icy handle of a broad ax and wrench its blade from the chapping stump. Then he continued on, heading toward the leaping light of the bonfire and the screaming of the woman he had promised to protect.

Dead vines and leafless branches pulled at his clothing as he tore through the thicket of the property's rear garden. The soles of his shoes were worn nearly through, and the coldness of the snow beneath his feet threatened to creep through the thin pads of leather. But Tyler ignored it. All that concerned him were the screams of the woman and the maddening thoughts of what she might be suffering at that moment.

Then, abruptly, he was there, at the edge of the flower garden. Just as in his last dream, Tyler witnessed the brutality that war could generate in the souls of men. He stared past the roaring bonfire to where the two bodies, male and female, writhed, one driving toward conquest while the other struggled for escape. He stood there for a long moment, taking in the ugly sight of rape. He was not the only one. Around the demon and his victim stood a semicircle of blue-clad soldiers. Some cheered their commander on, while others stood there quietly, as stunned by the act of blatant carnality as Tyler was.

Then the woman screamed again, breaking the spell of shock and disgust that had frozen Tyler in his steps. But as he moved forward, he knew that he was much too late to help her. In the glow of the firelight, he saw the man's arms bunch powerfully, his hands closing around the woman's gullet until his fingers nearly disappeared within the pale flesh of her throat. A single puff of frozen breath expelled from the woman's open mouth as her rapist's strong hands choked the last spark of life from her frail body.

Tyler shouted as he sprinted from the thicket and leaped over the high flames of the bonfire, oblivious to the heat that engulfed him. As he landed on the opposite side, he saw the man's body shudder with the release of his sadistic passion. Tyler stood over the two bodies—dead and alive—a moan of horrible loss escaping his throat. With a contempt he had never experienced before in his life, he stared down at the face of the murdering rapist. Under different circumstances, the man might have been considered strikingly handsome. He possessed the well-formed features of an aristocrat, his hair and muttonchop sideburns blond nearly to the point of whiteness, and his eyes a sharp hue of emerald green. But the ugly expression of pleasure and victory that creased his features made him look more like a beast from hell than a heavenly prince. There was a degree of pure evil in that face that Tyler could scarcely fathom, so intense and utterly complete was the extent of it.

A roar like that of a wounded bull barreled up from the depths of Tyler's throat as he lifted the heavy ax over his shoulder. Then, with a powerful swing, he brought it down upon the devil at his feet. The honed edge of the ax's heavy iron wedge found its mark a second later. It bit deeply into that leering face, splitting it cleanly in half. Past flesh and bone it traveled, unwilling to stop, until it burrowed into the tender mass of brain matter beyond. Even then, Tyler found himself wrenching the ax free and swinging it downward again and again, unable to stop himself. He knew that the act was pointless. The first blow had killed the evil colonel. But it was not until his rage itself had died that he lowered his brawny arms and let the bloody ax fall from his grasp.

Tyler fell to his knees in the snow and desperately tossed the mutilated body of the Union officer off the woman who had been shamelessly brutalized. He felt hot tears spring from his eyes as he stared down at the face of the one he had failed to save from dishonor and death. Her luxuriant auburn hair was matted with mud and snow, and her face was contorted in a death mask of horror and agony that was difficult for Tyler to even look at. He reached down and touched her pale face with a dark hand, then traced the ugly marks of the colonel's fingerprints that wreathed her throat just below the delicate jawline.

As he cradled the dead woman in his arms and cried like a motherless child, Tyler was aware of a tense silence above the pop and crackle of the bonfire. For the first time since he had entered the garden, he was again aware of the others who stood there. He looked up, and through the prism of his tears, saw them staring at him, their faces frozen in shock. But even as he regarded them, he saw the collective expression of bewilderment slowly change into outrage.

"He killed the colonel!" muttered a squat man with a profusion of knife scars across his face. "That filthy nigger . . . he done went and killed him dead!"

Tyler's attention shifted to a tall, bearded man wearing the uniform of a Union major. Apparently, he was the dead colonel's second-in-command. He took a couple of steps forward and glared sternly at Tyler. The look of contempt in his eyes was as clear and decisive as a death sentence.

"What shall we do with him, Major?" asked another soldier. This one was as thin as a rail, sported a mouthful of rotten teeth, and wore a brace of Colt Dragoon pistols on his hips.

The Union major turned away in disgust. "Do with him whatever you wish," was all that he said.

Then, like a pack of rabid dogs, they were across the garden and upon Tyler, the weight of them dragging him down to the frigid ground.

Tyler awoke with a cry on his lips. He sat up in a strange bed in an equally strange room. Confused, he tried to identify his surroundings. It was late in the afternoon; he could tell that by the waning light that filtered through the blinds of the chamber's single window. Slowly, he realized where he was. He was in the room Professor Hughs had reserved for him at the Franklin Holiday Inn just off Interstate 65. After visiting a couple of plantation sites with the Gants earlier that day, he had returned to the hotel to catch a quick nap before he joined them again for supper.

Shaken by the nightmare, he sat on the edge of the full-sized bed. Tyler brought his hand to his face and found his cheeks bathed in tears. He thought of the nightmare and the vengeful act of retribution he had performed within that dreamscape, and he felt sickened by it. It had seemed so real! The images, the emotions, the bite of the cold, and the hardness of the ax handle in his hands . . . all of it had seemed horribly authentic. The last lingering image of those angry soldiers also came back to him and he had to drive the memory away, it was so clear and threatening.

Tyler stood up and walked to the bathroom. Despite the coolness of the November day, his nightmare had thrown him into a panicked sweat. His clothes clung to his body wetly, causing him to feel grungy. He quickly undressed, then turned on the shower and stepped into its cleansing spray. As he stood in the jet of hot water, his muscles loosened and his body relaxed. But he still could not shake the grim images that had assaulted his mind during that strange dream. He kept experiencing them over and over again; the face of evil staring up at him, the violent murder of the sadistic colonel, and the mob coming for him, their fists clenched and their eyes burning with hatred. And there was also the image of the woman whose body he had held, the lovely, auburn-haired belle with the ugly fingermarks forever imprinted on the flesh of her pale throat.

Five minutes later, most of Tyler's tension had been washed away by the heat and spray of the shower. He stepped out and gingerly toweled himself off, still thinking about the nightmare. He recalled the name of Samuel again, called out to him by the maimed woman in the slave cabin, and wondered if it was some subliminal reference to his ancestor by the same name, the one whose home he was in the process of searching out.

As Tyler dressed, he decided he would share his dream with the Gants over supper that evening. Perhaps it held something important that he was unaware of, yet that would mean something significant to Archie or Alma. In any case, he could not help but think that he was having that particular nightmare for a specific reason. Maybe, if he could interpret it correctly with the help of the Gants, they might be able to avoid the dead ends they had encountered so far and successfully discover what Tyler had come to Tennessee to find in the first place.

That night, over a meal of chicken and dumplings at the Choices Restaurant, Tyler told Archie and Alma Gant about the dream he'd had that afternoon. After he had related the nightmare to them, detail by detail, he sat back and awaited their assessment. "Well . . . what do you think?" he asked.

Archie and Alma looked at one another, exchanging an expression that was a strange combination of excitement and seriousness. Archie turned his head and peered at the tall black man over the rims of his spectacles. "Tyler, you might find this hard to believe, me and Alma coming from such scholarly backgrounds, but we believe in the importance of dreams. We think that most dreams or nightmares have a definite psychic connection to reality. And this one seems more descriptive and potentially enlightening than any we've ever heard of before."

"What are you saying, then?" asked Tyler, anxious to hear their opinion.

"What we're saying is," continued Alma, "we think that something is influencing these dreams of yours. And since the central character that you are playing in this nightmare is a slave by the name of Samuel, it's possible that it is *he* who is responsible."

Tyler certainly was not expecting such a strange response, particularly from the Gants. "Wait a minute," he said. "Let me get this straight. You think that the spirit of one of my ancestors is influencing my dreams? Maybe painting a picture of what happened to him a hundred and thirty years ago?"

"Sounds kinda crazy, doesn't it?" chuckled Archie, lighting his pipe.

"I'll say!" said Tyler, shaking his head. "I'm not sure I can believe this theory of yours. I never was one for believing in ghosts and stuff like that."

"That's all right," said Alma. "A lot of folks don't. But take it from a couple of old-timers who have seen their fair share of strange things, some people can pick up psychic impressions during the course of their dreams, like a radio picking up signals. And sometimes those impressions can foretell the future, as well as replay things that happened in the past. Hindsight, you might call it."

Tyler thought about what she'd said for a moment. "Okay, I might buy that. But I'm not so sure about the ghost business."

Archie regarded Tyler through a cloud of Borkum Riff.

"This victim in your dream . . . the woman who was raped by the Union colonel?" he asked. "Are you certain about her description? Petite of build, with auburn hair?"

"Yes, sir," replied Tyler. He remembered her dead, glassy eyes and the fingerprints around her throat. "I don't think I'll ever forget her."

Archie glanced over at his wife. "What do you think, dear? Sound familiar to you?"

A slight smile crossed Alma's lean face. "Yes, it does." She turned back to Tyler. "Could you describe this plantation to us?"

Tyler frowned in concentration. "Well, it was after dark in my dream. I remember a row of slave cabins, a fruit orchard, and an old smokehouse with a tree stump next to it for chopping wood. I didn't see much of the plantation house itself, just its back wall at the edge of the flower garden, where the woman was murdered."

"Flower garden," repeated Alma softly. "Did it have a big oak tree right smack in the center of it?"

Tyler felt a chill run through him. "Yes, now that you mention it, it did."

Archie grinned like a lazy possum and puffed on his pipe. "Sounds an awful lot like Magnolia to me."

"Magnolia?" repeated Tyler, suddenly intrigued.

"A plantation about three miles south of here," Archie told him. "It wasn't much to look at for years, just a burnt hull of a plantation with a thicket around it. But just recently a lady writer named Laura Locke and her husband bought the place and restored it, turned it into a real showplace. And it fits the description of your mystery plantation to a tee."

New hope sprang into Tyler's eyes. "Do you think this Magnolia could be the place we've been looking for?"

"It might be," said Alma. "It certainly wouldn't hurt to take a trip over there tomorrow and take a look around. I'm sure Laura wouldn't mind the company. She did promise us a tour of the plantation grounds the last time we were there."

"I'll give her a call tonight and ask her if we can come over tomorrow afternoon," said Archie. "From the way they tell it, she and Rick do most of their work early in the morning or late in the evening, so they ought to be free in the afternoon. If they are busy, we can walk around the property ourselves."

"I'd sure like to get a look at the place," said Tyler. "Just to see if it does look like the place in my dream."

"And what if it does?" asked Archie. "Will that change your opinion about ghostly influences?"

"It might help," Tyler told them.

As they left their table and headed to the front counter to pay for their meals, Tyler felt both anticipation and a little dread concerning their planned trip to the plantation called Magnolia. Of course, he wanted to find the place where his ancestors, Samuel and Sassy, had lived as slaves. That was his sole reason for coming to Franklin. But in light of his bizarre nightmare, what if he were to encounter something that he had not originally bargained for?

He hated to admit it, but Archie and Alma's talk of ghosts had spooked him a little. Since discovering those forgotten letters in his grandmother's attic, Tyler Lusk had never viewed Samuel as anything other than a long-dead ancestor. But now, replaying in his mind the vivid images of his nightmare, Tyler found himself thinking that the Gants might be on the right track after all. Perhaps their talk of ghosts and influenced dreams was not so farfetched as he'd first believed it to be.

Chapter Twenty-One

The day that Jessica Heller had feared was finally at hand. She stood on the front porch of the plantation house, her delicate hands clutching an Oriental fan that her husband had bought for her during one of his purchasing trips. Jessica stood in the shade of one of the limestone columns, her heart heavy with sadness. She looked down at the bottom of the stone steps, where a dozen of the Hellers' slaves stood, respectfully awaiting the appearance of their master. One of the fieldhands, a towering Negro named Sebastian, held the reigns of Braxton's finest horse. The roan was as black as coal and the swiftest and surest of all the animals in the Heller stables. Jessica could scarcely bare to look at the empty saddle strapped to the horse's back. She knew that it would not be empty for much longer, and that was what distressed her so greatly.

Then, from within the house, she heard the sound of his boots on the risers of the staircase. She turned just as her husband strolled through the open doorway. Braxton was dashing in his knee-high riding boots and iron-gray uniform with the gold braid of a captain embroidered on the lower sleeves. His belt, which boasted a polished brass buckle with the initials CSA on its oval plate, held a cavalry sabre at one side and a holstered revolver at the other. On his head Braxton wore a high-peaked hat with a feathered plume stuck in its tasseled band. He removed the hat as he approached his wife and stood there regarding her with an expression of sorrowful regret.

"So," she said, hiding her dread beneath a lovely smile. "I see that you are ready to go."

Braxton stepped forward and took her in his arms. "To fight for the sake of the South, yes," he told her. "But believe me, I take no pleasure whatsoever in leaving you. If there were any other way, I would remain here at Magnolia, but you know as well as I do that that is not possible. Not if we are to survive the oppression that the North intends for us."

Jessica burrowed into his warm embrace, her tearful face against his chest. "Yes, I understand," she assured him. "It is your duty to do whatever you can to see that the South wins this struggle, no matter what the cost might be."

Braxton stared at his wife proudly. "I am glad that you support my decision to ride for the Confederacy, my dear. There are some women in Tennessee who don't understand the seriousness of this situation the way that you do."

Jessica did not say so, but there was still a part of her that wanted to retreat into her genteel world and deny that the mounting conflict between North and South was actually taking place. Her worse fears had come to be when news had reached Franklin of John Brown's raid on Harper's Ferry with the help of twenty-one freed slaves. Brown's violent assault had taken place two autumns ago, and since that time, the mounting argument over abolition had turned particularly nasty. The South's resistance to change and the North's insistence for conformity had split the country in half. The first Southern state to seceed from the Union had been South Carolina, in December. It was now the summer of '61 and Tennessee had been a member of the Confederacy for a month. Only days ago, Braxton had received news of the Battle of Bull Run in Virginia. It was then that he had decided to join the fight for Southern independence and contribute the military knowledge he had gained at West Point to help the cause of the Confederacy. That was where he was destined that sorrowful morning: to begin the long journey northward, to join Beauregard's forces in Virginia.

Jessica had done her best to support Braxton's decision, to be brave and unselfish. From all outward appearances, she appeared to be just that. But secretly she wished that Braxton could stay safely at Magnolia until the conflict had been resolved. But she knew that was too much to ask of a man like Braxton. His conscience would never allow him the luxury of cowardice. He was a man who preferred to be in the thick of things, especially if it was a cause that he thought to be just and right. Still, she could not help but fear for his life. Bravery and honor would not stop a musket's bullet or the honed edge of a sabre's blade.

Reluctantly, Braxton pulled away from his wife and checked his pocketwatch. "I'm afraid I must go," he told her. "I am to meet my brigade of volunteers at the Franklin courthouse at noon. After that, we have a long, hard ride ahead of us."

"Yes, you do," Jessica replied softly. "May God's mercy and my love go with you." Despite the presence of the slaves, she flung herself into his arms once again. "Promise me one thing, Braxton—promise me that you will come back to me."

Braxton took her face in his hands and delicately kissed her. When his face pulled away, his eyes were bold. "Don't worry about me, my dear. Hell, this conflict will likely be settled within a few weeks' time, if even that long. We'll teach those meddling Yankees to keep their opinions to themselves, and then I'll be back. You'll see. It won't be long."

"I hope that you are right," was all that she could say in reply.

Braxton turned away and descended the stone steps of the porch. He nodded to the slaves that had gathered to wish him well. Then, swinging atop his horse, he took the reigns from Sebastian. The master of Magnolia regarded the fieldhand sternly, yet with respect. "Sebastian, I want you to watch over Miss Jessica for me in my absence. I trust that you will take good care of her while I am gone."

The big Negro nodded, his broad shoulders squared proudly with the responsibility that had been bestowed upon him. "Yo' can shorely depend on me, Massa," he assured *him. "I'd jest as soon see mah'self dead an' buried than see a single hair harmed on Miss Jessica's head."*

Braxton reached out and shook the slave's callused hand, in appreciation of his loyalty. "I know that you would, and I thank you for that." The young captain then turned to Sebastian's mother, a hefty woman named Sophie. "You see that things in the household run accordingly, will you, Sophie?"

"Don't yo' go worryin' yo head none o'er things heah at 'Nolia, Massa Braxton," she told him. "I'll keep these heah niggers in line, or they'll end up wit' theah heads ringing ta da tune o' mah fryin' pan, dey will!"

Braxton could not help but laugh at the cook. "I know you will, Sophie. And I'd be obliged if you'd see to Miss Jessica's needs as well."

"Don't yo' fret none o'er Miss Jessica," said Sophie. "She'll be jest fine. We'll be prayin' fo' yo', Massa. Jest take care, all right?"

"I'll certainly do my best," he told her. As he reigned his horse toward Franklin, he paused long enough to turn in the saddle. He removed his plumed hat and waved to his beloved one last time. "I'll write," he called out to her.

"You do that," she replied. Then, as he rode away, she ran back into the house.

A moment later, Sophie found her on the sofa in the rear parlor, weeping into a velvet pillow. The big mammy sat down on the couch next to her mistress and cradled her sobbing form. "Ain't no use in cryin', Miss Jessica," comforted Sophie soothingly. "Massa Braxton . . . he'll do jest fine. What yo's gotta do is be strong fo' him an' tell yerself that he'll be back in no time a'tall."

Jessica wanted more than anything to be able to do just that, but she knew that she couldn't. "I've had a premonition," she confided to the old Negro cook. "A premonition that Braxton and I will never see one another again."

Sophie seemed appalled. "Aw, that just be plain ol' nonsense, Miss Jessica! Why, yo' jest wait an' see. Won't be long a'tall till Massa Braxton is ridin' back up dat road out yonder on dat' fine black hoss o' his, grinnin' from ear to ear."

Jessica Heller wished that she could feel as optimistic as Sophie, but that was impossible. The knowledge that she would never again see her husband after that day was etched permanently in her heart. Privately, she knew that her life with Braxton had come to an end the moment that he'd spurred his horse and sent it at a gallop through the lush summer shadows of the magnolia grove.

As she typed the last sentence of *Burnt Magnolia*'s twelfth chapter, Laura pushed her chair back from the word processor and appraised the text on the monitor screen with a frown. When she had begun on the new novel, she had been determined that the outcome of the book would be much more favorable than that of the actual event. But the further she advanced in the storyline, the more it seemed that the novel was writing itself. Laura had consciously attempted to keep the awful shadow of disaster at a mininum with each page she wrote. But strangely enough, the book almost appeared to be taking a dark turn of its own accord.

Laura could say the same about her life there at Magnolia. Ever since her bout of sleepwalking in the rear garden several nights ago, she had felt as if events at the plantation house had been wrested from her control. She felt an odd sensation of foreboding around the place. Where once she had seen only beauty and historical nostalgia, Laura now sensed something basically out of sync about Magnolia. If the mystery of the weeping woman beneath the oak tree had been the only factor, she could have handled it. She had felt no threat whatsoever from what was seemingly the wayward spirit of the long-dead Southern belle. Rather, there was something else there that disturbed her. She felt as if some other presence was there, a presence that held a potential threat for her and Rick.

She recalled the photos that had been laid face down, the rearranging of the frying pans, and the switching of the salt and pepper shakers. At first thought, such incidents seemed like innocent pranks. But the more Laura considered them, the more she became convinced that there was a definite degree of malice behind each one, directed particularly at her husband, more than at her. The rock through the windshield of Rick's truck proved that much.

Speaking of Rick, Laura had noticed some strange things about him, too. One was his continuing change in physical appearance and behavior. Due to his increasing interest in exercise, Rick was growing leaner and stronger. She could tell that during their lovemaking sessions, which had become more and more frequent since they'd moved to Magnolia. Also, his new mustache was growing thicker and his hair was a little longer than he customarily preferred to wear it.

But that was not all. Lately, his new attitude of boldness and spontaneity was slowly giving way to a brooding paranoia that worried Laura a bit. Yesterday, after she'd returned from her trip to Franklin, she had hugged her husband and smelled the faint scent of gunpowder on him. She would have contributed it to her imagination, but she had grown up around guns and hunting during her childhood and was certain of the scent. If Rick had chosen to bring a gun into the houshold, Laura was at a loss as to why he'd choose to keep that knowledge secret from her.

Laura stored what she had written that evening on microdisk, then sat in her chair for a while before leaving her desk. She had received a call from Archie Gant an hour ago, requesting a tour of the plantation grounds the following afternoon. Normally, she'd have preferred some advance notice of such a visit, but she'd agreed, sensing an urgency in Archie's voice. He had mentioned bringing along someone named Tyler Lusk, who was in Franklin researching his family history. From what Archie had told her, there was a good chance that Lusk's ancestors had been slaves at Magnolia. If that was the case, Laura knew she must do whatever she could to make him welcome and assist him in discovering the truth concerning his people.

She thought of the Gants and their interest in Magnolia,

both historically and otherwise. Laura knew it would be wise to inform them of the bizarre incidents that had plagued their life at Magnolia during the past few weeks. But she also knew that she would be unable to do that without Rick's agreement. Therefore, she knew it was necessary to clear the air with her husband concerning what was going on. If he denied that anything unusual was taking place, Laura was not so sure that she wouldn't confide in the Gants anyway, despite her husband's protests.

That night, after supper, Laura and Rick found themselves in the rear parlor as usual, relaxing before they went to bed. Rick watched an old Andy Griffith rerun on TV, while Laura read a Victoria Holt novel. As Rick's show came to a close, Laura knew that it was time to bring up the subject of Magnolia and the strange occurrences of the past three weeks.

"Rick," she said carefully. "Honey, we need to talk."

Her husband turned his head and regarded her questioningly. "Oh? What about?"

"Well, it just seems to me that a lot of strange things have been going on lately," she told him. "Things that are certainly out of the ordinary. Don't you agree?"

She expected him to laugh and deny that anything was going on, but he surprised her. A worried look crossed his face, and slowly he nodded. "Yes, you're absolutely right," he replied, picking up the remote control and turning off the television. "There have been a hell of a lot of strange things happening around here."

With that obstacle out of the way, Laura took the discussion a step further. "Rick, I've experienced some things recently that I haven't told you about. And I believe you have, too. Am I wrong?"

Rick stared at her for a moment, as if debating whether to be honest with her or not. Finally he made up his mind. "No, you're not wrong." He left his armchair and joined her on the couch. "I admit, at first I thought it was only our imagination.

But I don't know. I think it's about time to bring it all out into the open, don't you?"

Laura was surprised, but pleased by Rick's directness. "Yes, I do."

For the next half hour, they exchanged their personal experiences with the unknown since they'd come to Magnolia. Laura described her encounter with the weeping woman beneath the oak tree, while Rick told her of the phantom firelight that had originated from the magnolia grove and his puzzling discovery of the digging man in the open clearing. Both agreed that the ones they had encountered could only have been the spirits of Jessica and Braxton Heller, and that they'd both experienced the loss and anguish of those wayward souls upon contact with them.

"This may sound crazy, but I think they've *influenced* us somehow," Laura said. "How else can you explain your new mustache and the way your entire attitude has changed? I've read Ashworth's description of Braxton Heller, and believe me, you're becoming more and more like him every day."

"Good Lord!" whispered Rich, a glint of fear shining in his eyes. He regarded his wife carefully. "And what about you? Have you noticed any change in yourself lately?"

"Not mentally," she said. "But, physically, yes, I have. Have you noticed that my hair is a little darker today than it was yesterday?"

Rick nodded. "Yes, but I thought maybe you had something done to it at the beauty salon. Maybe had your hair tinted, or colored."

"No, whatever's happening to my hair, it's happening naturally, if you can call it that," she assured him. "I didn't realize it until the hairdresser pointed it out to me. My hair is changing its color . . . from the roots up. It's turning a shade of dark auburn."

Rick shook his head in bewilderment. "The same color as Jessica Heller's?"

Laura found herself wanting to deny it, but knew she could not. "Exactly."

They sat there in silence for a while, mulling over the revelation that there was, indeed, something of a ghostly nature taking place in their new home. Then Laura spoke again. "It isn't the spirits of Jessica and Braxton that frighten me the most. I believe their intentions are relatively innocent, whatever they might be. No, it's the *other* presence here that scares the hell out of me."

"So you've sensed it, too?" asked Rick.

"Yes," said Laura. "And I'm afraid that it doesn't like you very much. I mean, something has been acting hostilely toward you, what with the rock through the truck windshield and every photo of you in our bedroom ending up facedown."

"I'm afraid there's more to it than that," Rick told her. "Yesterday, after you left for town, I went up to my study and found an unwelcome surprise waiting for me. The cover painting I've been working on for that horror-western novel . . . it was completely destroyed. Someone . . . or rather *something* . . . had totally wrecked it. The canvas was slashed and splattered with red paint."

Laura's eyes turned bright with panic. "Oh, Rick . . . sweetheart, that scares me. What if it decides to hurt *you* next?"

The expression of concern and uncertainty on Rick's face suddenly gave way to a stern inner strength. "Don't worry. I won't let it go that far."

"Oh, and how do you intend to deal with it?" asked Laura incredulously. "With that gun you've been hiding from me?"

A trace of guilt emerged in Rick's eyes. "So you know about that, huh?"

"I didn't at first, but I smelled gunpowder on you yesterday," she told him. "Whatever possessed you to buy a gun, Rick? I know how strongly you're against them."

"Originally, I only bought it to use as a model for my painting," Rick explained. "But slowly I grew more and more fascinated with the blasted thing. Then, yesterday, after I discovered the ruined canvas, I decided it might be worth my while to learn how to load and fire it. So I did."

"You can't honestly believe it would fend off this disruptive spirit, do you?" she asked him. "I mean, what good are bullets against a ghost?"

Rick thought about it for a moment. "You're absolutely right. I don't know what possessed me."

"Braxton, perhaps?" suggested Laura.

"Maybe," agreed Rick. "But what do you think we should do about it?"

"I think our best bet would be the Gants. I think we ought to fill them in on what we've been experiencing here and ask their advice. I think they would know the best route to take in a situation like this."

"I guess you're right," agreed Rick, though a little reluctantly. "But I'd rather our trouble here not go any further than the Gants, at least, for the time being. I don't want the entire town of Franklin congregating on our doorstep, hoping to catch a glimpse of one of our so-called ghosts."

"I'm sure the Gants will be discreet about the matter," assured Laura. "I suggest that we talk to them about it tomorrow, when they come out to tour the grounds. Do I have your okay on that?"

Rick thought it over for a moment, then nodded. "I suppose so."

Laura looked relieved. "Good. Truthfully, I'd like to get this matter resolved as quickly as possible. Preferably before your trip to New York at the end of the month."

"Trip?" asked Rick, puzzled. Then, gradually, the blank look on his face gave way to realization. "Damn . . . I forgot all about it!" The trip Laura referred to was his scheduled attendance at a major horror and science-fiction convention in New York City on the thirtieth of that month. The convention really would not have meant much to Rick, except for the fact that he had been chosen as the artist guest-of-honor that year.

"Yes," said Laura. "I know how much you've been looking forward to it."

"It doesn't really matter," Rick told her. "I can cancel the trip."

"Nonsense!" said his wife. "That's a once-in-a-lifetime

honor! You've waited your entire career for a break like that."

"Then you can go with me," said Rick.

Laura shook her head. "I'd like to, but you know that's impossible, Rick. I'm too close to the deadline for this new book as it is. I really can't afford to put it on the back burner, even for a few days."

"I certainly understand that," replied Rick, thinking about his own backload of projects. "Then I guess we'll just have to take care of this situation before I leave."

Laura moved toward her husband and soon found herself in a tight embrace. They sat on the couch for a long while, silent, taking comfort in the closeness of one another. But despite the sense of safety their embrace provided, they both knew, deep down inside, that a threat stalked the grounds of Magnolia and the hallways of its manor, an unholy presence that for the time being was toying with them, much as a sadistic cat plays with a mouse before delivering the fatal blow.

Chapter Twenty-Two

The afternoon of November sixteenth was sunny and warm, a pleasant prelude to the promise of steadily dropping temperatures in the forthcoming weeks, according to several local weathermen. The Gants and Tyler Lusk arrived at Magnolia around one o'clock and were met on the front porch by Laura Locke. They embarked on the tour of the plantation house immediately, exploring the dense magnolia grove, then walking along the northern boundary toward the rear of the property.

By the time they stopped to study the stones of the Heller family cemetery, Alma began to notice that Laura seemed a little on edge for some reason. She could tell there was something pressing on her mind, something she wanted to share with someone. As they passed the fields that had once grown plentifully with cotton and tobacco, and Archie and Tyler started off toward the fruit orchard and the few remaining slave cabins that remained nearby, Alma took Laura aside. "I can't help but think there's something bothering you, dear," she said. "Is there anything you'd like to talk to me about?"

Laura was thankful that Alma was so observant, since she'd been struggling with the proper way in which to approach the Gants for help. "Yes, there is," she admitted. "Rick and I have been experiencing some unusual activity around here lately."

Alma was instantly intrigued. "You mean, psychic phenomena?"

"Exactly . . . and quite a bit of it during the past couple of days," said Laura. "To tell the truth, some of it has been downright frightening."

"Really? In what way?"

Laura ran her fingers through the back of her hair. "First of all, have you noticed any change in my hair color?"

"Why, yes, I have," said Alma. "I meant to mention what a nice color you chose."

"That's just the point," said Laura. "I *didn't* choose. My hair is changing to auburn . . . without any help from me whatsoever."

"Oh, dear," replied Alma, her face growing serious.

As they walked, Laura briefly filled Alma in on some of the mysterious things that had been taking place at Magnolia. She also told her about the more menacing aspects, like the smashed windshield of Rick's truck and the vandalized painting. "It scares me, Alma. Whatever is responsible for pulling those pranks, it seems to have a grudge against Rick. I'm afraid that it sincerely intends to harm him."

"It does sound as though Rick is a burr beneath this entity's saddle, so to speak," Alma agreed. She frowned as she looked around the vast grounds of the plantation. "You know, I've heard about every ghost story and tall tale concerning Magnolia, and they've always centered on Jessica and Braxton, never any other ghost. If there is another spirit here, then this would make Magnolia a site of multiple hauntings, which is an extremely rare occurrence in the field of parapsychology."

"I was hoping you could give us some advice about what to do," Laura said. "We're both pretty upset about the whole thing. We just want to resolve the matter and get on with our lives."

"I don't blame you one bit," Alma told her. "When we get back to the house, we'll all sit down and discuss our options. I believe Archie and I will be able to help you out."

"We'd certainly appreciate anything you could do," said Laura. She glanced down the pathway where Archie and Tyler stood, studying a partially collapsed slave cabin. "How about this guy? Can we trust him to be discreet? Rick and I would prefer that this business not be spread all over Williamson County."

"Don't worry," Alma assured her. "Tyler's a good man. Believe me, he's concerned mainly with discovering the place where his ancestors originated from. And hopefully, he'll find what he's looking for today . . . here at Magnolia."

Tyler peered into the shadowy depths of the old slave cabin, then closed his eyes. In his mind, he conjured the image of an injured woman lying on a bed of cornhusks, surrounded by a dozen frightened slaves. He could picture the scene clearly, every detail highlighted by the soft glow of a coal-oil lamp.

"What is it, Tyler?" asked Archie anxiously.

Tyler opened his eyes and again surveyed the dilapidated structure. Finally, he shrugged. "I'm not sure. It could be the slave quarters I saw in my dreams, or maybe not. It's difficult to say."

"What about the smokehouse and the chopping stump?" the old man inquired.

Tyler walked over to the rickety outbuilding. The smokehouse was little more than a framework of rusted tin and weathered lumber covered with honeysuckle and climbing ivy. He then crouched and studied the chopping stump that stood near the building's eastern corner. He noticed that a single bullet hole pocked one side and that tiny bits of glass and what looked like droplets of ketchup covered the top of the tree stump.

He reached out and touched the stump, and for a brief instant, felt the chill of a snowy night and the icy hardness of an ax handle in his hand. Then, just as swiftly, the strange feeling of déjà vu deserted him. "This seems more familiar. I believe we're on the right track."

Archie grinned as he puffed on his briar pipe. "Good. Now, let's move on to the garden at the rear of the house. Maybe you'll find something definite there."

They were starting toward the plantation house when Alma called out. "Archie, Laura and I would like to have a word with you for a moment, please?"

"You go on," Archie told Tyler, turning to join the two women at the far end of the fruit orchard. "We'll be there directly."

Tyler continued on down the pathway to the edge of the flower garden. Broad beds of bare earth, now covered with the husks of dead leaves, awaited the approach of spring and the bounty of iris, begonia, and daffodil the season would awaken. Likewise, leafless dogwood trees and gardenia bushes bordered the vacant flowerbeds, their own blossoms of snow-white concealed until the passing of winter. A quaint walkway of old-fashioned cobbled brick led from the back door of the immaculate white mansion and encircled the inner boundary of the garden. Standing directly in the center of that circle was an ancient oak tree that was perhaps four or five hundred years old. Its broad trunk was a good four feet in diameter, and its uppermost branches stretched ten or fifteen feet higher than the peak of the two-and-a-half-story plantation house.

As Tyler entered the garden, he felt a strange sensation grip him. He felt as if he had stood on that very spot, sometime long ago. Tyler closed his eyes and recalled the dream. He heard the shrill screams of the ravaged belle, the crackle of the bonfire, and the drunken cheers of the Union soldiers. In his mind's eye, he relived the nightmare, but this time he paid less attention to the atrocity that was taking place next to the fire and more to the general surroundings. This time he saw the rear wall of the big house, firelight playing sinisterly on its tall windows and whitewashed brick. And rearing over it all, like a silent and powerless spectator, was the oak, its branches covered with the frosty accumulation of a recent snowfall.

Tyler opened his eyes and compared the landscape of his dream with that which currently surrounded him. The positions of the house and tree seemed a little different in broad daylight, but he swore that they matched the place of his dreams closely enough. He turned and looked back the way he'd come. Even the smokehouse and the edge of the fruit orchard were in the same spot they'd occupied during the course of his nightmare.

His curiosity piqued, Tyler walked further on, stopping next to the trunk of the oak tree. It was cooler in the shade of the leafless branches, and he could not help but shiver with a sudden chill. Once again, he looked toward the direction of the plantation house. The afternoon sun was to his back, and on the thirty feet of ground and cobbled walkway that stretched between the tree and the house was cast the gnarled shadow of the skeletal oak.

Tyler's breath caught in his throat as he witnessed a peculiar illusion conjured by sunlight and shadow. One of the thickest and sturdiest of the oak's lower limbs seemed to support something. Tyler took a step closer. There was an additional shadow dangling beneath that of the limb, one that should not have been there.

The shadow of a man's body, suspended by a heavy rope, swung to and fro in the gentle autumn breeze.

Tyler closed his eyes and opened them again. The shadow was still there. He could make out the stiffened arms and legs of the body, as well as the oddly cocked head of a man whose neck had been snapped cleanly in half. Even as he watched, Tyler saw the body twitch once, twice, before finally growing still . . . deathly still.

Gathering up the nerve to turn around, he did so. But he found nothing suspended from the heavy limb that would cast such a bizarre shadow. Confused, he turned back around. The convoluted pattern of the oak stretched across earth and mortared brick, but the shadow of the hanging man was no longer there. The space beneath the limb was completely empty.

"What the hell was *that?*" he asked himself, although he could come up with no plausible explanation. Tyler closed his eyes several times, hoping to duplicate the strange effect, but it failed to repeat itself. The shadow of the oak tree remained exactly that and nothing more.

At that moment, Archie, Alma, and Laura entered the

flower garden and joined him. "Sorry that we took so long," said Archie, "but Laura had some interesting things to tell us. It seems that she and her husband have experienced some unusual psychic activity here at Magnolia during the past couple of weeks."

"Yeah," said Tyler softly, staring at the shadow of the oak tree. "I can relate to that."

Alma sensed that the young man had been shaken by something during their absence. "What is it, Tyler?" she urged. "You look as if you've seen a ghost."

Tyler turned toward the three, his eyes torn between fright and confusion. "You know, that might not be too far from the truth," he told her. He wondered if he should tell them about the mysterious shadow, knowing that it sounded too crazy to believe. But he told them anyway, providing every detail of what he had seen.

"Damn it!" cursed Archie with a scowl. "If we'd just gotten here ten seconds earlier, we'd have seen it, too!"

Tyler was surprised. "You mean, you actually believe me?"

"Of course," said Alma. "Take it from me, Archie and I have seen stranger things than shadows that aren't supposed to be there."

Archie surveyed the sturdy limb that stretched a good six feet over their heads. "Tell me, Tyler, what did this shadow look like? Could you tell what sort of man it was?"

"He was big, from what I could see," Tyler told them. "Tall and powerfully built."

"Hmmm," murmured Archie, his brain fast at work. "I can't recall ever hearing about anyone being hanged here at Magnolia during the course of the War."

"Maybe the phenomenon isn't related to that time period," offered Alma. "The Ku Klux Klan was pretty active in these parts at the turn of the century. This could be a manifestation of reflective haunting."

"Reflective haunting?" asked Laura. "What is that?"

"Sort of a psychic instant-replay of a particularly violent moment in time," Archie explained. "It's common at sites of brutal murder. There is no actual entity involved, only a brief visual reflection of a past event."

"That sounds frightening," said Laura.

"Yes, it certainly can be," agreed Alma. She, too, studied the limb of the oak. "As I was saying, perhaps this was a victim of the Klan. Someone they lynched from this tree."

"Maybe," said Archie, as he sucked on the stem of his pipe. "I just wish we could've seen it for ourselves."

Tyler looked around at the plantation grounds and its main house. "So, this place has a history of strange phenomena?"

"Yes, it does," said Alma. "Oh, most of the evidence has been nothing more than old wives' tales and childish ghost stories, but folklore usually always has a basis in fact. Now that we've had several people witness the phenomena at close proximity, maybe we can dispel all the myth and rumor, and get down to the truth of what is actually taking place here at Magnolia."

"But exactly how are we going to do that?" asked Laura.

"I suggest that we go inside and discuss it," said Archie. "I think Rick should be present, too. After all, just like you and Tyler, he has also experienced an important share of the phenomena. If we gather all the pieces of the puzzle, hopefully it will help us decide on the best course of action."

A half hour later, they were all sitting in the downstairs parlor of the plantation house's eastern wing. Archie, Alma, and Tyler sat on the Victorian sofa, while Rick sat in his armchair, looking a little sullen and nervous. Laura had taken time to brew a pot of coffee and now served it, passing out china cups and saucers to her company. Rick declined the coffee, but Laura poured herself a cup and took a seat in the hickorywood rocking chair next to the parlor fireplace.

At first, they all sat there in awkward silence, not sure how to begin their strange conversation. Then, Alma took the job of moderator and set the discussion in motion. "Laura, why don't you begin by telling us about your first visit to Magnolia, when you were a child? I believe that would be a good place to start."

Laura balanced her cup on her knee and slowly began to

tell of her trip to Magnolia on the Halloween of her twelfth year and her glimpse of the ghostly belle on the floorless balcony of the plantation house. After that, she related her latest experiences: the sound of footsteps coming from the upper floor and the puzzling erasure of the microdisk, the strange way her newest book had come to her as if it had practically written itself, and the eerie encounter with the weeping specter of Jessica Heller beneath the oak tree. She also told them of the events of the past couple of days: the prankish switching of objects in the kitchen and the mysterious changing of her hair color from honey blond to auburn red.

The next to relate his experiences at Magnolia was Rick. The artist was hesitant to discuss the matter at first, especially in front of a stranger like Tyler Lusk. Eventually, though, he relaxed a little and began to talk freely. He told them of the strange illusion of a raging fire that originated from the direction of the magnolia grove, as well as his encounter with the digging man in the clearing, a scavenger who held an unnerving resemblance to the pneumonia-inflicted Braxton Heller, who had performed a similar excavation of the plantation grounds shortly before his death. He also told them of his uncharacteristic fascination with the Colt Navy he had purchased in town and the feeling of impending disaster that seemed constantly to prey on his mind. All agreed that he was justified in feeling threatened, what with the vandalism of the truck windshield and the destruction of the cover painting.

Tyler was the last one to contribute to the discussion. He first described the shadow of the hanging man in detail, then began to tell them of the dreams he had experienced since discovering that his ancestors had originated in Franklin. He was describing his dream of the previous afternoon and was approaching the part about his enraged murder of the sadistic colonel when he was interrupted. Not by anyone who sat there in the room . . . but by someone whose presence they had been completely unaware of.

It began subtly at first. Tyler was halted in mid-sentence by the tiniest rattling of glassware. All eyes centered on the china serving set that occupied the coffee table in front of the couch. At first glance, they could detect nothing out of the ordinary. Then they noticed that Tyler's cup and saucer were vibrating due to some unseen force. Its motion grew more and more noticeable, until coffee began to spill over the rim of the china cup. Almost immediately, the other objects of the serving set—the floral coffeepot, cream decanter, and sugar bowl—also began to rattle.

No one said a word as the phenomenon gradually increased in intensity. Soon, coffee, cream, and sugar were erupting from the spouts of the decanters, splattering the table and those who sat around it. Suddenly, Archie's aged eyes narrowed and he called out to the others. "Everyone . . . away from the couch! Quickly!"

Tyler and Alma followed Archie's hasty retreat, apparently, just in the nick of time. A second later, the china serving set began to explode, one piece after another. Sharp fragments of jagged crockery flew like shrapnel, ripping into the cushions of the sofa where the three had sat only a moment before.

From that point on, the phenomenon only grew more frenetic and out of control. The next assault was launched on the framed photographs that lined the mantel over the fireplace. Every picture that bore an image of Rick was a casualty, the glass over the photos shattering with spiderweb cracks. Then the frames themselves flew off the mantel, as if violently flung by an unseen hand. Rick hit the floor as the framed pictures spun over his head. One shattered the screen of the television set across the room, while two others were embedded in the stylishly papered wall behind the armchair.

Before they could recover from the assault, another came just as swiftly. A thunderous pounding began to move around the perimeter of the room, as if the fists of an angry giant hammered at the walls from the other side. The force of the pounding grew until the very foundation of the parlor trembled. Plaster fell from the ceiling, while Rick's paintings and the framed covers of Laura's books dropped from the walls, taking the anchored nails with them.

"Oh, God, what is it?" cried Laura, her eyes bright with fear. "What's happening?"

No one was in the frame of mind to answer her at the moment. Abruptly, they were again under siege. A brass candelabra left its place atop a small side table and spun, end over end, across the room. Tyler ducked before the candlestick could crush his skull. Other objects began to leave their rightful places. Books shot from the shelves of the built-in cases like leatherbound missiles, while the door of a curio cabinet flew open with enough force to shatter its glass panes and wrench it completely off its hinges. A porcelain music box and several dozen knickknacks were flung, one by one, from the cabinet. Frantically, the objects spun through the open air of the parlor, dive bombing Laura and the others like a flock of crazed birds.

Most of the time they missed their marks, but other times they did not. Rick cried out as the music box struck him across the bridge of the nose, causing a steady flow of blood to trickle from his nostrils. Tyler was similarly assaulted. A heavy leatherbound edition of Dickens's *Great Expectations* swooped low and struck him forcefully across the right knee. The familiar agony of his old basketball injury returned and he rolled blindly on the carpet, clutching his leg. As he fought against the pain, he swore that he heard an echo of cruel laughter just beneath the thunderous pounding in the walls.

Laura cowered next to her rocking chair, too stunned to react to the barrage of objects that spun from mantel and shelf. Across the room, she saw Rick on his hands and knees, bleeding heavily from the nose. She watched as fear and bewilderment left her husband's eyes and something else replaced them. A moment later, she recognized the emotion that burned there. It was defiance, pure and simple.

Purposely, Rick rose to his feet, his face a mask of mounting rage. He raised his fists over his head, clenching them until the knuckles grew white with strain. Then, in a voice that Laura had never heard him speak in before, he yelled out.

"Stop it, you bastard!" he roared. *"Damn you, stop it this very instant!"*

For a moment, the force that loosed chaos within the walls of the parlor did not seem to listen. But then, abruptly, it all ended. The pounding on the walls, the airborne pelting of the room's decorations—it all ceased in the span of one swift and unexpected second.

At first, they could not move. They simply stood there or crouched where they had sought shelter, shocked into immobility by the pall of silence and calm that followed the violent phenomenon. Then, gradually, they discovered that the assault had, indeed, come to an end.

Laura climbed unsteadily to her feet and ran to Rick. She soon found his arms around her, strong and protective, as if promising to shelter her from any further harm. The Gants crossed the parlor to Tyler and helped him to the recliner. He sat there, cradling his throbbing kneecap in both hands, his eyes frightened. The parlor looked like a war zone. Wallpaper hung in tatters and the bare studs of the rafters could be seen overhead where plaster had fallen in large hunks from the ceiling. The floor was littered with fragments of broken glass and crockery, and the pages of books lay strewn upon the carpet, the volumes from the bookshelves having been literally torn apart.

"What was it, Archie?" asked Laura. She turned her head toward the elderly man, but made no move to leave her husband's embrace.

"A poltergeist," explained Archie, seeming out of breath. Exhausted, he sat down on the sofa and then jumped up just as quickly, a shard from the shattered coffeepot jabbing him in the butt from where it was lodged in the cushion. "A playful spirit . . . although I wouldn't hesitate to say that this one was more destructive than mischievous."

"Whatever it was, it was royally PO'd about something, that's for sure," said Tyler, rubbing his knee.

"He's right, you know," pointed out Alma. "Did anyone else notice that the brunt of the attack centered mainly on two people out of the bunch? Namely, Rick and Tyler?"

Rick probed tenderly at his nose. He was relieved to find it swollen, but not broken. "But *why?*" he asked. "Why did this . . . poltergeist, or whatever the hell you call it, decide to pick on me and Tyler more than the rest of you?"

Archie shrugged. "Who knows? Maybe you remind this entity of something in its past. Something that's painful or infuriating to it. Or maybe it attacked you because deep down it feels threatened by the two of you."

"Threatened?" laughed Tyler. "Yeah, I'm sure we scared the hell out of it, dodging and darting, and crawling around on the floor."

"Hey, I could be wrong," said Archie. "But tell me this—why did it pull in its claws when Rick stood up to it and demanded that it stop? Seems kind of peculiar to me."

Rick shook his head, his air of defiance suddenly giving way to frightened confusion. "Yeah, it does."

Laura pulled away from her husband's arms and looked around at the destruction that had taken place within the peaceful chamber of the downstairs parlor. The more she surveyed the damage, the angrier she became. "So, now what do we do? Will you please tell me that?"

"Our best bet would be to call in an expert," suggested Alma. "Someone who can investigate this matter objectively and hopefully eradicate the threat that's obviously present here. Someone who specializes in just this sort of phenomenon."

"I assume that you're referring to the parapsychologist you mentioned before," said Laura.

"That's right," replied Archie Gant, his eyes twinkling behind the lenses of his spectacles. "A man who has built his reputation by successfully investigating and, most of the time, solving Civil War hauntings all over the country. And perhaps the only person alive who's capable of ridding Magnolia of the evil that undoubtedly exists here."

PART THREE

A DARK SEED PLANTED

Chapter Twenty-Three

"There it is," said Bret Nelson, although he did not seem at all pleased. "Up ahead."

Wade Monroe ignored his assistant's cranky mood and looked ahead as he steered the Winnebago down U.S. 31, fifteen miles south of Nashville. The afternoon of November nineteenth was just as dark and stormy as Bret's attitude. A cold spell had replaced the warm weather of only a few days before and a steady rain fell, turning the asphalt of the road inky black with wetness. Wade peered past the sweeping arms of the windshield wipers and through the downpour saw a roadside sign that invited, *Welcome to the Town of Franklin—Established 1799.*

As the camper entered the town limits, Wade took in the surroundings, committing the layout of Franklin to memory. Steadily rolling pastureland and patches of dense forest now gave way to residential sections and apartment complexes. Next, the business district staked its claim. They passed a number of small businesses: a body shop, a Texaco station, and a fresh produce stand. Soon, the businesses grew larger and the buildings more stately as the circle of Public Square came into view beyond the next traffic light.

As they reached the town square, Wade took a moment to study the architecture of the surrounding buildings and the tall monument with the bronze statue of a Confederate soldier poised boldly atop its pinnacle. The Williamson County courthouse—a two-story structure of red brick and white trim—was located to the left, amid a stand of majestic oaks and sugar maples. Wade steered the Winnebago around the square and, to the west, saw the long stretch of Main Street with its twin rolls of old buildings and storefronts. At the far end, past businesses including a drugstore, a restaurant, a furniture store, and a movie theater, were the steepled structure of the First Presbyterian Church and a tree-lined avenue of various city departments and doctors' offices.

"Cheer up, Bret," said Wade, reaching over and patting his companion on the leg. "I know it was a long trip, but we're here, okay?"

Bret pushed his lover's hand away and stared through the rain-speckled windshield sullenly. "Hallelujah," he grumbled sarcastically.

"All right, that's enough!" said Wade, attempting to bite back his anger. He changed his original course for Main Street, swinging the big camper toward the courthouse and parking it in the front lot. He slipped the gear into park, then cut the engine. For a moment they sat in silence, listening to the steady pelting of rain on the roof of the Winnebago.

"What did you do that for?" asked Bret.

Wade gripped the steering wheel in both hands and watched rivulets of water roll down the glass of the windshield. "You know why," he told him. "I'm sick and tired of this shitty attitude you've had since we left Massachusetts. I don't know why you've reacted so negatively to this trip, but, truthfully, I'm growing more than a little weary of it."

"You know good and well why I objected to taking this investigation," snapped Bret. "I'm just thinking about you, Wade. You've been pushing yourself to the limit this year. Hell, we've performed fourteen investigations since January, and whether you want to admit it or not, it's beginning to take its toll on you."

"That's pure nonsense," scoffed Wade, although he was, for some reason, unable to meet his companion's eyes.

"No, it's not," said Bret. His face softened, the anger he had been carrying for the past thousand miles gradually changing into concern. "I can tell that you've been under a lot of strain, especially since the cleansing of that farmhouse in Kansas. You've grown more intense and less sure of yourself. And those damned nightmares you've been having lately . . . well, every time you have one, you grow more and more on edge. Don't try denying it, either. I know you better than you think."

Wade sat there and said nothing for a while. He hated to admit it, but Bret was right. He had not been feeling up to par lately, either professionally or emotionally. His brief but memorable encounter with the spirit of Elizabeth Saxton in the Applegate house the month before had seemed to set a disturbing trend of self-doubt and unhappiness in his life. Since October, Wade had been plagued by a series of disturbing nightmares that seemed to drag him down, more and more, with each new occurrence. They varied in setting, but were the same in sordid content. In the course of each, Wade played the part of a sadistic Union colonel who had a perverse appetite for torture, rape, and murder. Fortunately, the dreams always ended before the brutal act was performed, but still, he always awoke knowing what the eventual outcome of the particular atrocity would amount to.

The thing that had frightened him the most had been the incident at the battlefield near Petersburg, Virginia. His unexpected awakening in the tent of Cathy Hunter had shown him that the nightmares were having a negative impact on him, even to the point of causing him to play out the circumstances of his dreams. That, in turn, had sent him into a bout of depression and an increasingly heavy dependence on alcohol in order to relieve those melancholy moods.

He was aware of Bret's concern for him. He had tried his best to talk him into getting help, but Wade had neglected to listen. He kept believing that he could raise his flagging spirits on his own, though it seemed to be a hopeless battle. Every time Wade came close to regaining his confidence, he suffered yet another nightmare, twice as violent and degrading as the one before. Afterward, he just seemed to plunge even deeper into the depths of emotional despair.

Bret appeared to sense the thoughts that ran through

Wade's mind. "The reason I tried to get you to decline this investigation, was because I thought you needed a break. You certainly deserve one. We both do, considering our workload this year. I'm not blind. I've noticed the stress you experience every time we finish an investigation. I just thought it would be nice to take a few weeks off, maybe enjoy a quiet Thanksgiving and Christmas at home for a change. Then you could relax and recharge your batteries before we committed ourselves to another job."

Wade nodded and turned toward Bret. "That's what I was planning on doing," he told him. "But when this Archie Gant called me up the other day and described the phenomena that are taking place at this plantation . . . well, I just couldn't pass it up, Bret. I mean, we've always investigated one entity at a time before. This is a rare opportunity for us. Multiple hauntings at a single site, including a full-scale poltergeist attack witnessed by five people. Now, you can't truthfully sit there and tell me that doesn't excite you."

"I have to admit, it is intriguing," replied Bret. "But just promise me a couple of things, will you? First, try not to let this investigation affect you negatively. Try to approach it from a purely objective standpoint and try not to let it drain you emotionally, like that investigation in Kansas did. And second, after we're finished, let's take some time off. Maybe take a trip to Hawaii or Europe. Anyplace that has no connection whatsoever to the American Civil War."

Wade thought it over for a moment. "Okay, I promise . . . on both counts." He reached over and squeezed Bret's hand, and Bret squeezed back. "Now that we've cleared the air on that point, I suggest we locate the Gants' bookstore and get on with this investigation. Don't you agree?"

Bret smiled, his mood having brightened considerably. "Let's go," he said.

Wade started the camper back up, shifted into reverse, and, backing out of the courthouse parking lot, made a beeline for Franklin's picturesque Main Street.

* * *

The honking of a horn drew Alma's attention as she unpacked a UPS order of newly purchased books. She glanced through the front window to see a Winnebago pulling to the curb next to the bookstore. "Archie," she called, straightening her dress and patting her grayish-blond hair into place. "He's here!"

Archie was out of the rear office in an instant, shrugging a herringbone jacket over his wiry frame. He took his pipe from his mouth, tapped its smoldering contents into an ashtray on the sales counter, and slipped it into his pocket, out of sight. "Sure hope the gentleman is as nice in person as he seemed to be over the phone," he said, as he and his wife walked to the front of the shop.

They reached the door about the same time that it opened. A tall, blond man dressed in a heavy cardigan sweater, dark slacks, and a tan trenchcoat entered the bookshop, followed by a smaller man with glasses and a mustache. "I take it you two would be Archie and Alma Gant," inquired the first.

"That's right," replied Archie, extending his hand. "And you're Wade Monroe, no doubt. I've seen your face on too many magazine covers in the last couple of years not to recognize you on sight."

Wade shook Archie's hand and nodded politely to Alma. Then he turned toward the man behind him. "Oh, this is my right-hand man, Bret Nelson. He deserves just as much credit for my past successes as I do. Without his knowledge in electronic gadgetry, I'd probably still be sitting behind a desk at Harvard, instead of running all over the country, hunting for ghosts."

"Well, in that case, I'm certainly pleased to meet you, too, Bret," said Archie. "It'd sure be a crying shame if an illustrious parapsychologist like Wade here had ended up confined to some musky library, wasting his God-given talent for investigating psychic phenomenon."

"I agree wholeheartedly," said Bret with a smile.

Wade strolled into the center of the bookstore, marveling at the volume of information that was crammed within the limits of a mere four walls. "This looks more like an archive than a bookshop," he told the Gants. "And these artifacts are absolutely marvelous. I can tell that Civil War history is a labor of love with you two."

"You're right about that," Alma told him. "We seem to buy and collect more than we end up selling these days. But we don't really mind. We put away a nice little nest egg for our retirement while we were at Vanderbilt."

"I have to admit that I was honored when you called me concerning this investigation," said Wade. "I heard a lot of talk about you two around the university during my time there. Granted, Harvard has its share of pompous scholars, but they're quick to recognize talent and expertise . . . and both of you are well thought of in that respect."

"See, Alma?" chuckled Archie with a grin. "I told you we were going to get along just fine with this young fellow." The elderly bookseller walked to the sales counter and returned with a manila folder. "Here. I took the time to type you up a report on the history of Magnolia, as well as detailed accounts of the phenomena that have been experienced there. I thought it might give you a better idea of what you'll be up against."

"I appreciate your thoroughness," said Wade, accepting the folder. "Now, when can we visit this plantation that you've piqued our interest in?"

Archie fished his pocketwatch from his vest and flipped open the lid with a practiced thumb. "The owners of the property are expecting us around three o'clock. That should give us ample time to run across the street for coffee and a little conversation. And, if you've got a hankering for genuine Southern cooking, I'd highly recommend the pecan pie à la mode."

"That certainly sounds good to me," said Wade.

"Excellent," replied Archie with a nod. "Oh, by the way, before we head to the plantation, we'll need to swing by the Holiday Inn and pick up Tyler Lusk. He's the man I mentioned who saw the shadow of the hanging man. I don't know if that incident is even related to the other phenomena at Magnolia, but I thought you might be interested in it as well."

"It certainly sounds like it's worth looking into," agreed the psychic investigator from Massachusetts.

As they bundled themselves against the drenching rain and headed across Main Street to the Choices Restaurant, Wade found himself looking forward to the investigation to come. Certainly the circumstances of the multiple hauntings and the prospect of investigating—and hopefully banishing—a genuine poltergeist were more than enough to whet his professional appetite. But there was something else about the approaching evaluation of Magnolia that went beyond the mere interest of parapsychology.

Since Wade had received the call from Archie three days ago, he had, for some reason, felt drawn to this particular case more than to any other he had been offered before. From everything the Gants had told him concerning the phenomena at Magnolia, he was certain that this could very well end up being the most celebrated investigation of his career. But even beyond that, Wade felt a strange emotional connection to the place he would soon be visiting. In one sense he felt anticipation, while in another he felt something akin to dread.

Secretly, he somehow knew that his time at Magnolia could either bring a permanent end to the chain of disturbing nightmares he had been experiencing lately, or have a completely opposite and adverse effect—one from which he might never fully recover.

Chapter Twenty-Four

Shortly before three o'clock that afternoon, the Gants' Jeep Cherokee and Wade Monroe's Winnebago pulled off rain-drenched Highway 31 and drove along the paved lane leading to Magnolia. As they left the magnolia grove and parked in the circular driveway, Wade could not help but admire the main house with its tall limestone columns and immaculate white walls and trim. Both he and Bret agreed that it was one of the finest examples of antebellum architecture they had come across, and they had encountered many during the past seven years.

By the time they had left their vehicles and made it through the downpour to the front porch, they were met at the door by the owners. "Wade, Bret . . . this is Laura Locke and her husband, Rick Gardner," introduced Archie, once they had shed their wet coats and stepped into the inner foyer. "Laura, Rick . . . this is our famed parapsychologist Wade Monroe, and his assistant, Bret Nelson."

Wade stepped forward and regarded the lady of the house. Immediately, he was impressed with how lovely she was. Usually, he paid little attention to a woman's physical appearance. But that afternoon, Wade found himself paying more attention than usual. He matched her sunny smile with one of his own, and as he shook her hand, he was impressed by the softness of her touch. Even when their hands parted, Wade could not help but appreciate her simple beauty: her clear blue eyes and shoulder-length hair that was colored a unique blend of honey blond and auburn.

When he turned to shake the hand of Rick Gardner, he found little of the warmth that his wife had shown. The artist with the dark hair and mustache met Wade's firm grip with one of his own. Outwardly, Rick seemed polite enough, but still Wade sensed something cautious in the man's manner. He studied the expression in Rick's bluish-gray eyes and found a hardness there that was difficult to pinpoint. In fact, Rick seemed to be sizing him up just as much as Wade sized up him. The parapsychologist was normally an easy-going person who could get along with just about anyone. But upon meeting Rick, he felt an odd sense of dislike for the man. Exactly why he should react in such a way was beyond him.

"Welcome to our home," greeted Laura. "I'm glad you could take time out of your busy schedule to make it down here on such short notice. I don't think you know exactly *how* glad we are . . . right, sweetheart?"

Rick had not taken his eyes off Wade since he'd stepped into the foyer. "Yes," was all that he said in reply.

Wade ignored the man and turned to his wife. "I'm certainly glad that we didn't have any prior commitments either," he told her. "After Archie told me of the phenomena you've been experiencing, I knew we had to come. In fact, I'd guess that we're liable to investigate some phenomena here at Magnolia that we've never had the opportunity to since we began in this profession of ours. Wouldn't you agree, Bret?"

When his companion failed to answer, Wade turned around. He found Bret staring at him a little strangely. After a moment, his assistant answered. "Uh, yes, that's right. We've never investigated an actual case of multiple hauntings before."

"What about poltergeist phenomena?" asked Alma out of curiosity. "Have you ever encountered an entity like that before?"

"Yes, a couple of times," said Wade. "Once in an old bordello in New Orleans, and again in a Maryland farmhouse.

But what we encountered in both those places was pretty tame compared to the degree of activity that you claim happened here."

"What do you mean, *claim?*" asked Rick a little defensively. "Do you have some doubt about what took place in our rear parlor?"

"No, Mr. Gardner," said Wade. "What I meant was, the two examples of poltergeist activity that Bret and I investigated before were less spectacular than the incident Archie related to me over the phone. They were pretty innocent—levitating objects, disembodied voices, and the opening and closing of doors—and seemed to possess no danger. From what Archie has told me, your poltergeist has a particularly mean streak to it."

"You've got that right," said Tyler Lusk. "My poor knee is still smarting from the crack that spook gave it."

Bret turned his head and listened to the steady drumming of the downpour outside. "Well, it doesn't look like we'll be doing very much work outside today. That leaves out three of the main points of investigation—the digging man in the magnolia grove, the woman in the garden, and the shadow of the hanging man. I suggest we take a look at the parlor."

"Follow me," said Laura. As she led them through the entrance hall and down a narrow corridor next to the staircase, she turned and regarded the two ghost-hunters. "Archie suggested that we keep the parlor the way it was after the attack, so you'd be able to see the extent of the destruction firsthand."

"Good idea," replied Wade with a smile. "I certainly wish everyone involved in our investigations proved to be so considerate. Right, Bret?"

He turned to see his assistant subjecting him to the same odd expression again. "Yes," Bret finally answered. "I suppose so."

They entered the rear parlor. Wade and Bret walked around the room, examining the amount of damage that had been done within only a few minutes' time. Plaster, glass, crockery, and the torn pages of books littered the floor, while the walls and ceiling showed ripped wallpaper and exposed rafters. Wade paused where two of the framed photographs had been embedded in the drywall and wrenched one of them free. Beneath the shattered glass smiled the face of Rick Gardner, minus the mustache. "This poltergeist doesn't care much for you, does it?" he asked the artist.

"I'm not the only one it directed its attack at," said Rick. "Tyler here suffered his share of its wrath, too."

"That's strange," said Bret. "And none of the rest of you were harmed in any way?"

"We were scared half out of our wits," said Archie. "But it was Rick and Tyler who seemed to be this spirit's targets. What do you make of that, Wade?"

"Well, there could be a number of reasons," said Wade. "Maybe this entity was a racist during its lifetime. Maybe it resents Tyler's presence here simply because of the fact that he's black. Bret and I have encountered several bigoted ghosts in the last few years. Racism was a common emotion during the Civil War, both in the South and the North. And that hatred is so strong in some cases that it tends to resurface in the actions of some entities."

"But what about Rick?" asked Laura. "Why would this ghost dislike him so much?"

Wade turned and regarded the romance writer. "Spirits can just as easily exhibit jealousy. Maybe this entity has developed a crush on you. It would be understandable, really. I mean, you being as lovely as you are."

Laura blushed a little at the compliment. "Why, thank you."

Abruptly Rick stepped in front of Laura and confronted Wade, his arms crossed. "Okay, enough small talk. Exactly what is your game plan for getting rid of this crazy spook?"

The parapsychologist was growing tired of the man's apparent dislike for him, but refrained from saying anything derogatory. "Well, in the first place, there's no guarantee that we can 'get rid' of this entity," explained Wade.

"But I thought that was the whole point of you coming here," said Rick.

"No, Bret and I came here with the understanding that we were to investigate these phenomena, not play exorcist," said the ghost-hunter. "True, nine times out of ten, we find a positive solution and lead that spirit on to the level of existence where it should truly be. But that usually means a detailed investigation of the historical facts of the haunting site and an even more rigorous battery of scientific tests. If we can't uncover the reason why a spirit is bound to this realm, we certainly can't be expected to resolve the problem successfully, now can we?"

"Oh, this is great!" laughed Rick, shaking his head. "Just great! I thought you said this guy had a dependable track record, Archie."

The elderly bookseller regarded Rick like a stern grandfather would regard a tantrum-throwing child. "I assure you, Rick, Mr. Monroe has a very high success rate in relation to cases of this sort. I suggest you be patient and allow him and his assistant to do what they came to do."

Laura stepped next to her husband and, taking his arm, drove her fingernails painfully into the flesh of his tricep. "Yes, sweetheart, I agree with Archie. Now, why don't you just relax and hear Wade out?"

Rick pulled his arm from his wife's thorny grasp. "All right. I guess I'm just a little on edge, what with all this weird crap going on." He nodded toward Wade, although his eyes were still heavy with distrust. "Go ahead, Mr. Monroe. I'm all ears."

Sensing that the storm had passed, at least for the time being, Wade continued. "Well, first of all, I suggest that we investigate each of the individual phenomena separately. Since the weather forecast calls for more rain tomorrow, I propose that we investigate the poltergeist phenomenon here in the parlor and in the kitchen first. Then, when the weather clears sufficiently, we can set up our equipment outdoors and investigate the clearing in the magnolia grove and the places beneath the oak tree, where two of the occurrences took place. Then, from the data we gain from those studies, along with the historical information that Archie and Alma have provided, we should be able to come to a satisfactory conclusion concerning the entities that haunt Magnolia."

"That sounds fine to me," said Laura. She looked at her husband, an expression of underlying warning in her blue eyes. "Doesn't that sound okay to you, dear?"

"Just so he finds out what's going on here and does his level best to fix the problem," said Rick. "That's all I ask."

"We'll certainly do our best to give you the answers you're looking for, Mr. Gardner," assured Bret Nelson. "And, after that's done, I'm pretty sure that we'll be able to cleanse this house of its multiple presence."

"I agree," added Wade, although he was a little irritated at his assistant's promise. It was almost as if Bret had made a conscious attempt to smooth the rough ground between the psychic investigator and Rick Gardner.

"So, what type of tests will you be running here in the parlor?" asked Alma.

"I think we'll begin by trying to draw out this entity that attacked you," said Wade. "We'll set up our equipment—sensors, detection units, microphones, and cameras—and then set out the bait and wait for it to materialize."

"Bait?" asked Tyler Lusk. "What bait?"

"Why, you and Mr. Gardner, of course," said Wade. "Since you two seem to be the source of this spirit's anger, you would be the logical choice to act as bait."

"And have the damned thing kill us this time?" scoffed Rick. "Do you think we're stupid?"

"Believe me, I wouldn't think of putting either of you in any real danger," assured Wade. "You'll both be placed in a protective environment where this entity can't harm you. Trust me, you'll be completely safe during the course of the experiment."

"I'm all for it," said Tyler. "Come on, Rick. Don't be such a party-pooper. Where's your sense of adventure?"

Rick thought about it for a moment and seemed to come to the conclusion that his bravery might be questioned if he did not agree to participate in Wade's experiment. "Okay, Monroe . . . it looks like you've got your guinea pigs."

"Good," said the parapsychologist. "It'll take Bret and me several hours to set up our equipment, so I suggest we schedule the experiment for ten o'clock tomorrow morning. Any objections?"

When none were given, they walked around the parlor once again, then left the room. As the door was closed and the group moved on to take a look at the kitchen, the parlor's moderate temperature abruptly dropped a few degrees. Several of the loose pages on the floor fluttered in a chill breeze that should not have been there. And beneath the soft ruffling of paper, there was a sound akin to whispering laughter.

"I've never been so embarrassed in my whole life!" Laura fumed as she prepared for bed.

Six hours had passed since Wade Monroe and Bret Nelson had arrived at Magnolia. In the span of that time, Laura had treated the group to a thorough tour of the plantation house and then to a home-cooked meal. Around eight o'clock, Tyler Lusk and the Gants had left for the trip back to town. Despite Laura's insistence that Wade and Bret stay in two of the guest rooms upstairs, they had politely declined the offer, preferring to spend the night in the camper instead.

And, now that Laura and Rick were finally alone, the unspoken feelings between husband and wife were finally coming to a head.

"What?" Rick replied as he unbuttoned his shirt. "I don't know what you mean."

"You know very well what I'm talking about," Laura snapped. She took a flannel nightgown from the cherrywood chiffarobe and pulled it over her head. "I swear, Rick, I've never seen you act so rude before!"

"I wasn't being rude," Rick said. "Maybe a little overprotective, that's all."

"Overprotective about *what?*" Laura asked.

"About Monroe's interest in you, that's what," Rick retorted. "Or didn't you notice?"

"I noticed nothing of the kind," Laura said. "As far as I'm

concerned, Wade Monroe was the perfect gentleman today. If anyone acted like a jerk, it was you."

"Don't tell me you didn't notice how he looked at you. All the time he was here, he stared at you like you were the first woman he'd ever seen in his life."

"Your feathers just got ruffled because he paid me a few nice compliments," Laura said. She studied her husband for a moment, watching the angry way he pulled on his pajamas and climbed into bed. "I do declare, Rick, I believe you're jealous of the guy."

"That's a load of bull, and you know it," he grumbled.

"No, it's not," Laura said. A smile slowly crossed her lips. "You *are* jealous, aren't you? The way you were snorting and pawing down there in the parlor, I thought you just didn't like Wade. But now I'm beginning to see your behavior in a different light. It was jealousy, pure and simple."

Rick sat in bed for a moment, stewing in his own juices. Then, finally, a sheepish grin replaced the sullen frown. "Okay . . . so maybe I *was* a little jealous of Monroe. I mean, what red-blooded man wouldn't be? The guy has the face of a Greek god and the body of Arnold Schwarzenegger. Who wouldn't get a little defensive next to someone like him?"

"Defensive isn't the word that comes to my mind, Rick," Laura said. "Hostile and mean-spirited are more like it."

"Okay, I admit it," Rick agreed. "I wasn't on my best behavior. But I promise, I'll try to do better and treat him like a guest. Satisfied?"

"That's all I ask, sweetheart," Laura said. She climbed into bed and gave Rick a kiss. "I think that's the main reason why they chose to spend the night out in that camper. I don't think they felt welcome in our home."

"I'll ask them again myself tomorrow, if that'll make you happy," Rick offered.

"It would make me feel a little better." Laura pulled the heavy cover of the patchwork quilt over them both and snuggled close to him.

"By the way, have you noticed anything funny about Monroe's assistant?" Rick asked.

"What do you mean?"

"I mean, doesn't he seem just a little bit effeminate to you?" he said. "If you ask me, I think the guy is gay."

Laura considered it for a moment. "I have to admit, I noticed it myself." She smiled to herself and elbowed Rick playfully in the ribs. "Hey, maybe you don't have anything to be jealous about after all. Maybe Wade is gay, too."

Rick laughed. "Yeah, right. Mr. Testosterone? You've got to be kidding."

"No, really," said Laura. "I've heard that you can't tell with some. They might look as macho as John Wayne on the outside, but on the inside they're entirely different."

"Sorry, darling, but you're wrong on this count," Rick assured her. "If Monroe was homosexual, he certainly wouldn't have made eyes at you like he did."

"Can we just drop this subject and get some sleep?" Laura asked, tired of all this.

"You got it, sweetheart," Rick said. He reached over to the lamp beside his bed and, turning it off, settled in for a good night's sleep with his wife beside him.

Unbeknownest to Rick and Laura, a similar discussion was taking place in the Winnebago parked in their front driveway.

"You're crazy, Bret," Wade said for the third time since they'd locked the camper door behind them. "I don't know where you got such a dumb idea, but I wish you'd just forget it."

"I can't," Bret said. He sat at the table of the camper's main room, nursing a Michelob Light. "I was there, Wade. I *saw* how you were looking at Laura Locke."

"Oh, and just *how* was I looking at her?" Wade asked in annoyance.

"Well, for all outward appearances, you seemed to practically drool over the woman," Bret said angrily. "For Chrissakes, Wade, if I didn't know any better, I would say that you were *attracted* to her."

"That's a lie, and you know it, Bret!"

"Oh, do I?" Bret countered with a bitter laugh. "Since when do you go around complimenting the female participant of an investigation? Sure, she's beautiful, but normally you don't even pay attention to such things." A cruel expression bloomed in Bret's eyes. "You haven't turned bi on me, have you?"

For the first time since their relationship had begun, Wade actually felt like striking his lover. The compulsion to do so frightened the parapsychologist. Upset, he headed for the wet bar at the other end of the room. "I can't believe you asked me that," he said as he poured himself half a glass of bourbon and stretched out on the couch.

"I'm sorry," Bret said. "Maybe I shouldn't have. But I have to admit that it did cross my mind when I saw you fawning over Laura Locke like that."

"I don't want to hear any more about these silly delusions of yours," Wade told him sternly.

"I'm not so sure they're delusions," Bret continued. "I mean, if they were, then Rick Gardner is suffering from them, too. He sensed the same thing that I did. That was the reason he was so unfriendly."

"He just wants a fast solution to a tedious problem. His impatience came from his fear of the poltergeist that attacked him, and not from anything I might have said or done."

"You're wrong, Wade," said Bret. "He was green with envy, and rightfully so. You might not have been aware of the way you were acting toward Laura, but he was extremely aware—and so was I."

"Was that why you tried so hard to get on his good side and promise him results we can't possibly guarantee?"

"I did that because I was afraid for you," Bret said. The hardness in his eyes softened a little. "I don't know what it is about Gardner, but something tells me that he could be dangerous if pushed far enough."

"Come off it, Bret," Wade said in dismissal. "I'm no rutting buck trying to horn in on his territory. Now, let's end this discussion, right here and now!"

"I just want you to watch yourself around this guy," Bret

urged. "Be careful. And that doesn't go for just Gardner, either. This particular investigation . . . well, something about it bothers me. Something about this place and the prospect of tackling this case of multiple hauntings makes me uneasy."

"But why?" asked his companion. "Bret, we've been waiting years for an investigation of this magnitude to surface. Take it from me, everything will work out just fine with this case. We can handle anything those spirits throw our way. You have absolutely nothing to worry about."

"I hope you're right," Bret said, taking another sip of his beer.

Later, as Bret slept, Wade lay in bed and considered his lover's concerns. He had denied Bret's charges that he had developed an interest in the romance writer who had breathed new life into the plantation called Magnolia, but thinking back, he could no longer honestly say he had not been affected by her in some odd way.

He recalled the moment he'd stepped onto the porch of the main house and seen her for the first time. Never before had a member of the opposite sex stirred him as she had. He had noticed everything about her: her physical beauty, her intelligence, and her warm personality. All were things that he'd never really given much thought to when meeting other women during the course of his travels from the site of one haunting to another. His interest had simply not been geared in that direction . . . not until that afternoon.

Wade Monroe drove all thoughts of Laura Locke from his mind, although for some reason he found it difficult to do so. Instead, he focused on Bret's reservations concerning their approaching investigation of Magnolia. He had to admit that he, too, had felt a similar sense of foreboding about the place. Since arriving there, he'd felt as if he'd been under the watchful eye of some unknown presence—a presence that held no animosity toward him, but rather was amused by whatever attempt Wade had planned for the successful investigation of Magnolia.

If that presence turned out to be the destructive poltergeist who'd wreaked havoc on the downstairs parlor, Wade knew that he had his hands full. For secretly, he knew that the troublesome entity would do everything in its power to ruin Wade's chances for a satisfactory end to the most potentially challenging case that the parapsychologist had come across in seven long years of psychic investigation.

Chapter Twenty-Five

The morning of November twentieth found the downstairs parlor of the plantation house filled with an array of state-of-the-art equipment. Around the room stood tripods sporting the finest video and 35mm still cameras, along with a variety of ultrasensitive microphones and temperature sensors. There were also several ultraviolet scanning units and Geiger counters for detecting the passage of some unseen presence or a sudden rise in radiation levels. All of the equipment that had been meticulously positioned around the parlor was linked to a central bank of computer screens and detection monitors that had been set up next to the fireplace.

Bret Nelson sat behind the monitoring console, while Laura and the Gants stood in the parlor doorway, spectators of the test that was about to take place. Wade Monroe was in the process of finishing the last preparations of the experiment, which consisted of placing the bait—namely, Rick and Tyler—in their proper places. They sat in chairs in the center of the parlor, each surrounded by a booth of clear Plexiglas. The booths encased them on all sides, as well as overhead, and sported sufficient openings to provide outside air. If the poltergeist attacked them, as it had several days before, the unbreakable barriers would protect the two men from any harm.

"I believe we're ready to begin," Wade called. He checked a few last-minute details, then took his place next to his assistant. After receiving a nod from Wade, Bret donned a pair of headphones and readied the bank of monitors. He punched a series of numbers into the keyboard of the computer system, instantly placing the system into operation. The ultraviolet units shot their thin beams from one station to another, and the dozen or so automated cameras swiveled slowly back and forth on their motorized pedestals, sweeping the entire perimeter of the room.

They waited for fifteen minutes, silently watching for the least movement from the debris scattered across the parlor floor or the remaining objects that still sat on the bookcases and inside the doorless curio cabinet. When nothing had occurred within that period of time, Wade turned to Bret. "Any change in pressure or temperature?" he asked.

"No," replied Bret. "All readings are stable. No variation whatsoever."

Wade thought about it for a moment, then turned toward Laura and the Gants. "Was there anything that seemed to entice the appearance of the poltergeist before? Perhaps something that was said or done?"

"We were only sitting around the parlor, having coffee and discussing the phenomena that had been witnessed by Laura, Rick, and Tyler," said Archie. "Then, all of a sudden, things began to go haywire."

"Maybe there was something in your discussion that raised the spirit's temper," decided Wade. He turned to Rick and Tyler. "Can you both remember exactly what you were talking about just before the attack began?"

"Yes," replied Tyler. Rick agreed that he did, too.

"Then, let's try that," suggested the parapsychologist. "Rick, you begin first, followed by Tyler. And try to duplicate what was said, down to the very word, if possible. We want to provoke the entity the same as before."

For the next twenty minutes, Rick gave an oration of the phenomena he had witnessed during the past few weeks. When he came to the end of his experiences, Tyler then took up where Rick left off, detailing the nightmares he had suffered recently. A few minutes later, he, too, was finished. But no adverse occurrences had taken place this time. The atmosphere of the downstairs parlor remained calm, with no trace of spiritual activity.

"How about it, Bret?" Wade asked.

"Still no change," his assistant replied. He checked all of the monitors twice over. "All readings remain stable."

"What do we do now?" Rick asked impatiently. "I do have a backload of work to catch up on. I can't afford to sit in this cubicle all blasted day."

"Let's just give it a little longer," said Wade. "One point is common among spiritual entities—and particularly ones as troublesome as this poltergeist—and that is that they refuse to be rushed. They'll reveal themselves whenever they are good and ready, and not a moment before. I'm sorry that it's such a tedious process, but that's just the way it is."

"Great!" Rick grumbled. "So what you're saying is that we're going to have to play by this spook's rules, right?"

"At least for the time being," Wade told him. "But once we learn the cause of its haunting, we'll better understand its motives and be able to deal with it on our own terms."

For two more hours, they waited for the poltergeist to appear and launch an attack on the men in the Plexiglas cubicles. And, for two hours, absolutely nothing out of the ordinary occurred. Finally, Wade had Bret check the monitors one more time. When all readings appeared normal, he decided to end the session. "Well, it looks like this first experiment has proved to be a total bust," he told the others. "I'm sorry, but it appears as if this entity has no desire to show itself, at least, not this morning. We can try again tonight, if everyone is in agreement."

Everyone but Rick seemed to be in favor of repeating the experiment. "If it's not going to show up this morning, why do you think it would tonight?" he asked as he left the booth. "Can you tell me that? All I got out this test of yours was a numb butt and three hours of being bored half to death."

"I'm sorry that it didn't go as you'd hoped, Rick," said Wade, a little weary of the artist's attitude. "These sessions can prove to be tiresome, but that's just how it is sometimes.

I do think it would be in our best interest to try again, though. That is, if you truly want this situation resolved."

"Of course I do," Rick said. "And as soon as possible."

"Then I suggest that you stop your complaining and cooperate," Wade told him flatly. "All right?"

Rick brooded over Wade's rebuff, but gradually lost his anger and nodded. "Okay, we'll do it your way. But I hope we have better luck drawing that bastard out next time."

"So do I," the parapsychologist agreed. "I'm as anxious to get the ball rolling as you are."

Later that afternoon, after a lunch of coffee and sandwiches had been served in the dining room, Tyler and Archie broke away from the others and returned to the fruit orchard and the slave cabins that bordered it. The rain had stopped several hours before, but the clouds continued to hover darkly in the sky overhead, promising more showers that evening before the storm front moved further to the east.

Their reason for returning to the site was to continue what had been interrupted four days ago. The phenomenon of the shadow of the hanging man and the poltergeist attack had shaken them so much that they had neglected to resume their search for the slave cemetery, if, in fact, Magnolia had one on its property.

Tyler and Archie took to the dripping thicket directly behind the cabins, picking through acres of brush and bramble. A short time later, they found what they were looking for. In the center of a grove of hickory trees stood a few gravestones. Tyler was disappointed at first, for there did not seem to be more than ten or twelve left standing, and most of them were totally illegible.

"Don't get discouraged, Tyler," said Archie, placing an encouraging hand on the young man's shoulder. "If we don't find the answer here and Magnolia doesn't turn out to be the home of your ancestors, then we'll just try somewhere else. The truth will turn up eventually."

Tyler sighed. "I know . . . but something tells me that this *is* the place. I can just feel it."

"Well, let's tackle this boneyard and see if we have any luck at confirming that feeling of yours," suggested Archie.

They went to work. Tyler dried the limestone markers with a bath towel they had borrowed from Laura, then Archie placed a sheet of typing paper over each and traced off their inscriptions with broad strokes of crayon. Out of the first six, only two could be deciphered. The other four had been worn away by seasons of harsh weather.

The next five also produced little of interest. The twelfth and final stone, however, proved to be more revealing. They knew they were on the right track when the first stroke of the Crayola etched a single name in bright orange.

Sassy.

"Well, I'll be damned," Archie laughed around the stem of his pipe. "Looks like you were right after all."

Tyler's heart pounded in anticipation. "Do the rest of it."

Archie continued, and soon, the sheet of paper held the full inscription. It read: *Born ? — Died 1864, Servant to the Hellers, Mother to Samuel, God Rest Her Soul.*

"Well, that says it all," Tyler said in amazement. "I've finally found the place." He reached out and shook Archie's hand. "Thank you."

"I knew we'd find it eventually," the elderly bookseller said with a smile. He examined the inscription closely. "This is peculiar. The spelling and carving of the words on this one are first-rate, not haphazardly done, like most slave stones. I'd say this one was chiseled by a professional stonemason, most likely the one who did Braxton's stone in the Heller family plot. It appears that the Hellers' neighbor, Ashworth, must have come across Sassy after burying Braxton and had stones erected for both of them."

Tyler glanced around the patch of woods, but found no other stone. "Then apparently, Samuel was not found by Ashworth."

"I reckon not," agreed Archie with a frown. "Looks

like he'll join the ranks of the misplaced, along with Jessica Heller."

"I guess so," said Tyler uneasily. He turned and looked across the expanse of the Heller plantation. Even though the question he had come to Tennessee to uncover had been answered, he found himself confronting other mysteries—mysteries that he knew he must know the answers to as well. Like what had truly happened to the slave named Samuel, and where on the vast acreage of Magnolia his body had been laid to rest.

Chapter Twenty-Six

"I don't understand it," Wade Monroe said in frustration. He walked to the wet bar and poured himself another bourbon, his third that night. "We've done everything by the book, but so far, we've revealed absolutely nothing!"

Bret sat on the couch and watched as his companion paced back and forth across the Winnebago. He was silent as he, too, contemplated the lack of progress they had made in the investigation of Magnolia so far.

Three days had passed since they'd first arrived in Franklin, and during that time, they'd performed a battery of tests and held long periods of surveillance at the sites of the hauntings that had been witnessed by Laura Locke, Rick Gardner, and Tyler Lusk. The second session in the downstairs parlor had been just as fruitless as the first. After that, they had turned their attention to the outdoor locations. The rain had moved on and the skies had cleared, leaving the weather sunny, but increasingly cold. Wade and Bret had set up their equipment in the rear garden, as well as the clearing in the magnolia grove. But their efforts had so far proved to be pointless. No form of psychic activity had been detected at any of the sites. There were no weeping belles, no frantic scavengers, no shadows of hanging men who were not there. There was only hour upon hour of sitting in the cold, watching and waiting for something to take place. But, as of that afternoon of the twenty-second, the investigation of Magnolia had been a frustrating waste of valuable time.

"Perhaps we are not the ones at fault here," Wade said finally, taking a seat at the opposite end of the sofa. "If we are, it might be because of our own gullibility."

"What are you driving at?" Bret asked.

"Maybe these people are trying to pull some sort of elaborate hoax on us," Wade told him. "Maybe our tests so far have been correct and we've just been ignoring the obvious fact that there *are* no entities present at Magnolia."

"But why would they pull a stunt like that?"

Wade shrugged. "Who knows? Maybe they want to discredit me for some reason. Maybe they have something to gain by concocting this major haunting and then making me out to be a colossal failure when I can't properly investigate it."

Bret stared at his partner for a long moment. There had been times before when a particular investigation did not go according to plan, but never had Wade reached the point where he grew paranoid, accusing the others involved in some sort of secret conspiracy against him. "What possible reason would these people have for inviting us to investigate a bogus haunting? I mean, for the most part, they are very well-known people with extremely trustworthy reputations. Laura is a bestselling author, Rick is a popular artist, and the Gants—well, you yourself know their background. I'm not sure about Lusk, but he seems like a nice enough guy."

"Maybe you're right," Wade replied. He took another sip of straight bourbon. "But if these multiple hauntings are genuine, why hasn't our equipment picked up anything during the past three days? These are state-of-the-art cameras and sensors we're talking about here, not junk. In every investigation we've tackled, they've always picked up some trace of psychic activity, if not visually or audibly, then through some subtle change in temperature or radiation level. What have we detected here at Magnolia? Absolutely nothing! What conclusion can we possibly come to but that there is nothing concrete to investigate? As far as our monitors can tell, there are no otherworldly presences at this particular location."

"But what about the destruction in the downstairs parlor?" Bret challenged. "You saw that for yourself."

"Yes, I saw the aftereffects, but I did not actually see anything happen," said Wade. "Who knows, it might have a legitimate explanation. Maybe there was a substantial shifting in the foundation of the house. Or maybe it was a mild earthquake. The state of Tennessee does sit on a minor fault, and geologists have theorized for years that it's only a matter of time before a substantial tremor occurs in this area."

"Come on, now," Bret said. He stood, intending to make a trip to the kitchen to fetch something to snack on. "Do you really believe any of what you just said?"

"No, I suppose not," Wade said sullenly. "I guess I'm just trying to rationalize why we've drawn a blank as far as this investigation goes."

"Well, I'll tell you what I think," Bret said. "I believe there are entities here, but they are very shrewd and secretive. I don't think that they intend to reveal themselves until they're ready."

Then, unexpectedly and without prior warning, it happened.

As if on cue, the big window over the eating nook imploded, showering fragments of safety glass across the main room. The projectile that had shattered the window—a stone as large as a baseball—accompanied the glittering shards. It struck Bret a glancing blow behind his left ear, causing him to stagger forward, his eyes rolling back into his head. The force of the rock propelled him onto the couch, where he lay limply, facedown on the cushions.

"Bret!" Wade yelled. He cast his shotglass of bourbon away and dropped to the floor of the camper. As he crouched next to his fallen companion, the assault on the Winnebago continued. Another rock shattered glass, this time smashing through the narrow window of the camper's side door. Likewise, the brittle crash of destruction echoed from the Winnebago's windshield in the cab up front, as well as the window of the rear bedroom.

Wade ignored the chaos that rained around him and

checked Bret. He was still alive, but unconscious. The rock had split his scalp, and the entire back of his head was bleeding freely. "Oh, God!" he muttered, fighting against panic. He tried to think of the best course to take and decided that it was imperative to summon medical help as soon as possible.

He reached to where a cellular phone sat on a side table. He lifted it from its cradle, switched it on, and dialed 911. He pressed the receiver to his ear, expecting to hear an emergency service in Franklin pick up. But instead, there was a burst of crackling static that shot through his ear like a thunderbolt. Stunned, he dropped the phone to the floor. Wade was on the verge of picking it up and dialing again when he heard a soft snicker of laughter coming from the phone's speaker. It was an evil laughter, brimming with depravity and sadistic pleasure—the laughter of something straight from the depths of hell, or some fetid realm close to it.

Abruptly the camper began to shake. Its shocks and suspension began to creak as the vehicle rocked violently from side to side. Wade hung on for dear life. As boxes and cans fell from the kitchen cabinets and the contents of the camper's closets spilled into the narrow hallway, Wade was certain that the Winnebago would be overturned at any moment. But just as the jouncing of the camper reached that critical point, the motion stopped and the vehicle grew still.

Shakily, Wade got to his feet and crossed the main room to the side door. He laid his hand on the inside knob, but hesitated in turning it. He held his breath as he heard footsteps echo from outside. They encircled the camper once, twice, then stopped directly outside the entrance. On the opposite side of the door came the same laughter that had drifted from the receiver of the cellular phone only moments before.

Wade felt his adrenaline kick in, causing his heart to pound wildly. He had never been so frightened in his entire life. But something caused him to turn the knob of the door. He glanced over his shoulder and saw Bret lying there on the couch, unconscious and bleeding. He knew the only way he was going to help his companion was to leave the camper and go to the plantation house for assistance.

Bracing himself for the worst, Wade wrenched the camper door open and stared out into the darkness. The moment that the cold night air hit him, the laughter stopped.

Wade jumped down to the ground and stood there for a moment. It was much colder than the night before. According to the local weather forecasters, a severe cold front was sweeping down from the northwest. They were even predicting a chance of snow after Thanksgiving, which was only a couple of days away.

He listened, straining his ears for sound. An instant later, he heard the sound of heavy footsteps on the pavement of the circular drive, coming from the opposite side of the Winnebago. Cautiously, he started around the rear of the camper. As he paused to examine the crater in the rear window, Wade heard Rick Gardner call to him from the mansion's upstairs balcony.

"Monroe?" he asked. "What the hell's going on down there?"

The parapsychologist considered asking for help in investigating the footsteps, when he again heard the sound of snickering laughter, this time coming from the other side of the Winnebago. Wade thought of his injured lover, and suddenly anger overrode his fear. Fists clenched, he ignored Rick and stepped around the corner of the Winnebago, prepared for anything.

Anything, that is, but the sight that confronted him.

Monroe simply stood there for a moment and stared, his anger making an abrupt U-turn and changing again into a fear bordering on panic. For scarcely fifteen feet away from him stood a man surrounded by a brilliant aura of electric blue. He was tall and powerfully built, and was clad in the uniform of a Union colonel. Half of the officer's face was strikingly handsome—wreathed in platinum blond hair and bushy muttonchop whiskers—while the other half was horribly mutilated, showing ugly flaps of flayed skin and jagged shards of the fractured skull underneath. One of the man's eyes hung slightly askew, pointed blindly at the ground, but the other stared straight at Wade, flashing with fiery emotion.

"Who are you?" asked Wade, although he already knew the answer to his question. As the colonel took a step forward, the ghost-hunter could see the front of the Winnebago through the man's torso and upper limbs, and immediately knew that he confronted the poltergeist that had eluded him for the past few days.

The spirit laughed softly, and laying his hand upon the brass hilt of a cavalry sabre, withdrew it from its scabbard. Eerie blue light played along the length of the curved blade from point to haft. Then, with a hoarse yell of triumph, the entity raised his sabre overhead and charged straight at Wade.

The parapsychologist could not move; he was frozen to the spot. Wade had encountered many spirits during his career, but they'd always seemed harmless and unthreatening. This entity, however, seemed hellbent on launching a violent attack against him. He stood in indecision for a moment, not knowing whether to turn and run, or attempt to defend himself against the brutal spirit.

As it turned out, he had no time to react either way. Abruptly, the fifteen feet between them was gone and the ghostly colonel was upon him. Wade raised his hands defensively, even though he knew any resistance to the attack would be futile. He waited for the biting pain of the sabre's edge cutting into his flesh, but instead the spectral blade brought only a sting of intense cold. The sabre slashed downward, past his hands and arms, entering his left shoulder and upper body. A burning sensation like Wade had never experienced before seemed to rip through his lungs and heart, but it was an icy burning and not one related to heat in any way.

Wade dropped to his knees on the driveway. He urgently gasped for breath, his lungs seemingly frozen solid inside his chest. His heart pounded as the cold that engulfed him gave way to a flood of sickening emotions. They were emotions he was familiar with, but only in the darkness of his nightmares—emotions such as hatred and contempt, sadism and perverted desire.

Pushed nearly to the brink of endurance, Wade Monroe yelled out. Almost immediately, the emotions seemed to recede, not away from him, but somewhere deep inside him. He finally caught his breath and, lifting his head, looked around. The entity that had charged him, sabre in hand, was nowhere to be seen.

A moment later, Laura and Rick were standing next to him, their faces full of concern. "What's wrong, Wade?" asked Laura. "What happened?"

Still on his knees, Wade stared up at the two as if he did not recognize them at first. Then, finally, his vision sharpened. "We had a visit from our elusive poltergeist," Wade told them. "It attacked the camper. Bret is badly hurt. Could you please call an ambulance?"

"I'll be right back," Rick said. He left them and ran back into the house, heading for the telephone in the entrance hall.

Laura knelt next to Wade. "Are you all right?"

"I believe so," he replied. "Just a little shaken, that's all."

Laura reached out to help him up, but recoiled when she touched his arm. "Good Lord . . . you're as cold as ice!"

Shuddering, Wade climbed to his feet and leaned against the side of the camper to steady himself. He felt incredibly weak, as if his encounter with the poltergeist had sapped him of all his strength. His trembling grew in intensity, his muscles growing so rigid that they ached. Wade's teeth chattered forcefully and his entire chest seemed to seize up on him. For a moment, he was afraid he might suffer a heart attack if he was not warmed up quickly enough.

Laura seemed to sense the urgency in his eyes. "You're freezing to death!" she said. Then, without hesitation, she took him in her arms and pressed her body against his. On the surface, Wade knew that the act was basically an innocent one; simply the unselfish act of attempting to warm someone up before the shock of cold could set in.

But something else—something hidden down within him—reacted quite differently. He felt a warmth grow inside him, but it was not generated by the closeness of the woman's body. Instead, it was the mounting heat of desire. Stunned by the sensation, Wade attempted to fight it off, but it seemed much too strong to be quelled. He found himself returning her embrace as the crotch of his trousers grew tighter with expanding lust.

Then an impulse leapt full-blown into his mind, an impulse to wrestle Laura roughly to the ground, tear away her nightgown, and brutally force himself upon her. The thought of doing such a thing both disgusted and mortified Wade Monroe. Quickly, mustering the last bit of strength he had left in him, he pushed away from her. Stumbling, he caught hold of the camper's side molding and stood there, weak-kneed, gasping for breath.

Laura seemed to see his abrupt withdrawal in a different light. Embarrassed, she took a step backward. "I . . . I'm sorry," she said. "I was only trying to keep you warm . . . that's all there was to it."

"I know," Wade said. "Thank you. I'm feeling much better now." He took a couple of steps away from the camper and tested his balance. The bout of uncontrollable shivering had subsided and he felt his strength slowly begin to return.

Rick returned a second later. "The paramedics are on their way," he said. He regarded Wade curiously. "So, what happened? I saw you walk around the side of the camper, and then I heard someone yell. Did you see this ghost that attacked you and Bret?"

Wade did not know exactly why he chose to lie, but he did. "No, I didn't see anything," he told them. "I thought I heard footsteps, but I was mistaken. There was nothing there."

Rick seemed a little skeptical. "Are you sure?"

Wade's eyes flared in sudden anger. "Yes, damn it, I'm sure!" Almost as quickly, an apologetic look crossed his face. "I'm sorry. I'm just upset, that's all. Please, let's see to Bret. He was bleeding badly when I left him."

As they headed around the camper to the side, Wade heard the distant wail of a siren drifting from the direction of Franklin. The ambulance would be there in a matter of minutes. He turned and regarded the spot where he had encountered the sword-wielding ghost only a short time ago. He tried to recall the spirit's features, but try as he might, he simply could not remember them.

Wade knew at that moment that he must encounter the poltergeist again before his investigation at Magnolia was completed and lure it into revealing itself as it had only a short while ago. Then, perhaps he could discover the reason for the entity's violent attacks and make some progress toward ending its contempt and hostility toward the residents of Magnolia and those who had been invited there. For there was one fact that stood out very clearly in Wade Monroe's mind: the matter of the ghostly colonel was much too dangerous to be left unresolved. If it was, tragedy for Laura Locke and her husband was inevitable.

Chapter Twenty-Seven

On Thanksgiving Day, Laura Locke and Rick Gardner found themselves playing the role of hosts once again. At noon, their guests, Archie and Alma, Tyler Lusk, Wade Monroe, and Bret Nelson, who was recovering nicely from a mild concussion, were seated around the long table in the mansion's lavish dining room. The spread that had been laid out was traditional in every way. A roasted turkey sat on a garnished platter in the center, surrounded by bowls of green beans, cranberry sauce, corn on the cob, sweet potato casserole, and buttered rolls. Laura had used her finest china and glassware for the occasion, hoping to make the holiday an extra special one for those invited. After all, three of her guests were a considerable distance from home, and she hoped that her added effort would make them feel comfortable and content, instead of longing for family and friends.

After Archie had said the blessing and the meal was in progress, Rick began to carve the turkey, while Laura passed the bowls of vegetables and bread to her guests. Archie and Tyler commented on how wonderful everything looked and smelled, but Laura simply accepted their praise graciously. To say that she had spent considerable time in planning the preparation of the holiday meal would have been something of an understatement. She had spent the last couple of days shopping and cooking, doing everything she could to make everything perfect. Of course, Rick had done his share in helping her. The previous night and most of that morning, both had slaved in the kitchen until all the dishes were completed and the desserts of pumpkin pie and German chocolate cake were delivered piping hot from the oven. They had barely found time to set the dining room table before their guests arrived at a quarter to twelve.

As Laura helped serve the food, she glanced across the table several times. Directly across from her chair sat Wade Monroe. For some odd reason, the parapsychologist simply sat there staring at her, seemingly with no restraint at all. His attention bothered Laura a little. In fact, Wade's presence around Magnolia had given her a definite feeling of unease during the past two days.

Since the night the poltergeist had attacked the Winnebago, Wade's manner had changed. Instead of the polite and cultured gentleman Laura had first been introduced to, Monroe now seemed more brash and abrasive, especially when dealing with Rick and the other men. During a retesting of the downstairs parlor, Wade had berated Bret so severely that the assistant had angrily left his place behind the console of monitors and stalked out of the room. When Wade insisted on continuing the experiment, despite long hours of unproductive results, Rick and Tyler had also abandoned the session. Afterward, Laura had heard the parapsychologist, alone in the parlor, raving and cursing, yelling for the "damned ghost" to show itself, but to no avail. That alone had frightened Laura. Obviously, Monroe's curiosity in the haunting of Magnolia had grown after the assault on the camper and turned into an unhealthy obsession.

Even at that day's meal, Wade stood out from the others around him in appearance. He looked unkempt and near exhaustion. His hair was uncombed, and it looked like he hadn't shaved in several days. His eyes were darker and more brooding, and his face seemed ruddier than it had before. Although Laura could not say for sure, she suspected that Wade was drinking heavily. From the look of nervousness and worry on his face, she knew that her suspicions were probably close to the truth.

After passing the bowl of hot roasted corn to Tyler, Laura

glanced over and again found Wade's eyes on her. Since the night of the twenty-second, she'd noticed that Monroe's attention had been centered on her more and more frequently. Several times during the past few days, she had sensed someone watching her and, turning, found him standing nearby, simply staring at her, but brazenly so. It had gotten to the point where she had stopped taking her daily runs around the property, at least when she was alone. And whenever Rick took a trip to town, she made some excuse to go with him, afraid to stay at home by herself. Perhaps her fears were unfounded, but then again, maybe they were not.

"The turkey is delicious!" said Alma Gant, drawing her attention from the man across the table. "So moist and tender."

"I used an old recipe of my grandmother's," Laura told her. "You place the turkey in a roaster along with three stalks of celery, an apple, and a peeled onion, baste it in butter, then cook it in the oven for an hour. After that, you turn off the oven and—making sure you don't open the door—let it cook in its own juices overnight. Sounds too simple to believe, doesn't it?"

"Well, tasting is believing, that's for sure," said Alma. "I swear, my recipe file has grown fatter and fatter since I met you, Laura."

Conversation turned from the feast before them to other subjects. "Archie, I hear that you and Alma are going to St. Louis at the end of the month," said Rick, pouring himself half a glass of white wine.

"Yes, we're going to that auction we mentioned before," replied the elderly man. "We've had our eye on the diary of Major Hudson for quite some while now, and we think this time we have a very good chance of acquiring it."

Wade Monroe looked up from where he had been picking at his plate. "Hudson?" he asked, recalling the report that Archie had given him upon his arrival in Franklin. "Fredrick Bates's second-in-command?"

"That's right," Archie said. "I honestly believe that if we could get our hands on that diary, it would help unravel a lot of the mystery concerning what happened here at Magnolia on November 30, 1864. And it might even be instrumental in your own investigation, Wade."

"Oh, and why would you think that?" the parapsychologist asked, a little too brashly.

Archie was annoyed by the man's tone of voice, but he chose to overlook it. "Well, Alma and I have been discussing it, and we believe that we've figured out the identity of your rock-throwing poltergeist."

"Okay," Wade said, a glint of amusement showing in his eyes. "Please, tell me, who would it be?"

"Why, Fredrick Bates, of course," Alma said, a little defensively. "Just take a look at the facts. Bates took Magnolia under siege shortly before the Battle of Franklin; after the skirmish had ended, his troops left the plantation in flames . . . but apparently under the command of Hudson. What happened to Bates during that time is a complete mystery."

Wade eyed Archie skeptically. "So what you are saying is that Fredrick Bates suffered some terrible fate after coming to Magnolia, and now his ghost is wreaking havoc in attempts to gain vengeance for some wrong done it a hundred and thirty years ago." The parapsychologist laughed. "Oh, if it were only that simple!"

"I don't think Archie's theory is as off-base as you think, Monroe," Tyler spoke up, coming to his friend's defense. "But I suppose you have a better idea, right?"

"No," Wade admitted, his expression switching swiftly from hilarity to one resembling bitter melancholy. "To tell you the truth, I have no earthly idea what the identity of this entity is. And frankly, I don't care."

"But you can't really mean that, Wade," said Laura. "I thought that was how you dealt with phenomena like this. You explored its history and background, then attempted to discover a solution for exactly why it haunts a particular place."

"Well, yes, that *is* how I *usually* handle these matters," Wade told her. "But I've decided that this situation is much more different than the others I've explored. I think the best course of action in this case would be to bully the poltergeist into revealing itself, instead of trying to reason with it. It's a very cunning and savage entity; I've figured that out already. Perhaps more cunning than any spectral being I've encountered so far."

"What do you think, Bret?" Tyler asked. "Do you agree with Wade? Do you think the best way to deal with this spirit is to stoop to its level?"

Bret looked as if he was reluctant to join in the discussion. "Well, actually, our views differ on that point," he said. "In my opinion—"

Abruptly, Wade turned and glared at the man seated next to him. "Why should they give a damn what you think, Bret?" he asked sharply. "*I'm* the parapsychologist here. You're only an assistant, an overtrained errand boy more than anything else. *Your* opinion doesn't count—only *mine!*"

For a moment, everyone at the table was stunned into silence. Obviously angered by the comment, Bret glared back at Wade, then pushed his chair away from the table. "Excuse me," he apologized to the others, then stormed out of the dining room.

A moment after they heard the slamming of the front door, Alma regarded Wade sternly. "I think that was totally uncalled for," she told him, not afraid to speak her mind.

The look in Wade's eyes was challenging. "Oh, do you, Mrs. Gant?" he asked harshly. "I'm simply stating the extent of my qualifications. As far as assistants go, Bret is competent enough to twist a few knobs and read a few electronic monitors. But he is no parapsychologist. He doesn't have the foresight and depth of understanding necessary to successfully draw a lost soul out into the open and lead it toward its proper destination."

"That's mighty high talk," Rick said with a laugh. "Especially considering that you've struck out with every attempt to investigate this place so far. If you ask me, we could have done better if we'd looked in the Yellow Pages for help."

Wade's eyes flashed with rage. "If anyone should be faulted with the failure of this investigation, it should be you, Gardner, not me—you, and Mr. Lusk here."

"What?" Tyler asked in amazement. "Why do you think that?"

"I've come to the conclusion that your presence here is hindering my chances to communicate with this spirit, as well as the others that have been witnessed on the grounds," Wade told them. "Despite what happened before, it's clear to see that this entity is reluctant to duplicate its attack, particularly in front of both of you. Why that is, I'm not sure. But, in my opinion, there's only one solution to the problem."

"And what's that?" asked Tyler.

"You and Gardner must leave Magnolia," Wade Monroe said flatly. "And you must stay away until my investigation is completed."

"Like hell!" Rick said. "Do you actually think I'm going to leave my own home?"

"I'm afraid it's necessary, if you're truly serious about finding a permanent solution to this haunting." Wade turned and stared at Laura the way he had for the past couple of days. "Of course, Laura is welcome to stay. In fact, I encourage it."

The statement seemed to anger Rick even more. He stood up abruptly, nearly turning his chair over. "Listen to me, Monroe," he said warningly. "No one can dictate who stays in this house and who doesn't—no one but Laura and me. And believe me, if anyone's welcome here is growing thin, it's yours."

"You fool!" Wade said, standing up and facing the artist. "You can't possibly understand the magnitude of what's going on here. This isn't some simple case of disembodied voices and moving objects. This is a full-scale haunting of enormous proportions. And simply put, I'm the only one who could possibly resolve it. If you don't give me control of this situation, and I mean *complete* control, this investigation is doomed to failure. And then where the hell will you be? Back to square one, with a murderous poltergeist on your hands, that's where. Then you'll be on the phone, begging me to come back and do the job right . . . on my own terms."

Again, stunned silence filled the dining room. Then Laura

spoke up calmly, but firmly. "Mr. Monroe . . . I'm sorry, but I must ask you to leave. I won't tolerate such rude behavior in my home."

"That's right," Rick said. "So why don't you jump in your camper and head on back to Vermont, or wherever the hell you came from!"

"No," Laura said, despite her husband's statement. "I do want this matter resolved. You and Bret can stay and finish your investigation. But get one thing straight—who goes or stays here at Magnolia is *my* decision, not yours."

The anger and contempt in Wade Monroe's eyes faltered, then finally gave way to an expression of brooding uncertainty. Without another word, he turned and left the dining room, heading toward the front door.

"Arrogant cuss, ain't he?" Alma said, shaking her head.

Laura's show of strength suddenly crumbled and she tossed her fork down on her plate with a clatter. "A great Thanksgiving this turned out to be," she said bitterly.

"It's not your fault, Laura," Tyler assured her. "Everything was perfect . . . until Monroe started to mouth off."

Archie removed his spectacles and polished the lenses on the front of his shirt. "I don't want to sound like I'm defending Wade's behavior, but I think there's something you ought to know. I was talking to Bret yesterday, and he told me that Wade has been out of sorts lately. He's been suffering a string of bad nightmares for the past month and has been hitting the bottle a little too hard. Bret thinks that he might be burning out on parapsychology and that the strain of taking on case after case, with no rest in between, is pushing him toward a nervous breakdown."

"Oh, great!" Rick said. "What you're saying is that we could have a potential nutcase on our hands!"

"No," Archie clarified. "Just a man who's seen a hell of a lot of strange things in a relatively short period of time, and who doesn't know exactly how to deal with it. I suggest we be a little more patient with Wade. He might be coming across like a self-righteous asshole now, but he's the best in his field, and I think it would be worth your while to overlook his behavior and let him do his work. Within reason, of course."

"I suppose so," Rick admitted reluctantly. "But there's something about the guy I don't like. I can't put my finger on it, but I still feel like he can't be trusted."

Privately, Laura shared her husband's doubts concerning Wade Monroe. He had seemed like a capable professional upon his arrival, but that impression was slowly deteriorating. The more Laura considered his unstable behavior—the way he showed disdain for Rick, while treating her with increasing interest—the more she became convinced that he was a man to be watched, and watched closely.

Chapter Twenty-Eight

A couple of days after the incident on Thanksgiving, Rick knocked on the side door of the Winnebago. He waited a few moments, mulling over what he had to say in his mind and wondering if the extent of his concern was more imaginary than anything else. But when the door opened, he knew that he had to speak his piece and set a few things straight, before they got out of hand.

"Yes?" Bret Nelson asked. The man looked a little distraught and pale, as if he had been up half the night worrying about something.

"I'd like to talk to Monroe," Rick said, attempting to keep his temper in check. "I have a few things I'd like to discuss with him."

Bret stared at the artist for a moment, as if he were well aware of the purpose of Rick's visit. "I'm afraid he's asleep right now," Bret told him.

"Then wake him up," Rick said. "This is important."

Bret stepped out of the camper and softly closed the door behind him. "I don't think you understand. Wade . . . well, he had a little too much to drink last night. I don't think it'd be wise to wake him up right now. He's been a real bear lately, especially when he's suffering a hangover."

"I don't care," Rick insisted, impatience flaring in his eyes.

"Well, I do," Bret said firmly. He could see that Rick was upset, perhaps on the verge of pushing his way into the camper and rousing the parapsychologist from his drunken sleep. "What do you want to talk to him about, anyway?"

"Some things have been said and done during the past couple of days that concern me," Rick said. "I believe you know what I'm talking about, too, don't you?"

Bret hesitated, then nodded. "Yes, I do." He motioned for Rick to step away from the camper. "Can we talk in private?"

Rick looked as though he wanted to have it out with Wade Monroe himself, but he grudgingly complied. "I guess so," he finally said.

A minute later, the two men were standing beneath a magnolia tree at the edge of the grove. "All right," Bret said. "What's on your mind?"

"Plenty," Rick said. "First of all, I don't like how the course of this investigation is going. I mean, there seems to be no pattern to how Monroe is conducting his experiments."

"Yes, I know what you saying," Bret agreed. He thought of the past couple of days and how the meticulously planned investigation of Magnolia had, for some reason, turned into a disorganized mess. Since Wade's arrogant statements at the dining room table, the parapsychologist seemed to have grown obsessed with the poltergeist that had attacked the downstairs parlor and the Winnebago. The other entities—those of Jessica and Braxton Heller—had been utterly ignored, despite the obvious importance of their presence at Magnolia. Wade had focused solely on the troublesome spirit and on no other aspect of the multiple haunting. The parapsychologist had abandoned his original notion of using Rick and Tyler as bait to draw the entity into the open, instead banning the two from participating in or attending any further sessions. Also, his normally stringent process for the investigation of a phenomenon had become erratic and unpredictable. He had eliminated one piece of equipment after another, sure that they were the cause of the poltergeist's reluctance to reveal itself. Whenever Bret protested the changed methods, Wade would fly into an uncharacteristic rage and again remind him that he was merely an assistant and not the one who made the final decision as to how an investigation was to be conducted. The repeated belittling of his expertise hurt Bret, both professionally and personally. He never knew that Wade had it within him to be so cruel and abusive.

"Something else that bothers me is Monroe's behavior," Rick said. He studied Bret's face and saw that he had hit a nerve. "What's wrong with the man? Does he normally act like such an arrogant asshole?"

"No, really, he's usually a very kind and gentle man," Bret told him. "It's just that he's overextended himself this year, as far as investigations are concerned. He's been under a tremendous amount of strain lately."

"That's what Archie told me," Rick said. "I can understand someone in a position such as his feeling a lot of pressure, what with the type of profession he's chosen. Hell, I know how it feels to be pressed to the limit, due to deadlines and a growing demand in popularity. But despite all that, it doesn't give him the right to behave like he has."

"You mean the way he has treated you and Tyler?"

"No, I can handle that," said Rick. "It's the behavior he's shown toward my wife that I'm talking about."

"I don't know what you mean," Bret lied.

"Then you're as blind as a bat," Rick said. "Monroe's had his eye on Laura since he arrived. And he hasn't been too damned subtle about his interest in her, especially during the past few days. Hell, the man can't keep his eyes off her."

Bret had also noticed Wade's apparent attraction to the romance writer, but he did not let on to Rick that he had. "I think you're mistaken, Rick," he said. "Wade's no ladies' man, not by a long shot. Believe me, it's just been a misunderstanding on your part."

"No, it hasn't, and you know it," Rick said angrily. "Anyway, what do you mean, 'He's no ladies' man'? He sure acts like some horny Casanova when he's around Laura, and he doesn't seem to care who sees it."

"I assure you," Bret repeated, going out on a limb in order to calm the jealous husband. "You have absolutely nothing to worry about. Wade is incapable of feeling anything for your wife. Just take my word on that."

Rick's eyes narrowed. "And why is that? Maybe Laura was right after all. Maybe you two do have some sort of relationship going. Is that it?"

"That's all I have to say on the matter," Bret said, afraid of revealing too much to Rick. "Just try to put up with him for a few more days, okay? Then, hopefully, we'll be finished with our investigation and out of your hair for good."

"I just want to make sure that things don't get out of hand while I'm in New York," Rick said. "See that it doesn't. Do you understand?"

"I promise," Bret said.

When Rick Gardner had made his way back across the circular driveway and into the plantation house, Bret stood beneath the magnolia for a while and wondered if he could truly keep such a promise. He recalled the sleepwalking incident in Virginia and was aware that it could happen here as well. Bret had awakened then and saved his companion from a potentially explosive situation before it had a chance to take place. But what if he slept through one of Wade's nocturnal prowlings this time? What if Wade suffered one of his interactive nightmares and got to Laura before Bret could intervene? The very thought of such a thing happening scared him. For if Wade did act out his dreams once again, Bret wasn't too sure that he could prevent him from carrying it out this time, given the parapsychologist's current state of mind.

"Let us in!" boomed a baritone voice from outside. "By the authority of the federal government, I demand that you open these doors immediately!"

Jessica Heller stood at the head of the winding staircase, listening to the pounding of fists against the bolted doors of sturdy oak and the stern voice that roared just beyond them. She had expected something disastrous to take place when she had heard the movement of troops, marching en masse, along the main road earlier that day. Jessica now knew that the rumors that had been circulating for several days were true: Hood's Confederate Army was on its way north to take

Nashville back from the Union, while the federals waited for them in Franklin, intent on fighting to retain possession of the state capital.

"What shall we do, Miss Jessica?" asked Sophie from below. The cook and several of the other servants stood nervously in the entrance hall, at a loss for what to do.

"Let those Yankee bastards stand in the snow and freeze to death, for all I care!" said Jessica, speaking loudly enough for those outside to hear.

"Very well!" came the thunderous voice of authority once again. "Then we shall have to enter by force!" Jessica could imagine the commander turning to his men. "Knock the doors down!"

The sound of a battering ram slamming against the oaken doors echoed through the house. It was a sinister sound, one that quickened the heart and sent a shudder of dread through one's body, in dire anticipation of what was certain to follow next.

Jessica stood on the upper landing, her frail hands tightly clutching the banister. She wished that her beloved was there with her at that moment, but she knew it was futile even to think of such things. She had not seen Braxton since he'd ridden off to join the Confederacy three summers ago. She knew that he was still alive; he wrote to her whenever he found the opportunity. But for the past year, his letters had grown fewer, due to the Union Army's tightening hold on the Southland.

Her train of thought was interrupted as the ram finally finished its job. Both doors crashed inward, littering the marble floor of the foyer with twisted iron and ragged shards of splintered wood. Then, like a wave, those who had intruded upon the snowy grounds of Magnolia burst through the open doorway and streamed into the house.

Several of the soldiers—cavalry men, from their dress and demeanor—pushed the gathering of slaves away. In their wake strolled a tall, powerfully built man clad in the uniform of a Union colonel. The man was handsome, sporting a mane of blond hair and thick sideburns, but there was a cold cruelty in his eyes that revealed the ugliness that dwelled within. He was carrying a long-barreled revolver in one gauntleted hand, while the other held a cavalry sword. As he entered the hall, he looked around as if searching for the one who had denied him and his men access to the house upon their unwelcome arrival.

Jessica was afraid, but she spoke out nevertheless. "What do you want here?" she demanded boldly.

The officer's attention was drawn to the head of the stairway. He showed none of the courtesy she was accustomed to, neglecting to remove his hat as he took a step forward. "I am Colonel Fredrick Bates," he told her with an air of pompous superiority. "By the order of General Thomas of the Union Army, I have been given instructions to seize this dwelling for use as a command post during the skirmish to come." The way he said it, it was clear that he was none too happy about the part he was to play in the approaching battle.

"You have no right!" Jessica yelled from above.

"Oh, we have every right in the world to do whatever we damn well please," Colonel Bates told her. "Besides, what do you rebels expect, after the disloyalty and treason you have shown your country? We intend to use this dwelling for the purpose I've stated, and when the battle is over, confiscate whatever supplies and livestock we deem necessary to aid us in our journey to Nashville."

Jessica knew there was no use in protesting. After all, what could a Southern belle and a handful of frightened slaves do against a battalion of battle-hardened cavalry men? She studied the soldiers who stood around the entrance hall below. They were a motley crew, to be sure, not at all like she'd have expected defenders of the Union to be. The men were unshaven, they carried the unconventional weapons of marauders instead of legitimate soldiers, and they stank of sweat and whiskey. Only the colonel and his right-hand man, a bearded major, possessed the poise and polish that the Northerners were customarily known for.

Suddenly, Jessica found Bates's eyes upon her. They roved across her petite body, lingering at the bodice of her silken dress. Jessica knew the expression that blazed in the man's eyes; it was the burning of sexual desire. With growing alarm, she realized the colonel's intentions toward her.

"Major, secure this house and make a full inventory of the horses in the stable out back," he said. A cruel grin crossed his whiskered face as he started toward the foot of the stairway. "I have some business to attend to."

"Yes, sir," replied the major, turning away to relay the orders to the rest of the men.

Colonel Bates returned his revolver to its holster, but kept his sabre in hand. But before he could reach the staircase, Sophie broke away from the other slaves and cast herself upon the steps, blocking the man's path. "Yo' mustn't do it!" she pleaded. "Pleeze, leave Miss Jessica be!"

A contempt like nothing Jessica had ever witnessed before leapt into the colonel's eyes. "Filthy nigger!" he growled. "I'll teach you to defy an officer of the Union Army!" And before Sophie could escape, Bates acted. Brutally, he brought the sabre down with all the force that his muscles could muster. The blade sliced cleanly through flesh and bone, hacking her left leg in half, just below the knee.

Jessica's screams of horror mingled with the agonized cries of her most loyal slave. Mortified, she stared down at the jet of blood that shot from the stump of Sophie's leg, as well as the twitching length of the severed limb itself.

"Mammy!" yelled one of the slaves from the gathering that had been confined to the opposite side of the foyer. Despite the attempts of several calvarymen, the brawny form of Sebastian broke away. He crossed the hall, pushed the laughing colonel aside, and knelt next to his wounded mother. Quickly, he gathered the screaming woman up in his arms and started toward the rear of the house. Two or three cavalrymen pulled pistols and walked toward him, intending to bar his way.

"Let them go!" said Bates with a wave of dismissal. His eyes burned almost feverishly at the sight of blood and mutilated flesh. "They are of no concern now." He then turned his attention back to Jessica. Even through her terror, she felt relief, for the desire he had shown before seemed to have

abated, at least for the time being. "I'll deal with you later," he called to her, then strolled into the living room, where the crystal decanters of Braxton's liquor cabinet beckoned to him.

Frightened, Jessica fled along the upstairs corridor to her bedroom. Slamming the door behind her, she securely engaged the lock and sat on the canopied bed. As tears bloomed in her lovely eyes, she wondered what she might do to prevent the colonel from eventually mounting those stairs and coming for her. But in her heart, she knew that she could do nothing. She could do absolutely nothing but sit there and await the inevitable.

Laura's anxiety seemed to match that of the character in her novel as she stored her latest chapter on microdisk and paused for a breather. She did not know exactly why she had suffered such a mood of gloom and unease during the past few days. She attributed a good part of it to the embarrassing incident in the dining room on Thanksgiving Day. She simply could not erase the image of Wade Monroe standing there, his eyes livid with arrogance and contempt as he faced her husband. There had been the potential for violence between the two men; she had sensed that immediately. And she was not sure that it would not have come to that, if she had not intervened and asked Monroe to leave.

But that single altercation wasn't the only reason for Laura's nervousness. During the past couple of days, she had noticed that Wade's interest in her had seemed to increase, almost blatantly so. When Monroe was away from his experiments—which had seemed to have grown increasingly bizarre and unorthodox, in comparison to his earlier sessions—he tended to roam the plantation grounds, never straying far from the house. Several times, while she worked on her novel, she had glanced out the study window to find Wade standing on the lawn below, staring up at her.

She had found herself deliberately trying to avoid the man, but still, he seemed to be uncomfortably near, whether she liked it or not. Although he and Bret had not been invited to share meals like before, they were still allowed in the house in order to conduct their investigation. Even then, whenever Wade spoke to Laura, there always seemed to be some suggestion of lewdness in his words; innuendos of a sexual nature that had been made more than once. Laura knew that Rick was aware of what was going on and that he did not like it one bit. Sooner or later, Rick was sure to confront the man about his inappropriate behavior.

One particular incident during the past few days preyed on Laura's mind, but it was not one that involved Wade's unwholesome interest in her. Nonetheless, it was an occurrence that Laura simply could not forget.

The previous night, she had been working late in her study, editing and polishing a couple of chapters of text. When she finished, she went downstairs and checked to make sure that all the doors were locked. When she came to the front entrance, she caught a glimmer of light through one of the side windows. Keeping well back in the shadows, Laura had peered out into the night.

Wade Monroe leaned against the front bumper of the Winnebago. He held a butane lighter before his face and, as she watched, slowly passed the flame back and forth in front of his eyes. There was an expression of grim determination on his features, as if he were desperately looking for the answer to some perplexing question somewhere within that flickering tongue of bluish-yellow flame.

At first, Laura was sure that Wade had gone completely over the edge. But then she realized what he was actually doing: the parapsychologist was holding the lighter up to the plantation house in front of him as if attempting to get an idea of how the mansion would look engulfed in fire.

That single image of Wade Monroe staring through the flame of a cigarette lighter continued to disturb Laura as strongly now as it had then. But she had chosen not to tell Rick about what she'd seen. Her husband was jumpy enough about flying to New York and leaving her home alone as it was. If she'd told him, Rick would have insisted on canceling his trip, and she simply could not let him do that. Careerwise, the convention was just too important for him to pass up.

Rick had tried to talk her into accompanying him to New York several times in the past few days, but she'd decided against it. Her work on *Burnt Magnolia* was going too well for her to take a sudden hiatus from it, even a brief one. The writing came with a fluidity and ease that was unparalleled in comparison to that of her other novels. Frankly, she was afraid that if she paused, even for a short while, the strange flood of inspiration would leave her and she would never be able to recapture it.

Still, the prospect of being alone at Magnolia with Wade Monroe on the premises continued to frighten her a little. She was determined not to let it bother her, however. She slid open one of the drawers of her computer desk and lifted a pad of stationery. Underneath lay a loaded .38 revolver. She had found the snubnose in her late father's footlocker while rummaging through some boxes they had stored in the attic upon their arrival at Magnolia. As far as she knew, Rick had no knowledge of the gun, and she preferred to keep it a secret from him. True, his attitude toward firearms seemed to have changed, but he would probably have worried more about Laura accidentally shooting herself than her having to actually use it against someone else.

She picked it up and frowned. The revolver was old. Its blued finish had nearly been worn away down to the bare metal, and the cartridges she had thumbed into the cylinder's six chambers had been tarnished green with age. She just hoped that the thing would fire if she ever had to put it to the test.

The thought of having to resort to such an act of violence made Laura more uneasy than ever. Secretly, she hoped that all her fears and suspicions were nothing more than unfounded paranoia on her part. But considering what she had noted in the behavior of Wade Monroe during the past few days, she knew that she was correct in taking whatever precautions she deemed necessary to stay safe until Rick returned from his trip.

Chapter Twenty-Nine

On the morning of November twenty-ninth, Tyler Lusk parked his rental car on Franklin's Main Street, intending to see the Gants off on their trip to St. Louis. But as he climbed from the vehicle, he was surprised to find a county patrol car parked in front of the rare and used bookstore.

As he crossed the street and stepped onto the curve, he saw that the center pane at the front entrance's glass door had been shattered. Archie was standing out in front, talking to a Williamson County deputy as the law officer filled out a report. "What happened here?" asked Tyler, as he walked up to them.

"A dadblamed burglary, of all things!" Archie told him. Tyler could tell by the flush of anger in his cheeks and the way he gnawed on the mouthpiece of his pipe that the elderly man was upset. "Alma and I came in at nine, as usual, and we found the glass broken and the door standing wide open. Never would've expected it in a town like Franklin, but I reckon I shouldn't be too surprised, what with how things are these days."

"Don't you have a burglar alarm?" Tyler asked.

"Why, hell, no! Never thought we'd have cause to need one," grumbled the old man.

"What did they get?"

"Wasn't much of value in there to take, except those Civil War antiques of ours," said Archie. "And out of all of them, the thief only stole two things. A cavalry sword, and an old black-powder revolver . . . a Colt Army .44."

The deputy, who's name tag read *Craven*, glanced up from the report he was finishing. "Smith's Gun Shop down the street a piece was broken into, too," he said. "Hank is still going over his inventory, trying to figure out what the burglar took. As far as he can tell, they didn't take any guns or archery equipment." Deputy Craven cast a suspicious eye at Tyler. "I don't believe I know you. Are you from out of town?"

"Aw, he's all right, Tom," assured Archie. "He's the fella I've been telling you about, the one who's in Franklin researching his family history. And he's made good progress, too. We're ninety-five percent sure that his ancestors hail from Magnolia."

"Jesus, that place again!" said Craven, shaking his head. "Heck of a place for your kinfolk to have come from." The officer double-checked the form he had just completed. "Well, Archie, it looks like I have everything I need. I'll sure let you know if anything turns up. Oh, and I suggest you install an alarm system as soon as possible. If you'd had one, it's likely the fella would've been scared off and he wouldn't have broken into Smith's place right after he left yours."

After the deputy was gone, Archie and Tyler entered the bookstore, careful to step over the broken glass scattered across the threshold. Once inside, Tyler found Alma standing next to one of the display cases. The glass pane of its hinged top had also been smashed. Between a couple of bayonets and a number of brass buckles and uniform buttons were the empty spaces where the sabre and pistol had once been on display.

"Told you we should've had those things insured," Alma said, directing her statement at her husband. "But no, you said it'd just be a waste of money. I recall you said the same thing about putting in a burglar alarm, too."

"Come on, old woman!" Archie moaned, raising his liverspotted hands in surrender. "The law's already given me an earful! Believe me, I've seen the error of my ways. It just doesn't pay to be a skinflint, at least not as far as security is concerned."

"So, what about your trip?" Tyler asked. "Are you still going?"

"Can't see how we can leave just yet," Alma said. "I just called the glass company and the man I talked to said it would be late this afternoon before he could bring a replacement pane for that door. We can't possibly go until it gets here."

"Why don't you two go on and let me take care of it?" Tyler suggested. "You've certainly done enough for me. Let me do this one thing for you in return."

"Are you sure?" Archie asked.

"Of course," the young black man assured them. "I know how much this auction means to the two of you. Besides, if you do get ahold of Major Hudson's diary, it might just give us a clue as to what happened to my ancestors, Samuel in particular."

"You're right about that," Alma replied, buttoning up a heavy woolen coat. "If we're lucky, it ought to give us the entire story as far as what happened at Magnolia during the time of the Battle of Franklin."

"I'm sure Laura and Rick would be grateful for any information they get," said Tyler. "Especially if it helps get that loony ghost-hunter out of their hair."

"Yes," Archie said with a nod. "Wade Monroe seems to have been more of a hindrance than a help, as far as the hauntings at Magnolia go. Can't figure it out, though. I'd heard from dependable sources that the man was a genius in his field, and a real nice guy to boot. But instead, he's proven to be incompetent and annoyingly arrogant. I reckon his fame must have come more from hype than actual fact."

"But you said his assistant told you that he's been under a lot of emotional strain lately," Tyler said. "Maybe that's why he's behaved so strangely."

"Maybe so," Alma allowed. "But that still doesn't give him an excuse for being such a cranky and conceited son of a bitch . . . pardon my French."

Tyler accompanied the Gants to their Jeep Cherokee. As Archie climbed behind the wheel and fastened his seatbelt, he took his wallet from his jacket pocket. "Here's a spare key to the bookstore and enough money to pay for the glass for the door. I'd appreciate it if you could stop by every so often while we're away, just to check up on the place. And if you want to stay a while and do a little reading, feel free."

"I just might take you up on that," Tyler said. "I noticed you had a nice section on black history in there." He closed the Jeep door for the old man. "When should you be back?"

"Late tomorrow, more than likely," Archie told him. "The auction doesn't take place until nine o'clock tomorrow morning, and it'll probably be noon before it's over and done with."

"If we leave by one o'clock, we ought to be back in Franklin by tomorrow evening," Alma said. "That is, unless the weatherman's forecast turns out to be the gospel truth and it snows, like he said it might. Then we'll probably get back later."

Tyler recalled hearing the weather forecast on the radio during his drive over. The Tennessee Weather Service forecasted the possibility of sleet and snow during the next two days. If the weather did grow that severe, it would be the first time in a long while that Tennessee had experienced such a heavy snowfall during the month of November. But considering that the temperature had barely topped forty degrees that morning, Tyler knew that the forecast had a very strong chance of coming true.

"You folks take it easy and have a safe trip," he told them.

"We'll see you when we get back," replied Archie. He started the Jeep's engine and shifted it into gear. "And hopefully we'll have some good news for you."

"That would be nice."

Tyler waved at the two as they made their way down Main Street, heading in the direction of the interstate. As they circled Public Square and faded from sight, Tyler pulled his coat tighter against the cold and returned to the bookstore to await the arrival of the glass-fitter.

* * *

That night, Tyler Lusk again experienced the nightmare that had plagued his sleep during the past month. But unlike before, this time it did not end abruptly, but led to a very definite and startling conclusion.

Once again he was leaving the drafty structure of the slave cabin, spurred into the cold and snow by the screams of a woman. The familiar rage filled him, quickening his pace as he ran down the snowy pathway of the fruit orchard to the dark hull of the smokehouse. He paused next to the chopping stump, wrenched the broad ax free, then continued onward.

A moment later, he was at the edge of the flower garden. The scene was the same as before, etched in the flickering light of a blazing fire; the tall rear wall of the plantation house, the sturdy column and gnarled limbs of the oak tree, and the cheering crowd of drunken soldiers. And the focal point of the entire occurence was there as well, each hideous detail revealed. The body of the Southern belle, her gown hiked up around her waist, struggling for escape, while the powerful body of her attacker bucked mercilessly above her, bringing shame and agony with each brutal thrust.

Again, the ugly scene of rape stoked an anger within Tyler, and he tore through the brush, heading toward the Union colonel and his helpless victim. But halfway across the garden, Tyler knew that he was too late to save the woman. The officer's strong hands encircled her neck and squeezed. Her screaming was cut short and there was a wet snap from somewhere within her throat, the ugly sound of a fragile windpipe being crushed beneath powerful fingers. Then there was the frosty expulsion of the belle's last breath as it exited her open mouth.

With a shout and a leap, Tyler was over the flames of the bonfire and standing over the two. Again, he stared down at the demonic face of sadistic pleasure, glistening with sweat, eyes blazing like unholy hellfire. The very sight of that evil visage evoked the same reaction as before. Tyler lifted the ax overhead, then brought it down with all the force he could muster.

The heavy blade did its damage. The edge bit deeply, obliterating that horrible smile of sick triumph. Again and again the ax descended, even though the rapist had been slain by the first deadly blow. Eventually, Tyler felt the rage fade and the strength drain from the muscles of his arms. The murderous ax slipped from his grasp and fell to the ground, speckling the snow with blood and gore.

Wearily, Tyler dropped to his knees. He rolled the lifeless body of the dead colonel away and stared at the woman who had been raped and strangled. Hot tears sprang from his eyes, and mournfully he cradled the woman in his arms. Then the spell of his loss was broken by the realization that there were others who had laid witness to the brutal rape . . . as well as the savage slaying of their commander.

Angry yells of accusation were voiced, followed by calls for retribution. Tyler looked up and saw a single face of control among those of the leering mob. But no compassion was shown him. The Union major simply gave the drunkards what they wanted and turned away.

Instantly they were upon him, bearing down on him with the sheer weight of their number. He felt the pain of the blows they inflicted, delivered by fist, boot, and gun barrel. He felt panic overcome him. He struggled to find a route of escape, but there was none. The angry soldiers were too many and too tightly packed. The assault failed to let up. It only increased in its fury, bruising his flesh and breaking his bones. Tyler felt what little strength he had left begin to leave him. His head swam as the barrel of a Springfield rifle repeatedly pummeled his skull. He felt blood trickle warmly from his split scalp, bathing his battered face. Then his eyes swelled shut and the night and the fire and the mob of soldiers faded into blackness.

Tyler felt himself being lifted upward, off the snowy earth and into the open air. He heard the neigh and snort of a horse and, a moment later, found himself dumped into the cradle of a cavalry man's saddle. Confusion reigned for a moment, then the high thrill of pure terror as something thick and coarse was slipped around his neck. As the cord was tightened, Tyler realized that it was the loop of a hangman's noose that encircled his throat.

He struggled, attempting to pull his head from the noose, but the rope did not give. If anything, it grew more constricting, cutting off his ability to breathe. Tyler gasped and tried to draw air, but he could find none. The last thing he heard was a great roar of bloodlust rising from the men around him, as well as the slap of a gloved hand across the rump of the nervous horse. He felt the mount surge forward while the rope tightened further, dragging him bodily from the saddle.

After that, there was a sharp jerk downward, a brief explosion of pain at the base of his skull, and a quick descent into a darkness much more complete and final than that which his swollen eyes had cast him into.

Tyler awoke so violently that he rolled from his bed and landed on the carpeted floor of the hotel room, entangled in sheets and blankets. He lay perfectly still for a long moment, flat on his back, afraid to move as a burning sensation traveled along his neck and down the length of his spine. Then, just as quickly, the pain diminished, leaving only a muted soreness.

Slowly, he pulled the bedcovers from around him and sat up. He groaned in discomfort. It seemed as if every muscle in his body was sore. He recalled the punishment that he had suffered in his nightmare and felt as if he had actually been subjected to such a brutal beating.

Shakily, he got to his feet and walked toward the bathroom. Once he made it there, he leaned against the vanity and turned on the light. Tyler expected to find his face swollen and bleeding, but it looked the same as usual. That was, except for the sheen of panicked sweat and the lingering expression of terror that shone in his eyes.

Tyler tore the cellophane off a hotel drinking glass and filled it with water. He drank half a glassful before his breathing slowed and his heart began to beat at a slower pace. He splashed cold water on his face, then left the bathroom.

He sat down heavily on the bed and stared around the hotel room. Strangely enough, he felt a presence there that was not his own—a presence that was alien, yet was as familiar to him as his ownself. Then, little by little, the sensation of there being someone else in the room began to fade. A moment later, Tyler was certain that he was truly alone.

He sat there in the darkness and considered the ending of his recurring nightmare. Ever since he'd witnessed the phenomenon of the shadow of the hanging man he had suspected the identity of that powerfully built form, but he was unwilling to accept the fact. Now there was no denying it. The one who had been brutally lynched from the limb of the towering oak tree was none other than his ancestor of generations past, a loyal slave by the name of Samuel.

Tyler thought of the nightmare, of its horror and brutality, and knew that he was being subjected to those awful images for some distinct reason. He felt as if perhaps the spirit of Samuel was responsible. But why was his dead ancestor haunting him in such a cruel manner? And what was he trying to tell him? Or rather, warn him about?

As he considered those questions, Tyler Lusk knew that there was only one place where the answers could be found. He knew that he had to return to Magnolia and take another look around. Perhaps then he would discover something of importance that had eluded him during his past visits there.

Chapter Thirty

About the same time that Tyler Lusk awoke from his nightmare, Bret Nelson also woke up. Groggily, he sat up and laid his hand on the side of the bed that his lover usually occupied. Wade was not there and apparently had not been there for some time. The sheets were cool to the touch.

Bret groaned in disgust and climbed out of bed. He figured he would find Wade where the parapsychologist had chosen to spend most of his nights since arriving at Magnolia—drinking shot after shot of straight bourbon in the Winnebago's main room. As Bret crossed the darkened bedroom and entered the narrow hallway, he felt his anger rise. He was tired of his companion's new routine. During daylight hours, Wade divided his time between attempting to draw out the poltergeistal entity and constantly putting Bret down; at night, he totally shut himself off from the outside world, drinking too much and brooding silently.

As Bret made his way to the front of the camper, he decided that he had had enough of Wade's fluctuating moods. He had to find a way to bring back the old Wade he had known for seven years, or at least discover an explanation for the man's drastic change in behavior.

Surprisingly enough, he did not find Wade where he expected to. The couch Wade always occupied was empty. He quickly checked the liquor cabinet beneath the wet bar and found that his suspicions had been on the right track: there was an unopened bottle of bourbon missing from the shelf.

Obviously, Wade was engaging in his new favorite pastime. But where?

He checked the camper's bathroom and the cab up front, but found that Wade was nowhere in the Winnebago. Grumbling beneath his breath, Bret dressed and bundled up in a goosedown coat. Then he left the camper and stepped down to the hard surface of the paved driveway.

The front of the plantation house stretched above him, but it was dark and quiet at that late hour. The night was as black as soot. Dense snowclouds hung low in the sky overhead, promising the precipitation that the forecasters had predicted. Bret stood there for a moment, allowing his eyes to grow accustomed to the gloom. Then he set out in search of his missing companion.

It did not take long to find him. As soon as Bret rounded the rear bumper of the Winnebago, he saw the light of a fire deep within the magnolia grove. Alarmed, he jammed his hands in the pockets of his coat and started toward the flickering glow. Dead magnolia leaves rustled around his feet as he made his way toward the center of the grove, ducking low limbs still plentiful with thick, brown-edged leaves.

When he finally reached the site of the mysterious glow, he could not believe his eyes. Wade sat on the ground, legs crossed Indian-style, not more than three feet from a crackling fire fueled by dead leaves and broken branches. The man's face was as expressionless as stone, but his green eyes were livid as he sat staring into the flames and drinking from the now half-empty bottle of bourbon.

"What the hell are you doing out here?" asked Bret. "It's below freezing tonight. You'll catch pneumonia for sure."

"I've found it, Bret," was all that Wade said in reply.

Wade's contemplative tone of voice disturbed Bret for some reason he could not quite identify. "What do you mean?" he asked. "What have you found?"

"The solution to the problem," explained Wade calmly. "That nasty problem that we've been busting our asses trying to solve for the past week."

"You mean the poltergeist?" Bret asked.

"Of course!" Wade growled. He glared at Bret as if he were an idiot, then his expression softened and he turned his eyes back to the crackling flames of the campfire. "But it won't elude us any further. No, I've figured it all out."

"And what is that?"

Wade seemed annoyed that he had to explain his discovery to Bret. "Simply put, if Archie Gant's theory is right about the poltergeist being the spirit of Colonel Fredrick Bates—and I've just about reached the conclusion that it is—then there has to be some reason for its restlessness; some motive for its apparent contempt for those who live at Magnolia. I've given it a lot of thought over the past few nights, and I believe I know the reason why."

Bret said nothing. He simply stood there and waited for his companion to continue.

"It hungers, Bret," Wade told him, his eyes sparkling with excitement. "It hungers for that which it missed, due to the sudden circumstances of its earthly demise. It hungers for death and destruction. It hungers for fire."

"Do you mean to tell me—?" Bret began.

"Yes," Wade said. "It desires to witness that which it was denied a hundred and thirty years ago—the burning of Magnolia."

Bret realized what Wade was driving at, and the very thought of it frightened him. "You can't seriously be considering what I think you are. If you are, then you're crazy."

"I should have expected such a reaction from you," Wade Monroe snarled irritably. "I'm not talking about the entire destruction of the plantation house. We could set part of it on fire just long enough to draw the entity out of hiding, then put it out before any real harm was done. In fact, we could set up our equipment and do it tonight. Right now."

"Without the permission of Laura or Rick, I take it."

"You know very well they wouldn't condone such an experiment," Wade said. "Not willingly."

"And rightly so," Bret told him. "You're talking about arson, Wade. Destruction of private property for the sake of an experiment that might or might not work. It's not worth the risk, and you know it."

"You're wrong!" Wade roared. He stood up, his expression dark with mounting anger. "It *is* worth the risk. You don't seem to realize that this is the most important investigation of my career, Bret. This is the most active form of poltergeistal haunting that we've ever encountered. We experienced its fury firsthand . . . or did that knot on the back of your head make you forgetful?"

"I think *you're* the one who's become forgetful, Wade. You seem to have lost sight of the true nature of this investigation. This is a case of multiple hauntings, not just one. You seem to be totally ignoring the other entities here. Instead, you're obsessed with this bully of a ghost. And in the process, it's turning *you* into a bully."

"What are you talking about?" Wade demanded.

"You know what I'm talking about," Bret said. "Since you arrived here at Magnolia, you've grown more abrasive and demanding, even downright belligerent. At first you treated this investigation objectively, but in the last week you act as if this poltergeist's failure to materialize is some personal insult to you. Your rude behavior has alienated everyone involved, including me. I don't know what's wrong with you, Wade, but whatever it is, you need help."

The rage in Monroe's eyes grew in intensity. "Oh, that's what you'd like to do, isn't it, Bret?"

"I don't understand," Bret said, taking a cautious step backward.

"Yes, you do!" Wade shouted. "You'd like nothing more than to talk me into thinking that I'm suffering some sort of nervous breakdown. Then you could check me into a mental hospital and claim all the victory for yourself. Yes, I've suspected what you've really been up to all along."

"That's pure nonsense," Bret protested. He took another step back as Wade started menacingly toward him. "Listen to yourself. You're talking irrationally, love."

Before Bret knew what was happening, Wade struck. His right fist lashed out, slamming into Bret's jaw with the force of a hammer blow. Stunned, Bret stumbled backward and fell on his back in the magnolia leaves.

"Don't call me that!" Wade growled. "Don't ever call me that again, do you understand?" He regarded Bret as if he were some sort of hideous bug. "I don't know what possessed me to feel anything for you in the first place. You're so soft and weak, so utterly stupid! And what we shared together . . . well, it was perverse. Perverse and unnatural!"

"You're wrong, Wade," Bret said, the man's words stinging him like slashes from a knife. "We loved each other! Our relationship was for real."

Wade bent down and, grabbing the front of his assistant's coat, hauled Bret bodily to his feet. "Our relationship was a damned lie, and that's all there is to it! God, you disgust me!"

Bret opened his mouth, but he was not given the opportunity to say anything more. Wade struck him again, backhanding him across the mouth hard enough to split his lower lip and draw blood. Bret's head rocked back with the force of the blow, but that was not the end of it. The big man continued his assault, refusing to let up. Wade released his hold on Bret's coat to free both hands. Blow after blow came savagely, battering Bret's head and midsection.

Even after Bret had doubled over and fallen back to the ground, Wade refused to stop. Angrily, he kicked Bret in the stomach several times, bringing grunts of pain and cries of protest. As he lay there curled up on his side, Bret looked up at the man who stood over him. The glow of the fire reflected on the face of the psychic investigator. Never before had Bret seen such an expression of hatred on Wade's face. He actually looked as if he was enjoying the punishment he was inflicting on him. Bret suddenly found himself fearing for his life. Considering Monroe's strength and stature, there was a very real possibility that he could actually beat Bret to death, if he chose to.

But fortunately, he did not go that far. Wade's anger seemed to lose its steam and was slowly replaced by disgust. "You repulse me!" he said with a shake of his head. "I don't want to see your face again, do you hear me? Take your stuff and get the hell out of my sight!"

"But where will I go?" Bret asked. Feebly, he got to his feet, despite the pain that throbbed throughout his body.

"I don't care!" Wade told him, seemingly on the verge of exploding again. "The camper is in my name, so I guess you'll have to make it to town on foot. I just want you out of this investigation and out of my life as soon as possible."

"You can't be serious," Bret said, attempting to reason with the man he had shared everything with for the better part of a decade.

"I am," Wade told him coldly. "Deadly serious. I suggest you go, before I lose my temper again and end up killing you this time."

Bret said nothing in reply. There was really nothing to be said. As tears came to his eyes, he turned and started toward the Winnebago to gather what few belongings he could comfortably carry to Franklin. He considered rousing Laura and Rick and asking for assistance, but thought better of it. If he did involve them in his and Wade's quarrel, the truth of their relationship was bound to come out. And if that happened, there was no telling what the unstable parapsychologist might do in retribution.

Wade Monroe watched as his former assistant and lover disappeared into the shadows of the magnolia grove. The very thought of the intimacy they had shared sent a shudder of nausea through him. "Filthy queer," he growled, turning away in disgust.

A moment later, all thoughts of Bret Nelson had passed. He was back before the blaze of the campfire, bottle in hand, eyes centered on the heart of the crackling flames. In his mind's eye, he pictured an elegant and stately manor standing amid the fire, its tall limestone columns blackening and its interior expelling smoke and cinder.

He found himself smiling at the thought, but fortunately, decided not to act on such compulsions that night, no matter how strongly they nagged at him. No, for the time being, he would be content with his drinking and scheming.

But ultimately, he knew it would not be very much longer until he put his theory into practice. Not much longer at all.

It was well past two o'clock in the morning when Bret Nelson finally completed his three-mile trek and reached the Franklin city limits.

By the time he stumbled through the front door of an all-night convenience market, he was nearly frozen half to death. He stood in the warmth of the store, unable to control his shivering. He attempted to drop the nylon gym bag that held what little clothing he had hastily packed, but his fingers seemed too numb to function properly. He clutched the webbed strap tightly like a drowning man clutching at a life preserver.

"Can I help you with something?" asked someone at the front counter.

Bret looked over and saw an overweight woman with dark hair and thick-lensed glasses eyeing him nervously. Obviously, the beating Monroe had inflicted on him was apparent in the way of cuts and bruises. "Uh, no thanks," he said. "I just came in to warm up." He glanced up at the end of the counter and saw a Bunn coffeemaker with two steaming pots sitting on its twin warmers. "How much is the coffee?"

"Sixty-nine for a small, eighty-nine for a large," the clerk told him.

He dug his wallet from his back pocket and paid for a large cup. Soon, he was standing beside a display of cold and flu remedies, sipping the strong brew. Before long, his trembling stopped as the coffee began to warm him up.

"Were you in some sort of accident, mister?" the clerk asked out of curiosity.

"You might say that," Bret said, not wanting to elaborate. He stood there for a while, trying to decide what to do about Wade. He considered calling the Gants, but remembered that they had left for St. Louis early that morning. And there was no need to call Tyler Lusk at the Holiday Inn. He was a nice enough person, but there was no cause to involve him in such business.

He thought of Wade's unstable theory on how to coax the poltergeist from its hiding and the threat it presented to the residents of Magnolia. He also recalled the hatred and anger Wade had exhibited during the beating he had given Bret. There was no doubt about it: given his current state of mind, Wade was a potentially dangerous person to be around. Bret had the aches and pains to prove it.

As he finished the last of his coffee, Bret spotted a pay phone at the rear of the market. He walked to the phone and dug a quarter from his pocket, but decided not to drop it in the slot. Even though Wade had treated him badly and had physically assaulted him, he found that he could not bring himself to call the police. He cared too much about the man to do a thing like that.

But he knew he had to do something, if it was only to warn Laura and Rick that something tragic might take place. He opened his wallet once again, dug through several notes he had stored in an inner pocket, and found a scrap of paper bearing the phone number he needed. He deposited the quarter, dialed the number, and waited for the ringing on the other end of the connection. When it finally came, he debated on whether to hang up or not. But he did not have time to change his mind. Someone picked up the phone on the second ring.

"Hello?" came a sleepy voice he recognized as belonging to Laura Locke.

He opened his mouth to speak, but was unsure of what to say. In his mind, he pictured Wade again, face hard with anger and contempt, only a hairsbreadth away from murderous rage. His heart pounded as the fear for his safety returned in full force.

"Hello?" repeated the woman on the other end of the line. "Who is this?"

Bret knew he had to say something before she hung up the phone in frustration. "Be careful," he told her, then returned the receiver to its cradle, breaking the connection.

Which was what he intended to do, too. He decided the best thing for him to do was break his connection with the whole sorry business of the investigation at Magnolia and his falling-out with Wade. Then maybe he could put the hurt of his companion's harsh words and painful blows behind him.

"Is there a bus station anywhere in town?" he asked the clerk as he returned to the front of the market.

"There's a Trailways station three or four blocks down the street," she replied.

"Thank you," he said. He shelled out more change for another jumbo cup of coffee, then, bag in hand, started down the deserted street for the bus station.

PART FOUR

THE ANNIVERSARY

Chapter Thirty-One

Rick Gardner pulled back the cuff of his shirt sleeve and checked his Seiko. It was half past seven. "Looks like I have about twenty minutes until my flight. How about a cup of coffee?"

"Okay," Laura agreed.

Rick had already checked in his baggage that morning of November thirtieth and all that remained was the boarding of his Delta flight to New York. They walked through the busy terminal of Nashville's Metro Airport, past a newsstand and gift shop specializing in Grand Ole Opry and country music souvenirs, until they came to one of the airport's smaller restaurants. Both were quiet as they found a table and ordered a couple of coffees.

"Are you sure you won't come with me?" Rick finally asked. "We could check at one of the desks and see if we could book you a later flight. You could run home, pack a bag, and join me in New York this evening."

"Really, I'd like to, sweetheart," Laura said. "But this book is moving along so well, I'm afraid to leave it right now. You understand how it is to have a sudden burst of inspiration. I'm afraid it'll fizzle out if I don't stick with it. Sorry."

"No need to apologize," Rick said. "I certainly know how fickle the creative process can be." The waitress brought them their coffee. Rick took his straight and black, while Laura doctored hers with cream and two packets of Sweet & Low.

"You don't seem very excited about this trip," Laura said, after taking a sip of her coffee.

"Sure I am," Rick said. "This is the chance of a lifetime. It's not every day I'm invited to be artist guest-of-honor." He stared through the window. Above the expanse of the multiple runways hung a blanket of thick gray clouds that was darkly ominous with the promise of snow. They had spotted a few stray flakes during their drive to Nashville, but so far, nothing of real substance had materialized.

"Then what's the problem?" Laura asked. She could not help but be bothered by the brooding expression in her husband's eyes.

Rick pulled his attention from the snowclouds and centered it on his wife. "I'm just a little worried about you, that's all."

Laura reached across the table and squeezed his hand. "Hey, I'll be all right."

"I hope so," he said, forcing a lame smile. "I've just been a little jumpy. First, with this ghost business, then with the way that asshole Monroe has been acting."

Laura nodded. "I know, but don't worry. I can handle him."

"Can you?" he asked. "I don't mean to scare you, honey, but I don't like the way he's been acting toward you. He can't keep his eyes off you, and some of the remarks he's made have been downright vulgar. I still say we should have dismissed him from the investigation when we had the chance."

"I thought we already agreed that we wanted this matter resolved," his wife reminded him. "I know he hasn't measured up to his reputation so far, but Archie still thinks he's qualified enough to find the answers to these multiple hauntings, so I think we should let him continue—at least for a while longer."

"Multiple hauntings," Rick mused, with a shake of his head. "Do you realize that other than the attack on Monroe's camper, there hasn't been a single occurrence since the guy arrived? Maybe Monroe has offended those spooks as much as he has everyone else and driven them off with his arrogance alone."

Laura laughed. "Maybe you're right."

Rick sat there silently for a moment more, sipping his coffee. When he spoke again, his eyes were serious. "Laura, if something should happen, I want you to call the sheriff's department immediately, understand? Don't hesitate. It's better to be safe than sorry, you know."

Laura could see that her husband was taking Monroe's apparent infatuation for her very seriously. "All right. I promise."

"And another thing," continued Rick. "That black powder gun I bought . . . I took it out of the cabinet in my studio and stashed it downstairs in the kitchen pantry. It's on the shelf behind the canned vegetables and it's fully loaded. I just wanted you to know where it is, just in case."

"Okay." Laura neglected to tell him that she already had the matter of self-protection covered. Her father's .38 snubnose was still in the drawer of her computer desk.

An announcement came over the speaker system, calling for the passengers of Delta's next flight to New York to assemble at a particular gate. "I reckon that's me," said Rick.

They quickly finished their coffee and left the restaurant. Soon, they were at the corridor leading to the boarding gate. "Have you got your ticket?" asked Laura.

A glint of sudden panic shown in Rick's eyes, then turned to relief when he withdrew the envelope from the inner pocket of his jacket. "Yep. It's right here."

"Have a good time and I'll see you when you get back," said Laura.

"I'll call you when I get there," promised Rick. They both shared a lingering kiss, then Rick joined the crowd that was boarding the plane at the far end of the corridor.

Laura waved to Rick one last time before he disappeared into the cabin of the 727. Turning, she walked across the main lobby and left the terminal, heading for the parking lot.

Once she was back on the interstate and heading home, Laura felt a sensation of sadness and dread engulf her. It did not hit her without warning; in fact, it had been building all that morning. She could not figure out exactly why Rick's leaving should affect her so strongly. They had been apart before, sometimes for a week or more, do to conventions and autograph tours. But this time felt different than it had before.

She tried to rationalize the feeling of abandonment. Maybe it was because this was the first time they would be apart since moving to Magnolia. Or it might be due to the trouble at Magnolia itself—the hauntings that had taken place there and the threat of the poltergeist. Perhaps she was afraid to return home and face the prospect of encountering another occurrence alone, with no support from her husband.

Laura considered what Rick had said about the sudden inactivity of the spirits that had been seen around Magnolia. He was right: since the arrival of Wade Monroe, they seemed to have purposefully refrained from revealing themselves. In fact, except for the troublesome poltergeist, they had only made a single appearance each, and absolutely nothing had been seen of them since. Rick had encountered the spirit of Braxton Heller in the magnolia grove only once, just like she had encountered the weeping form of Jessica beneath the oak tree that one occasion and that was all.

As she drove, Laura glanced at her reflection in the Saturn's rearview mirror. As of her awakening that morning, the mysterious transformation of her hair color had reached its completion. It was now a striking shade of rich auburn. She thought again of the phenomenon; of how it had begun directly after her contact with the spirit of the weeping belle. Come to think of it, the writing of *Burnt Magnolia* had increased in clarity and intensity the day after the encounter, almost doubling her pace. It had always taken four to six months for Laura to complete a manuscript, but only a month's time had elapsed since she'd began her latest novel, and she was already nearing the end. At first, she had attributed it to a sudden surge of inspiration, but now she was not so sure of that assessment.

She recalled an idea that had come to mind before, a suspicion that the spirits of Braxton and Jessica had somehow influenced her and Rick, causing them to act and resemble the long-dead Confederate officer and his beloved wife. But the more she thought about it, the more Laura became convinced that some form of possession, even if it was subliminal, had taken place. Perhaps that was the reason why the story of Jessica Heller's life was coming to her so freely. Maybe it had nothing to do with imagination at all, but the prompting of a source that had experienced those events first-hand.

Just the thought of such a thing happening to her, somehow taking place within her soul, fascinated her. Had she somehow accepted the essence of Jessica's spirit when she'd reached out and touched that ghostly hand? And had Rick experienced the same melding with Braxton when he'd spotted the digging man in the magnolia grove? She recalled Rick's drastic alteration in attitude and appearance directly following that night and decided that there was a good chance that he had.

If such a thing had happened, however, then why were Braxton and Jessica still not at peace? If they had discovered each other through Laura and Rick, surely they would have moved on to their rightful places in the hereafter. Perhaps even now, they existed as they had during the past hundred and thirty years. Perhaps they were condemned to roam the earth, but on entirely different planes of existence, constantly searching, but unable to find one another.

The very thought saddened Laura. She considered how it would feel to search for Rick, knowing that he was somewhere just beyond her sight, but unable to make that crucial connection due to some spiritual state of limbo. It would be tragic, even maddening, to a point.

But if that was truly the case, then there must be something blocking the bridge between those two realms of coexistence, some mysterious factor that separated the spectral lovers and prevented them from meeting. As Laura switched from Interstate 40 to Interstate 25 and headed south for Franklin, she decided that she would speak to Wade Monroe about her theory. Perhaps what she had to tell him might, in some way, lead to the solution of the haunting of Magnolia, at least as far as the spirits of Braxton and Jessica Heller were concerned.

Chapter Thirty-Two

When Tyler Lusk arrived at Magnolia around eight-fifteen that morning, he found the circular driveway in front of the plantation house empty except for Rick's pickup truck. Laura's Saturn and Wade Monroe's Winnebago were both absent from their usual spots.

Tyler parked his rental car near the mansion's long front porch and stepped out into the cold. He gathered his coat around him, trying to drive away some of the November chill. The morning was unseasonably cold; it was only thirty-five degrees at that hour and, according to the weather forecast, the temperature would likely drop below freezing before noon.

He mounted the steps, crossed the porch, and pressed the doorbell. After a few minutes of waiting, he decided to try knocking instead. He took the loop of one of the heavy brass knockers and rapped it against its metal plate several times. Inside, he could hear the thunderous echo of the knocker's report, but that was all. The noise rang hollowly through the rooms and corridors of the big house, but it did not conjure the sound of footsteps hurrying to answer the door.

Tyler checked his watch, then decided that Laura and Rick had probably already left for Nashville. He knew the artist was leaving for the convention in New York that morning and figured that Rick had likely booked an early flight. If so, Laura had probably already taken her husband to the airport and was on her way back home.

He took a quick peek through a couple of the downstairs windows, then left the porch. Tyler considered his dream of the night before and his reason for making the trip to Magnolia that day. He did not know exactly what he had come there to find, but he knew he would not find it loitering on the mansion's front porch. He took a brick walkway that circled around the eastern end of the house, heading for the flower garden at the rear. He decided that Laura would not mind if he simply walked the grounds and took another look around.

Tyler soon found himself in the garden. It looked even more barren and desolate in the gloom of the blustery autumn day with the dark threat of snowclouds hovering overhead. He walked to the towering oak that stood, ancient but sturdy, in the very center of the garden. He pressed the palm of his hand against the trunk. Its bark was rough and cold to the touch. Tyler stared up at the curved limb that stretched several feet over his head. It was from there that the shadow of the hanging man had originated.

"What is it, Samuel?" he asked out loud. "What is it that you're trying to tell me?"

Tyler really expected no response to his question, therefore he was not disappointed when he was answered only by the whistle of a cold wind through the naked branches of the big oak. He studied the limb once again and absently rubbed the back of his neck. The sensations of his dream returned, affecting him as strongly as before; the exit of the horse from beneath him, the sudden jerk downward, and the tightening of the noose around his throat.

He was on the verge of starting toward the dilapidated cabins and the slave cemetery beyond when he heard the roar of an engine drift from the far side of the plantation house. At first, he figured it was Laura returning home from her trip to Nashville. But on second thought, he decided that the vehicle was much larger than Laura's Saturn sedan. He stood there beneath the tree and listened as the engine idled for a moment, then grew silent.

Before long, the driver of the vehicle appeared around the side of the house. Wade Monroe stopped midway across the garden, a stern expression on his handsome face. Tyler was shocked at how the man looked. He had been a little lax as far as his physical appearance was concerned during the Thanksgiving dinner, but that morning he looked much worse than he had a few days ago. Wade's clothing was rumpled and wrinkled, as if he had slept in them several nights in a row. His blond hair was uncombed, he sported two or three days' worth of stubble on his cheeks and jaw, and his eyes, wreathed with the lines and dark circles of someone well past exhaustion, were a stark shade of blood red.

"What the hell are you doing here?" demanded Monroe.

At first, Tyler could not believe that the man had spoken to him in such a way. "Pardon me?"

"You heard me the first time, nigger," the parapsychologist snarled. He took a single step forward, a step full of deliberate malice and perhaps a degree of menace. "I asked you what business you have here."

Tyler bristled at the use of the word "nigger." He had once thought Wade Monroe to be a man incapable of crude prejudice, but it seemed that he had been mistaken. "I just thought I would stop by and have another look around Magnolia," he said flatly. "Laura gave me her permission to visit anytime I felt like it. That's what I decided to do this morning."

Wade's green eyes glittered with an underlying emotion that Tyler could only identify as hatred. "I thought I told you to stay away from here," he said coldly. "Your absence is necessary if I'm to complete this investigation properly. It is plain to see that the poltergeist resents your presence here . . . the same as I do."

"Well, I'll tell you one thing, Monroe," Tyler said, unwilling to back down. "I really don't give a damn what you like or don't like. The truth is, I have just as much right being here as you do. And if you ask me, *you're* the one who's hampering this investigation. I thought you had the right game plan at first. But lately, I've come to realize that you don't have a clue as far as solving these hauntings is concerned. And I think Laura and Rick feel the same way I do."

Wade approached the young black man until they stood

only a few feet from one another. "You're right when it comes to Gardner. He's too ignorant and self-absorbed to realize just what is taking place around him. I'd expect him to doubt my professional abilities, if only out of petty jealousy. But I'm certain Laura doesn't share her husband's shortsightedness. She knows what I'm capable of. She knows that I'm the best man for the job."

"You're probably right," laughed Tyler, "if you're talking about sexual harassment. I swear, Monroe, you've proven yourself to be the biggest jerk I've ever come across. Flirting with Laura . . . and right in front of her own husband. If I were Rick, I'd have whipped your ass a long time ago."

"Don't you think it's natural to desire a woman like Laura Locke?" Wade asked bluntly. "Don't tell me that you haven't thought about it yourself, Lusk. It would only be natural, being what you are."

Tyler felt his anger build. "What do you mean by that?"

"You know what I mean!" Wade growled. "It's a perversity that's been bred into you black bastards. You desire white women more than those of your own race. You'd like nothing more than to rape Laura Locke, wouldn't you? You'd like nothing more than to overpower her and violate her in every way imaginable."

The black man stared at Monroe in disgust. "That's a damned lie, and you know it," he retorted. "What the hell *are* you, Monroe? Some sort of damned Klansman?"

Wade failed to reply. He simply took a step forward, an angry grimace splitting his unshaven face. "I'm through talking to you, nigger," he rasped softly. "Now, I suggest you leave before I end up throwing you off this property myself. And if I am forced to resort to that, I might just end up hurting you. Hurting you very badly."

Tyler felt like letting loose and striking the insolent ghost-hunter. But the glint of pure meanness that shined clearly in Monroe's eyes prevented him from acting on such an impulse. He smelled the sour odor of liquor on the man's breath, but knew that drunkenness had little to do with his behavior. No, Wade's bigoted statements and apparent hatred of Tyler had more to do with blatant arrogance and cruelty than anything bordering on intoxication.

Suddenly, Tyler knew what it felt like facing a true racist. He recalled what others of his color had endured in the past: the taunting of white students on the sidewalk of a newly desegregated school, the physical cruelty inflicted by bigoted lawmen sporting attack dogs and firehoses. He had always thought that he truly understood what they had gone through. But now he knew that he had been wrong all along. Seeing the injustice pictured on television or reading about it in books was nothing in comparison to staring it nakedly in the face.

"What about it, Lusk?" Wade Monroe asked contemptuously. "You're trying my patience."

Tyler stepped out of the man's range, but more out of caution than fear. "Archie made a mistake when he involved you in this business," he told Monroe. "You're a dozen times worse than that damned poltergeist. And sooner or later, Laura is going to realize that. Then she'll kick your lily-white ass off her property and your sterling reputation will be totally shot."

Wade took a threatening step toward him, his fists clenched into tight, angry knots. "Get the hell away from here, nigger," he warned, his eyes dangerous and full of mounting rage. "And stay away . . . if you know what's good for you."

Tyler Lusk said nothing else. He simply walked past the parapsychologist and kept right on walking. As he made his way around the side of the house to the circular driveway, Monroe's undisguised threat remained foremost in his mind. He knew that the man was not bluffing. If Tyler did show up at Magnolia again, Wade would act on his threat, and violently so; he was sure of that.

As he climbed into his car and started the engine, a flurry of snowflakes began to dart from the sky above. The snowfall began sparsely, then grew in speed and volume. By the time Tyler reached the end of the driveway and pulled out on the main highway, snow had already began to accumulate on the ground and cling to the branches of the magnolia trees.

Tyler headed in the direction of Franklin, bitter over his confrontation with Wade Monroe and his retreat from Magnolia. There had been no dishonor in his departure, but still he felt as if he was running away from the bigoted ghost-hunter and his threats of violence. Cursing beneath his breath, Tyler told himself that there was really no need even to return to Magnolia. He had found the information he had traveled to Tennessee to find. He had discovered the location of his ancestral home and his ancestors' burial places. All that was left for him to do was to wait until the Gants returned from St. Louis, and if they had acquired Hudson's diary, to find out what had actually happened to Samuel and Sassy. After that, there would be nothing to keep him there in Franklin. He could fly back to Michigan, satisfied that his sojourn to uncover his family history had been a success.

But even as he thought it, he knew that he could never leave truly satisfied—not until he unlocked the mystery of those terrible nightmares in which he played the part of the unfortunate Samuel. And, despite everything he told himself, he knew that the key still remained at the place he had just left. It was still there . . . somewhere at Magnolia.

Chapter Thirty-Three

Laura arrived home a little after ten that morning.

The predicted snowfall began fifteen minutes before she reached the Frankin city limits. By the time she had driven through the heart of town and made the three-mile trip to Magnolia, the snow began to mix with sleet. The frozen mixture gradually began to adhere to the road, promising hazardous driving conditions within the next hour or so. Probably by late afternoon the state highways and interstate systems would be nearly impassable.

Fortunately, though, Laura made it home with no trouble at all. She parked her Saturn behind Rick's pickup truck, then ran to the front porch through the freezing sleet and snow. She fumbled with her keys, unlocked the front door, and ducked inside. The entrance hall was warm and inviting, and she found herself thankful that she had made it home before the worse had hit. Laura was not a good driver on icy roads; she knew that from past experience. More than once she had slid into a ditch or found herself a victim of a fender-bender due to particularly rough weather.

Laura shed her coat and hung it on a brass hook beside an oval mirror in the main foyer. Then she went to the kitchen. She made herself a cup of hot chocolate to help drive the chill away and leafed through a copy of *Cosmopolitan* she had bought at the supermarket the day before.

After she finished her cocoa, Laura felt the urge to write. But she knew before she could actually sit down and work, she had to know if her routine would be interrupted by Wade Monroe and his ongoing investigation. She dreaded going out into the cold again, but knew that it was necessary. She returned to the entrance hall, donned her coat again, then stepped out onto the front porch.

The snow was coming down more heavily than it had a half hour ago. Light patches covered the grass and powdered the limbs of the magnolias that surrounded the plantation house. As she stepped onto the driveway, she found the pavement wet and a little slushy. She knew that it could change drastically if the temperature dropped another five or ten degrees. Then that coating of slush could freeze and turn into a solid sheet of ice.

Carefully, Laura crossed the driveway to the Winnebago. She knocked on the side door of the camper, but at first received no answer. She could not see into the vehicle. The windows that had been shattered by the poltergeist's rock-throwing attack were covered with sheets of heavy cardboard secured in place with duct tape.

Laura knocked again, gritting her teeth against the icy wind that engulfed her, snaking past the warmth of her coat and ruffling her long, auburn hair. She was turning to go back to the house when she heard the door's lock click behind her. A moment later the door opened and Wade Monroe stood in the doorway, dressed sloppily in faded jeans and a filthy sweatshirt that looked as if it had been worn and slept in for several days. Another thing drew Laura's attention: the man held a bottle of bourbon in his right hand. She could tell that Monroe had probably been drinking steadily since late last night.

"Ah, Laura," Wade said. "What a nice surprise." His eyes roamed over her from head to toe, more blatantly now than before. "To what do I owe this unexpected visit?"

Laura drew the folds of her coat more tightly around her, not only to keep the cold at bay, but to obscure Monroe's view of her as well. "I was just wondering if you'll be conducting any experiments today? If you are, I need to know. I was planning on doing some writing this afternoon."

Wade took another swig from the liquor bottle and shook his head. "You know, I really haven't given it much thought. But given the deterioration of today's weather, I really don't think so. I can't set up my equipment outside, and there's really no need to hold any more sessions inside the house, either. I believe the potential for uncovering any psychic activity in the downstairs parlor has decreased considerably. Wherever that damned poltergeist is hiding, it's not anywhere inside the house. I'm pretty sure of that."

Laura was surprised by Wade's statement. "What are you saying? That you're giving up?"

"Good heavens, no, my dear!" Wade said with a laugh. "I'm only regrouping, that's all. Plotting a different strategy for dealing with the collective entities of Magnolia. And believe me, I'm beginning to realize that a more drastic course of action is required to draw them into the open."

That bothered Laura a little. "What do you mean by 'drastic'?"

"I mean, in part, giving them what they want."

"And what is that?" she asked.

"Something to entice them into revealing themselves," replied the parapsychologist with a sly grin. "Perhaps even a reenactment of sorts."

For some reason, Laura did not like the sound of that. "What kind of reenactment?"

Wade's smile faded and he seemed to clam up all of a sudden. "I really haven't made up my mind yet," he told her brashly.

Glancing past Monroe, Laura noticed that the inner room of the Winnebago was dark. Suddenly, a question came to mind. "Where is Bret?" she asked.

The grin returned, this time edged with touch of contempt. "I'm afraid that Mr. Nelson is no longer part of this investigation."

"What do you mean?"

"Unfortunately, I found that his services were no longer required," Wade told her. "In other words, I fired him."

"But whatever for?" Laura asked, surprised.

"Let's just say that there was a substantial difference between our views concerning the direction this investigation should take. A difference that was really beyond discussion. So I had no choice but to dismiss him."

"Don't you think that was a little severe?" she asked. "I mean, he was only trying to help."

"No, he wasn't," Wade said flatly. "If anything, he was trying to hinder our investigation. Bret wasn't quite as trustworthy as you might have thought. He had ulterior motives that were very dishonest in nature. In fact, he had hopes of discrediting me and claiming the glory of this investigation all for himself."

"I don't believe that," said Laura.

Monroe's eyes suddenly flared. "Are you calling me a liar?"

The man's expression scared Laura. "Uh, no," she said quickly. "Of course not."

"I didn't think so," said Wade with a smirk. He stood there for a moment, staring at her shivering form. "It must be quite cold out there in the snow. Why don't you come inside and have a drink with me? A shot or two of bourbon will certainly drive the chill from your bones."

Laura swallowed nervously. "No, I don't think so."

"Come on, Laura," Wade beckoned. "Come inside and let me warm you up."

"Really," Laura said, taking a step backward. "I have to get back to the house—"

Before she could finish her sentence, Wade Monroe's free hand darted out and caught her by the wrist. "Please, Laura," he said softly. "I insist."

Laura struggled to break his hold, but his fingers refused to yield. "Let go of me!" she demanded.

"Why?" he asked playfully. "That's why you came out here in the first place, isn't it?"

"Of course not!" Laura declared. The pressure of his grasp slowly turned into pain as his fingers tightened.

"Come now! Tell the truth," Wade urged. "I know that you've been thinking along the same lines that I have. You want me just as badly as I want you. I've seen it in your eyes, the way that you smile at me when your husband isn't looking."

"That's a lie!" Laura yelled. "Now, let me go! You're hurting me!"

"And I bet you like it, too, don't you?" Monroe continued, his eyes feverish with desire. "I bet you *like* to be hurt. You like it rough, don't you? You tease a man until he can't stand it any longer, just so he'll lose control and take you by force. Is that it? Is that the way you like to play, Laura?"

"Stop it!" she screamed, and with a lurch backward, succeeded in breaking the man's iron hold. She staggered back a couple of steps, putting a safe distance between her and the camper. Nearly in tears, she glared at the man who stood in the side doorway. Wade Monroe simply laughed and took another swallow from the bourbon bottle. "Rick was right all along," she finally said, her voice cracking with emotion.

"About what?" Wade asked with a grin.

"You're crazy and you can't be trusted," she said. "I want you off my property, Mr. Monroe. *Right now!* Do you hear me?"

"But what about the investigation?"

"Considering what just happened, I'd rather take my chances with the ghosts," she told him truthfully. "Now, get out of my sight, or I swear, I'll be forced to call the police."

A frown of mock hurt crossed the parapsychologist's face. "Very well," he said with a sigh. "But you'll regret it. Believe me, once that poltergeist returns, you'll wish I was still around."

"I don't think so," Laura said. "Now, please, just go."

Wade Monroe said nothing else. He simply stared at her for a long moment, grinning from ear to ear. Then he closed the side door of the camper behind him. Laura retreated to the porch just as the Winnebago's engine roared into life. She saw the man studying her from the side window of the cab as he made a slow turn along the circular drive and headed toward the highway. The same oily smile remained on his face, a disconcerting smile full of amusement and malicious promise.

Quickly, she entered the house and locked the double doors behind her. She stood in the entrance hall for a while, trembling not from the cold, but from her encounter with Wade Monroe. She stared down at her left wrist and saw that the red fingermarks were gradually darkening and turning into bruises. She thought of what could have happened; of how easily Wade could have dragged her bodily into the camper and locked the door. And then what? She drove the ugly images from her mind and turned her thoughts to other things. She ascended the stairway, heading for her study and the book that awaited completion within the limbo of the computer disks.

When she reached the second floor, Laura decided to double-check the driveway. She entered the master bedroom and went to the French doors that led to the balcony. Beyond the frosty panes and steady snowfall, the circular driveway and the lane that led to the highway appeared to be completely empty. There was no sign whatsoever of Monroe's Winnebago.

She left the bedroom and continued on down the hallway to her study. But even when she had taken her place behind her desk and cued up the latest chapter of *Burnt Magnolia* on the computer, Laura could not seem to drive the incident from her mind. She kept recalling the inexplicable look of desire in the psychic investigator's bloodshot eyes, as well as the brutal hold he had subjected her wrist to. And there was something else as well. Something that she had not even realized until that moment.

While standing in front of the open door of the camper, Laura had smelled a peculiar scent coming from inside the Winnebago. It had been a teasingly familiar odor that she had not been able to identify at first. But, now, thinking back, she suddenly realized what it was.

It had been the strong scent of gasoline.

Chapter Thirty-Four

Rick Gardner found himself traveling along Highway 31, not in his pickup truck or his wife's car, but strangely enough, on the back of a powerful black horse.

The animal moved along the two-lane stretch of rural road at an even trot. But was it actually the state highway? He couldn't really tell. The road was covered with a crusty blanket of snow and ice; so much, in fact, that the center and border lines were nonexistent, and he could hardly distinguish the avenue itself from the snowy drifts of the surrounding countryside.

It was early morning. He could tell that by the gray light that washed across the Tennessee sky. Traces of clouds hung overhead, but there were not nearly so many as there had been the day before. It was that storm front that had rolled in from the northwest the previous day, enveloping the expanse of Williamson County and the surrounding area in the heaviest snowfall the state had seen in a decade or two, especially in the month of November.

He spurred the horse onward as the town of Franklin grew further behind him. The number of residences decreased, giving way to a desolate landscape of barren pastureland and dense patches of heavy forest. As he approached one such patch of woods, he realized that he was nearing his own home. Magnolia lay three miles south of town, a good half mile from the closest neighbor. To say that it was an isolated stretch of land would almost be an understatement. Any crime could have been committed on the plantation ground, and at least for a while, gone undetected.

That seemed to be the fear that Rick possessed the most that moment, as he urged the horse along the length of frozen highway. A dread like none he had ever experienced before sat in the pit of his stomach, its presence only increasing with each mile he traveled. By the time he reached the turnoff leading to the plantation, his anxiety had reached a fevered pitch. In his heart, Rick knew that tragedy had struck Magnolia . . . and struck hard.

As he rode down the lane that led to the main house, Rick was assaulted by the sights and smells of wholesale destruction. The magnolia grove was no longer the lush stand of stately trees that had once grown there. Instead, only charred trunks bearing a few smoldering branches stood along the front drive. The bittersweet odor of burnt magnolia hung heavily in the air, causing the horse beneath him to snort and grow skittish. The scent of burning affected him as well. The feeling of dread increased tenfold and his heart began to pound wildly in his chest. But despite his fears, he steeled his nerve and bore his heels into the flanks of the dark stallion, sending him forward at a gallop.

"Oh, dear God in heaven!" was all that he could manage to say as he approached the circular drive and the structure that stood just beyond.

The first things that he saw were the two vehicles parked in the driveway: Laura's Saturn and his pickup truck. Both were no more than smoking hulls of blackened metal now. The next thing that drew his attention was, of course, the plantation house itself. That is, if it could still be referred to as such.

The tall structure had suffered the same fate as the car and the truck. Sometime in the past twenty-four hours it had been engulfed by fire. Its towering limestone columns and brick walls were sooty and black, and the windows stood empty of wood or glass. They gaped at him like wide, sightless eyes, perhaps accusing him of arriving too late to prevent its destruction. He shifted his shocked gaze to the front entrance.

The double doors of sturdy oak hung askew on their hinges, revealing only a choking mist of smoke and ash beyond the threshold.

Numbly, Rick swung down off the horse and, on trembling legs, approached the building. When he reached the open doorway, he paused for a moment. Smoke stung his eyes and brought tears. "Laura?" he called out weakly. His voice echoed through the ravaged structure, bounding off charred timbers and crumbling walls, sounding very hollow and small.

He checked the rooms of the lower floor. The parlor, living room, and kitchen were all empty, their furnishings either missing or reduced to mounds of ash and cinder. His panic built as he returned to the entrance hall. Without consideration for his own safety, he bounded up the curving staircase. Halfway up, the steps collapsed underneath him. He felt his feet punch through boards weakened by fire. Fortunately, he caught hold of the railing before he could plunge completely through. The banister creaked, having grown unsound. But despite its frailty, it held firm. Rick pulled himself up and continued to the second story, proceeding at a more careful pace.

He found the upper floor to be as complete in its devastation as the lower had been. The roof had caved through in several places overhead, exposing naked rafters and the cold gray light of the sky beyond. The corridor that he traveled was cluttered with debris. Its floor—once constructed of sturdy hardwood—had also been ravaged by flame. Several times, he hud to leap over craterlike holes that descended into smoky darkness, always afraid that the rest of the floor would give way beneath him. But luckily enough, the beams remained true, even though they creaked and lurched in their weakened state.

Rick entered the master bedroom, finding that its door, like those in the foyer downstairs, had been ripped from its hinges. The room had been consumed by fire as well. The furnishings stood around the blackened walls, little more than thin frameworks of smoldering cinder. The canopy bed looked like the dark bones of some sacrificial animal. Tatters of burnt cloth dangled from the frame of its canopy, shifting gently in a frigid breeze that blew through the shattered opening of the now nonexistent French doors.

"Laura!" he cried again, more frantically this time. He entered the hall and cautiously made his way to his wife's study. The room was empty and darkened with soot and cinder, just like all the others he had explored since entering the house. He crossed the floor to Laura's computer desk. Little remained, only a few charred boards and blackened books, their pages shriveled by the heat that had engulfed them. Amid the carnage he found the half-melted console of his wife's word processor. The screen of the monitor was still intact, except for a single flaw in the very center. It took a moment before Rick realized that the hole in the middle of the screen had been made by a bullet.

Suddenly, Rick lost what little composure he had left. Wildly, he turned and ran back down the upstairs corridor, leaping over the holes in the floor and scrambling down the rickety staircase. "Laura!" he screamed wildly. "Where in heaven's name are you?"

His mad search for his missing wife led him through the kitchen and out the back door. Abruptly, he stopped in his tracks, finding himself standing in the rear garden. The big oak no longer stood where it had for centuries past. Now it was only a jagged black stump. And the circular garden had been altered, too. Stretching around him, to the border of the garden and even beyond, were dozens of earthen mounds. It did not take him long to recognize what they were. They were newly dug graves, hastily filled and left unmarked.

For a long moment, Rick Gardner could only stand and stare at the intimidating number of burial mounds. Then something drew his attention: it was a single shovel standing a few yards away, its spade wedged firmly into the frozen earth. It seemed to beckon to him, taunting him to take it in hand and try his luck, no matter how futile the effort might seem.

In a daze of mounting grief, he walked to the shovel,

yanked it from the ground, and faced the task before him. Then, picking one site out of a multitude of others, he buried the edge of the spade into the earthen mound and began to dig . . .

"Sir?" came the voice of a woman. "Sir . . . are you all right?"

Rick awoke abruptly and sat up in his seat. "Huh? What's wrong?"

The Delta stewardess stood in the aisle, her pretty face full of concern. "You were talking in your sleep," she said. "Were you having a nightmare?"

Rick thought back to the dreamscape he had just left. The images that plagued him during his sleep returned in full force: the grove of blackened magnolias, the fire-ravaged plantation house, the single bullet hole in the monitor screen, and most of all, the garden of graves, waiting to be uncovered. "Yes," he said. "A nightmare."

"Can I get you anything?" she offered. "Something to drink?"

"Water, please," he replied gratefully.

The flight attendant smiled at him, then went to get the water. Rick breathed deeply and rested his head back against the seat. He glanced around at the other passengers. The ones in the opposite row paid him no attention. He looked at the passenger next to him. The overweight businessman seemed totally oblivious to what Rick had suffered in his sleep. He had his nose buried in a copy of the *Wall Street Journal,* frowning at that morning's stock market report.

Rick thought of Laura and felt a strange sense of unease overcome him. The terror of running through the burnt-out house, searching for his missing wife, lingered in the back of his mind. He told himself that there was nothing to worry about, that it had only been a stupid dream. But another part of him was not so sure that it should be so easily dismissed. The more he thought about it, the more it seemed as though the incident he had dreamed about had been more of a premonition than just a nightmare.

"Here you go, sir," said the stewardess, appearing next to his seat. She handed him a plastic cup of icewater.

"Thank you," he said. Rick took a swallow of it, cooling his parched throat. Then he looked back up at the flight attendant. "Could you tell me when we'll be landing?"

The woman checked her wristwatch. "It shouldn't be more than an hour."

Rick nodded. "Thanks."

As the stewardess moved along the center aisle, attending to the needs of the other passengers, Rick thought of the nightmare again and found that he could not shake the feeling of nervousness he had awakened with. The dream had only increased the concern he had felt over flying to New York and leaving his wife behind. He decided that there was only one thing that would ease his mind: the first thing he would do when he disembarked at Kennedy would be to give Laura a quick call, just to make sure she was all right. Only when he heard her voice would his fears be eased. Then he would be able to hail a taxi and make the trip to Manhattan without further worry.

Chapter Thirty-Five

At eleven o'clock that morning, Archie and Alma Gant left St. Louis and started the long journey home to Tennessee.

Their trip had been a successful one. The auction had gone smoothly, and when the item they had been waiting for, the diary of Major Alexander Hudson, had appeared on the block, they'd bid shrewdly. There had been an instant of heated competition between them and a professor from a university in Louisiana, with bids being bandied back and forth at rapid pace. But eventually, the scholar had backed down when the bidding had reached the lofty price of eight thousand dollars. The rap of the auctioneer's gavel had finalized the deal, and before long, the Gants had paid for their new treasure and were back on the road again.

"I can't believe it," Archie said for the umpteenth time since they'd hit the interstate. "I can't believe we actually have the thing, after all these years."

"Well, here it is," smiled Alma. She opened the flap of a padded envelope and carefully withdrew the diary. The book was roughly the size of a paperback book, was a good two inches thick, and was bound in a brown leather cover that was cracked with age. "Not much to look at, but it's what's inside that counts."

"You've got that right," said Archie. "I just hope it answers some of the questions that have been nagging us for the past few years. We certainly paid enough for the thing."

Alma ran her wrinkled hands along the cover of the diary.

"Yes, but I'm sure it'll be well worth the price. Especially if it helps solve the mystery of Magnolia."

Archie eased into the center lane and passed an eighteen-wheeler as if it were standing still. He recalled the forecast of snow in Tennessee the day before and wanted to get back home before the roads grew too hazardous. True, they really were not in any great hurry, but he was sure that Laura Locke and Tyler Lusk were eagerly awaiting their arrival back in Franklin. Obviously, they were anxious to learn what Hudson's diary had to reveal concerning the plantation called Magnolia and its past residents.

The elderly man glanced over at his wife. Alma simply sat there, holding the book in her hands and staring at it with awe. "It ain't gonna sprout vocal cords and start talking," he told her. "Open the blamed thing and start reading. I'm anxious to find out what's inside."

Alma Gant took her reading glasses from her purse and perched them atop the bridge of her nose. Then she opened the book and read the opening caption that was scrawled across the yellowed page in a bold, elegant hand.

"The Journal of Alexander J. Hudson," she began, reading out loud. "Major of the Union Army of the United States of America."

Archie grinned to himself as Alma continued, reciting one passage after another. He knew it would be a while before they reached the point in history that they were most interested in, but then, quite a few miles of monotonous freeway lay ahead of them, too. Hopefully, the reading would go fast and the mystery would be solved before they rolled into Franklin later that evening.

Once again, Wade Monroe found himself in the midst of a nightmare. As usual, he wore the uniform of a Union colonel and possessed the grisly appetites of desire and bloodlust that he had experienced during his dreams of the past month or so. But there was a very distinct difference in this current ex-

cursion into the realm of his subconscious: this time he found himself in a place that was familiar to him.

Wade stood in the living room of Magnolia's plantation house. The chamber was decorated differently. Rich furnishings that had been imported from Britain and France graced the room. Examples of the finest art that money could buy decorated the walls and the mantel over the fireplace. Paintings and sculptures crafted by some of Europe's most talented artists drew Wade's interest. He studied them with the eye of a man who appreciated such things. It was plain to see that the owners of the plantation also had tastes along the same line. He made a mental note to take the objects that he liked the most when his assignment had ended and it was time to move on.

The distant thunder of cannonfire drew his attention and he walked to one of the front windows. Although he could see nothing beyond the grove of magnolia trees, he knew that a battle was taking place, out of view, several miles away, in the township of Franklin. Wade felt a sudden burst of anger grip him, causing him to down a glass of Tennessee sipping whiskey and pour himself another just as quickly. He was puzzled as to why the emotion should possess him so very strongly, until the reason finally came to him: he was enraged by a command given by his superior, the order to stay put at Magnolia, while the rest of the Union Army participated in the skirmish further northward. The very thought of being denied the chance to test his mettle in battle nearly drove him to the point of madness. It was not fair, not when the chance of acquiring a promotion was so close at hand.

He stood next to the roaring fire of the hearth, his rage building with the crack and boom of each distant cannon. He thought of the house he and his brigade had seized and contemplated how they would leave it when the battle had ended. Past images of similar mansions came to mind, stately structures that had been stripped of their treasures and then torched. He recalled the sight of those flaming pyres: the crackle of the fire and the rich scent of burning flesh drifting on wings of cinder and ash. And with that final act of retri-

bution, he would always savor the afterglow of the atrocities that had taken place before the first drop of coal oil had been spilled and the first torch lit. Atrocities such as rape, torture, and murder, as well as others that were much more deviate and heinous in nature. Taboo appetites that could only be justified in the depraved mind of a true madman.

One such appetite resurfaced as Wade finished off the decanter of liquor and left the room. As he entered the entrance hall, he felt the familiar heat of desire possess him. He thought of the woman who had stood at the head of the stairs, and he felt his loins stir at the memory of her creamy skin, her auburn hair, the modest swell of her bosom. Lust took over then, like a wild animal hungering for sustenance. He knew that he must act upon it, right then and there, just as he had countless times before.

Wade looked around the foyer. It was decorated differently from the hall he was accustomed to. The chandelier was much more elaborate and glowed with the light of a multitude of candles, instead of electricity. Also, the floor was constructed of marble slabs, instead of carpeted wood. He spotted a splash of crimson next to the staircase and walked over to it. Kneeling, he studied the blood of a slave he had taken his sabre to several hours before. He removed his glove and ran a finger through the puddle. The blood had congealed and was tacky to the touch. He stared at the redness on the tip of his finger and considered raising it to his lips. He considered blood to be the rich nectar of victory and had tasted it many times before. But he refrained from partaking of it that night, simply because the one who had shed it had been of a race he considered to be of a lower order than that which he himself belonged to. With disgust, he wiped the blood from his hand and donned his gauntlet once again.

He looked around the entrance hall and noticed that some of the furnishings were missing. He listened closely. From the garden at the rear of the mansion, he could hear the roar of a bonfire and the laughter of his men. He could guess what they had been up to. Some had probably slain several of the cattle and feasted on cooked beef, while others had gone to the slave quarters and taken their pleasure with some of the plantation's finer wenches. Then the brigade had returned to the house, carrying off its furniture and building a fire to keep them warm that night. He knew that the ragtag band of calvarymen had confiscated several cases of whiskey during one of their recent pillages and were probably in the process of getting drunk at that moment. That was okay with Wade, though. He felt no anger or resentment toward them. They, too, had been denied the chance to fight that day, so he figured that they deserved to be allowed a little freedom to act upon their desires.

Which was what he intended to do at that moment. He had grown tired of drinking for that evening. Now his hunger for carnal conquest had returned. He thought of the belle at the top of the stairway—the lovely, auburn-haired woman with the face of Laura Locke—and he felt his need build until it was nearly unbearable.

He wasted no more time. A predatory grin crossed his handsome face, and one by one, he climbed the steps to the second floor, eager to meet the challenge of his next conquest . . .

Wade Monroe awoke with the same burning need for brutality and desire that he had experienced in his nightmare. But this time, his emergence from the dreamscape was different. He did not rebel against the emotions that accompanied him from his sleep, but welcomed them instead. He recalled the lust for blood and burning destruction, as well as the ache for carnal revelry, and saw them as a natural part of himself, instead of feelings that should be denied.

He rose from where he had fallen asleep on the couch and stretched. The main room of the Winnebago was littered with empty bourbon bottles and stank of liquor and sweat. But the squalor only seemed to fuel his sordid desires even more.

Wade made his way back to the rear bedroom. When he got there, he knelt next to the bed and slid open the storage drawer underneath. There, beneath folded shirts and underwear, lay several objects he had hidden there but had forgotten about until the moment of his awakening. He withdrew the objects—a long cavalry sword with scabbard and a Colt Army revolver—and laid them almost reverently upon the unmade bed. Then he gathered the things he had stolen from the gun shop. He emptied the contents of a paper bag onto the mattress: a full can of black powder, a box of lead balls, and several round tins of percussion caps.

As Wade loaded the gun—expertly, although he had never handled such a firearm before in his life—he thought of the other supplies that he had procured earlier that morning. The two five-gallon cans of gasoline that were currently stashed in one of the storage closets of the camper's hallway.

Soon, the pistol had been loaded and slipped into the waistband of his pants. Taking the sword, he made his way back through the belly of the camper to the cab. Once there, he looked through the windshield at the parking lot of a Piggly-Wiggly store. The snow continued to fall at a steady pace and was already adhering to the pavement.

Wade Monroe buckled himself in and started up the vehicle. As he pulled out onto Highway 31 and started southward, he checked the small calendar he kept handy in the pocket of the center console. The significance of today's date was not lost on him. For it was November thirtieth—the anniversary of the siege of Magnolia—and it was time to celebrate.

Chapter Thirty-Six

Laura Locke found herself in the midst of a writing frenzy—one that, frighteningly enough, she found that she could not control. Her fingers worked the keyboard of her work processor at a frantic pace, sending the final chapter of *Burnt Magnolia* in a direction she had originally hoped to avoid.

Jessica Heller sat on the feather mattress of her canopy bed, dressed in one of her finest silk gowns. But sleep was the furthest thing from her mind at that moment. For the past hour she had listened to the roar of the bonfire that had been set in the rear garden, as well as the shouts and dirty laughter of drunken soldiers. She recalled the paradise that Magnolia had been during the first years of her marriage to Braxton and wondered how, in such a short span of time, it had deteriorated into the site of tragedy and wantonness that it had become that night.

She recalled the horrid wound that the Union colonel had inflicted upon Sassy and wondered if the woman was still alive. She also wondered if any of the other slaves had suffered a similar fate. Jessica had heard screams echo from the direction of the slave quarters several hours ago, as well as the laughter of Bates's cavalry. She could only imagine what filthy acts had been committed there, fired by too much liquor and the mounting of desires long denied by the isolation of war.

Jessica rose from the bed and went to the French doors. Beyond the frosty panes, she saw that the snowfall had stopped. Darkness had fallen, but that had not stopped the battle that was being fought three miles to the north. She thought of her neighbors in Franklin—the Ashworths, Carters, and McGavocks—and wondered if they had survived the brutal clash between blue and gray.

Her fear for the safety of others was replaced by that of her own, however, when she heard the distant sound of footsteps on the stairway. Jessica moved away from the French doors, and clutching a post of the bed for support, listened as the footfalls grew nearer, making their way steadily along the outer hallway. Her breath caught in her lungs as the drumming of heavy-soled boots paused outside the door of the master bedroom.

Jessica expected to hear the baritone voice of the Union colonel, demanding her to unlock the door and let him in. But apparently, he was in no mood for negotiation. He decided to forgo any demands and cut right to the matter at hand. The crash of a boot against the door's side panel caused Jessica to cry out in alarm. The door held firmly at first, then weakened when the boot struck a second time. A moment later, the lock gave way and the door was flung open. From the darkness of the outer hallway emerged the powerful form of Fredrick Bates, his face ruddy from drinking, his eyes burning with insatiable desire.

"No!" yelled Jessica, recoiling from the man. "Leave me alone!"

The only response she received from her protest was cold laughter.

She turned, perhaps intending to retreat to the French doors and the balcony beyond, but she never got that far. Before she knew it, the officer was upon her, grabbing her roughly by the wrist and spinning her around to face him.

Jessica expected for him to fling her upon the bed and have his way with her, but the cruelty in his eyes told her that it would not be that simple. He intended to humilate her before she was forced to submit to his lewd desires.

"My men were unable to admire their commander in battle this day," he said bitterly, his eyes flashing with rage. "But they shall witness this conquest. They shall watch every minute of it!"

"No!" she screamed once again, but there was no reasoning with him. Bates tightened his hold on her wrist and dragged her struggling form into the hallway and down the curving staircase.

She nearly escaped his grasp when they reached the kitchen. She felt his hold loosen and began to fight to free herself. She succeeded in wrestling her wrist from his steely fingers, but that guaranteed absolutely nothing. Bates laughed cruelly, and raising his arm, struck her viciously with the back of his hand. Before she could regain her footing, she stumbled backward and crashed through the multipaned doorway that led from the kitchen to the walkway of the rear garden.

Stinging pain engulfed her as shards of glass sliced at her skin and clothing, bringing blood. Stunned, she landed on her back in the snow. Through eyes brimming with tears, she stared at the shattered door. A moment later, Bates stepped boldly into view. The lust in his eyes had only increased with the act of violence he had just committed.

"Gather around, boys!" he called out to those who stood near the bonfire, drinking and telling obscene jokes. "Gather around and watch your commander in action!"

Soon, Jessica found herself surrounded by a mob of filthy soldiers, eager to witness the act of brutality their colonel was on the verge of committing. Fear and shock drove away the discomfort of pain and cold as Jessica turned her eyes back to Fredrick Bates. The officer with the serpentine eyes and muttonchop whiskers laughed harshly as he stood above her and began to unbutton the front of his uniform trousers.

Jessica began to scream as the man fell upon her, pressing her into the snowdrift with the weight of his body. But there was no one within earshot who would come to her rescue.

Desperately, she craned her neck and stared at the soldiers who gathered around them. Most watched the crime with delight, laughing and cheering their commander on, while those who seemed sickened by the act remained silent, afraid to speak out.

Then, with a single brutal thrust, the violation began. Jessica's screams grew shriller and her struggles more frantic, but they were of no help to her. The powerful hands of Fredrick Bates encircled her slender throat and began to slowly squeeze the life from her as the driving degradation of her rape continued with no sign of letting up . . .

Through an act of sheer willpower, Laura pulled her fingers from the keyboard. Her hands quivered with physical strain, aching to complete the horrid scene, word after lurid word. But she would not allow them to continue. With a lurch backward, she rolled her chair away from the computer desk, putting some distance between her and the screen of the monitor.

"What am I doing?" she asked herself. "What's happening to me?" The tendons of her hands flexed with painful spasms, like a junkie's in the throes of painful withdrawal. Her fingers continued to type in midair, as if continuing the story, despite the absence of a keyboard. What was being dictated through the channel of her possessed hands at that point, Laura could only guess. But secretly, she knew that it was even more brutal and devastating than the last few sentences she had allowed herself to write.

Then, abruptly, her hands stopped moving under their own power. They relaxed and relinquished their control to her once again. Frightened, Laura cradled them in her lap, feeling them tingle as if they had suddenly gone to sleep. "Oh, God," was all that she could manage to say.

She was turning her eyes to the lines of text on the amber screen of the monitor when the power went out. The word processor and the standing lamp next to her desk . . . both died in a single instant.

Normally, the loss of such a significant amount of text would have upset her, but not this time. Instead, she felt relieved that the ugly scene of rape she'd just typed was no longer there. She had certainly not intended to write it. Upon reflection, it almost seemed as if someone else had been writing through her, someone who had actually lived through the humiliation and brutality. Or was "lived" too premature a term to use in this case?

"Jessica?" she called out softly. But if the spirit of the Southern belle heard her, it gave no evidence of its presence.

Laura left her chair and crossed the study. She stepped into the hallway and tried the light switch. The domed fixtures that hung along the ceiling of the corridor remained dark.

She continued down the hallway to her bedroom. The power was off there as well. The lights failed to work, and the display of the digital alarm clock on the nightstand was blank. Apparently, the entire house was devoid of electricity. But for what reason?

A sensation of unease suddenly possessed her. Laura retreated to the study, and opening the desk drawer, withdrew the .38 revolver. She stuck the gun into the pocket of her sweater, then entered the hallway once again.

A moment later, she had descended the back staircase to the kitchen. A sudden burst of cold air told her that something was amiss. She found the back door standing halfway open. The wood around the deadbolt was splintered, as if someone had forcefully pried it open.

Frightened, Laura grabbed a chair from the breakfast nook and wedged the edge of its back under the knob of the back door, securing it in place. Then she entered the utility room to the left of the kitchen. Again, she found her suspicions justified. When she checked the fuse box, she found that most of the fuses had been taken. As if that was not enough, the carton of spare fuses that Rick had set on top of the water heater for just such an emergency was also missing.

Laura suddenly wondered if the intruder who had forced his way inside and deprived the house of its electricity was still around, perhaps lurking in some shadowy corner, ready to grab her. She placed her hand in the side pocket of her sweater. The gun was still there where she had put it, fully loaded. She hated the thought of having to use it, but knew that she would if she was forced to.

Cautiously, she left the utility room and crossed the kitchen to the phone that hung on the wall next to the pantry door. Quickly, she lifted the receiver and punched the preset button that would instantly dial 911. She was no longer hesitant about calling the local police. The broken lock and the stolen fuses were reason enough to alert the sheriff's department.

But unfortunately, she was denied even that act of precaution. For, no matter how many times Laura tried, she could not raise a dial tone.

The phone was completely dead.

Rick Gardner hurriedly crossed the cavernous lobby of John F. Kennedy International Airport, heading toward the bank of pay phones that stretched along one wall.

All were in use but one. Luckily, he reached it before any of the other passengers could tie it up. He took out his wallet, found his AT&T charge card, and placed a call home.

When he found the line busy, he hung up and tried again. With each fruitless attempt to reach Laura, Rick grew more and more certain that something was wrong. He thought of the nightmare he'd had during the flight to New York and knew that he had to talk to his wife, if only to give him peace of mind.

He decided to call the operator. Rick quickly explained his problem to her. "My line at home is busy," he said. "Could you please break the connection for me? This is an emergency."

"There will be an extra charge for that service," the operator told him.

"I don't care. Just do it, okay?"

A moment later, the operator returned. "I'm sorry, sir, but there is no connection to break. The number you are trying to reach appears to be out of order."

A sensation of cold dread hit Rick like a punch in the stomach. "Thank you," he said, then hung up the phone. He stood there in indecision for a moment, debating on what to do next. Then he found another number in his wallet and put in a call to Gant's Bookshop. That did not work, either. He let the phone on the opposite end ring a dozen times before he realized that the Gants were probably still in St. Louis. Frustrated, he hung up.

Rick Gardner stood in the busy terminal for several minutes, at a loss as to what to do next. He thought of Laura and somehow knew that she was in some sort of danger. He also knew that he had to forget the convention and return to Tennessee as soon as possible.

He rushed to the Delta ticket desk. After waiting in line for ten minutes, it was finally his turn. "What can I do for you, sir?" asked a perky blonde.

"I was wondering if there might possibly be an opening for your next flight to Nashville?" he asked nervously.

"I'll be glad to check for you," she said politely.

Rick stood there as she punched up that afternoon's schedule on a computer terminal, certain that the flight would be completely booked. But luckily, that was not the case. "We do have a cancellation on Flight 286. It should be leaving in thirty minutes. Would you like me to book you into that vacancy?"

"Yes, please," Rick said in relief. He slipped his Gold Mastercard from his wallet and pushed it across the counter to her.

A few minutes later, Rick had his ticket in hand and was sitting in the waiting area, eager to board the flight back home. He thought of trying to call Laura again, but knew it would do no good. He had a feeling that something bad was taking place at Magnolia at that moment. He just hoped that he made it back in time to prevent the worst from happening.

Chapter Thirty-Seven

After discovering that the phone was dead, Laura carefully made her way back upstairs. She checked both the phone in the master bedroom and the one in her study. They, too, were dead.

It did not take her long to figure out the best thing to do: she would jump in her car and drive to the sheriff's station in Franklin. Laura hated the thought of having to drive in such bad weather, but she liked the idea of staying in the house with an intruder lurking about even less. Quickly, she gathered up her purse, coat, and gloves, then headed downstairs to the main entrance hall.

She donned her coat, dug her car keys out of her purse, then cautiously opened the front door. As she stepped out onto the porch, she saw nothing out of the ordinary at first. The circular driveway was empty, except for her car and Rick's truck, and there was no sign of anyone around.

It was only when she descended the steps and started for the Saturn, that she froze in her tracks. There, standing out clearly against the snowy surface of the driveway, were footprints. The tracks—which appeared to have been made by a large man—led from the magnolia grove, crossed the drive, and encircled both vehicles parked in front the house.

Afraid of what she might find, Laura walked slowly toward her car. Her heart began to pound and panic began to blossom in the back of her mind when she spotted the Saturn's tires. All four had been slashed to ribbons, clear down to the wheel rims. Instantly, the option of taking Rick's truck sprang into mind, but the saboteur had been thorough. The tires of the pickup were also flat and beyond repair.

Laura took a few steps beyond the disabled vehicles and studied the ground. The tracks led around the western side of the house, making a beeline for the back door. Obviously, the intruder had slashed the tires first, then cut the telephone line and broken into the house to pull the fuses.

"Who the hell would do such a thing?" Laura asked herself, although she had a pretty good idea already. Her suspicions were confirmed as she turned toward the magnolia grove. At the end of the driveway that led to the highway was parked the white-and-tan Winnebago that had stood in her driveway for nearly two weeks. It was positioned horizontally across the paved road, blocking the way from both directions.

"Monroe," she whispered. Even given his harrassing behavior earlier that morning, Laura still would not have expected him to go to such an extreme. Sure, he had made a pass at her, even to the point of nearly molesting her, but she would never have suspected that her rejection would cause the man to slash her tires and cut off her access to the outside world. Suddenly, she realized just how dangerous Monroe really was, and that he was capable of almost anything.

Laura turned and started back toward the front porch. As she mounted the icy steps, her attention was drawn by the rattle of metal. She glanced toward the western end of the house. Standing there, next to an evergreen bush, was Wade Monroe. The man was dressed in his trench coat, sweatshirt, and blue jeans, but he wore two additional objects around his waist that sent a thrill of terror through her: one was a cavalry sword in a brass scabbard that swung from the loops of his belt; the other was a pistol, which had been haphazardly stuck in the front of his waistband.

Wade smiled. It was not a nice smile. "I'm back, Laura," he said.

She wasted no time. As she scrambled up the slick steps and crossed the porch, Laura could hear the crunch of his footsteps in the snow. He was coming after her.

A moment later, she was inside the house with the double doors closed and locked behind her. But as she crossed the entrance hall, she knew that such precautions would not dissuade him. She jumped as the boom of a gunshot echoed from the opposite side of the doorway. The bullet punched a hole through the side panel of heavy oak, sending splinters of wood across the foyer floor. A second shot struck the steel plate of the deadbolt, buckling the metal.

Laura could think of nothing to do but retreat to the upper floor. She knew that it was a stupid move to make, but there was no time to come up with a better route of escape. As she bounded up the curve of the staircase, she grappled with the buttons of her winter coat. The .38 snubnose was still in the pocket of her sweater. Why she had not transferred it to the pocket of her coat was a mystery to her.

She was almost to the head of the stairway when a third shot rang out. This time the bullet was more effective. She turned her head in time to see the shaft of the deadbolt bounce across the floor, having been driven from its moorings by a lead ball. A moment later, Wade Monroe was through the door, long-barreled pistol in hand.

Laura continued up the stairs. As she reached the landing, she flinched as another shot rang out. The bullet struck the railing only a foot in front of her, shearing off a sliver of wood seven or eight inches in length. Laura fell to the floor and lay there for a second, peering through the support rods of the banister.

Wade grinned at her from the foyer below, a heavy pall of gunsmoke hovering above his head. He thumbed back the hammer and readied the gun for another shot. "I'd advise you to give it up right now, Laura," he said. "If you don't, I may be forced to hurt you."

"Screw you!" Laura yelled. She rose to her hands and knees and swiftly began to crawl to where the landing joined with the upstairs hallway.

A second before she reached the concealment of the corridor, another shot was unleashed. This time it was more accurate. The bullet smashed through one of the support rods of the railing, then traveled onward, hitting Laura in the side of the left foot. The round ball punched through her fleece-lined boot and lodged deeply in her instep.

Laura cried out, and with a lurch forward, made it into the hallway, out of Wade's view. As agony burned through her foot from ankle to toes, she looked down and saw a steady flow of blood pour from the hole in her boot. *Oh God!* she thought at the sight of her injury. *I've been shot! The bastard shot me!*

Knowing that she had no time to waste, she continued to crawl along the upstairs hallway. The door to the master bedroom was only a couple of yards away, but it seemed like a hundred. Each time she moved her left leg, white-hot pain shot through her in sickening waves. She glanced back and saw that she left a smear of fresh blood behind her, like the trail a snail leaves in its wake.

She felt like giving up. She felt like surrendering to the pain that made it so excruciatingly difficult to even move. But Laura knew she could no afford to do that. Already she could hear the sound of Monroe's footsteps drumming on the staircase as he made his way to the second floor. Driving the pain from her thoughts, she scrambled madly for the doorway of the master bedroom. She reached it at the same moment that Wade appeared at the top of the stairway.

Laura slumped against the doorframe and stared at the man. Wade simply stared back at her, his hands busily reloading the cap-and-ball revolver. "Aw," he said with an expression of mock concern. "You're bleeding, Laura. What a shame." Slowly, a devilish grin replaced the frown of regret. "Stop running from me, and I promise, I won't make you bleed any more."

From the glint of pure meanness in his emerald eyes, Laura could tell that he was lying about his intentions. "You son of a bitch!" she yelled at him. Then, crawling through the doorway of the master bedroom, she slammed the door behind her.

Frantically, she locked it and made her way across the bedroom floor. She groaned in pain as she pulled herself up on the bed and propped her foot on the curved edge of the cherrywood footboard. The hole in the side of her boot continued to bleed freely, giving no indication of stopping.

As she began to loosen the bootlaces, she heard the sound of Monroe's footsteps as they casually made their way along the length of the upstairs hallway. She recalled how easily he had made it past the deadbolt of the front doors and knew that the one on the bedroom door was not nearly as sturdy as the other. Immediately, she thought of the .38 Special. She quickly finished unbuttoning her coat and found the gun in the pocket of her sweater. The revolver felt as heavy as lead in her right hand as she cocked the hammer and aimed it at the center panel of the door.

She listened as he grew nearer. From the corridor, she could hear the stealthy pace of his approach, as well as something else she could not quite believe that she was hearing. Monroe was cheerfully whistling an off-key tune of some sort. It seemed familiar at first and it took a while before she identified exactly what the song was. He was whistling a Civil War battle hymn called "Rally Round the Flag," a favorite with soldiers of the Union Army.

Eventually, though, both the whistling and the steady procession of footsteps stopped . . . directly in front of the bedroom door. The knob rattled as he tried to gain entrance. "You might as well let me in, Laura," said Monroe from the other side. "What will happen will happen. There is no need to delay the inevitable."

"I'd get away from here as fast as I could, if I were you," Laura told him. "Somebody was bound to have heard those gunshots. The police are probably coming to check it out right now."

The parapsychologist laughed. "Out here, in the middle of the boondocks? I doubt that very much."

Laura knew he was right. Magnolia was a good half mile from any of the neighboring farms along Highway 31. Besides, it was hunting season, and the distant crack of a gunshot was common at this time of year.

The doorknob jiggled again, but the lock held firm. "Oh,

well," said Monroe with an exaggerated sigh. "I guess I'll just have to shoot the door open, the same as I did downstairs."

Laura's hand trembled as she continued to aim the .38 squarely at the center of the door. "Don't try it!" she warned.

"And why not?" Monroe asked playfully.

"I have a gun."

There was a moment of silence, then the man laughed again. "I believe you're bluffing."

Laura heard the crisp click of the pistol's hammer being cocked on the opposite side of the door. She knew that she could hesitate no longer. Before the man who stalked her could shoot out the lock, she pulled her trigger first. She cried out as the .38 bucked in her hand, its stubby barrel belching noise and fire. A hole the size of a dime appeared in the center panel of the bedroom door where the bullet hit and went through.

Suddenly, the tables were turned. It was time for Monroe to be cautious. Laura heard him yell out, then begin to curse loudly. It sounded as if she had hit him, but not fatally so. "Go away!" she said again, her voice steadier than before. "I swear to God, I'll shoot again!"

She listened closely. Monroe's cussing stopped, and she heard his footsteps retreat a safe distance down the hallway. "Don't get comfortable," he warned her, his voice edged with anger. "I'll be back."

Laura relaxed a little as she heard him descend the main staircase to the floor below. Obviously, the knowledge that she, too, had a gun in her possession had taken some of the wind out of Monroe's sails. But she had a feeling that it would not last long. The parapsychologist was not behaving rationally, so she knew that she could expect the unexpected. She had, at least, bought herself a period of reprieve, if only a short one.

The danger having passed for the time being, Laura turned back to the injury that Monroe had inflicted. She finished loosening the laces of her boot, then tenderly eased it off of her foot. She did the same with her sock—even though it hurt like hell—and examined the wound. It looked as bad as it felt. The ugly hole was located halfway between her instep and the sole of her foot. The bullet was still lodged somewhere inside. From the severity of the pain, Laura guessed that some bones had been broken and some ligaments torn. But luckily, the bleeding was slacking off, so it did not appear as if the slug had damaged any major veins or arteries.

Although she dreaded it, she knew that she must clean and bind the wound. Carefully, she attempted to stand up, thinking that she might be able to hop on her good foot, but that did not work. She ended up losing her balance and falling flat on her face.

"Okay, let's try the simple method," she told herself. On her hands and knees, she crawled across the bedroom floor to the adjoining bathroom. Soon, she was sitting on the lid of the commode with a bottle of hydrogen peroxide in her hand. "This is going to hurt," she said, then poured the antiseptic into the open wound. She was right, it did.

When the burning pain had diminished into a dull throb, Laura breathed deeply and continued. She opened a first-aid kit she had taken from the cabinet beneath the vanity and found a box of sterile gauze and a roll of medical tape. Carefully, she pressed the gauze against the entrance wound, then bound it in place with the tape. Blood began to seep through the packing, but not nearly as badly as before.

As she sat on the commode and attempted to gather her wits, Laura closed her eyes and wondered what Wade Monroe would try next. She was scared, almost to the point of tears, but she refused to surrender to the terrifying turn of events. She was stronger than that, or at least she thought she was. She guessed that she would just have to wait until Monroe made his next move to see if her nerve was as reliable as she believed it to be.

Laura also found herself thinking of Rick. How she wished he had never taken that trip to New York earlier that morning! But despite all her wishes, she could not escape the truth of the matter. She was here, held prisoner in her own house, and he was there, with no earthly idea of the dangers she was facing.

Chapter Thirty-Eight

Around three o'clock that afternoon, Archie Gant pulled off an exit along Interstate 24 near Paducah, Kentucky. He spotted a Texaco station amid the oasis of motels and fast food restaurants, and pulled up to the self-service island of gas pumps.

The trip home had gone smoothly, until they'd left Illinois and crossed the Kentucky line. Once they had entered the western part of the Bluegrass State, the temperature had grown colder and light snow flurries had begun to dust the interstate. By the time they reached Paducah, the snow grew heavier, coating the surrounding countryside with an inch or two of accumulation.

As Archie shifted the Jeep into park and cut the engine, he stared through the windshield. Snowflakes were coming down as big as goose feathers and gradually adhering to the pavement, signaling a gradual drop in temperature. A little snow on the road did not worry him. The Cherokee was a four-wheel-drive and could go where a normal car or truck could not. But he knew that its dependability would be tested if the snow turned to sleet and they found themselves traveling on a solid sheet of ice. One instant of lost control could send them skidding into a drainage ditch . . . or beneath the wheels of a tractor-trailer rig. That was what worried him the most.

He turned to his wife. Alma was engrossed in the writings of Major Alexander Hudson. Since leaving St. Louis, she had read nearly half of the private journal. So far, the passages had proved to be more historical in nature than anything else. Hudson had spent much of the diary detailing the battles he had participated in under the command of General George H. Thomas, as well as the strategies implemented and the end results. During the first hundred pages of the journal, little was said concerning Fredrick Bates or the brigade of cutthroat cavalrymen that Hudson had helped command. From the passages Alma had read to him, Archie had gotten the impression that Hudson had suffered the misfortune of being assigned to a brigade whose activities he detested, but he had not informed Thomas of Bates's indiscretions, perhaps afraid of retaliation. Hudson could very well have been a basically decent and God-fearing man who had unwillingly been subjected to serving alongside murderers, rapists, and madmen.

"The snow's really coming down," Archie said for the third time in an hour. "You know, it really would be safer if we just checked into a motel and stayed the night. It'll be getting dark soon, and things are bound to get worse before they get better."

Alma looked up from the diary and glanced out the window. "Maybe, but I still feel like we ought to get home, and as soon as possible. Don't ask me why . . . I just do."

Archie had long been a believer in women's intuition, especially where Alma was concerned. Several times in the past, she had acted on her feelings, choosing to forgo her husband's common sense. And almost every time, she had been correct in doing so. Alma's instances of intuition had led to several historical and archeological discoveries during their younger days, and had gotten them out of more than one jam. So if his wife was determined for them to stick to their plan to drive straight through to Franklin, then he knew it was probably in his best interests to shut up and listen to her.

"I'll be back in a minute," he told her. He buttoned his coat, pulled his hat down over his ears, and quickly ducked out of the car. The freezing temperature hit him like a slap in the face. From the bite of it, Archie was sure that it was in the mid-twenties and falling fast.

Spryly, he ran to the combination gas station and convenience store. Once inside, he paid the attendant for fifteen dollars' worth of regular unleaded, then returned to the Jeep. The two minutes it took to fill the Cherokee's tank were pure agony to the elderly man. An icy wind cut through his clothing as if he were completely naked and the handle of the gas nozzle felt numbingly cold to the touch.

Finally, the last of the gasoline was in. Swiftly Archie placed the gas cap back on and jumped back into the shelter of the jeep. "It's colder than a well-digger's butt out there," he said. Archie turned back to his wife. "Alma, are you sure about—?"

He stopped speaking the moment he saw her face. In the fifty years that he'd been married to the woman, he'd never seen such a peculiar expression on her face. It was a cross between excited triumph and dreadful realization. It was as if she'd discovered the answer to some great mystery, but one that had turned out to be extremely unpleasant.

Alma stared back at him. "I found it," she said softly.

"Found what?" Archie asked although he had a pretty good idea what she was referring to.

"The passage about the Battle of Franklin," she said. "And, most important, the one concerning the siege of Magnolia."

"So what does it say?" Archie urged, his heart beginning to pound.

Alma stared at the page where she had stopped reading, then handed her husband the diary. "Go ahead," she said. "Read it. Then tell me if I'm wrong about wanting to get back to Franklin as soon as possible."

Archie took the book and began to read the passage that Alma had indicated. A few minutes later, he had finished the page and a half of handwritten text. "Well, I'll be damned," was all he could manage to say.

"No," Alma said. "But someone else could very well be . . . if we don't get back on that interstate and head for Tennessee."

"I see what you mean," Archie said. He handed the book back to her and wasted no more time. He shifted the Jeep into drive and headed for the ramp that would put them back on I-24.

It was four-thirty that afternoon when the Delta flight from New York finally landed at Nashville's Metro Airport.

By the time Rick Gardner disembarked and reached the lobby of the main terminal, he was a nervous wreck. He was convinced more than ever that something bad had happened at Magnolia. He could not explain why he felt that way; there was just something in the back of his mind that told him that danger stalked the plantation grounds. And there was something else as well. Rick had the definite feeling that Laura had been hurt in some way.

The first thing he did upon arrival was to try his home phone again. He used one of the terminal's pay phones, but again, the number kept conjuring the monotonous tone of a busy signal. Angrily, he slammed the receiver back onto its cradle, drawing some odd glances from the people around him.

He walked to one of the terminal's huge windows. Snow fell steadily from the pale gray sky, covering the runways of the airport with a treacherous coating. He was lucky that his flight had been able to land as smoothly as it had. Flights during the next few hours could be delayed or canceled if the weather continued to deteriorate.

Rick turned and eyed the Avis rental counter at the far end of the lobby. He was determined to get home and, as far as he knew, there was only one way that he could possibly do that.

Forty-five minutes later, he started a rented Ford Tempest and pulled it out of the airport lot, heading for the ramp that would put him on the interstate. It had taken some quick talking on his part—as well as a few white lies—to get the man at the Avis counter to even rent him the car. He had been forced to make up a story about his wife being severely injured in a traffic accident to convince the fellow to release one of the vehicles to the threat of hazardous driving conditions. Rick had also been required to leave his American Express number to act as a substantial deposit, nearly twice the amount that was normally required.

As Rick slowly drove down the snowy ramp, he mapped out the route he would be taking. First, he would get on I-40 and head due west. Then he would take the loop and make the connection to I-65. After that, it would be a fifteen-mile drive south to Franklin.

Yes, it seemed very simple. That was, until he actually reached the entrance to Interstate 40 and found the traffic to be literally bumper-to-bumper. He suddenly realized that it was the middle of rush hour and felt his hopes for a speedy trip begin to falter. The drive to Franklin would have been difficult enough in such severe weather, but it seemed twice as tedious with the prospect of wall-to-wall cars, all traveling at a snail's pace of fifteen miles per hour or even less.

It took Rick five minutes to find a gap in the long line of vehicles, but finally he was part of the congested flow. It was not long before he was swearing beneath his breath and honking his horn in impatience. The feeling that Laura was in danger had not diminished at all. If anything, it only continued to grow stronger.

"Please, Lord," Rick whispered. "Just get me there in time, that's all I ask." Then he grew silent as he gripped the steering wheel with white-knuckled hands and stared at the endless line of taillights that stretched ahead of him.

Chapter Thirty-Nine

Wade Monroe finished the last of a decanter of sherry, draining it to the very last drop. Angrily, he rose from where he sat in a wingbacked chair and flung the crystal container at a wall. It shattered into glittering fragments as it hit. Then he staggered back to the liquor cabinet and chose another decanter, this time one partially filled with Scotch.

As he removed the decorative top and cast it away, he made his way to an oval mirror that hung on one wall. He turned his head and cursed. The single shot that Laura had fired at him had almost been a fatal one. The bullet had punched through the center panel of the door and caught the lower half of his right ear, tearing most of it away. Tenderly, he touched the ragged edge of the torn cartilage and hissed as a burst of renewed pain flared up. Dried blood coated the side of his neck, as well as the shoulder and right lapel of his trenchcoat. That alone stoked his anger, since he had paid over five hundred dollars for the raincoat.

Monroe tipped the decanter and took a long swallow of Scotch, although he detested the taste of it. "The stupid bitch," he growled, turning away from the mirror. "She'll beg forgiveness for what she did before this is all over with."

He had spent the last four hours in the living room downstairs, drinking and licking his wounds, so to speak. But now, his rage began to burn again, more powerfully this time. He felt his desire for the woman upstairs nag at him again, as if taunting him, daring him to return to the bedroom and finish what had been interrupted so abruptly. He wanted to give in to the burning in his loins, but he knew better than to act on such a foolish impulse. He had come within a hair's breadth of death several hours before. Next time, Laura's aim might be truer and he might be much less fortunate.

Still, his sudden attack of rationality did not quell the resentment he felt. With a roar of anguish, he set the decanter on a table, then drew the cavalry sword from its scabbard. Furiously, he ran around the room, swinging the sabre with broad, powerful strokes. The curved blade slashed the drapes of the windows into ribbons and mutilated the cushions of the loveseat and matching chairs until ragged mats of cotton and foam were strewn about the room.

Even then, his wrath did not diminish. If anything, it blazed even stronger than it had before. He returned the sabre to its sheath, took another swig from the bottle of Scotch, and then, grabbing the wingbacked chair, burst into the entrance hall. He cursed loudly as he made his way down the corridor beside the stairs and into the kitchen.

"I'll show that whore that she can't mess with me!" he yelled. With a heave of muscular arms, he sent the heavy chair crashing through the bay window of the breakfast nook. It landed with a thud in the snowy garden, twelve feet from the base of the oak tree. Monroe refused to stop there. He also tossed the Windsor chairs and circular breakfast table through the open windowframe, along with a dozen or so of Laura's cookbooks that sat on a small bookcase near the back door. Soon, a pile of paper and furniture was heaped in the center of the snowy yard.

Monroe walked to the kitchen's hearth and, spying a kerosene lamp of antique brass sitting on one end of the mantel, snatched it up. He marched back to the bay window and climbed through. The snow had stopped, but the temperature seemed even colder than it had before. His boots crunched in the drifts of newly fallen snow—it was three inches deep in some places—as he approached the pile of furniture and torn cookbooks. Then, wrenching the glass chimney from the lamp, he produced the Zippo lighter from his coat pocket and set the cloth wick aflame. He watched it burn for a second, then with a roar of outrage, flung the entire lamp at the jumbled heap.

Suddenly, kerosene and fire spread in all directions. Only a few moments passed before the entire pile had ignited. Monroe stood before the fire, gloating as the expensive handcrafted furnishings turned into additional fuel for the blaze. Before long, the flower garden was illuminated by the crackling fury of a full-scale bonfire.

Monroe stood before the blaze, relishing the feel of the heat against his face. It seemed to conjure images in his mind, images of death and destruction, of stately mansions and fields of cotton engulfed in flame and clouds of billowing smoke. It also re-ignited the maddening urgency of his passion once again. He felt the desire return, along with the knowledge that to act on such whims might bring a fatal shot from Laura Locke's gun.

He stared into the flames for a while, then turned away, his eyes livid. Shucking the Colt Army from his waistband, he stalked back to the house.

Laura reclined on the canopy bed, her back and shoulders propped against the headboard of hand-carved cherrywood. She held the .38 Special in one hand, her eyes constantly shifting from the bedroom door to the entranceway that led onto the balcony. The pain in her foot still throbbed, but it was not as intense, since she'd taken several Tylenols.

She glanced at her wristwatch in the gloom of evening. It was six o'clock. The snow had stopped, but the clouds still crowded the Tennessee sky. An eerie blue light was cast over the countryside, and Laura knew that it would not be long before the darkness of night followed. That was what she feared the most: being confined there in the bedroom in pitch blackness with the threat of Wade Monroe lurking somewhere outside.

Laura thought of Rick. It had been nearly ten hours since Rick's flight had left for New York. She knew that he'd tried to call her upon reaching Kennedy Airport and wondered what his reaction had been when he was unable to get an answer. She knew that he had not gone about his business and attended the convention as planned. Knowing him, he was probably worried sick about her, given what had taken place at Magnolia during the past few weeks. Whether he was concerned enough to actually book a return flight home was what occupied Laura's mind the most. She found herself grasping at the chance that her husband was on his way home at that moment, that he would appear in the nick of time like the proverbial knight in shining armor. But she knew that she could not afford the luxury of harboring such optimistic fantasies.

As she sat in the gathering darkness, stranded without the benefit of electric light, heat, or phone, Laura caught a scent of something. A half hour before, she had heard the sound of Monroe throwing a tantrum downstairs. First, there had been the shattering of glass—perhaps the breaking of a bottle—followed a few minutes later by a larger crash that sounded like the smashing of the breakfast nook window. The destructive noises had alarmed her, but not as much as the strong odor of burning that had suddenly appeared out of nowhere.

Instantly, her conversation with Monroe at the door of the Winnebago came back to her, along with his cryptic statement about performing some sort of reenactment. Frightened, she rose from the bed, and steadying herself with the help of the bedroom's furnishings, she made her way to the French doors.

When she unlatched one of the double doors and opened it, the scent came to her more powerfully than before. Also, she noticed two things that had eluded her in the sanctuary of the master bedroom. One was the dark vapor of woodsmoke drifting over the peak of the plantation house, while the other was the definite crackle and roar of a large fire originating from somewhere in the back yard.

What is he up to now? she wondered to herself, although whatever it was, she knew it was certainly something sinister in nature.

She considered crossing the balcony to the railing to investigate the source of the smoke further, but she never received a chance. Before she could take a single step, a shot rang out. A bullet glanced off the decorative banister, shearing a fragment of wood from the ledge of the railing. She retreated inside an instant before a second shot tunneled up through the floor of the balcony, traveling at a treacherous angle and shattering one of the panes of the French doors. Shards of glass spun throughout the bedroom, glittering in the dimming light of evening. One of the fragments hit Laura across the face, slicing a shallow groove from her left cheekbone to just below her earlobe. Crying out from the sudden sting of pain, she stumbled backward and, losing her balance, fell to the bedroom floor. Her injured foot twisted underneath her, bringing a fresh burst of agony, as well as renewed bleeding.

As she struggled to fight against the pain, Laura heard uproarious laughter drift from the driveway below. "I'm still here, Laura!" called out Wade Monroe. "I just wanted to remind you of that!"

"You crazy bastard!" she wailed, sitting up. "Why don't you leave me alone?"

That seemed to stoke Monroe's sadistic sense of humor. "I don't believe so, my dear," he said with a chuckle. "I'm afraid that I'm here for the duration. At least, until I get what I came back to get."

Laura was about to ask him what that was, but she already knew. An image of Monroe's drunken, sweating body weighing her down, his strong hands working at her jeans, attempting to gain access, abruptly crossed her mind. The thought sickened her, for she knew that was his ultimate goal. Whatever else the parapsychologist did to her or Magnolia would only be icing on the cake.

Suddenly, Laura's disgust turned to anger. Enraged, she crawled to the French doors, pulled herself up, and stepped out onto the balcony. "Monroe!" she called, her voice trembling with emotion.

Beyond the railing of the balcony, she saw the man appear at the edge of the magnolia grove. He grinned broadly, holding the .44 revolver in his right hand. "Yes, Laura?" he asked eagerly. "Are you prepared to surrender now?"

"Fat chance!" Laura said. She lifted the .38 from where she held it at her side and unleashed a volley of gunfire.

Wade's expression of triumph turned into one of panic as bullets thudded into the snowbank around him. Before any of the slugs could find him, he leapt back into the concealment of the magnolia grove.

Laura laughed harshly. "You'd better stay away from me, Monroe!" she screamed, close to hysteria. "Stay away or I swear, I'll kill you next time!"

Before the man could shoot back, Laura ducked back into the bedroom and closed the French doors behind her. Unsteadily, she made it to the canopy bed and collapsed there just as her injured foot gave out. For a moment, she simply lay there laughing so hard that tears came to her eyes. The sight of Monroe jumping into the grove like a frightened rabbit caused her to laugh even more.

Then, as the humor of the situation diminished, a sobering thought suddenly came to mind. She sat up on the bed and stared down at the smoking gun in her hand, suddenly aware that she had made a terrible mistake. With shaking hands, she disengaged the .38's cylinder and pressed the ejection rod, spilling the contents of the six chambers into her lap.

Frantically, she made a quick inventory. "No!" she moaned. "No, damn it!"

Laura instantly knew that her momentarily loss of control on the balcony could have very well brought about her last chance at survival. For, upon checking the gun, she found that five of the casings were now empty.

Unfortunately, that meant that she had only one cartridge left to defend herself with. She only hoped that would prove to be enough when Monroe chose to strike again. And Laura had a feeling it would not be long before he attempted to do just that.

Chapter Forty

It was after seven o'clock when Rick Gardner finally escaped the bumper-to-bumper traffic of Interstate 65 and took the exit ramp to Franklin.

As he eased along the icy roadway and turned onto U.S. Highway 31 North, he was aware that he still had quite a distance to go. A good mile or so of rural countryside lay between him and the actual boundary of the city limits. Then, once he made it through Franklin itself, there were still three more miles of highway to travel before he reached Magnolia.

The tedious two-hour drive on the icy interstate had grated heavily on his nerves. His urgency to get home and put his worse fears to rest had grown into an obsession that overshadowed everything else. Laura's lovely face intruded on his thoughts every few seconds, along with the horrible images of smoldering desolation that he'd encountered during his dream on the flight to New York. His heart ached at the thought of such a thing taking place, but not because of the plantation itself. No, his fear was for Laura's safety and that alone. He loved the woman deeply, so much so that he would risk his own life for her.

He nearly did just that when he came within a mile and a half of the Franklin city limits. As he rounded a particularly sharp curve, the tires of the rental car hit a slick patch of ice. Rick felt the rear of the Tempo swing to the left, and in a sudden panic, he wrestled with the steering wheel, hoping to stabilize it. But the icy road was much too treacherous at that point. The car spun around twice, then slid to the side of the road. A moment later, the Tempo ended up nosedown in a drainage ditch. The impact of the crash was minimal—the car suffered only a smashed headlight—but unfortunately, the Tempo was lodged at an angle that provided no traction to its tires. It was plain to see that the car would remain there until a tow truck pulled it free.

"Damn!" Rick yelled at the top of his lungs. He unbuckled his seatbelt and opened the car door. After a few moment's effort, he finally climbed up the steep embankment to the far side of the ditch.

He stood there in indecision for a moment, searching along the highway for the glow of approaching headlights. As far as he could tell, the road was totally deserted; no cars traveled from either direction. He waited another minute or two, then looked across a pasture to where a collection of buildings stood. Rick recognized the place as a thoroughbred horse farm owned by one of the members of the Franklin City Council.

Carefully, he climbed over a barbed wire fence and started across the snowy pasture. As he neared the massive stock barn, he paused to catch his breath. He had originally intended to walk to the two-story farmhouse that stood a hundred yards further on. But the closer he got to the barn, the more urgent his need to reach Magnolia grew. Soon, it reached a point that pushed all rational thought from his mind. His desperation was so great that he did something that he would normally have considered unthinkable.

Rick went to the front of the stock barn and tried its sliding door. It was unlocked. Quickly, he ducked inside and felt along the side wall for a light switch. He found it a second later. Several 100-watt bulbs blazed into life along the barn's cathedral ceiling. The sudden illumination roused several of the stabled horses from their sleep, causing them to snort and grow restless.

He went from one stall to the next until he found the animal he was looking for. It was a magnificent horse; a coal-black roan with a white star in the center of its forehead.

Without a second thought, Rick went to a wall where a collection of saddles and riding tack was located. Although he knew absolutely nothing about horses and had never ridden one, he found himself working with the knowledge of an experienced horseman. He saddled the horse, led it from its stall, then escorted it through the barn door into the night.

Rick gave his act of horse theft no further thought as he swung atop the roan and, taking the reigns in hand, spurred the animal forward with a kick to the flanks. He sent the horse from a trot to a full gallop. By the time they reached the gate that led onto the property, Rick knew that there was no need to stop. He urged the horse to leap and it did, clearing the gate with no trouble at all. The black stallion slid on the icy surface of the highway for a second, then regained its footing.

"Let's go, boy!" Rick urged. Then, an instant later, both man and horse were speeding along the snowy avenue of Highway 31 for Franklin.

Tyler Lusk had taken Archie Gant up on his offer to explore the shelves of the rare and used bookstore.

It was a little past seven-thirty that night when he sat on the stool behind the sales counter, snacking on diet cola and potato chips, and reading a pictorial history of Malcolm X. He was a third of the way into the book when a peculiar sound echoed from the direction of Public Square. It was a hollow, thundrous noise that was not at all familiar to an urbanite such as himself.

He laid the book down; curious, he walked to the front of the bookstore. Tyler reached the front door just as the source of the mysterious sound came into view. Even then, he found it hard to believe his own eyes.

It was Rick Gardner on the back of a pitch-black horse. He was hunkered down in the saddle like a jockey, a grim expression on his mustachioed face.

Tyler watched as the man spurred the horse down the center of Franklin's empty main street, ignoring every traffic light he came to. He watched as Rick made the end of the street, then reigned the horse onto the road that would take him southward out of town.

At first, Tyler wondered if he had actually seen what he thought he had. Rick Gardner was supposed to be in New York at that moment, attending the horror and science-fiction convention that was honoring him. Instead, he was clinging to the back of a black horse that galloped urgently along Main Street.

Tyler walked back to the sales counter and took a long gulp of his soda. He knew that he was not asleep, so what he had seen must have been real. And from the direction Rick was heading, it was evident where he was bound. He was on his way to Magnolia.

Tyler returned to the stool behind the counter, staring at the Gants' address book, which lay next to the cash register. He finally picked it up and thumbed through the pages until he came to the "L" listings. He found Laura Locke's address and phone number a second later.

He debated whether to make the call or not, then decided it wouldn't hurt. He dialed the number and received a busy signal. He hung up, then tried again a few minutes later. Again there was that monotonous tone on the other end of the line.

"I wonder what's going on?" Tyler asked himself. He picked up the volume on Malcolm X again, but found that he could not get back into his reading. The image of Rick Gardner's frantic horse ride along Main Street simply would not leave his mind, nor the ominous melody of the busy signal.

Tyler closed the book and sat on the stool for a while, indecision preying on his mind. He did not know exactly why, but he had the distinct feeling that something potentially disastrous was on the verge of taking place at Magnolia. He also felt that if he investigated that suspicion on his own, his involvement could turn out to be dangerous, particularly for him.

He left the sales counter and again walked to the entrance

of the bookstore. Tyler peered through the frosty panes, but the street remained empty. He thought of Archie and Alma. They were past due, probably on account of the snowstorm. "Wherever you are, I hope you get here soon," Tyler said beneath his breath. "It looks like we have trouble on our hands, and you two might be the only ones who can put a stop to it."

Chapter Forty-One

Wade Monroe had endured enough. The time to act was at hand.

It had been an hour since Laura had fired at him from the upper balcony of the plantation house. In that time, Monroe had clung to the shelter of the magnolia grove, afraid to reveal himself. But now he was tired of cowering in the shadows.

Boldly he stepped from the stand of trees and stood at the edges of the circular drive. He expected Laura to reappear at the French doors and begin firing again, but she did not. The balcony remained unoccupied and the glass doors leading into the bedroom remained closed.

Monroe turned and made his way along the drive to the Winnebago. A moment later, he was inside the camper. He went to one of the storage closets in the narrow hallway and opened it. Inside sat two five-gallon cans of gasoline. He hefted one in each hand, then left the Winnebago.

Soon he was at the plantation house. "I'm back, Laura!" he shouted up at the balcony. "And I'm tired of playing cat-and-mouse with you! It's time to do what I came here to do. It's time to recreate the glorious downfall of Magnolia!"

When he received no answer to his declaration, Monroe continued with his work. He unscrewed the cap on one of the gas cans and thoroughly doused the circular drive with raw fuel. He did the same with the front porch, then continued to pour the gas, in a steady stream, through the double doorway and into the entrance hall.

He made a complete tour of the downstairs—moving from living room, to parlor, to dining room, to kitchen. The can was empty by the time he reached the breakfast nook. Monroe cast the container away and, gripping the other in his right hand, climbed through the shattered frame of the bay window. The bonfire continued to blaze, if not quite as powerfully as it had an hour before. That did not bother Monroe, though. He had another fire in mind, one that would make the bonfire seem like the flame of a candle in comparison.

Monroe uncapped the second can, and making his way around the mansion, doused the walls and the bordering shrubbery with gasoline. The fumes of raw petroleum filled the ghost-hunter's nostrils, making him even more giddy than the alcohol had. He laughed as he stomped through the snow, splattering gas on the whitewashed brick and the painted wood of the windowframes. Finally, he was back were he'd began; in the circular driveway. He emptied the last of the fuel on Laura's car and Rick's truck, then flung the empty can away.

"My work down here is finished, Laura!" he called up to the balcony once again. "All that needs to be done is to light the match. But first, I must deal with you. The scenario would be incomplete without the conquest of Magnolia's mistress, don't you agree?"

Monroe listened for a reply, but again there was none. Only silence came from the room beyond the balcony. The parapsychologist thought of Laura again—of her supple, feminine body and her long spill of rich auburn hair—and felt the heat of desire awaken in his loins again. With a husky laugh, he started toward the front entrance of the gas-soaked manor.

He had taken only a couple of steps when his attention was drawn by a sound behind him. Monroe was unable to identify the noise at first. Then, a consciousness much older than his own recognized the drumming staccato that echoed from the far end of the driveway.

It was the sound of horse hooves thundering against the frozen ground . . . and it was coming straight toward him.

At seven-fifty that night, Archie and Alma Gant finally rolled into Franklin. They had said little to one another during the drive home, particularly after reading that single, illuminating entry from the diary of Major Alexander Hudson. The enormity of what had actually taken place at Magnolia on the night of November 30, 1864, was foremost in their thoughts, as well as the grim task that had to be performed once they returned to the restored plantation.

Archie parked the Jeep in front of the bookstore and cut the engine. As he and Alma prepared to leave the vehicle, Tyler Lusk burst from the front entrance, struggling into his coat. From the look on his face, they could tell that he was both relieved by their return and excited by something that had happened during their absence.

"Am I glad to see you two!" said Tyler. Before they knew it, the black man had opened the passenger door and squeezed into the back of the Jeep.

"Nice seeing you, too, Tyler," said Alma. "What's got you so keyed up?"

"I'll explain it on the way," he said. "Right now, we have to get to Magnolia as soon as possible."

Archie and Alma exchanged tense looks. Archie wasted no time. He shifted the Jeep into drive and headed down Main Street. "What's going on, Tyler? What's happening at Magnolia?"

"I'm not sure," he replied truthfully. "A little after seven, I saw Rick Gardner riding a jet-black horse down the middle of Main Street, hellbent for Magnolia. And, right after that, I tried to call Laura several times. The line was busy . . . or out of order."

"That doesn't sound good," Alma said.

"No, it certainly doesn't," Archie agreed. When he reached the end of Main Street's business district, the elderly bookseller made a left turn and headed down the snowy lane of Highway 31.

When they passed the sheriff's office, Tyler reached over the seat and put his hand on Archie's shoulder. "Shouldn't we stop and get some help from the police?"

"No," Archie said. "They wouldn't be of any help in a situation like this. The only stop we'll be making before we reach Magnolia is my nephew's place. He's a landscaper and ought to have the tools that we'll need."

"Tools?" Tyler asked a little confused.

"Yes," Alma said. "Three shovels and a couple of pickaxes."

"But I don't understand."

Alma undid the brass clasp on the padded envelope, withdrew the ancient diary, and quickly found the right page. She handed it over the seat to Tyler. "Read that passage there and you'll understand why."

Tyler took the diary, and in the pale glow of the Jeep's domelight, began to read.

After the brutal slaying of Colonel Bates and the execution of the slave who had killed him, I had a decision to make. The men wanted to leave the Negro hanging from the tree, but despite the atrocities I have been made privy to in the past few years, I found that I could not allow the man to be left in such a sorry state, even if he was but a lowly slave. Therefore, despite the protests of the men who are now under my command, I had the body cut down and laid out beside those of Bates and the woman who had been violated and murdered.

Almost immediately afterward, I received a dispatch from General Thomas, in need of reinforcements and requesting our presence on the battlefield. Given little time to do what needed to be done, I was forced to act hastily. Although it was against my moral conscience to do so, I had no choice but to inter the remains of the three as swiftly as possible . . .

Tyler stared at the last sentence of the entry, unable to believe what he was reading. "Oh, my God," he muttered. "Is this for real?"

"I'm afraid so," said Archie. "Now you know the grisly truth, as well as the reason for the multiple haunting of the plantation grounds."

The realization of what had taken place hit Tyler like a slap in the face. "Do you mean to tell me . . .?"

"That's right," the old man replied grimly. "Three people died that night at Magnolia . . . but only one grave was dug."

Chapter Forty-Two

Wade Monroe turned and peered through the gloom at the horse that swiftly approached from the direction of the highway.

It was a fine thoroughbred roan, coal-black, with a white star on its forehead. But the animal itself was of no importance to Monroe. Rather, it was the one who crouched low in the saddle, peering past the horse's windswept mane, that concerned him the most.

A moment later, he was able to distinguish the man's features: the shaggy black hair, the full mustache, and the piercing eyes of bluish-gray. They belonged to the last man in the world Wade Monroe would've expected to see there that night.

Without a second's hesitation, Monroe drew the Colt Army from the waistband of his trousers and extended it at arm's length. He waited until the rider came within fifty feet of the circular driveway, then snapped off a single shot. The .44 pistol boomed, belching fire and thick black smoke. Despite the darkness and distance, the lead ball found its mark, burrowing deeply between the horse's eyes. The animal made no noise as its front legs collapsed, sending it and its rider into an awkward somersault. Monroe watched as the man attempted to leap from the saddle. But before he could jump clear, his left foot got caught in the stirrup. The dying horse rolled twice, then crashed to its side, pinning the man underneath.

Laughing, the parapsychologist cocked his revolver again and ran toward the dark heap that lay thirty feet away. When he got there, he found the horse breathing its last. Its sides rose a couple of times, then grew deathly still. Monroe stared at the animal's face. Warm vapor drifted from its flared nostrils and its dark eyes grew glassy and sightless.

Cautiously, Monroe leveled his pistol and stepped around the dead horse. "Damn it!" he cursed, when he failed to find Rick lying where he'd expected him to be. There was an impression in the snow where the man had frantically dug himself out from under the animal's dead weight, as well as footprints leading off into the woods.

Angry, Monroe stepped to the edge of the magnolia grove and fired a couple of blind shots into the darkness. "I know you're out there, Gardner!" he shouted. "Do you hear me?"

Only silence answered him. If Rick Gardner was hiding nearby, he was not foolish enough to speak out and reveal his position.

"I don't know how you came to be here, Gardner," called Monroe, "but you've wasted your time. No one—not even you—will stop me from doing what I came here to do tonight. If you attempt to stop me, I will not hesitate to kill you. Do you understand?"

Again silence stretched through the close-grown stand of magnolia trees.

Monroe fired another warning shot. "I'm serious, Gardner!"

Cursing beneath his breath, he turned and marched back up the driveway. As he approached the plantation house, the strong odor of gasoline filled his nasal passages, reminding him of the task he had come to perform at Magnolia that night. Monroe turned his thoughts from the hindering presence of Rick Gardner and vowed that he would not be stopped. No, if it took his very last breath, Wade Monroe was determined to ravage the mistress of Magnolia and leave her beloved home in fiery ruins before the night was over.

* * *

Rick Gardner leaned against the trunk of a maple tree, no more than a stone's throw from the eastern end of the plantation house.

He fought against the pain in his right leg. It had felt numb at first, after the horse had fallen on it, but now the feeling was returning to the limb and it hurt like hell. He felt his pants leg and found the material tightly stretched. His leg was swollen to nearly twice its normal size.

But he knew that he had to ignore such a handicap. He thought of Laura and what she would suffer at the hands of Monroe if he were to let the pain slow him down. He recalled how crazy the man had appeared standing in the circular driveway, armed with sword and pistol, his green eyes wild with lust and depravity. Before leaving for New York, Rick had viewed Monroe as a crude flirt with a drinking problem and really nothing more. But now he saw him in an entirely different light. Now the parapsychologist seemed more like a sadistic madman with the potential to wreak the worst kind of havoc.

Rick knew that he could wait there no longer. He had to get to the house. He took a step away from the tree and felt a pain like none he had ever experienced shoot up the length of his leg. He nearly collapsed in agony, but knew that he could not allow himself to do that. He breathed deeply, then limped through the trees toward the side of the manor house.

He reached the eastern wall without being seen. He leaned there for a long moment, gulping in breaths of cold air in an attempt to clear his head. When the pain had diminished a little, he continued onward, inching his way toward the back corner of the plantation house and the flower garden beyond.

When he reached the garden, he found the bonfire blazing brightly, no more than a dozen feet from the oak tree. It looked as if Monroe had used some of the mansion's furnishings to fuel the fire.

Rick cautiously edged along the rear wall until he reached the back door. He tried to enter, but the door opened a couple of inches, then held firm. Rick noticed that the bay window had been shattered, so he decided to take that route instead.

It was difficult climbing through with his injured leg, but he finally made it. He stumbled across the kitchen floor, making his way to the pantry as quietly as possible.

A moment later, he was inside. He went to a center shelf and rummaged frantically behind a roll of canned goods. At first, he was certain that Monroe had found the gun he'd hidden there and that it had been the Colt Navy that had slain the black stallion. But suddenly his hand closed around the rectangular case, right where he'd left it. Relieved, he opened the case and withdrew the 36-caliber revolver. Rick emptied the case's compartments, placing the powder flask, loose round balls, and tin of percussion caps in his coat pocket. Then he left the pantry and crept across the kitchen to the corridor that led to the entrance hall.

Wade Monroe stood in the living room of the plantation house, emptying the last of the Scotch from its crystal decanter. The liquor settled his nerves a little, and he felt his resolve return. Gardner had been an unexpected diversion in that night's celebration, but he could not let the artist ruin things for him. He had to continue with his plans as scheduled.

As the last of the alcohol burned in his stomach, Wade reloaded the spent chambers of the Colt Army with powder, balls, and caps. He thought of Laura again, cowering in the master bedroom upstairs. The image of the frightened woman fueled Monroe's passion and his need to dominate her grew even stronger than it had before. He knew that she was armed, but that fact seemed to be less disturbing to him now. With a loaded gun in his hand and a belly full of liquor, Monroe felt invincible. He was prepared to take any chance necessary in order to finish what he'd come there to do.

He tossed the Scotch bottle away, then left the living room. As he crossed the entrance hall and started toward the staircase, someone called out from the direction of the kitchen.

"Stop right where you are, Monroe!" warned the voice of Rick Gardner.

"You're a fool, Gardner!" the ghost-hunter said with a laugh. He raised his gun at arm's length and cocked back the hammer.

But, before he could pull the trigger, the flash of gunfire bloomed from the darkness of the corridor, along with a brittle crack. Monroe's heart leapt into his throat, and blindly, he fired back. As he started for the foot of the curving staircase, a second shot rang out. This time the bullet came closer to its mark. Monroe cried out as white-hot pain burned across this left side, just below the ribcage. He reached underneath his trenchcoat and felt the warm wetness of fresh blood flowing from his torn sweatshirt. The wound was shallow, but it still stung like fire.

Monroe snapped off another shot, then reached the stairway. He bounded up the carpeted steps, aware of dark motion beneath him. He dropped to his knees as another shot was unleashed. He ducked just in time. The slug skimmed the ornate banister, splintering the handrail and puncturing the wall beyond, at the exact spot where Monroe had stood a second before.

"It's no use, Gardner!" the parapsychologist called out as he crawled up the stairway on his hands and knees. "You won't be able to stop me!"

"I'll see you in hell before I let you harm Laura!" Rick told him. Then the gunfire continued, filling the darkened house with flashes of fire and the sulfurous stench of burnt powder.

Chapter Forty-Three

Archie Gant pulled the Jeep off the icy highway and into the drive that led into the heart of Magnolia. He eased on the brakes and came to a skidding halt when the Cherokee's headlights revealed the Winnebago blocking the way several yards ahead. Archie considered trying to drive around it, but found that to be impossible. The magnolias grew too heavily on either side, leaving only a couple of feet between their snow-laden branches and the bumpers of the big camper.

"Looks like we'll have to go the rest of the way on foot," he said, cutting the Jeep's engine and unbuckling his seatbelt.

Together, all three left the Jeep and gathered the shovels and picks from the rear of the vehicle. Then they started toward the columned structure of the plantation house.

Halfway there, they heard the crack of gunfire echoing from the mansion. "Lord help us!" Alma said. "I hope we're not too late."

"Don't even say that!" Archie said, goosestepping through the high snowdrifts. "Now move that skinny ass of yours. We've got work to do."

When they reached the circular drive, the sound of gunfire had grown more plentiful. It sounded as though a full-scale battle was taking place inside.

"Shouldn't we go in and try to put a stop to it?" Tyler asked.

Archie stared at Tyler as if he were crazy. "What are you gonna do? Bat away the bullets with that shovel you're holding? Don't be silly. There's only one way we can stop it, and that's to right the wrong that was done here a hundred and thirty years ago."

Although it was difficult, they turned their attention away from the gunfire that roared inside the house. The stench of gasoline hung heavily in the air, and again the severity of what was taking place that night was confirmed. They hoped they had arrived at Magnolia in time to prevent some horrible tragedy from taking place—or rather, some ghostly form of reenactment.

The three made their way around the side of the house to the rear garden. When they rounded the corner of the mansion, they stood there for a moment, surveying the snowy garden and the crackling bonfire that had been ignited a short distance from the house. When they turned their eyes to the towering oak tree, they felt their hearts pound with excitement.

"Will you look at that?" Tyler whispered.

There, dangling from the sturdiest limb of the ancient oak, was the ghostly apparition of a hanging man. It did not manifest itself as an indistinguishable shadow this time, but as a detailed form etched in lines of eerie blue. The man—a tall, powerfully built black dressed in threadbare clothing—swayed gently back and forth on his spectral rope. Tyler took a step forward, attempting to get a better look at his long-dead ancestor. When he got near enough to see the slave's face, he was surprised at how similar it was to his own features.

"Samuel," he said softly. "Tell us. Tell us where you're buried."

For a moment, the hanging man continued to dangle from the limb of the oak tree. Then, abruptly, the ghostly rope parted. The form of Samuel did not fall, but rather drifted downward, sinking into the snow-covered earth until it vanished from view.

They ran to the spot below the tree. "This is it," Archie said. "This is the place."

Tyler took his shovel and stuck the edge of the spade into

the snow. There was a steely clank as it hit the bricked walkway underneath. "Looks like this isn't going to be as easy as we thought."

A renewed volley of gunfire echoed from the plantation house. "We don't have any time to waste," said Archie. "Pry the bricks up. *Hurry!*"

Tyler scraped away the three-inch blanket of snow, revealing the icy bricks that lay underneath. "Hand me that pick," he said. When Alma handed him the tool, he went to work, burying the point of the pickax in the connecting mortar and making his way through the surface of the garden walkway brick by brick.

Five minutes later, he had cleared away a good-sized section of the cobbled walk, revealing the bare earth underneath. "Okay, here we are," he told them.

"Then let's get to work," Archie said.

The crack of gunfire and the rise and fall of angry voices drifted from the direction of the house as the three took their shovels in hand and began to dig.

The desire had turned maddening. Wade found himself tearing at his clothing and growling like a wild animal as he made his way slowly up the winding staircase. He thought of Laura waiting upstairs: of soft, creamy skin waiting to be mauled and bitten, and a slender throat waiting to be crushed by powerful hands. And with the agony given, there would be ecstasy received. Violation and death, in exchange for one flashpoint moment of pleasure.

He reached the top of the stairs, and without any regard for his safety, stood up. Almost immediately the boom of the Colt Navy echoed from the entrance hall below. Monroe grunted as a lead ball nicked his leg just above the kneecap, but he did not curse the pain. Instead, he greeted it as he would an old friend. Laughing maniacally, he aimed his gun downward, searching for a glimpse of his adversary.

A moment later, through the gloom, he caught the pale circle of a face approaching the foot of the stairway. Monroe pulled the trigger. The Colt Army bucked in his hand, unleashing its deadly projectile toward the lower floor. He grinned when he heard a yelp of pain and saw the form of Rick retreat back down the side corridor, toward the kitchen.

"I'm coming for you, Laura!" Monroe yelled in a voice that was not his own. "I'm coming for you right now!"

Then he cast his pistol aside and, drawing the cavalry sabre from its scabbard, began to walk down the hallway toward the master bedroom.

Chapter Forty-Four

The revealing clang of steel against bone sounded from the hole they had labored on since arriving at the oak tree in the rear garden.

"I've hit something," Tyler said. He reached down and ran an exploring hand over the object. It took him a few seconds to realize that it was a human femur bone.

"Stand back, Tyler," Archie told him. "Let's let Alma tend to this. She knows more about skeletal remains than both of us put together."

"Thanks for the vote of confidence, old-timer," she said, as she knelt in the four-foot hole and began to examine the leg bone. "This one belongs to a big man, well over six and half feet tall." The elderly archaeologist carefully dug in the cold earth with her bare hands, extracting other bones, some whole and some fragmented. She laid them meticulously at the edge of the hole, keeping them in a single pile. When she eventually pulled a filthy skull from the soil, she held it up in the flickering glow of the bonfire and studied it. "The skull of a man with decidedly Negroid features."

"Samuel," Tyler said excitedly.

Alma laid the skull with the other bones she had extracted. "We have to keep these remains separated. If we don't, we'll fail at what we're trying to accomplish."

"We understand," Archie said. "Now, get on back to work. We're running out of time." From the plantation house came the crack of a single gunshot, followed by a cry of pain.

Alma sank her wrinkled hands into the earth once again and continued her careful excavation. A few moments later, she discovered the blade of a pelvis. "This belonged to a woman," she said in satisfaction. "Poor Jessica, more than likely." She handed the bone to Archie, who started a separate pile next to the remains of Samuel.

Soon, all the feminine bones had been successfully extracted and accounted for. "Now, let's find the third one," said Alma.

Archie and Tyler watched as the elderly woman continued to burrow at the dark earth with the tenacity of a mole. Then, a minute later, she grunted in triumph. She held up another skull. Half of it had been brutally shattered. "Found it. The skull of a Caucasian male, roughly thirty to forty years of age."

"Fredrick Bates," said Archie.

Alma returned the last skull to the depression she had lifted it from and covered it back up with earth. "Okay, this will be the burial place of Bates. That leaves the other two to be taken care of."

"I'll see to Jessica," Archie said. He removed his coat, and using it as a makeshift sling, began to pile the skeletal remains of the Southern belle in its folds.

"I'll take care of Samuel," Tyler told them. "It's the least I can do for the poor guy." He followed Archie's example, removing his winter coat and loading the pile of bones inside, then tying the garment's sleeves together.

"You fellows know where to put them," directed Alma, her eyes grim. "No need to bury them deep. Just plant them and make sure the remains are thoroughly covered with earth. And afterward, be sure to say a prayer over the graves."

"What sort of prayer?" Tyler asked.

"I don't reckon it really matters. The Lord's Prayer is a good one, if you're familiar with it. If not, just improvise. The whole point is to bless the ground that the remains are being committed to; to offer some parting words of peace to the spirits who have been denied their rest for so long."

"We'll do our best," Archie said. He heaved the bundle of

bones over his back, picked up his shovel, and headed into the darkness beyond the garden. Tyler wasted no time. He followed Archie's example and set off for the thicket beyond the orchard and the slave cabins.

"Just do it, and do it fast," Alma said under her breath. She glanced back at the house, unnerved by the sudden stretch of silence that dominated the interior of the structure. "I don't think we have very much time."

Then she climbed out of the hole, took hold of her own shovel, and began to fill in the grave of Fredrick Bates with heaps of cold earth.

Rick stumbled into the shelter of the kitchen and collapsed on the floor. He clutched at his left shoulder, biting against the pain that burned there. Blood coursed through his splayed fingers, slowing slightly at the pressure he applied. Still, the wound was serious enough to frighten him. He was concerned that if he did not stop the pace of the blood flow, he would bleed to death before he could save Laura from the threat of Wade Monroe.

With some effort, he lifted himself to his feet and staggered to a drawer in one of the oak cabinets. He knew what Laura kept there: potholders, dishrags, and drying towels. He took one of the towels and awkwardly fashioned it into a crude tourniquet. Rick slung it underneath his armpit and wound it tightly around the bullet hole. Using both his free hand and his teeth, he tied a knot and examined the results of his frantic first aid. After a moment, he deemed his action to be a success. The bleeding slowed to a creep, then stopped completely.

Overhead, he heard the heavy drumming of footsteps on the floor above. He did not have to guess twice about who they belonged to. He listened as the footsteps moved along the upstairs hallway. He instantly knew where they were headed.

Although his left arm throbbed from the severity of the shoulder wound, Rick fought against the disabling pain and quickly reloaded the empty chambers of his Colt Navy. The process seemed to take an eternity, but finally it was done.

Rick tightened his grip on the curved butt of the revolver, then cautiously made his way up the rear stairway that led to the mansion's upper floor.

Laura sat on the edge of the canopy bed, gun in hand, listening as the sound of footsteps echoed along the outer hallway.

Several confusing things had taken place in the last fifteen minutes. Gunfire had roared downstairs, and from the difference in resonance, she had determined that it had originated from two entirely different guns. Obviously, a gun battle of some sort had raged between Monroe and a second party. But exactly who that second party could have been was a mystery to her.

The last gunshot fired was followed by a yell of pain, then the sound she now heard: the distinctive rapping of footsteps on the hardwood floor of the upstairs hallway.

Laura held her breath as the one outside made his way down the corridor and came to a halt directly outside the door of the master bedroom. She listened intently. From the other side, she could hear raged breathing, labored more by the excitement of mounting passion than from actual physical exertion.

"Go away!" she warned. Laura lifted the .38 Special and aimed it at the center of the door. "Remember, I've got a gun. You know that I'll use it if I have to."

She hoped that her threat would incite some reluctance in the man who stood outside the bedroom door. But instead, it only seemed to amuse him. A peal of laughter roared from the hallway; a laughter more cruel and purely evil than any other she had ever heard before. It was followed by the crash of a heavy boot sole against the door. In spite of the added precaution of the deadbolt, the door gave way. It swung inward, revealing the man who had terrorized her for the past few hours.

Wade Monroe entered the room, filling the chamber with his fierce presence. Looking at him at that moment, Laura could not believe that he was the same courteous, refined gentleman who'd arrived at Magnolia on the nineteenth of that month. Now he resembled a rabid animal more than anything else. His clothes were torn and reeked of gasoline, while his face was set in a predatory snarl. His emerald eyes burned with a mixture of emotions: anger, lust, and triumph. Laura's gaze shifted to the bloody stump of his mutilated ear and wondered if the shot she had fired through the door a short time before had caused the injury.

"It's time, Laura," Monroe savagely growled. Then, sword in hand, he started toward her.

Laura had no chance to issue another warning. He was nearly upon her when she tightened her grip on the revolver and squeezed the trigger. The gun barked in her hand, but its aim was thrown off by the trembling of her hand. The bullet punctured the bicep of Monroe's left arm. Soon, the sleeve of his tan trenchcoat was drenched in fresh blood. But the expression of carnal hunger in his face did not change. It was as if he was so consumed with desire that he was completely oblivious to the injury that had been inflicted upon him.

Her last bullet gone, Laura found herself at a loss as to what to do next. She flung the gun at Monroe with all her might. The revolver glanced off his forehead, opening a gash over his right eye. But just as before, he totally ignored it. He merely laughed, grinning with sadistic glee.

"There is no use in running, Laura," he told her. "I will have you, just as surely as I will burn this house and everything around it to the ground. I missed out on its destruction once before, but I'll be damned if I'm denied that chance this time!"

Laura stared into Monroe's brilliant green eyes and suddenly realized that she was looking at someone entirely different from the man who actually stood there. It was not Wade Monroe who advanced on her, but a wanton and murderous spirit that had somehow taken control of the parapsychologist's physical being. And from some source deep within herself, she recognized the face of that destructive demon and identified him by name.

"Bates!" Laura said, as she began to crawl backward over the mattress of the canopy bed.

"Yes, it is me!" replied a voice that held no resemblance to that of Wade Monroe. "And you know what I have returned for . . . don't you, Jessica?"

The same feelings of terror and dread that Laura had experienced upon touching the apparition of the weeping woman came rushing back, and suddenly she knew the answer to the mysteries that had plagued her for the past few weeks. The changing of her hair color, the ease with which she had penned her latest novel . . . both had been a result of the entity that lived within her . . . the spectral essence of a tormented Southern belle with auburn hair.

But the awe of that realization did not last long. It was replaced by panic as Monroe suddenly reached the bed. Laura had nearly made it over the opposite side of the bed when the man tossed his sword aside and roughly grabbed her ankles. She struggled to escape, but his hold was too strong. Inch by inch, she was pulled back across the mattress, until she found herself directly underneath him.

Laura screamed and fought, clawing at Monroe's face and eyes. But the man ignored the painful scratches that her nails inflicted. He roared with laughter and backhanded her across the face. Laura's head rocked with the force of the blow. Stunned, she fell back, unable to summon the strength to continuc her struggling.

The terror of the act that was being committed resurfaced when she felt Monroe's strong hands grapple with the fly of her jeans. Soon, the zipper had been disengaged and she felt the garment being wrestled from her body. "No!" she screamed. "Don't!"

Again, only cruel laughter answered her pleas for mercy. Laura smelled the stench of his liquored breath and saw the blaze of unbridled desire flare even more brightly in his eyes than it had a moment before. Then his right hand reached toward her bikini panties, the fingers yearning to tear the flimsy material away.

But before that could happen, the sound of movement came from the bedroom door, as well as a voice. It was the last voice in the world that Laura expected to hear at that terrifying moment.

"Let go of her, you bastard!" Rick Gardner demanded.

Chapter Forty-Five

At the sound of Rick's voice, Wade Monroe cast his lust for Laura from his mind, aware of the danger that confronted him. He moved his right hand from the woman's hips and gripped the hilt of the sabre in his hand. Then, quickly, he whirled, a shout of rage bellowing from his throat.

Even though he held his pistol at arm's length with the hammer cocked and ready, Rick was unprepared for Monroe's swift reaction. The parapsychologist spun on his heels, swinging the sword with all the force his muscles could muster. Luckily, the edge of tarnished steel struck the gun across the barrel, sending it flying from Rick's grasp and into a far corner of the room. If the blade had hit the artist's arm instead, there was no doubt his hand would have been completely severed from his wrist.

Rick backed up a couple of steps, ducking low as the madman swung wildly with the wicked blade, hacking at the air above his head. He knew that eventually Monroe would find him and deliver a debilitating or even fatal wound. He was determined not to let that happen. Beyond Monroe, Rick saw Laura's face in the gloom, full of terror. He had to survive the attack, if only for her sake.

He crouched and waited for the man to swing once again. When Monroe did just that, burying the edge of the sabre into the frame of the door, Rick acted. He tackled the man, slamming his good shoulder into Monroe's abdomen. As the two stumbled toward the bed, Rick reached up and grabbed the ghost-hunter's wrist. Even then, he found it difficult to gain the upper hand. Monroe was much stronger than he was. He felt the man's muscular arm bending downward, nearly driving him to his knees.

Monroe seemed to sense Rick's weakness. He roared with arrogant laughter and increased his leverage. But just as Rick seemed on the verge of submission, a strange boldness blazed in his eyes. As if tapping into some unknown reserve of strength, Rick grinned defiantly and began to match Monroe's physical power. A moment later, he had actually surpassed it. Rick's hold tightened on Monroe's wrist and he bore backward, unwilling to let up. Again and again he slammed the back of Monroe's hand against a post of the cherrywood bed, until finally his fingers loosened their grip on the sword. The sabre spun from his grasp and slid across the bedroom floor, landing beneath the chest of drawers.

Unarmed, the two men continued their assault against one another. They fell to the floor, wrestling and fighting. As Laura watched in horror, they rolled past the bed, toward the French doors.

Having reached the Heller family graveyard a few minutes before, Archie Gant finished digging a grave next to the marble stone of Braxton Heller. The hole was a shallow one—scarcely two feet deep—but he knew that it would be sufficient for the next step he must take.

Quickly, he emptied the contents of his winter coat into the hole. The skeletal remains of Jessica Heller settled against its dark bed of raw earth, the skull staring up at him. Then, without a moment's hesitation, he grabbed the shovel again and began to fill the grave.

Soon, the bones were totally obscured from view. Archie tossed the shovel aside, then knelt between the two graves, one ancient, the other fresh. "Braxton, Jessica," he said grimly, "I hope that this simple act brings the peace you both have sought for so many years. Find each other, and then go on to where you rightfully belong."

Then he clasped his hands together and, bowing his head, began to pray. "The Lord is my shepherd, I shall not want . . ."

Five feet from the French doors, Rick Gardner and Wade Monroe separated. Each one rolled away from the other and rose unsteadily to his feet. They took a moment to catch their breath and size each other up. Then, as their eyes met, burning with mutual rage and animosity, they surged forward again. The two collided with a fury of swinging fists, bruising flesh and drawing blood.

As Laura watched the brawl, she was aware that it was not actually her husband and the parapsychologist who were at odds at that moment. No, in reality, it was two entirely different beings who fought tooth and nail, two beings who'd awaited that moment of violent confrontation for well over a century . . . a grievous and vengeful Confederate colonel named Braxton Heller, and a sadistic officer of the Union Army by the name of Fredrick Bates.

Tyler Lusk shoveled the last of the earth into the grave of Samuel and patted it down even. He had chosen the best spot in the slave cemetery: directly next to the grave of Sassy.

"Find the peace you need to go on, Samuel," he whispered softly. "You've done your part . . . now it's time for you to rest."

It had been years since Tyler had attended church. He tried to remember the Lord's Prayer, but it did not come easily. Instead, he recalled a simple prayer that he had been taught in Sunday school class when he was a child. Folding his hands and sinking to his knees in the snow, he began to recite it out loud.

Rick and Wade battled one another savagely, landing blows time after time, until their knuckles split and grew swollen.

Even then, they refused to slack up. They continued to fight, growing ever nearer to the French doors.

A moment later, Monroe grinned through blood-drenched teeth and delivered a roundhouse punch to the side of Rick's jaw. The blow sent the artist flailing backward. He collided with the double doors, crashing completely through. Stunned, he fell to his back on the balcony floor, amid cascading shards of glass and fragments of wood molding.

Wade Monroe wasted no time. He laughed crazily and rushed through the open doorway, his hands outstretched. Rick shook his head, clearing his senses just in time. He waited until Monroe was nearly upon him, then kicked out and buried his feet in the man's midsection. With all the strength his legs could muster, he lifted Monroe off his feet and flipped him completely over. The parapsychologist landed on his back near the balcony railing with enough force to drive the wind from his lungs.

Wearily, Rick rose to his feet. By the time he turned to face Monroe, the parapsychologist had recovered also. He stood next to the railing that looked out onto the circular drive and the dark grove of magnolias beyond. There was a sadistic smile on the man's bruised and bloody face, and the brilliant light of triumph in his emerald green eyes. Throwing his head back, Monroe cackled loudly and without restraint.

Rick took a threatening step forward, his fists clenched tightly. "What the hell are you laughing about?" he asked.

"I'm rejoicing, you fool!" Wade Monroe growled. "For despite your pitiful attempts to stop me, I have won nevertheless!"

Rick was puzzled at the man's claim to victory, until he saw the object that Monroe withdrew from his pocket. It was a Zippo lighter of chromed steel. With a flick of his thumb, the flint was sparked. From the mouth of the lighter leapt a yellow-blue flame.

"No!" Rick screamed. In the frigid night air, the stench of gasoline was nearly overpowering. "Don't do it!"

"Just try and stop me!" Monroe called. Then, laughing, he turned toward the edge of the balcony.

* * *

Close to exhaustion, Alma Gant finally covered the hole beneath the oak tree and let the shovel drop from her aching hands. Breathing heavily, she collapsed on top of the mound and lay there for a long moment. From the far side of the plantation house, she heard a laughter more frightening than any she'd ever heard during the course of her long life.

"Lord in heaven," she called, closing her eyes and clasping her hands. "Here lie the earthly remains of a truly evil man. A man who walked in the footsteps of Satan and was the cause of countless tragedies and deaths. Whether his immortal soul will spend eternity in paradise or hell, well, that's up to you. But whatever you intend to do, Heavenly Father, please do it quickly . . . before this entire place is destroyed!"

In desperation, Rick ran toward Monroe. He leapt at the man, grabbing at the man's right hand. But the lighter was beyond his grasp. Laughingly, Monroe held it a couple of feet over the edge of the balcony railing. Below lay the gas-soaked drive and the trail of fuel that led throughout the lower story of the plantation house. He knew that the touch of a flame—even a single wayward spark—would ignite the gasoline, sending a wave of consuming fire throughout the entire structure.

Teasingly, Monroe loosened his grip on the lighter, letting it slide, little by little, through his fingers.

"Oh, God, no!" Rick whispered, as he strained to reach Monroe's hand. "Don't let him do it!"

Then, just when all hoped seemed to be lost, something strange happened. Something that was totally unexpected, either by Rick Gardner or Wade Monroe.

Some unseen force propelled Rick backward. He was thrown to the balcony floor, where he landed near the shattered portal of the French doors. In stunned silence, he watched as the triumphant expression on Wade's face changed into one of complete horror. His body grew rigid and his mouth yawned wide as if intending to unleash a bloodcurdling scream. But no such sound escaped his throat.

Instead, a spout of pure energy shot from the man's open mouth. Rick watched as the geyser of electric blue light rose into the darkness of night and hovered, for a long moment, in mid-air. It slowly took shape, changing into the form of a man, a Union colonel with an expression of terror and defeat on his mutilated face.

With a mournful wail, the spirit of Fredrick Bates pulsed brightly, then gradually faded from view. A heat like that from a blast furnace washed across Rick's face and the stench of raw sulfur assaulted his nostrils. Then that, too, had gone the way of the murderous wraith.

Startled, Wade Monroe breathed deeply. He felt something slipping from the palm of his sweaty hand and, seeing the Zippo there, quickly tightened his fingers. If he had acted a second later, the lighter would have fallen to the gas-soaked driveway below, setting into motion a chain reaction of destruction.

"Lord help me!" he muttered, falling to his knees on the balcony floor. Tearfully he closed the lid of the Zippo, banishing the threat of the lighter's flame.

Rick stared at the man. All hatred for him was gone. Rick now saw Wade Monroe for what he had really been: an unwilling tool in the spectral hands of a murderous entity.

"Rick," someone called from behind.

He turned toward the doorway that led into the master bedroom. His wife stood next to the bed, supporting herself with the help of a cherrywood post. "Laura," was all that he could manage to say in reply.

But before he could go to her, he saw something incredible take place. An aura of brilliant blue seemed to encircle Laura, then gradually move away from her. In frightened fascination, Rick watched as the ghostly form of a Southern belle began to walk toward him. She did not resemble the brutalized woman that Laura had described to him. The marks of violence were absent, as well as the torn nightgown. Instead, she was delicately beautiful, her auburn hair hanging in ringlets around her lovely face, her shapely body clothed in an ankle-length dress of the finest silk and lace. And in one delicate hand she held an Oriental fan.

The closer she came, the more Rick felt as if something odd was taking place within him. He felt an odd sensation of separation, then a similar aura of blue light surrounded his body. A moment later, he watched in awe as the form of a man stepped away from him. He was a handsome gentleman with dark hair and a full mustache, dressed in the uniform of the Confederate Army. Slowly, the colonel walked toward the open doorway.

Both Rick and Laura watched as the two spirits approached each other. A hundred and thirty years of isolation had separated them, but that barrier was present no longer. They paused a few feet from one another, their eyes filled with joy.

An instant later, the two embraced. As their lips met, they seemed to merge, becoming as one. Then, with a brilliant flash of light, their presence on this earth was no more.

For a moment, Rick and Laura could only stand there, dazzled by the reunion they had just witnessed. Then the shock wore off and their eyes met. Soon, the distance between them was gone and they were in each other's arms. They embraced for a long time, refusing to let go. As they kissed, they realized that they shared something very special with Braxton and Jessica Heller, something that could not be denied.

It was a love that would last for eternity.

Epilogue

Almost a month had passed since the near-fatal anniversary of Magnolia. December had come, softening the memories of that terrifying night and replacing them with the anticipation of the holiday season.

It was Christmas Eve when Laura Locke and Rick Gardner heard a knock at the front door. "I hope it's him," said Laura, as she excused herself from her guests. With the help of crutches, she left the remodeled parlor, crossed the entrance hall, and opened one of the doors of sturdy oak.

When she saw who was standing on the front porch, she smiled. "I was wondering if you would change your mind and take us up on our invitation."

"Don't think that I didn't give it a lot of thought," Wade Monroe said, as he entered the house. "At first I thought it might be better if I never came back, considering what almost happened here. But I finally decided that it would be better if I faced it, rather than deny that it ever took place."

"I agree," Laura said. She reached out and took his hand. She was surprised to find that it was trembling. "I'm glad you decided to come."

Wade lowered his eyes a degree, unable to look the woman directly in the face. "Laura, I want to say again how very sorry I am . . ."

"Please," Laura said, interrupting him. "I've told you before, you owe me no apologies. It wasn't you who did all those things. It was the spirit of Fredrick Bates."

"Yes," the man meekly replied. "I suppose you're right."

"Then let's put the matter behind us and get on with the celebration," Laura suggested. "After all, it *is* Christmas."

Wade glanced around the entrance hall. It was decorated with garlands of holly, candy canes, and bright red ribbons. He regarded the festive surroundings with an air of sad resignation and simply nodded. Then he accompanied his hostess down the corridor to the parlor.

When he entered the room he found it decorated similarly to the foyer, with the addition of a Christmas tree and stockings hanging from the mantel. But his attention did not linger on the decorations for very long. Instead, he regarded the other occupants of the parlor, feeling more than a little self-conscious and nervous.

The one he had been the most apprehensive about encountering turned out to be the first one to greet him. Rick walked up to him and extended his hand. "How are you doing, Wade?" he asked.

Wade searched the artist's eyes, but found no trace of malice or mistrust there. Finally, he accepted his hand. "Much better," he replied. "Thank you for inviting me."

"Just our way of saying that there are no hard feelings," Rick said with a smile.

"You don't know how much I appreciate hearing that," Wade said.

"How's the arm doing?" Rick asked.

Wade laid his hand on the bicep of his left arm. "It's healing nicely. And your shoulder?"

"Gives me fits in this cold weather, but I'll tough it out." Rick waved toward a tray of bottles and glasses on the coffee table. "Can I get you something to drink? I recall that you're partial to bourbon, right?"

Wade shook his head. "Not any longer. I haven't had a single drink since I left Magnolia."

"That's wonderful," Laura said. "I'm so glad that you're getting back on track again."

Wade smiled sadly. "There are a few matters I haven't

been able to resolve just yet. I still have some broken fences that need to be mended."

He walked further into the room. Suddenly, the other three occupants of the parlor stood and gathered around him, greeting him with hugs and handshakes. Alma and Archie Gant were there, and Tyler Lusk. Wade had half expected to receive a cold shoulder from them, especially considering the bigoted remarks he'd made toward Tyler. But apparently all three had come to grips with the reality of what had actually taken place at Magnolia the month before and held no grudge against him.

As they sat around the Christmas tree, drinking hot chocolate and catching up on things, their conversation turned to what each was currently involved in. "I'm not working at the bowling alley any longer," Tyler told them. "Professor Hughs was so impressed with how the search for my family history turned out that he offered me a position as his assistant. Of course, I owe a debt of gratitude to the Gants here. I never would have gotten as far as I did without their help."

"Ah, fiddlesticks!" Archie bawked. "All we did was drive from one graveyard to another and trace the headstones with a box of crayons. No big deal, really."

"Not to you, maybe," Tyler said with a laugh. "Now, what have you two been up to since I saw you last?"

"Oh, business as usual at the bookstore, mostly," Alma said. "Archie finally got that alarm system installed. Cost him a pretty penny, and he's been bitching to the high heavens about it, but at least we feel a little more secure now."

"There is one project that the old lady and I have been toying around with," Archie added. "We're thinking about collaborating together on a book about the haunting of Magnolia. Of course, the text will mostly deal with the history of what took place here during the Civil War, as well as the actual hauntings themselves. We really don't intend to elaborate on what happened during the thirtieth of November. We've decided to make this more of a scientific journal for training parapsychologists, rather than a piece of sensational garbage."

"I commend you for that," Wade said sincerely. "And rest

assured, I'll be more than happy to assist you in any way possible."

Alma exhibited a rare smile. "We'd certainly welcome any input you'd like to give us," she told him. "What about you, Wade? What have you been doing lately?"

Wade's mood seemed to darken a little. "Not very much, really. I haven't accepted any investigations since Magnolia. Oh, I've had plenty offered to me, but I just can't seem to get back into the swing of parapsychology. I guess one reason is because I'm only one half of a team now. You just don't realize how important someone can be until they're gone."

Laura exchanged a knowing glance with Rick. "Oh, I don't know, Wade. Sometimes things have a way of working out when you least expect it."

"What do you mean?" Wade asked, his melancholy turning into puzzlement.

At that moment, the sound of a car echoed from the drive outside, followed by a knocking on the front door. "Why don't you answer that, Wade?" Laura suggested. "I believe someone is here to see you."

Wade searched his hostess's face and suddenly realized what she had done. "It's Bret, isn't it?" he asked hopefully.

Laura nodded. "Merry Christmas."

Wade looked as if he was at a loss for words. "Thank you," he said, as he rose from the sofa and walked toward the hallway. "Thank you very much."

When he was gone, the remaining guests turned back to the conversation at hand. "What about you two?" Alma asked. "What have you been cooking up?"

"Well, we're both caught up on our backload of projects," Rick said with a laugh. "Laura finished *Burnt Magnolia,* which her publisher expects to be her most successful novel so far, and I've finished the illustrations for that horror-western project." He glanced fondly at his wife and smiled. "So what about it, sweetheart? Do you want me to tell them or do you?"

"Tell us what?" Archie asked, grinning around the stem of his pipe.

"Well, it seems that Rick and I were working on a collaboration of our own, and we didn't even know it until only a few days ago," Laura said, blushing slightly.

Alma's eyes widened. "You don't mean to say—?"

"Yes," Laura said. "I'm pregnant."

Suddenly, Rick and Laura were being subjected to hugs and pats on the back. "But how far along are you?" asked Alma.

"A little over a month," Laura told her.

"So that means—"

"That's right," Rick replied. "The child was conceived when Laura and I were . . . you might say . . . not exactly ourselves."

"So exactly whose is it?" Tyler asked. "Yours and Laura's . . . or Jessica's and Braxton's?"

Laura and Rick looked at each other and smiled. "Who knows? Maybe all four of us had a little bit to do with it."

As Wade and Bret entered the parlor and the Christmas celebration got under way, Laura and Rick stood with their arms around one another. Every now and then, they looked up at a painting that hung over the mantel. It was a portrait that Rick had painted from memory, a portrait of a ravishing young woman with auburn hair and a dashing, mustachioed man dressed in a uniform of gray.

And as they stared up at that painting, they found themselves thinking that they would not mind at all if they had a daughter with the poise and beauty of a Southern belle, or a son with the courageous spirit of a Confederate colonel.

About The Author

After twelve years as a blue-collar worker, Ronald Kelly has exploded on the horror scene, exploring the darker side of Dixie and sharing his own style of Southern horror with readers across the nation. The author of *Hindsight, Pitfall, Something Out There, Moon of the Werewolf*, and *Father's Little Helper*, Kelly has had short fiction published in numerous horror magazines, as well as in several major anthologies, including *Dark Seductions, Gauntlet, Shock Rock*, and *Cold Blood*. He currently lives in Antioch, Tennessee, with his wife, Joyce. You may write to Ron c/o Zebra Books.